SINCE
1854

MECHANICS' INSTITUTE
LIBRARY & CHESS ROOM

WITHDRAWN

57 Post Street, San Francisco, CA 94104
(415) 393-0101

Also by Sergio de la Pava

A Naked Singularity

Personae

Lost Empress

Lost Empress

||||||||

(a protest)

Sergio de la Pava

MECHANICS' INSTITUTE LIBRARY
57 Post Street
San Francisco, CA 94104
(415) 393-0101

Pantheon Books, New York

This is a work of fiction. Names, characters, places, and incidents either are the product of the author's imagination or are used fictitiously. Any resemblance to actual persons, living or dead, events, or locales is entirely coincidental.

Copyright © 2018 by Sergio de la Pava

All rights reserved. Published in the United States by Pantheon Books, a division of Penguin Random House LLC, New York, and distributed in Canada by Random House of Canada, a division of Penguin Random House Canada Limited, Toronto.

Pantheon Books and colophon are registered trademarks of Penguin Random House LLC.

Library of Congress Cataloging-in-Publication Data
Name: Pava, Sergio de la, author.
Title: Lost empress : a novel / Sergio de la Pava.
Description: First edition. New York : Pantheon, 2018.
Identifiers: LCCN 2017049323. ISBN 9781524747220 (hardcover).
ISBN 9781524747237 (ebook)
Subjects: LCSH: Football team owners—Fiction. Football teams—Fiction.
Convicts—Fiction. BISAC: FICTION/Literary. FICTION/Visionary &
Metaphysical. GSAFD: Humorous fiction.
Classification: LCC PS3616.A9545 L67 2018. DDC 813/.6—dc23.
LC record available at lccn.loc.gov/2017049323

www.pantheonbooks.com

Jacket spine image: DigitalVision / Getty Images
Jacket design by Kelly Blair

Printed in the United States of America
First Edition

2 4 6 8 9 7 5 3 1

MAY 2 4 2018

For the lost and unknown

MAY 2 4 2018

Lost Empress

Prologue

||||||||||

Empyreal Dissonance

Because it will remain true, even then: that we will only see before affect after, only sense the immediate, and dumbly feed on the invisible other.

And in 2042 a woman with indeterminately colored eyes will suffer the first known case of mass reverse amnesia (codified thereafter and for the first time in DSM-XI). Meaning she will one day wake to find that while her perception of her surroundings is unchanged, she's now perfect stranger to all who knew her. This absence of external recognition both perfect and consistent.

She will look in mirrors. It will still look like her; will still *be* her, right? She will move through confusion and space. Her head will hurt as if from a blow. Everything will look the same but nothing will cohere into meaning. Yet this absence of meaning will clearly apply to her alone. The clockwork of the world will continue to grind forward and she will more and more feel like disinterested observer.

Although there will be freedom too. Because if no one knows who you are today that means no one knows who you *were*. Magnifying greatly the power of self-reinvention inherent in something like starting a new job or moving to a new school. Also the freedom that comes from realizing it may all just be a game. After all, if you can wake one day to find you've been converted into a complete unknown, then it seems fair to posit that, when it comes to existence, really anything at all is in play.

She'll agonize, through tears, about whether life is screwball comedy or soap opera, will feel like those are the only two options. But how truth could equally underpin both.

Let me explain. Was Mathematics invented or discovered?

Formalists (invented) and Platonists (discovered) will still not have agreed (true advancement will not come where you'd like, it will stay confined to things like pixels). Of course, the only reason the question will remain relevant is that Math will continue to be so unreasonably effective at describing the natural world. So, to take a classic example, Newton will seemingly invent calculus (some debate, Leibniz?) and others, centuries later, will discover that it accurately, to an extreme level, depicts our physical reality, which reality of course is decidedly not a Newtonian invention. See? One possible explanation is that although it felt like an invention what Newton was actually doing was discovering a truth and that's why his *invention* has persisted.

The afflicted woman will focus intensely on this issue but ultimately conclude that Life is neither, it's endurance. Your new reality is formed hourly or even more frequently and the universe has approximately zero interest in how you feel about that fact, only what you emit in response.

She will look into a still, standing body of water and address her reflected self.

She will conclude that, finally, it's Beauty will destroy us all.

She will, she'll decide, endure.

Every Thing in Everything

↔

Everything in Every Thing

88

||||||||||

Let us then have, in these pages, an entertainment. Not strictly one, but principally so. Let wit and peals of laughter distract to the point of defiance and leave for elsewhere the desultory analysis of decay and devolution.

Now, no one who's had any degree of intelligent seasoning doubts that thick women are the highest life-form. They better warp space-time, creating a gravitational pull ambient attention cannot resist. Men are embarrassing by comparison.

Reason is that Woman gives ample indication of being superior to Man in every respect save one. First, the obvious: women are far more physically beautiful than men. But they also are more kind, generous, selfless, emotionally perceptive, diligent; the list could go on until reaching aggression and purely physical strength. What happens with a properly thick woman is she negates the one traditionally male advantage to result in terrestrial angels.

So what has been the social response to this universally ignored truth? Simple, if enough people often enough say that up is down, black is white, good is bad, it will begin to seem that way to auditors so that eventually women will prefer looking like ironing boards than Jayne Mansfield or Rita Hayworth and ask who this most benefits and who's in position to make it so?

Although it bears stating early what will later seem a priori true: when we say *women this* or *people that* we are not including tall, thick, impossibly magnetic Nina Gill.

. . .

The current tidal rise of food-oriented programming is a repulsive obscenity. What makes that dispiriting machine hum is an inexhaustible supply of self-regarding illiterates who are either unaware or unconcerned that an indefensibly substantial portion of their world is right now wasting into their pained final exhale as organ after organ shuts down from lack of food, so that these desinent victims will adopt a desperately expansive definition of that term, *food*, to include things like insects and twigs. And while that occurs, far away, morons preen before a camera to berate someone with self-esteem issues because of their risotto.

Berating is a way to stardom and the *stars* then trade on that to open establishments that feed people an image more than anything else. Places like BALLS in Hoboken, NJ, or Henri Deuxfleur's (Hank Doof until a week before his television debut) *fusion* take on the *classic* sports bar and *Americana* and *comfort food* and *traditional* and point made, right?

And about a week after Super Bowl XLIX, so February 2015, Nina Gill walks into BALLS to audible gasps from the almost entirely male patrons. And she's got a monopoly on their eyeballs as she walks directly to the main bar, elbows aside two idiots, and sits on the only stool she can bear in the place.

BARTENDER

Nina, you're here!

NINA

And you're there. Can you guess what comes next?

BARTENDER
(*pouring a shot*)

Already a step ahead of you.

NINA

Shoot for half step behind.

BARTENDER

And thrilled to see you. Our boss, your boyfriend, has us like *this* waiting for your arrival. Some major announcement apparently.

NINA

I knew it, he's turning this place into an institute for the advanced study of Russian literature. Better put down the whiskey sours and start boning up on your *Anna Karenina*.

BARTENDER

My Annie Kawhatiwhat?

NINA

Withdrawn.

BARTENDER

No, I believe this announcement involves a very valuable circular object.

NINA

What? He's going to concede and purchase a cock ring?

BARTENDER

My God. You kiss your mother with that mouth?

NINA

Not in too long a while.

The way someone can reflexively say something, without thought, then experience that something echo with its unintentional truth value. He is still talking but she is living in that echo. Then she notices it.

NINA

Hell's that?

BARTENDER

Ah, you probably think it's a wall-size television. Incorrect, that television *is* the wall. No mere partition either, you're looking at the world's first load-bearing television.

NINA

By the way, I'm forty-two. So if you use the word *boyfriend* around me again, I'll have to snap your fat neck.

BARTENDER

Okay, but doesn't look like you'll be saying *boy*—uh, using that term anymore. I mean once he makes his announcement.

NINA

Shut it, give me volume, I want to hear this.

On the screen is one of the National Football League's signature programs, *Inside the NFL*, and their season wrap-up show. Over highlights of the recently completed Super Bowl an announcer uses an absurdly stentorian voice to detail the championship victory of the Dallas Cowboys, their third consecutive. Eventually he appears to get carried away with the rhetorical excess until coming almost completely unglued before recovering and reminding everyone that the Cowboys are truly America's Team. Specifically:

ANNOUNCER

Up only ten with twelve minutes to play, the Cowboys and their impeccable quarterback, Tom Laney, turned to perhaps the most feared unit in the history of organized sports. Comprised of five men and nearly a ton of mauling beef, the Cowboys' offensive line imposed their will on Denver like the Nazi regime invading Poland, leaving devastation in their wake in perhaps humanity's most merci-less display to date.

BARTENDER

Did he just say?

ANNOUNCER

To hoist the trophy for the third straight year and in the process
once again establish themselves, beyond a scintilla of doubt, as . . .
America's Team.

Back to the studio, where the host announces that following the break they
will bring you an interview with Daniel Gill, president of the Cowboys
and the NFL's point person with respect to the ongoing labor negotiations.

BARTENDER

And that America's Team crap drives me nuts. Jersey's part of the
universe, ain't it?

NINA

I'd have to do the math.

BARTENDER

And I don't know anybody round here can stand the goddamn Cowboys.

NINA

A cogent objection.

BARTENDER

Still, you got to hand it to them. Three in a row. First team in NFL
history. They're unbeatable.

NINA

No, they're highly beatable, just not by the numbskulls currently
populating that league.

BARTENDER

Here comes the boss.

Deuxfleur walks towards Nina, a small black felt box weighing down his hand. This is going to be great is what surrounding people seem to be thinking.

HENRI

Nina, you look as lovely as ever!

NINA

How would you know?

HENRI

Huh?

NINA

You've only been looking at me for a month or so, right?

HENRI

Oh, of course. You certainly keep me on my toes.

NINA

I'll try and get you back on your heels.

HENRI

I don't understand.

NINA

I know.

A genuine crowd of BALLS employees has gathered around the bar for the big announcement. Nina notices them and becomes visibly, although reluctantly, uncomfortable.

NINA

Listen, Hankie, I don't think you're going to want a public airing
of—

HENRI

Nina, the heart is a fickle organ.

NINA

(*aside*)

Not your only one.

HENRI

That's why it's so important to listen to it when it speaks.

NINA

Think it's more important you listen to your ears right now.

HENRI

Now, I don't have to tell you the kinds of options I have with respect
to women.

NINA

Only if you want me to know, and I'm betting you do.

HENRI

But needless to say there are a great many women who would love to
be in your position.

NINA

Many are, though I don't know how great they are. As to what positions they love—

HENRI

(*confused*)

Let me just spit it out.

NINA

Please, but watch your aim.

HENRI

Will you marry me? Nina?

Here is heard the expected female squeal of delight. Problem is, as
the seconds pass, it becomes apparent that said squeal emanated from
interested bystanders and not Nina, whose response is by far the most
relevant. Not that she's giving any indication of being aware of that fact.
Seconds that resemble hours mount. Nervous laughter.

NINA

Think I'm going to pass.

A palpably pained deflation then the crowd quickly disperses in response
to the extreme discomfort of the situation, all except the bartender, who's
trapped by the setup of the bar. The bartender is Fran Quinn, and despite
having just completed three decades as a Bronx EMT, this is the worst
thing he's ever seen. He wants desperately to be elsewhere, but the bar
has only one potential point of escape (that swingy trapdoor thing), and
that's precisely where Nina's nonchalant elbow rests not far from Henri's
slack jaw.

Still, if he can just . . . maybe . . . sneakily . . . slide under.

This does not go well. To attempt to negotiate himself through the
opening under the trapdoor, Fran first bends his knees to drop into a
pained haunch. From there he tilts forward to commence a kind of crawl.
But due to his considerable girth his drop into a haunch has caused all
his ventral fat to quickly migrate up towards his reddening head like
toothpaste being squeezed up a tube. This taxes his already overburdened
shirt collar to the point that his oxygen supply begins to be cut off and of
course the quickest solution to that is the immediate hand-off-a-hot-stove

raising of his head but this raising is violently met by the aforementioned swing door, which lifts a bit, pushing Nina Gill's elbow up. But because that elbow is attached to Nina Gill and she doesn't like being moved, even slightly, she immediately pushes her elbow back down with extreme prejudice, in essence repeating the blow to Fran's head and resulting in his anguished plea to the gods of slapstick for a cessation to his protracted physical torture as he rolls onto his back in the form of a pranked turtle. At least this animalistic yowl serves to jar Henri out of his mute daze.

HENRI

I don't understand, you're saying no?

NINA

No. I mean yes. Yes, I'm saying no. I'm repeating the no. Saying yes to your question regarding whether I'm saying no.

HENRI
(recovering)
Fine! You know, I didn't want to use the O word.

NINA

Oh, don't worry. I was still having them in my spare time. I just don't believe in faking, too selfless.

HENRI

I meant old, you're old! Think you'll ever have this opportunity again? Remember you're a woman, every day you get less attractive.

NINA

That's okay, every night I recover. Now get the hell out of my establishment.

HENRI

This is my place!

NINA

Guess you're right, but certainly you wouldn't begrudge me finishing my drink.

HENRI

You would stay and finish your drink?

NINA

If you insist.

HENRI

This woman's impossible!

Deuxfleur storms off trying to invent words for what just happened as EMT-turned-booze-slinger Fran rubs the top of his head and stares vacantly at the receding pitiable figure, so vacantly that Nina has to snap her fingers at him.

NINA

Wake up, pork chop! You heard the man, unlimited tequila on the house for having broken my heart and all.

FRAN

Oh my God, that was horrific.

NINA

You're welcome.

FRAN

You're like an assassin. You act like you've done that before.

NINA

I guess we could celebrate reaching double digits.

FRAN

What? You're not saying.

NINA

What?

FRAN

That you rejected a marriage proposal just to reach double digits.

NINA

No! (*whispering*) Not entirely. Hey, two here (*tapping her shot glass*). And turn that up again.

The promised interview with Daniel Gill is occurring on *Inside the NFL* and the announcers are blowing fulsome smoke up his ass for having won three straight titles even though, at the time of this interview, Daniel Gill has not perspired in about seven months:

ANNOUNCER

Is this Cowboys team the greatest NFL team ever?

DANIEL GILL

Frankly, I'm not familiar enough with the history of the league to say, but I know that our success on the field has generated unprecedented revenue for—

ANNOUNCER

Well, let me stop you there because that's what's on the mind of every NFL fan. We've heard a lot of posturing, is there going to be a work stoppage?

DANIEL

The truth is, the current system, while great for the players, is simply unworkable for the owners. As we speak there are unforeseen revenue streams that must be factored in and an appropriate split of that revenue, one that is commensurate with the—

Fran shakes his head in disgust and raises the remote to change the channel until Nina violently stops his hand.

ANNOUNCER

Don't know if this would qualify as a criticism or not, but many around the league say that it is actually your sister, Nina Gill, no longer with the team, who is most directly responsible for your team's unprecedented success.

As they speak, a picture of the sister is on the screen and an openmouthed Fran is alternating looks at the two Ninas as if at a tennis match. In the studio, Daniel Gill squirms in his seat a bit at the mention of his sister then forces a phony smile while looking down at some papers in front of him.

ANNOUNCER

That she was the one with all the football acumen. That she made all personnel decisions and even contributed to the coaching of players and the devising of game plans. Is this accurate? Are you just a caretaker winning with someone else's team?

DANIEL

I would say that while Nina certainly contributed greatly, no one person is bigger than the organization. The media tend to overrate one person's effect. The Cowboys are the premier NFL team and we expect that will continue for the foreseeable future.

A hurled shot glass suddenly destroys the screen.

NINA

I'm sorry, were you watching that?

Nor is that the end of the destruction either. Because whatever load that television was intended to bear, it didn't count on doing so as shards of screen collapsed in on themselves and out onto the floor.

And for a moment there (the sound of groaning wood was quantifiably sexual, but maybe everything is) it does almost feel as if the entire place will come down around them.

People are rushing out in disaster-movie egress but Nina doesn't move. She knows it's not all coming down. But she kind of wishes it would.

87

|||||||||||

Why islands, like extreme outlier Manhattan, where Nina retreated to following the Great Hoboken Barpocollapse, have such imaginative hold is due to the related concepts of insularity and simplicity.

The insularity is of course nearly tautological. It's almost the definition of an island that you are in a state of underinfluence.

And because variegated influences are a complexifying force, their absence has the opposite simplifying effect.

But while the battle between simplicity and complexity may rage eternal and unabated, there's no denying that (a) complexity is superior in every meaningful respect to simplicity and (b) simplicity, by often providing warm understanding and the yummy sensation of the proper piece smoothly falling into the proper place, can at times be superior to complexity, basically giving lie to the above (a)'s assertion and establishing that humans are more likely to longingly yearn for the simple; although the really complex is fun too, but not always.

So islands can help do this, the creation of simplicity. For example, the desert island. The mere concept of it can reduce the complexity of all recorded music or all bound language for example into the five or ten recordings or bindings worthy of existence on it.

Also, on that kind of island, humanity can restart everything, even society itself. So there's the philosophical concept that people should strive to form the society they would wish to live in if they were about to be reborn as one of its marginalized members. Those types of thought experiments almost always aided by imagining a clean-slate island rather than the overwhelming complexity of our modern age and world.

Though, truthfully, none of the preceding has any great relevance to this: where Nuno DeAngeles is from, in that neglected place, there's only one island, only one possible referent for the nominative phrase *The Island.*

Thing is, he never thought it'd be him sitting in one of those blue and white buses with the dangerously thin shell, slack chains on his and the other passengers' ankles. Never thought he'd be staring dead-eyed at the window stained from raindrops (no, teardrops!) and located inches from his faintly reflected face as that island magnetically pulls another bus to it (always with the buses this island; impel then expel them in great numbers through its rigidly metallic membrane with a result to the world of nameless loss).

Fine. The only moment of weakness he allows himself is when, from the suddenly-congested-at-three-in-the-morning northbound FDR, he looks up high as possible on a luxury building to see its penthouse apartment, the one with wall-size windows and the grandest possible piano therein, and for a brief, blurry moment imagines life on the other side of the chasm between his masticated New York City Department of Correction bus seat and that piano stool.

86

||||||||||

The very stool, it turns out, Nina Gill sits on while playing the third movement (not the goddamn first) of Beethoven's fourteenth piano sonata and occasionally positioning her mouth so she can drink from a nearby snifter without raising her hands from the keys and, again, three in the morning.

She sits and plays and seethes and drinks.

Seethes because playing she cannot help but look at the wall across from her. The wall features exclusively the works of Salvador Dalí. A surreal medley of rhino horns, tesseracts, elephants, and eggs. It's pleasing. The large ink splotch and the rest depicting Christ on the cross with a black 1965 in the bottom right corner. Pleasant. It's all pleasure, in fact, except for the one empty quadrilateral absently framing empty space. That emptiness is why she seethes. Seethes so loudly it takes far too long to hear the apologetic knocking at her door.

NINA

What is it?

BRYANT

I'm Bryant. From downstairs?

NINA

How exciting, are you introducing yourself to everyone in the building or just lucky me?

BRYANT

No, just, two things. First, piano at four in the morning?

NINA

Pianissimo at three, don't exaggerate.

BRYANT

Is everything okay? You look, do you need to talk?

NINA

Oh, criminy. What are you trying to do? Position yourself as like my gay confidant?

BRYANT

Gay?

NINA

Because the last thing I need is—

BRYANT

Gay?

NINA

A little mascoty—

BRYANT

Gay? I'm not gay, why would you think I was gay?

NINA

Oh. Okay, well, glad we cleared that up. You want to be referred to as straight.

BRYANT

I don't want to be *referred* to as straight, I am straight.

NINA

Then you'll have no problem being referred to as such (*ushering him out*).

BRYANT

Right but . . . what?

NINA

It's really not appropriate for me to be here alone with a straight man, what will people say?

BRYANT

Speaking of which, now that you realize my high degree of straightness, is there any chance. You and I. Could?

NINA

No, none. Wait (*she checks him out head to toe*). Yeah, none.

BRYANT

Oh, one more thing. This was delivered to me by accident. It looks official, I'd open it if I were you.

NINA

Thanks, I was wondering what you would do in my unprecedented situation. Can you show me how you'd do it?

Confused, he starts to open it and, when she doesn't stop him, removes an official-looking letter.

NINA

What would you do next? You know, were you me?

BRYANT

Read it?

NINA

Demonstrate.

BRYANT

Let's see, it's from a law firm. In Manhattan. Littman, Ligursky, and Leib.

NINA

They sure sound litigious.

BRYANT

The presence of one Ms. Nina Gill—

NINA

Present.

BRYANT

Is requested at a mandatory—

NINA

Which is it?

BRYANT

Estate settlement meeting wherein and wherefore the wherebys and whatnots *failure to appear shall constitute the waiver of all rights and claims thereunder;* anyway it's on the thirteenth. Tomorrow, no *today* is the thirteenth!

NINA

Let me see that (*snatches it*). Relax, Nancy, *February* thirteenth.

BRYANT

Yes! Today's February thirteenth!

NINA

February? Already? Interesting.

BRYANT

This meeting's in six hours.

NINA

I'll be there, off you go then. And don't worry about the piano, play as loudly as you wish.

BRYANT

But.

She closes the door and resumes seething but now it's a bipartite seethe.

85

||||||||||

The perils and procedures of ghost calls are covered early and often in the training and subsequent life of a 911 operator. Sharon Seaborg is 911 Operator 7744 and occasionally ghosts still scare her. But not like at first. At first a call that came in, provided no information, then hung up, could send her into a tailspin.

Back then nonresponsive silence did not feel devoid of meaning, it felt as if meaning itself had placed the call then lost interest in participation. Ghosts would cause early Sharon to imaginatively fill the emptiness, but always with these horrific invented scenarios she found she was quite good at generating; *a gift for imagined pessimism* her ex-mother-in-law once helpfully called it. And the next morning checking the paper almost expecting confirmation, something like

Legless Woman Runs Out of Time

A Bronx woman, who a decade ago lost both her legs following a vicious assault by her boyfriend, was killed yesterday in the apartment of that same man, when he savagely beat her to death using one of her prosthetic legs.

Miranda Johnson, 39, apparently crawled on her belly to dial 911 during the assault but was then unable to speak into the line to provide any information. 911 Operator 7744 was unavailable for comment but her inability to procure that information is being viewed as a proximate cause of the tragedy.

Silvan Dennison, of the Bridgeport, Connecticut, Dennisons, was in custody last night.

Oh yeah, Ms. Johnson was five months pregnant at the time. No word on whether the right or left leg was used.

Not that there was any need, really, to *invent* grim horrors when their shared universe was always at the ready to actualize true ones. Relentless horrors that accumulated in everything but effect.

Because it turns out that human reactions to certain mildly complicated activities, like answering 911 calls for a living, disturb in their lack of significant variance. Which explains why someone interacting with an experienced 911 operator will almost certainly be struck by what seems to be their pretty blatant rudeness but is in fact just the gem the activity builds through constant, call-by-call, polish.

At any rate, current Sharon will take a ghost any day over those calls that establish a calamitous setting then abdicate. Calls like

People v. Dell Morkevich 911 Transcript

911: 9-1-1, Operator Seaborg, what is your emergency? Hello?
Unknown: Yes, I just watched a car drive right into a bus stop, didn't even slow down.

911: Is anybody injured, sir?
Unknown: Some guy's wearing the car, does that answer your question?

911: Location please?
Unknown: Twenty-third and Third Ave.

911: We're sending units and an ambulance.
Unknown: Don't bother, send a hearse.

911: Your name, please?
Unknown: I don't want to get involved.

Call disconnected, recording ends.
  –Intern 8311

Which spurs her into action as follows. But one thing the resulting Sprint Report won't depict is the bizarre happening that she will be dealing primarily with one Larry Brown. As in the ex-partner of her recently exed husband, Hugh Seaborg, and not the basically infinite number of other possible EMTs.

********************* Thurs. 02/12/15 *********************

INCIDENT RECORD I MAN   2   13B T60   1156   F07876 A

10-53H   PED STRUCK   P2   HOSP/RMVD

ROUTING.D B   ANT   WSF   CCD   UF61   CC

3 AVE

E 23 ST——E 24 ST

DUPLICATE JOB NUMBER F07877

02   T60   2356 @DBALTNEXTEMS*——TRAP——PIN——IFO

JAMBA JUICE STORE——STS VEH CRASHED IN BUS STOP—
    OPR 1849

05   E100   2356 @*18 EMS LOGGED

05   E100   2356 @*14 EMS VIEWED

25   E100   2356 @A8633112117911 8633

05   E100   2356 @*20 ETA UNK

91   D41A 2356   0REP1 10-91   1356 @*

91   D03A 2356   13E   10-92C 1540 @*

05   T60   2356 @BA*A5747——VEH STILL ON SCENE——
    AIDED MALE——RO 8747——ANON——WIRELESS——
    SPRINT——310 3RD AVE NW SECTOR COS. WPH2
    LAT.040.738549 LON.-073.980254 OPER 7744-CP60

05   T19   2356 @DBAF*AC SAME STILL WAITING CELL
    SITE——AT&T MOBILITY 151 E 23 ST S SECTOR COS.
    WPH2 LAT.040.740610 LON.-073.897342 OPER 1120-CP19

05   T60   2357 @T*

05   T111   2357 @DBF* ANOTHER CALL SFC MALE PIN
    TRAP VEH INOPERABLE MALE DRIVER LOC

05   T34   2357 @DBF* ANC MC WILLIAMS STS DRIVER
    HIT BUS STOP MALE AT LOC BLEEDING NO MEDICAL
    ASSIST ON SCENE ADV ASAP OPR 1059-CCP23

05   T34   2358   @B* COWEN SHAWN 646 334-1892 CELL
SITE TMOBILE 231 THIRD AVE SECTOR S COS.WPH2
LAT.040.739192 LON.0083.767980 OPER 1120-CP19

05   T34   2358   @B* COWEN SHAWN 646 334-1892——MC
STS NOT INVOLVED——N LEAVING LOC——OPR 1120-
CP19

05   D03A   2358   @D*

05   T25   2359   @DBF* ANOTHER CALL FC STS SAM ELOC-
STS PED STRUCK AT TH ELOC-ADV FC POLICE EMS
ASAP-OPR 1120

05   T60   2359   @DBF* STS AIDED MLE STS GUSHING
BLOOD OUT OF FACE N HEAD AIDED HAS LOC OPR 1849

05   T92   2359   @D*

05   D03A   2359   @*

05   D03A   2359   @D*

05   T92   2359   @D*——SPCT LEVI PLATOON——SPCT
PRESTON

05   T60   2359   @DBF*FC——AUTH OF SEC E CONFIRMED
PED STRUCK-PLZ RUSH THE BUS——D1849

05   T60   2359   @DBF*FC——MALE HISPANIC BLEEDING
FRM HEAD N FACE——HIT BY BMW——151 E 23 ST S
SECTOR COS.WPH2 LAT.040.740610 LON.-073.897342 OPER
1849

05   T60   0001   @DB*FC——AUTH OF SEC E CONFIRMED
PED STRUCK——PLZ RUSH THE BUS——D1849

05   T60   0001   @DB*FC——ANOTHER CALL—BLACK
BMW——RAN UP ON SIDEWALK——AND CRASHED
INTO BUS STOP——PERP MW ASLEEP——WHT SHIRT

05   T60   0001   @BA*A5747——VEH STILL ON SCENE——
AIDED MALE——RO 8747——ANON——WIRELESS——
SPRINT——310 3RD AVE NW SECTOR COS. WPH2
LAT.040.738549 LON.-073.980254 OPER 7744-CP60

12   D03A   0002   13E 10-84   0002 @*

05   T60   0004   @DB*FC——STS EMS JUST ARRIVED ON
SCENE

05   T60   0004   @DB*FC——SPCT LONG NTFD D7744

```
05   T60   0005   @*
05   T60   0005   @DB*FC——STS EMS ON SCENE AIDED
     MALE CONSCIOUS
05   T60   0006   @DB*FC——0REP1 10-91 0006
05   T60   0007   @DB*FC——SEC E REQ SGT TO LOC——
     AIDED MALE WITH NUMEROUS LACERATIONS TO
     HEAD N FACE——JAWS NEEDED——NOT LIKELY——
     D7744
05   T60   0008   @MU*——SGT ONSENE——7744
05   T60   0009   @MU*——JAWS ASAP——7744
05   T60   0010   @MU*——OPS SIT NTFD——SPCT
     LONG——7744
05   T60   0010   @*
05   T60   0011   @*
05   T60   0011   @N*
05   T60   0012   @DBNS*——PLS HAVE PATROL SUPV 10-1
     OPS——OU——NS——7744
05   T60   0016   @DB*FC——STS EMS ON SCENE——
     REVISE——AIDED MALE WITH LACERATION TO
     ABDOMEN
05   T60   0018   @DB*FC——AIDED = MALE HISPANIC 47 YO
05   T60   0020   @DB*FC——AIDED IS LIKELY
05   T60   0018   @DB*FC——MALE HISPANIC 47 YO
05   T60   0108   @DB*FC——BODY REMOVED TO
     BELLEVUE
14   B01A   0111   @*
```

This kind of unsettling stuff has to stop. Or she has to lose the ability to unsettle. And the circadian anomaly that is the 23:05 to 06:55 shift doesn't help. Because everything just seems *worse* at, say, three-forty in the morning. Maybe it's because the ambient, still silence is prospectively mirroring what comes immediately after all endings and this intuition causes us to counter the resulting dread with mental noise in a way that simply isn't necessary when the sun is flaring life out into the sky and everything is crackling with responsorial noise. Sweet, occlusive noise.

84

||||||||||

Nina Gill dislikes sunlight intensely and countenances dilatory human activity even less. This is currently problematic because she is as hungover as a person can be and achieving this while only somewhat standing in the remarkably luminous reception area of a high-level law firm, where she is told a Havisham Esq. will be with her shortly.

She sits on a sofa and slowly slinks into an almost fully reclined pose. She could even sleep, she finds, except she is having trouble with the painful immanent brightness of the room, from which she resolves to shield her eyes through various methods of varying efficacy while mentally cursing the negligent absence of her shades (two giant black spheres only barely resolving into the shape of glasses). First, she predictably raises her horizontal hand to the fore of her head as if saluting a military superior. But while this does create some coveted shade, it also has the disadvantage of requiring muscular exertion that while admittedly minimal is nonetheless sufficient to ensure that, in her condition, it cannot be sustained. Next, she is, in contravention of all possible sense, raising her left foot to block the photonic beams emitting from the primary culprit. Aside from the obvious objection that this is even more physically exertive than her first attempt, there's the usually-little-attended-to-by-her question of what others are experiencing as a result of her actions, which in this case amounts to something strongly suggestive of pornography so that she drops the foot. Now she makes the nearly startling discovery that this law firm feels the need to provide *two*, count 'em, two coatracks—one on each side of the sofa. The only possible response then is to tilt each rack towards its twin until the tops conjoin above the sofa and their contents spill down to create a rudimentary coat canopy that resolves the Spotlight v. Shade battle conclusively.

But the moment Nina Gill settles deeply into the darkened slumber that is the just reward of the successful artist, the evil receptionist informs her that Mr. Havisham will see her now. Nina rises reluctantly, parting the odd curtain to emerge as if to applause. But even this minor disturbance, the parting, is enough, after a two-second delay, to disturb the structure's fragile ecosystem such that the entire metallic-fibrous mess implodes with maximal commotion and significant disruption to all nearby attempts at the practice of law. She continues, leaving ample destruction in her wake.

Nina walks into Havisham's office. Seated there is her brother and he's surrounded by a team of lawyers. Havisham seems friendly enough as Nina takes a seat.

NINA

I see you have your usual phalanx of lawyers, Daniel. Well, this time you're going to need them. And I'm glad there's so many of them, because none of them looks individually capable of operating a toaster.

ANONYMOUS LAWYER #1

We didn't come here to be insulted, Mr. Havisham.

NINA

Oh? Where do you usually go?

MR. HAVISHAM

All right, let's get started. Ms. Gill, can I assume you have no representation?

DANIEL

Of course not, see what I mean? Who shows up for something like this without representation?

NINA

How dare you? Really! My attorney is outside using the restroom. Is that okay with you gentlemen, the party of the worst part? As soon as she returns we can begin and not a moment before.

Everyone just sits there without saying a word. How much time passes? Enough to vault past uncomfortable and into unambiguous embarrassment.

NINA

Well, I believe I need to use the restroom myself so I'll thank you to excuse me briefly.

She walks out into the reception area in desperation (any woman she picks will be known to Havisham) to see a young woman stepping through the aforementioned destruction to deliver greasy brown paper bags to the receptionist. Spotting the deliverer's Brown University sweatshirt she approaches it aggressively.

NINA

You attend Brown?

DIA

(*excited*)

Yes! How'd you know? Oh (*remembering the sweatshirt*) duh. I'm Dia, a potential grad student there potentially writing my potential thesis on—

NINA

I'm Brown too, class of unintelligible mumbling.

DIA

What?

Nina is looking at Dia, estimating her size.

                        NINA

What are you about four foot ten?

                        DIA

I beg your pardon, I'm almost average height!

Nina grabs a jacket off a nearby chair and violently places it on Dia.

                        NINA

Listen, Dina, us Brownies have to stick together.

                        DIA

Dina?

                        NINA

So come with me.

                        DIA

What? Where?

                        NINA

You're my lawyer, beyond that don't be nosy.

                        DIA

I don't know, a legal career?

                        NINA

More like a legal five minutes, try to follow.

                        DIA

Got you, but where did I go to school?

NINA

The hell are you talking about? No one's asking that.

DIA

Well, it's a little hard to get into character when—

NINA

Fine, what law school do you want to have gone to?

DIA

I'm thinking Princeton. Yeah, Princeton Law, the very bastards who rejected me must now watch as—

NINA

Fine! Princeton Law it is, but let me do all the talking, Counselor.

Nina and Dia enter. The balance of power has swung as, to the astonishment of the room's inhabitants, Nina did have a lawyer and, at a minimum, she is nearly as striking as Nina.

NINA

Okay, only now can we begin. This is my attorney, Dina, um, Rousseau, and she graduated top of her class Princeton Law so don't try anything funny, Daniel's crew.

ANONYMOUS LAWYER #2

Princeton doesn't have a law school.

NINA

Of course not, that's what makes it so impressive (*shoots Dia a dirty look*). All right, Havisham. Let's get to it, we're busy women.

HAVISHAM

Yes (*clears throat*). I believe we should, in fact, begin. Mr. and Ms. Gill, as you know, your father's holdings are extensive and his health is failing.

Nina seems mildly surprised at the failing health part.

HAVISHAM

The net worth of these holdings is estimated in the billions and as his only two heirs some thought must now be given to what will be done with your rather, um, sizable inheritances . . .

As Havisham speaks, Nina allows her imagination free rein. What will she do with billions? She daydreams the following:

The President of the United States is in his war room surrounded by numerous generals and only the highest-level members of his staff. On a giant screen appears Nina. Forming a semicircle behind her are heavily armed half-monkeys-half-robots looking menacing in support of their evil leader.

NINA

Lastly, unless the actor who so deftly portrayed Cousin Oliver on beloved seventies sitcom The Brady Bunch *appears within the hour in this lair and performs skillful cunnilingus on me and my henchwomen I will detonate the device, thereby destroying North and South America and leaving only Central America, or as it will thereafter be known: America.*

She has missed something.

HAVISHAM

Ms. Gill? Ms. Gill, is that acceptable?

NINA

Oh, yes, well, pending the approval of my obscenely compensated attorney, of course.

Everyone looks at Dia, who is oblivious and appears to be working on a particularly thorny issue with one of her fingernails.

HAVISHAM

Okay, well, moving on we arrive at the football-related holdings, which I understand tend to be the greatest source of contention.

NINA

Only since my brother decided he was a football man.

DANIEL

No, I'm a businessman, but football happens to be the best business the family's involved in.

NINA

Yes, so good that you lead a contingent hell-bent on locking out the players.

DANIEL

Well, that's neither here nor there.

NINA

Agreed, it's everywhere.

HAVISHAM

At any rate, perhaps the following clause can lay your dispute to rest. It reads as follows: *Mr. Worthington Gill, desiring, above all, a seamless familial transition as regards football ownership, hereby decrees that Nina Gill will forthwith assume sole ownership of the football team.*

NINA

Yes! I knew Pop wouldn't let me down! In your smug face, Daniel!

Nina is doing a celebratory dance that is directed primarily at her brother but also occasionally at his legal representation. Dia at first only observes closely but soon is caught up in the spirit and joins in with skillful complementary movements.

HAVISHAM

Ladies, please. If you would be so kind as to allow me to finish. Nina Gill will forthwith assume sole ownership of the football team here-inafter referred to as the Paterson Pork.

NINA

I'm sorry, come again with that pork part?

ANONYMOUS LAWYER #2

What's wrong, Miss Football, never heard of the Pork?

NINA

The hell you driving at, Havisham?

HAVISHAM

Apparently, in addition to owning the Dallas Cowboys, Mr. Gill owns or now I suppose *owned* the Paterson Pork of the IFL.

NINA

The what-now?

HAVISHAM

The IFL or Indoor Football League.

ANONYMOUS LAWYER #1

Surely you've heard of it, Ms. Gill. Along with the league's perennial doormat, the Pork?

Laughter.

NINA

And this concerns me why?

HAVISHAM

Concerns you, Ms. Gill, because the Pork is yours.

NINA
(*hopeful*)

Along with the Cowboys?

HAVISHAM
(*sympathetic*)

No. I'm sorry, but ownership of the Cowboys will be transferred to Mr. Daniel Gill alone.

Nina collapses into her chair. Dia hasn't been paying the greatest of attention but she knows enough to sense that Nina is crushed by developments. As a member in good standing of the bar she has a professional obligation to react. She rises.

DIA

This is outrageous, I object!

HAVISHAM

Objections aren't really appropriate in this forum but—

DIA

I demand that whatever negative consequence has befallen my client be immediately rescinded and that this be done in a trebled fashion and *tout de suite* as we say in the courts of this great land, which incidentally is *our* land! Moreover, you can expect a happiest corpses petition from me before lunch unless and until my client is granted full ownership of that cowpoke thing she wanted.

DANIEL

Okay, I think we're done here.

NINA
(*rising*)

We are done, yes. But let me leave you with this parting thought, gentlemen. Pork . . . is no longer just the other white meat. Pork will soon be the name of a championship football team.

All snicker except Daniel.

                          NINA

Same goes for the IFL or whatever that concoction is called.

                          DANIEL

Listen, Nina.

                          NINA

One more thing, Daniel. When the Pork are parading down the
Canyon of Heroes don't expect an invite.

                          DANIEL

Listen, don't be like that. Come back to the Cowboys and run all the
football, I won't interfere. Just stay out of the business side, that's all I
ever asked. That's a good offer, Nina. Consider it.

                          NINA

Considered, now listen to *my* offer. Because once I walk out that door
it's gone. Transfer full ownership of the Cowboys to me. You can still
have all your fun with your little oil wells and leveraged derivatives
or whatever, but the team must be mine and mine alone. Otherwise,
well, I think you know.

She purposely stops talking and just looks at Daniel. Daniel's attorneys
are doing more incredulous snickering. Is this woman clinically
delusional? Daniel, however, is not laughing. He appears to be seriously
considering it.

                          DANIEL

I can't, Nina. There's just too much money involved and I have no
confidence that you would respect that in the slightest.

NINA

Okay then, we'll see how that works out for you. Let's go, Ms. Rousseau.

Dia doesn't stir.

NINA

Ms. Rousseau! (*staring at Dia in expectation*)

Now everyone is staring at Dia until finally she realizes she's supposed to be Rousseau and jumps up.

DIA

Yes, Counselor, let's go! I mean, I'm the counselor, let's go, Client. I mean, Ms. Gill. (*quietly*) Let's go.

They leave together, through the reception area, affecting an air of great dignity.

FEMALE (*O.S.*)

Hey, isn't that my jacket?

They are in a nearby RapidPark, where Nina approaches her car.

DIA

My God, that was intense! Lawyering is brutal, even when it's just *pro boner*.

NINA

You definitely threw some boners in there.

DIA

So what now?

NINA

Now?

DIA

I mean.

NINA

Are you applying for employment?

DIA

I'm . . . not sure. What's the position?

NINA

Quit that deli job, I'll halve your salary then double it.

DIA

So you'll pay me what I'm making now?

NINA

Well done, just making sure. You're hired, and I'll double it for real.

DIA

But what's the position?

NINA

Sidekick, what else?

DIA

That's . . . not . . . a real title.

NINA

You said your degree was in marketing.

DIA

Never said that.

NINA

Which is perfect because we need someone to market the hell out of the Pork if we're going to take down the NFL. You'll have full autonomy; as long as you run every single thing by me. Come.

DIA

Coming! Aren't first days on the job so exciting?

83

||||||||||

Travis Mena, MD, needs those initials to mean a lot but is strongly starting to suspect they don't. MD, MD, MD, repeat it often enough and it starts to sound like *empty*. Travis is sitting in Bellevue Hospital Emergency Room and it's the first time this shift he's had a chance to think. He's thinking that if those initials aren't magical then it's just *Travis*—the same boy who would obsessively pluck his eyelashes out— as the only resident at one of the fulminating hot spots of the universe with the attending again nowhere to be found.

He's not ready for this, accompanying initials or not.

There's a joke: *What do you call the guy who graduates last in his medical school class? Doctor.* As in, same thing you call the graduate chosen to nervously enunciate platitudes at the commencement.

Maybe that's supposed to be a testament to the training; but to someone who's been intimately subjected to it, the *training* is like everything surrounding it, unimpressive. For four years he impressed no one; but while that failure to impress certainly impressed him, evidence of sound ambient judgment is at least mildly impressive, the fact that his failure to impress made no lasting impression only served to impress upon him how wildly unimpressive the whole enterprise was.

The world hums by on illusion. He felt he could declare that as a fact in general force. But he also conceded that, if pushed, he could only respond with arguments drawn from his small medicinal slice of it.

Take, as example, the process that got him sent to Bellevue in the first place. The recent med school grad must begin a residency, but where? It's not simply a case of apply then, if lucky, pick. Because, in a process that may have no real-world analogue, what matters is not what the applicant wants but rather how well the quantum of want it has towards an entity aligns with that entity's amount of reciprocal want.

Which, upon further reflection, maybe suggests the analogue of romantic love and courtship, where a substantial portion of early interaction in that field consists of the participants trying to gauge the precise equation applicable to the reactants that are each party's perhaps fluctuating level of interest and the reactions that tend to endure are the ones where a sweet-spot valence is achieved early on.

So what happens is the applicant identifies say a dozen residency programs and interviews at them. Now comes the weird part, where the applicant ranks the programs in order of preference and the programs do the same with their interviewees. Incredibly what then controls is a *matching* system whereby the new doctor goes to the program that will result in the respective rankings agreeing and which, here, resulted in Travis Mena attending the place he least wanted to attend while that place got the resident it least wanted.

Why Bellevue was last on Travis's list was his desire to continue skating. Because one cannot walk into a place like Bellevue Hospital, as Travis did for the first time the day of his interview, and inhale anything but urgent intensity. Problem with intensity is it runs counter to the vast network of passive entitlement that turns Travis Menas into doctors. Because the story of Mena becoming a doctor was one less of achievement than of inertia. The invisible force that can and did subtly propel the only child of Dr. Ben Mena from elite school to elite school with elite prep courses that got him into other elite schools where he could join organizations that lament the direction the country is taking, where hard work is no longer paramount, when in reality the speaker has no genuine relationship with that concept, is nothing if not effective.

Thing is, that effectiveness has its limits. And someone trying to extend it into the wrong arena may find that suddenly all anyone cares about is results, not things like reputation or prestige.

For Travis, the seeds of this truth began to germinate his previous shift, when, despite his best efforts, he somehow found himself immersed in a first night of a trauma surgery rotation at a Level I trauma center. And, worse, no one could find the attending when they brought in a forty-seven-year-old wearing those blue-collar overalls. But with its entire midsection essentially consisting of a lance surrounded by the wearer's mealy pink and gray insides.

82

‖‖‖‖‖‖‖

What would education look like if its ultimate goal were incarceration? Where would it occur? There are many fertile possibilities. For example, in East New York, Brooklyn, you have Cypress Hills Houses, a housing project made up of fifteen seven-story buildings that at times seem more penal than anything the New York City Department of Correction could ever devise.

Locations like that (where shots were once fired during a mayoral press conference announcing a crackdown on guns) are their own kind of special training. Nuno's from Cypress and starting at age thirteen has extensively engaged in precisely the kind of conduct that generally results in incarceration. He has watched as pretty much everyone he knows fulfilled that expectation so he has, over the years, spent significant time imagining what it must be like to be *in*. And this has not been fanciful imagining either but rather the kind that seems based on at least probability. The expected result might be someone for whom sudden incarceration would not be the all-out electric shock it would be for others.

But there are events for which there is no such thing as adequate preparation and one of them is the suddenly savage restriction of your motility. Because freedom is one of those things only adequately experienced in the negation, as with its sudden absence. That squeezing the prisoner feels is the sensation of their soul dying.

The bus with Nuno rattles over the only bridge to Rikers Island and he forces himself to observe. The razor-wire coils only a certain way—the DNA of the island. This is a darkness that truly descends. A sudden desperation radiates from his skin. He is being held and claustrophobia fills his lungs. This is low-grade terror but still terror and his response is an agonized search for dissociation.

Nuno thinks how his only ally now is René Descartes. Descartes basically started that whole mind-body dualism and this is the only out he sees right now. If two things are separable then it stands to reason that one can intentionally separate them.

Nuno is going to do this. They can put him in Rikers but they can't make him live there. There's two of him and only one's going in.

But which of the two is making that decision? He wants to say his mind but that, he knows, is question begging. There's only a mind to make the decision if the duality exists; if it doesn't, the question is meaningless.

The point is there's no choice involved, where the body goes there goes the mind, giving great support to those who argue against the duality's existence. And if the duality exists despite the absence of choice then, viewed that way, the body itself is a form of prison, no?

And if that's the case then an actual prison loses a lot of its potential to cause pain. Or does this further imprisonment only aggravate what is already a serious lesion?

What's that thing where someone suddenly realizes that targeted attention has been directed at them for some time without their knowledge and that sudden realization somehow allows you to rewind in a sense and experience some of what you missed the first time? He thinks of angels. Angels!

"*Of angels?*"

The screamer is a corrections officer. Nuno, a heavy noticer, sees H. SEABORG on his chest, bursting arms, and a strange packet peeking out of his back pocket.

"DeAngeles?"

He says nothing, just reads at a closing distance from the packet.

"Nuno DeAngeles!"

"Yeah, here."

"Not a good start, son. This is not a place for fucking daydreaming."

"Probably true."

"Oh shit, that *Nuno DeAngeles*? You get protective custody?"

"What?"

"I'm looking at your card, your lawyer could have requested PC, you know. You're gonna need that."

"I agree, protective custody is needed. Everybody here, all fifty thousand of them—"

"Twelve thousand."

"—is going to need protection from me. Take care of that, will you, Officer?"

"Funny guy."

CO Hugh Seaborg said this not in the service of sarcasm but because it was true, he actually grinned. And Hugh had found so little amusement during his months working the island, his recent assignment to *transport* doing nothing to alleviate this absence, that even as he did it, he felt he was actually exaggerating this little exchange into a respite from tedium.

Although it *was* the kind of thing you told the wife about when you got home, in the case of the overnight shift, the next afternoon.

She wasn't a great audience for this kind of thing and he was no born storyteller but even he would know enough to start with something like *Guess who I drove in last night?* Then he could have added a little nugget about the experience. The PC thing would work good there.

None of that will be necessary. And what better evidence that he was having trouble adjusting to this fact than these kinds of constant false starts where he will think of what he's going to say to Sharon only to remember, with a sudden chest jump, that far as he is concerned there is no Sharon and only barely a six-year-old named Donnie?

Had that Nuno kid actually placed his hand on his shoulder, a massive breach, while he was peripherally aware of the intrusion but somehow disinterested in preventing it?

Why would he . . .

Barely a Donnie . . . no Sharon. Not *under the eyes of the law,* whatever that means. No marital home just a no-fault house in Paterson, NJ, with alienated irreconcilable affections, and he remembers that lawyers get rich using words no one else understands except the judge that pays them.

81

||||||||||

Years back, when Sharon Seaborg was shopping for a house, the first in her family to do so, she chose near Route 80 in Paterson because of her almost certainly misguided belief that genuine horror relies on a cloak of secrecy, so that nothing truly horrific could ever occur so close to a major thoroughfare.

Though maybe the original purveyors of the Indoor Football League, those many uneventful years back, were relying on something similar when they chose the location of their headquarters then poured not a penny thereafter into its maintenance.

Nina and Dia arrive at that building in Paterson, New Jersey. It doubles as team offices for the Pork as well as IFL headquarters. In a second-floor office, at a desk buried in paper, is the league commissioner, who, grooming-wise, looks as if he was recently rescued from a deserted isle. They knock and go in.

DIA

Mr. Gordon? Eric Gordon? Commissioner Gordon?

GORDON

Yes, all of the above! Who is it? What do you want? And how'd you get past security?

DIA

Security? You mean the three-legged dog out there?

GORDON

Right, Tripod. How'd you evade him?

DIA

He was sleeping.

GORDON

Damn narcoleptic dog!

NINA

Listen, Gordon. As enthralling as this interaction's been, I'd like to skip ahead a bit. I'm Nina Gill, new owner of the Pork, and you are hereby relieved of your duties as IFL commissioner.

GORDON
(*excited*)

Really? Relieved? Oh, that's the perfect word for it, what a relief! I do feel compelled to train my replacement, of course, so here.

He hands her a truly giant binder overflowing with paper.

GORDON

Everything you could possibly want to know about the league but were afraid to ask is in there.

He's walking out with an energy he displayed no evidence of before.

GORDON

Good luck, Commissioner Gill. You'll need it!

DIA

I didn't know you had the authority to fire him.

NINA

Me either, I just liked the sound of it.

DIA

This is exciting, you're the new commissioner!

NINA

Thrilling.

DIA

Listen, I know I've only been in your employ like twelve hours but . . . being that . . . when . . .

NINA

You want a promotion, don't you?

DIA

Just that *sidekick* sounds so menial.

NINA

Fine, you said your degree is in administration.

DIA

I didn't.

NINA

You're deputy commissioner, with another doubling.

DIA

Oh, my word! This is so unexpected.

NINA

You lobbied for it.

DIA

I'll need to be trained of course.

NINA

Sure, it's a two-pronged training program.

DIA

I'm all ears.

NINA

Okay, three-pronged, first prong is don't say things like *I'm all ears.* Second, I like my coffee like I like my men, black and bitter. And lastly, here (*hands her the binder*). Learn this like your life depends on it, because it genuinely does.

DIA

I'm on it!

NINA

Really? Because it looks to me like you're just standing there with that goofy grin on your face. See you tomorrow, Deputy, try to keep the league solvent until I return.

The next day around noon Nina returns to find that Dia has slept there, which strikes Nina as not the safest sequence of events, poring over the binder while watching the twenty-four-hour sports network and listening to the twenty-four-hour sports radio.

DIA

You know, this league's not as pathetic as you think.

NINA

More?

DIA

Less.

NINA

How's that coffee coming?

DIA

Middle shelf, extreme left.

NINA

Impressive.

DIA

I'm serious about the league. Listen up. Twenty teams and except for ours all are located in a place with no NFL or even high-level college presence, but these are places with legitimate football pedigrees.

NINA

Yet I'd never heard of it.

DIA

No TV hurts, of course, but look at this! Every team plays in a legitimate facility, some of the premier arenas in the country.

NINA

Arenas, ugh, indoor football, and exclusively to boot.

DIA

And in the summer, which seems weird because I associate football with, like, the changing leaves and cold, you know?

NINA

You and everyone else. But what do you expect them, I mean *us*, to do? Play at the same time as the NFL?

A song comes on the radio. The song is *new* and the song is good because it was a good song forty years ago and now the best part of it has been stolen, or rather *sampled* while a person with an undeniable talent that is rhythmic more than musical in nature is using that talent over the preexisting part. Problem is the only accepted way to display that talent is through language, and talent in this limited rhythmic area not only is not predictive of talent in the language arena but almost seems to contraindicate the very absence of same. But Dia's head slides side to side in a situation where the language involved can't even be said to rise to the level of incidental, unless you're the sort for whom words are always paramount.

NINA

Hell's this?

DIA

This is Young Scuzzy, he's been shot fifteen times and served five different terms of imprisonment. Or maybe it's the other way around. Anyway, today his searing musical portrayals straight from the streets hold a cracked mirror to—

NINA

I mean *what* is this? Did you hear what he just said about your sister?

DIA

I don't have a—

NINA

Do we have the ability to control the precise notes that come out of that thing?

DIA

We do, indeed.

NINA

I'll take care of it then. In the interim let's pretend the device only plays the rests between notes and, to be clear, the rests are silence.

                    DIA

I know what you're going to say, about classical music and how it
relates to this.

                    NINA

That?

                    DIA

That it's vastly superior.

                    NINA

If by *that* you mean high examples of it then no sane person disputes
that.

                    DIA

I think I might dispute it.

                    NINA

Precisely.

                    DIA

But also, I guess, sometimes things like superiority don't even matter's my point. Sometimes you just want a mindless distraction, a
convenience store chocolate bar. And if all we had were Brahms and
Mahler, music could never serve that function—the one pop music
fills so ably.

                    NINA

By that reasoning though, whenever pop music tries to be more
than convenience store chocolate it makes itself irrelevant, since we
already have Wolfgang and Ludwig for that.

                    DIA

Maybe.

NINA

No.

DIA

No?

NINA

No, because of two things.

DIA

Auto-Tune.

NINA

Language.

DIA

And dancing.

NINA

And the human voice.

DIA

That's what I meant.

NINA

Language and the human voice are why we sometimes just need this lesser iteration of Music.

DIA

(*pointing up at the television*)

Oh, look! I've been waiting for this, your brother called a press conference to give an update on their labor situation.

Before many microphones set up outside NFL headquarters in Manhattan, stands Daniel Gill, surrounded by furious media activity. He pulls out a small sheet of paper and reads:

DANIEL

Regrettably, the union's latest position is so unacceptable, the players
would continue to retain fifty-six percent of the revenues as called for
in the just-expired collective bargaining agreement that resulted in
a tripling of revenue, that the owners have no choice but to lock out
the players effective immediately. No questions at this time, unless it's
from one of our TV partners in private. Thank you.

A commentator indicates that:

COMMENTATOR

According to my sources, the owners intend to play serious hardball
with the union and are willing to sacrifice an entire season if need be.

Nina mutes it.

NINA

You say your degree's in journalism, huh?

DIA

No.

NINA

I want you to use all your newspaper, radio, and television contacts—

DIA

I don't have any.

NINA

—to schedule a press conference for tomorrow morning. Poor Daniel, maybe we can get him a job in the IFL parking cars or something.

80

||||||||||

The problem for Jorge de Cervantes was they all claimed to be some variation of QUIK. This made it difficult for the mere mortal in charge of a parking garage to differentiate it from competitors so that the numbers go up. And up enough that those who look at them will attribute the rise to the manager's actions and not to amorphous wave-like fluctuation.

His idea, and he put it into effect literally the day he was at long last properly promoted, was a name change to the stronger RapidPark. What a language, man, with seventeen words where maybe one or two would do. A fact his son adored. But easy for him to feel that way, the language having naturally arisen in him, not violently injected into him from a foreign source. The language kept disorienting him enough that part of the above choice was probably just the similarity to the Spanish *rápido*.

The name change was cosmetic, but not solely so as it was coupled with a renewed, almost surgical, devotion to the efficiency the new name promised.

On the slight chance any condescension may arise, understand that the parking of cars in an indoor, downtown Manhattan parking garage is a highly complicated operation requiring constant and precise neural calculations that then marry almost athletic motor tasks undertaken with attendant time pressure and minimal error-supporting margins. And there was a chance—not a certainty, just a definite chance—that Jorge de Cervantes was the world's foremost expert in this activity, the chessy maneuvering of aluminum alloy rectangles into and out of impossibly constrained spaces.

The story of Jorge de Cervantes was now history and it was a history of work, little but. And because real work is done by hands, not fingers or words, he could look at his hands, look through the various discolorations and hypercolorations, the palms under layers of dead human leather, with unpredictable but permanent swellings and indentations, and see how much those hands had held and done, how they'd become inured to decades of abuse, yet how little all that activity had accrued to his benefit.

From age ten delivering newspapers in Manizales, Colombia, all the way up to a parking spot in a Bogotá bank, it'd all been steady if unsatisfying progress. A bank is a relatively calm place without uniforms or name tags and he had an office and a comely secretary and the only thing that kept this from developing into static long-term comfort was the bank's location and the banker's impatience at the notion that everything is just more big-time in America.

What Jorge failed to realize is that this seductive element would have very little daily relevance to a person who has, in essence, rewound time to when they were unskilled fodder for exploitation. So suddenly this quasi-American found himself, for example, obeying cartoon chickens at a fast-food restaurant. These places are highly regimented work environments, but approximately zero percent of the precision involved is directed towards the achievement of employee safety or comfort. So almost always an increase in a workstation's intensity (the electronic board above featured animated depictions of what they sold and they stacked like poker chips on top of each other to inform him what level of intensity he needed to sustain [e.g. a cartoon chicken flexing a double biceps pose conveyed the need for more grilled chicken sandwiches]) resulted in cuts, burns (the back of his right hand would eventually be covered only by what comes after the skin that grows hair), and especially twisted ankles—the floors of these places, like working on the surface of a giant bar of soap. And, oh, you had to punch out to use the bathroom.

From there he moved on to janitor. The bleach used to inundate the floors of the glassy office building was so potent, and utilized to such excess, that it emptied the user's nose in what felt like a deluge of brain tissue but, notwithstanding that, the user had no discretion to reduce the amount involved—it was assumed you had no abilities beyond certain predetermined motor tasks, the rules had to be in place for everyone, with no variance.

Dishwasher, restaurants don't have time to use automatic ones.

Factory worker. The existence of enough commerce that a factory could *specialize* in the creation of bags and he could operate its forklift until one day the steering wheel slipped out of his hand and circled violently to brutalize his thumb.

Steelworker. Bethlehem Steel had a location in Hoboken, NJ, then they didn't. Then they had none anywhere.

Driving a van. Deliveries in impossibly clusterfucked Manhattan needed to be made by commercial vans and their drivers, not trucks.

Cabdriver. Unfortunately, the only money to be made in the taxi-cab game is for the owners of the medallions, not the drivers who rent them.

And, lastly, a parking garage, where the discovery of a latent yet significant talent in his mid-forties was almost unnerving.

But because de Cervantes was not one to let a talent, no matter how obscure, go unexploited, he set about honing this odd ability to position cars optimally. And, God knows, he was always a worker so he also just outworked everyone around him until the garage was, in a sense, his. He even sometimes let himself think that this might be his final stop. I mean, he wasn't the owner, true, but he was making more than ever before; no garage got you your car faster and no place on Earth demanded more automotive babysitting.

So, he had taken to asking himself, *What's the problem?* This meant *Why does he feel this way inside?* Because if it was undoubtedly true that the external signifiers were as good as they'd ever been (a closing date within the month on a Bergen County house; fine, no palace, but still a universe away from Paterson. An eighth-grade son trouncing the academic competition. A fifth-grade daughter with a superluminary smile and nature. That former secretary, now wife, gleefully making extensive interior decoration projections), it was also true that he'd recently made the mistake of glancing then looking at the abyss and there was a definite danger of progression into a stare. He was asking the dreaded *why* questions and inappositely asking them at a time when celebratory satisfaction was more appropriate.

He had, he saw, intentionally reduced himself to the physical. Eighteen Years, at times it felt like a prison sentence. He was from a family of intellectuals. Colombian politics, literature, academia. Damn, if anything, he was probably the most so inclined. But for eighteen years he'd instead set up this giant impediment (the fluctuating legality of working and in a quixotic language that wouldn't fully yield) that ensured only what he'd come to view as a life of subservience.

Imagine a special kind of incarceration: self-chosen but impossible to retract. It's true he'd tried to parole himself once. A summer in Colombia. Still a Colombian citizen. Seven years in. Look at this giant house, he'd said. Isn't it better than an apartment in Jersey City? He was weak. A four-year-old cries and back they go to the apartment.

His son and daughter are Americans. He never will be. He could make it so on paper but not where it counts, and with a pervasive racism sometimes the only partial defense is a kind of resigned acceptance masked as humor. Because what's the alternative, an endless enmity?

He goes to church these days and it only feels like more subservience. Wake up and grind, then repeat. The *sequence = repeat, repeat, repeat . . .* and like in *Siphonaptera* he was never sure what size flea he was, only that he had to continually prey and be preyed on. To what end?

Better not to think too greatly on it. Forty-seven years old, that kind of thinking was a luxury. Kierkegaard said meaning is *created* not *found*. No way Søren said that, but someone, somewhere, sometime, probably did. And, if not, Jorge de Cervantes said it and it wasn't all that difficult to locate the meaning he'd tried to create. He'd done nothing less than figure out an entire country.

Success in Colombia had been insufficient because every time you turned on the television or went to a damn movie there was that *puta* country taunting him again, the same five buildings and bridges but still. Here what matters are things like prestige and certification and he can't get those. But Nelson can, Gisella too. Nelson, for one, is maniacal. This recent realization had defused the house slightly as he stopped trying to exert even minimal control over an individual who, if he were a plant, would probably resent the sun. But the positive charge to all that was a will that would one day doubtless manifest itself in the above-cited prestigious certifications that would allow his son to absentmindedly hand the keys to a car worth more than the person parking it makes in a year. A decade or so away, and maniac or not, the kid was all heart, so that no way his aging father would still be parking cars. In the meantime, to them he was like a record that skipped and skipped and the only song that played extolled education, although in this limited mercenary way—education to then teach poetry (his sister) or chemistry (his brother) was not something crying out for repetition.

But an abyss does not become one through lack of patience. If all that was required was waiting, in this case for a thirteen-year-old to mature, anyone could endure it. No, a true abyss can only emerge through the desaturation of meaning. So, here, the suspicion that there may be no appreciable difference between becoming the guy with the car or not. Worse, that a lifetime spent trying to acquire the car achieves only a higher order of emptiness.

He had looked at, through, then *past* the surface—the quotidian distractions that deaden a mind's eye from underuse—to see only coldness. Cold that his recent highly inexact computation had revealed he'd grossed less time in the presence of his children than of his father, a man he'd seen shot dead when he was eight years old. Cold that there'd been nothing remotely transcendent about that experience, only animate matter becoming dumbly inanimate seconds later. Cold, mostly, that even those children, whose vitality often jumped into his tired face to result in a form of guilt, would one day also deanimate fully and all that then seemed so critical would simply vanish.

His most recent life (sixteen hours a day) spent inside a parking garage. No sun or wind. Only mufflers, exhaust pipes, rattling noise, smoky pestilence. And none of it theoretical or mere potentialities. Those noxious things were always the Present and they struck with the peculiar force of that element. So if he said something like *Today I inhale these fumes but tomorrow my son enrolls in one of the premier high schools in the Northeast* it wasn't that those premises weren't factu-

ally true, they were, it was the very real fear that these valid premises might nonetheless logically induce nothing while the fumes and
cinder-block walls rely on no syllogism; they just assault through Repetition, a force so potent it can cleave giant wounds into the globe
using only water.

Lacking wings to fly
Using dreams he flies

In reality he walked. Walked on dirty concrete. So late or early,
so dead of winter, even Manhattan almost whispered conspiratorially.
Walked because of a faulty fuel pump that couldn't be replaced until
Friday's payday. Walked in the resigned manner of someone finally
getting off of overwork. In the direction of a secretive bus stop. Giant
unfeeling cylindrical worms to shuffle the forgotten back and forth
anesthetically.

And it wasn't that he then developed an inhuman headache so much
as he suddenly realized he'd had one all day but had been too busy to
notice.

Then it went away. It and only everything we call all. A sped-up
evanescence so sudden and complete it most resembled flight.

79

||||||||||

We call something the *head* of something else when we want to indicate its primacy: *Nelson de Cervantes will graduate head of his class at Charles Riley Elementary in the spring; Daniel Gill has been selected by his fellow owners to head their effort on a new CBA; Sharon Seaborg's application to be head of all operators at her location was wholly ignored.* Or when someone *heads* wherever they're *heading* maybe to *head* something off but usually in an effort to get *ahead*.

Consonant with this, the *head* of the human body is the head. And primacy therein belongs to the brain (yes, over the face). Inside the brain, the primacy question becomes more problematic. What has traditionally been given prominence in that organ is maybe undeserving.

Neurons everyone knows but less understood are glial cells (the *glue* assonances are mistakenly intentional). Everywhere else people use frequency and prevalence to judge importance. With the brain, however, people have collectively decided to pretend it's 1940 and grant paramount status to neurons despite the fact they account for only about ten percent of the brain's cells (incidentally the inspiration for the oft-repeated claim that humans use only ten percent of their brains—the kind of claim that, in each instance of its incessant repetition, constitutes unintended support for itself). At any rate, a subset of glial cells is astrocytes—so named because of their astral shape—and our story intersects with the story of a certain astrocyte.

It is an underappreciated truth of our common existence that even the most complex and widespread processes can be reduced and reduced in search of an origin until reaching an inciting singularity—the sole individual or event that ignites, however innocently, the sequence whose end product may offer no clue to its successful deconstruction. Here, the individuated inciter was a single astrocyte, one of about 3.8E + 18 in the tristate area at the time.

This cell wanted to, in medical parlance, *escape senescence*. The way a cell does this is by mutating into a cancerous cell (the method by which cells do *that* is being skipped). And a cancerous cell is no different from a healthy one in that it has a ticking cellular clock it wants to obey through cell division, which division here created more cancerous progeny because the various applicable defense mechanisms all failed until the result was a colony of cancer cells—a disordered mass of cells literally crawling all over each other so crazily the mayhem chokes the life out of any nearby attempts at beneficent processes. So cancer will be the result but so what, right? There's much can be done these days, no? No.

Because remember that we're talking about astrocytes. Cancer there means glioblastoma and glioblastoma means, among other things, that nothing can be done. Because if cancer is a killer, glioblastoma is the motherfucker even killers fear. So while you'll hear references to *cancer survivors*, the living don't speak of glioblastoma in the past tense. Instead it grows and grows in the very deepest tissue of their brains until one of its resulting tumors impinges enough on some area of the surrounding brain to produce the kinds of symptoms that can be ignored no longer, then a series of steps ensues, but steps designed solely to get you maybe another year of life.

All of which means that the actions of this single astrocyte, in inciting a necrotic spiral with the opposite of a surprise ending, were the equivalent of God capriciously deleting a human from existence.

78

||||||||||

Divine intervention is the only thing can maybe save Dia. But she has her pride and won't even ask. She has pride but no media contacts whatsoever, so her creation of a viable press conference is going abysmally. Still, no chance she's going to ask Nina for help/guidance. Nina, whose idea of motivation consists of presuming wild success so that the person charged with bringing it about is supposed to almost feel like they're fulfilling a prophecy more than effecting anything. This method has not worked with Dia, who feels nothing lofty, only impending abject failure.

Failure like the next day, when Nina arrives at the location of the press conference (a conference room in the Secaucus hotel where NFL players visiting nearby architecturally horrific MetLife Stadium stay during the season). She enters directly into a backstage area where she meets up with Dia, who wears, most saliently, apprehension.

NINA

Okay, it's very simple. You stand next to me with the occasional nod. When I indicate I'm bored you pretend you just remembered another engagement I have, whisper in my ear, and we terminate. Got it?

DIA

I feel I should warn you about the, um . . . sparse attendance. I mean, the *Paterson Palimpsest* is here of course.

NINA
(*sarcastically*)
Of course, how could they miss it? Who else?

DIA
That's just it, he's the only one.

NINA
He?

DIA
(*partially pulling the curtain aside*)
See?

Nina looks and sees a single elderly man inexplicably sitting in the last row despite having his pick of seats. He is half asleep and remnants of the food spread sit on his heaving chest.

NINA
The hell is that?

DIA
I know, I'm sorry.

NINA
Did you do *anything* I said or is he related to you?

DIA
I tried, it's just that, well, when I would say the IFL a lot of laughter would ensue.

NINA
Listen closely, please. We're going to pretend the somnolent man out there is unrelated to the task I gave you. You're going to notify

his next of kin then you're going to arrange a press conference for this afternoon. That's right, a chance at redemption. Now this is where the close listening part comes in. Because when you schedule *this* press conference you're going to say that the Gill family has a major announcement to make regarding the NFL and its work stoppage. The key letter here is *N. N* as in *NFL* and not *I* as in *I better get the result I want or I'm going to kick your ass*, we good?

> DIA

Brilliant, I love it! They'll think—

> NINA

Go!

Dia starts to runs out.

> NINA

Wait, one more thing.

> DIA
> (*running back*)

Yes?

> NINA

Listen to this whenever possible.

> DIA

Oh, my word. A gift.

> NINA

No, an album.

> DIA

An album as gift, really touching if you think about it.

NINA

Then don't. Do you call it a gift when a professor hands you the textbook?

DIA

That's even better! It's like you're taking me under your wing.

NINA

Not that either, just listen to it, will you?

DIA

Song to a Seagull, if you say so.

NINA

And none of this wing business either.

DIA

You're right, we're much more like equals than that. What we have is—

NINA

About to end ignominiously if you don't leave this instant and accomplish your menial task!

Dia runs away apologetically. Nina comes out from behind the curtain and looks at the slumbering old-timer; she goes to the podium and its microphone.

NINA

—B three!

REPORTER
(*jumping up*)

Bingo!

Daniel Gill is in his office. This office measures eighteen hundred (1800) square feet. To put this in context, the apartment de Cervantes was preparing to move his family out of is one thousand (1000) square feet and the move would've been into a twelve-hundred (1200)-square-foot *house*; Sharon Seaborg's nine hundred (900) square feet at least felt more ample with the recent excision of Hugh Seaborg; the Bellevue Hospital ER reception area is nine hundred eighty (980) square feet; and an NYC subway car can fit about two hundred and fifty (250) people into its six hundred (600) square feet and about twenty Rikers Island cells like the one Nuno DeAngeles sits in would fit in that car.

Gill's feet are on his desk, he does Barker Black footwear exclusively, and he is watching footage of his televised statement the day before, mouthing along with the words and thinking it was a pretty impressive performance if he does say so himself. His secretary comes in.

SECRETARY

Sorry to interrupt, Mr. Gill. But we're receiving a great many calls wanting to confirm this afternoon's press conference and wondering if you would comment beforehand.

DANIEL

You're a little late aren't you? You mean yesterday's media event.

SECRETARY

They're saying three p.m. today. They want to know what this big announcement is the Gill family is going to make regarding the work stoppage.

DANIEL

That's crazy, I'm the Gill family, there's no announcement. Thank you, Ms. Spinn.

She leaves. Daniel restarts the footage of his performance, only now he's not watching as intently as before, he's thinking. Thinking how odd that the media would make such an easily avoidable error. Then he realizes something as the tension builds on his face.

DANIEL

Nina!

Now there's a palpable flurry of activity. The assembled media are ravenous. Is it possible that a mere day after Daniel Gill announced the lockout the parties have come to an agreement? Is Gill going to announce an attempted deathblow to the union by proactively canceling the upcoming season? All possibilities seem in play and the facility can scarcely contain the sea of eager humanity. As Nina approaches the podium with Dia at her side there is surprise in the crowd that it's Nina and not Daniel.

NINA

Thank you for attending, though from the looks of this crowd I can't imagine you had anywhere else to be. I'll be brief in deference to today's shortened attention spans. As you know, yesterday, my brother, Daniel Gill, announced the NFL's lockout of the players and there has been much speculation that the league intends to cancel the upcoming season unless it can get the union to bend over, uh, capitulate to their demands for a radically restructured compensation scheme. Naturally, football fans are concerned that there will be no professional football come fall.

I'm here to announce, no *guarantee*, that there absolutely will be professional football on Sundays this fall. Specifically, in my dual capacity as commissioner of the IFL or Indoor Football League and as owner of its Paterson Pork, I am announcing that the IFL, that most beloved of America's football leagues, will be playing a sixteen-game regular season to commence the first Sunday of September and to conclude with a championship game the last Sunday in January.

In other words, we, America, will lock out the NFL. The resources of the IFL are limitless. Consequently, the quality of play this fall will be indistinguishable from that of the just-concluded NFL season. Well, with a few differences. IFL teams will not operate at a profit. Any revenue accrued will go the players, you know, those guys who agree to cripple themselves in the future and risk paralysis and brain damage for our entertainment? Should some accidental profit somehow occur it will be distributed to the charities identified in the handout you are now receiving.

Moreover, IFL football will be real football. Played in the harshest of elements by the harshest of men in front of rabid fans who don't have to skip a mortgage payment to attend. Our referees will understand that they are there to prevent and punish serious infractions that affect the competition, not engage in protracted litigation involving obscure minutiae of the rule book, which rule book is about ten percent the size of the current NFL one.

Well, that's it for now. There's a lot more information in the packets you've received. The relevant notion is this, folks. People love football, not the NFL. They tolerated the NFL because it gave them football. Now it doesn't, so forget them. The IFL is the present and future of this sport and it remains the greatest, truest, *team* sport despite the best efforts of numbskulls like my brother. I apologize for him, he may have been adopted. Questions?

REPORTER
Just to be clear, you're no longer affiliated with the NFL despite your father's continued ownership of the Dallas Cowboys?

NINA
Good sleuthing, Scoop. I haven't been in the NFL for four years. I am the owner of the Paterson Pork, a once-proud franchise that has fallen on hard times but which will soon be ascendant.

REPORTER # 2

When were they proud? Says here they've never had a winning season.

NINA

You can be proud without success, that kind of pride. Next?

REPORTER # 3

Are you saying your league will compete with the NFL for players?

NINA

That's exactly what I'm saying. Our pockets are deep and our vision is clear. Let's say you're not under contract for next season, you're a college grad who was going to enter their draft or a free agent looking for one last contract, well, the IFL will definitely be in business in September, which means you will definitely be getting paid. Can they say that?

REPORTER # 4

Will these games be televised?

NINA

(*flirtatiously*)

Of course, silly. Oh and no local blackouts or any of that other nonsense either.

REPORTER # 4

Televised by whom?

NINA

Well, that has yet to be determined, but an obscene number of filthy-rich entities are vying for that honor as we speak.

REPORTER # 5

You mentioned playing in the elements, but isn't this an *indoor* football league? That would seem to preclude elements.

NINA

Oh, a wise guy in the press corps, eh? All right then, I'll do you the honor of answering your question just before I revoke your press pass and have you beaten within an inch of your life (*gasp in audience*). Just kidding, you can keep the press pass. Next? (*whispering to Dia*) I'm bored, get ready.

REPORTER # 5

Um, the elements question?

NINA

Okay, well, I have many high-level meetings to attend so at this time I'm going to introduce the IFL's deputy commissioner, Dia Rousseau, who is amply able to answer any further questions you might have.

Dia is mortified as Nina abruptly leaves. She had not been warned that this was a possibility. She reluctantly approaches the podium. The press corps feels emboldened by the departure of the intimidating Nina and they begin to pepper Dia.

REPORTER # 3

Says here your last name is Nouveau, who's Rousseau?

DIA

It is Nouveau, but it's sometimes pronounced Rousseau, you can see where the confusion would lie.

REPORTER # 5

What on Earth?

DIA

Okay, truth is she decided Rousseau and I've been too scared to correct her, I think you can see why.

REPORTER # 5

Still looking for an answer to that elements question.

DIA

I think Commissioner Gill answered it perfectly, we will have
weather. (*She smiles and looks around, quite pleased with herself.*)

REPORTER # 5

How?

DIA

How? How else? We will have the globe's foremost weathericians
flown in from Bangkok, Bangladesh, the . . . Bangles.

REPORTER # 2

That's not a geographic location.

REPORTER # 3

And *weathericians* isn't a word.

DIA

And they will provide weather in the following fashion. Before each
game a wheel, the Weather Wheel, will be spun, and through that
manifestation of chance the artificial weather for the ensuing game
will be determined.

REPORTER # 1

What?

DIA

Of course, at other times the element of chance will be removed. For
example, there will be no archaic coin flips in the IFL. Every team
has a mascot and those mascots engage in a pregame physical duel to
determine which team will receive the ball first.

REPORTER # 3

How is that—

DIA

And now is as good a time as any to announce the halftime entertainment at our championship game, which game will feature the positively brilliant musical stylings of Radiohead. That's right, math geeks, Radio goddamn Head! Additionally—

Dia notices Nina, who has just walked back into the room to hear the Radiohead announcement and is signaling for Dia to stop by miming a throat-slashing.

DIA

Okay, I see my time is up so . . .

REPORTER # 5

What time? You can go as long as you want.

DIA

My temporal allotment being what it is I think I'll leave you guys with this little inspirational nugget. Ummmmmm (*notices Nina and her apoplectic expression*) bye!

REPORTER # 5
(*to fellow reporter*)

Ooh, that *was* inspirational.

77

||||||||||

CO Hugh Seaborg is subject to a great many forces but none motivates him to action quite like abject fear. This time the sequence of events engendering the fear is linearly straightforward. The organization of corrections officers intentionally apes that of the military—as if in at least partial admission that what is being waged is war. And the equivalent of his commanding officer has impulsively assigned him a simple task now grown hopelessly convoluted through the use of negligence, his.

Inspired by the revelation that Hugh's fucking grandpappy Something Seaborg was the original inspiration for the creation and promulgation of the *Rikers Island Inmate Rule Book*—an admittedly inspired codification of the particulars of widespread systemic control designed to quell the desperation of the caged by raising the tools of confinement almost to the level of scientific precepts—this inferior superior has, in a most coercive manner, named Correction Officer Hugh Seaborg subhead of *The Committee to Meet a Few Times Then Tepidly Agree to Certain Mild Recommendations That Couldn't Possibly Backfire on the Recommenders Concerning the Latest Amendments to the Inmate Rule Book, Which Recommendations Will Almost Certainly Be Pointedly Ignored by the Relevant Attorneys but Which Will Allow Those Attorneys to Declare That Those on the Alleged Front Lines Were Closely Consulted.* Or so one of the committeewomen calls it.

Normally who cares? But he has incredibly misplaced the packet he was given with the tentative rule book, the island blueprints and CADs, insufficiently complex security codes, his notes, and sundry other irreplaceable addenda. He says *misplaced* only he knows said packet was safely ensconced in his back pants pocket as late as the last transport of his previous shift.

The one where the kid from the news with the weird name got off last. The kid who believe it or not touched his shoulder. The kid who . . .

The kid who could've easily been one of the all-time great *cannons* had he continued in that direction. In terms of natural talent and learned command of the applicable principles divorced from action, he was unsurpassed. The problem was ultimately one of insufficient reps. Because truth is Nuno's not one to work well as part of a team so his time in a wire mob (a group of thieves larcenously working together) was never built to last. Too many moving parts, and they never seemed to move in the precise trajectory he wanted. Often literally too.

How many times had he explained to teammates that the moving distraction, to best hold the mark's attention, should form a parabolic arc? The human eye will follow something moving in an arc without constantly returning to its origin point but this is not so when the object is moving in a straight line. Yet, incredibly, this simple concept would elude the *stick* charged with creating the distraction and often at the most inopportune times. Granted this never resulted in actual detection but only because Nuno would quickly sense the inefficiency and abort the lift. Besides, detection was beside the point. If three or four people have chosen to collaborate on a highly simple procedure like the lifting of some fuck's wallet, mere respect for craft should be enough to ensure that it be executed at the highest level possible. But the other two or three never saw it that way and whose opinion on the matter should control? He thought the star's, so he started working alone (*single o*), then not at all when the lack of violence began to disturb him.

And Nuno hadn't planned on giving up that inactivity his first night at Rikers. But there it was, a CO spewing orders at him, how offensive, while a rather interesting packet announced itself from his back pocket.

What was most delicious? The lift itself—relatively simple yet no less beautiful for its simplicity, and in its urgent audaciousness a sufficient jolt to jerk him out of what was threatening to form into full-blown existential crisis—or the fact that he would have to retain the property through what promised to be highly invasive searches?

Or maybe it was that when he finally has a chance to review the packet in his cell he can't quite believe its contents. A highest-quality *get* out of fucking literally nowhere. And that high quality related not just to its obvious utility to someone with his plans but also to the epic stress its disappearance must be causing the rightful owner. It's almost enough to make him feel bad for the dude, who hadn't come across particularly bad, unlike some of these other fucks.

But then he thinks, Fuck you, don't devote yourself to caging others and you wouldn't have to worry about it, and just resumes reading.

New York City Department of Correction

CITY OF NEW YORK

DEPARTMENT OF CORRECTION

Adopted Amendments to the

Inmate Rule Book

Section I Chapter 1 of title 39 of the Rules of the City of New York

is REPEALED, and a new Chapter 1 is added to read as follows

CHAPTER 1

INMATE RULE BOOK

& 1-01 Introduction

This chapter sets forth rules relating to inmates of New York City

Department of Correction ("Department") facilities. All inmates will also be

provided separately with detailed information relating to their

incarceration, including the subjects covered in section 1-02 of these rules.

§ 1-02 Rights and Privileges

(a) *Property*

When you first come to jail, any property that is taken from you that

involves a criminal offense may be forwarded to the appropriate law enforcement agency for possible criminal prosecution and subject you to disciplinary action. Property taken from you that does not involve a criminal offense will be identified, receipted, stored and returned to you after your discharge from Department custody. Upon incarceration, you will be given more information about what property may be kept in jail and how to get other property back after discharge.

(b)   *Recreation.*

The Department may limit your right to participate in recreation for a security related reason in accordance with State Commission of Correction standards (9 NYCRR § 7028.6). Upon incarceration you will be given more information about how and when the Department can limit recreation.

(c) *Religious rights.*

You may attend religious services with general population inmates unless you are found to pose a threat to the safety and security of the institution, including if the Department finds it likely that you will disrupt the service. Upon incarceration, you will be given more information about your religious rights in jail in accordance with New York City Board of Correction standards (§ 1-08)

(d)   *Telephone calls*

The Department may limit your telephone calls if they constitute a threat to institutional safety or security, if you abuse the telephone regulations or in accordance with a court order. Upon incarceration, you will be given more information about your rights to telephone calls.

If you are affected by a determination made pursuant to this subdivision, you may appeal such determination to the New York City Board of Correction by providing written notice. Written notice must also be provided to the Department of Correction and the Facility. You may also submit any additional relevant materials for the Board's consideration. The Board will issue a written response upon the appeal within five (5) business days after receiving the appeal

(e) *Visits.*

The Department may revoke, deny or limit your contact visits if they constitute a serious threat to institutional safety or security. Upon incarceration, you will be given more information about your right to visits and the permitted schedules of those visits.

If you are affected by a determination made pursuant to this subdivision, you may appeal such determination to the New York City Board of Correction and to the Commanding Officer by providing written notice. You may also submit any additional relevant materials for the Board's consideration.

The Board, or its designee, will issue a written decision upon the appeal within five (5) business days after receiving notice of the requested review.

§1-03 Rules of Conduct

(a) Introduction

This section sets forth the behavlor that is prohibited by Department of Correction {"Department") facilities. The grade of each offense is listed. The acts of conspiracy, attempt, and accessory will be punishable to the same degree as the actual offense involved

(b) Definitions

(1) "Accessory" shall mean assisting in any way in the violation of a Department rule, before, during or after such violation.

(2) "Any person" shall include. But not be limited to uniformed and civilian Department staff, medical staff, contractors and their employees, volunteers, visitors and inmates.

(3) "Attempt" shall mean any act that is intended to and tends to lead to a violation of a Department rule. .

(4) "Contraband" shall mean any Item that is not sold in the commissary that is not on the approved list of permissible items, that is possessed in more than the approved amount, or that the inmate docs not have permission to possess. Contraband includes items that may disrupt the safety, security, good order and discipline of the facility Any item that is

illegal for an individual not on Department property to possess is also illegal to use or possess on Department property. Possession of contraband may subject an inmate to criminal prosecution as well as disciplinary action. Any person who tries to introduce contraband into a facility may also be subject to criminal prosecution.

(5) "Conspiracy" shall mean an agreement between one or more person to violate a Department rule

(6) "Good Time" shall mean a discretionary reduction of up to one third of the term of commitment for a definite sentence or certain civil commitments, as allowed by the New York State Correction Law

(7) "Security Risk Group" shall mean persons such as gang members, intended or actual contraband recipients, and weapons carriers or users, whose actions violate laws or established rules of conduct or persons who belong to groups whose purpose is antithetical to established law enforcement authority.

(8) "Unauthorized group" shall mean five or more inmates remaining in close physical proximity to each other when not authorized to do so by Department personnel.

(c)   *Prohibited conduct*

(1)   *Arson (setting fires)*

Grade I:

100.10. An inmate is guilty of arson when he or she intentionally starts or attempts to start any fire or causes or attempts to cause any explosion.

(2) *Assault and Fighting*

Grade I

101.10 An inmate is guilty of assault on staff when he or she injures or attempts to injure any staff member. Or when he or she spits on or throws any object or substance at any staff member Assault or attempted assault on staff is always a Grade 1 offense.

101.11: An inmate is guilty of Grade 1 assault when he or she injures any other person, or when he or she spits on or throws any object or substance at any other person.

101.12. An inmate is guilty of Grade I assault on an inmate when he or she injures any other inmate. Or when he or she spits on or throws any object or substance at any other inmate.

101.13 An inmate is guilty of assault with a weapon when he or she uses any item to assault or attempt to assault any person.

101.14. an inmate is guilty of Grade I fighting when he or she engages in a physical struggle with another inmate that results in injury to any person

Grade II:

101.16· an inmate is guilty of Grade II assault when he or she attempts to injure any person other than a staff member, without using a weapon, but does not cause injury.

101.17: An inmate is guilty of Grade II fighting when he or she engages in a phvslcal struggle with another inmate that does not result in injury

Grade III:

101.18: An inmate is guilty of Grade III fighting when he or she engages in a non-violent physical struggle with another person such as horseplay, boxing, wrestling or sparring.

(3)   *Bribery*

Grade I

102.10   An inmate is guilty of bribery when he or she gives or attempts to give any benefit, including but not limited to money or valuable items, to any person, with the intent of influencing that person's conduct or obtaining a benefit for himself or herself.

(4)   *Contraband*

Grade I

103.05 Inmates shall not possess any tobacco-related products including, but not limited to, cigarettes, cigars, loose tobacco, chewing tobacco, rolling paper, matches, and lighters.

103.07 Inmates shall not sell, exchange, or distribute tobacco-related products including but not limited to cigarettes, cigars, loose tobacco, matches, and lighters.

103.08 Inmates shall not make, possess, sell, or exchange any amount of alcoholic beverage.

103.10: Inmates shall not make, possess, sell or exchange any type of contraband weapon. Any object that could be used as a weapon may be classified as a weapon.

103.10.5: Inmates shall not possess or transport Department-Issued razors outside the housing area.

103.10.6 Inmates shall return all Department-Issued razors after shaving is completed in accordance With Department or facility procedures. Razors shall be returned in the same condition as received, for example, blade and handle shall be intact.

103.11 Inmates shall not make, possess, sell, give or exchange any amount of narcotics, narcotic paraphernalia, or any other controlled substance.

103.12 Inmates shall not make, possess, sell, give or exchange any type of escape paraphernalia where there is the likelihood that an item can be used to attempt an escape, it may be classified as escape paraphernalia. Keys, possession of identification belonging to another person, or fictitious person, transferring an inmate's identification to another, possession n of employee clothing, or any other articles which would aid in an escape. or which suggest that an escape is being planned, are contraband

103.12.5: Inmates shall not possess any type of electronic telecommunication and/or recording device or any part of such instrumentt, whlch is deslgncd to transmit and/or receive telephone, electronic, digital. cellular Or radio communications The term utelecommumc.lllon device" shall include, but not be limited to, any type of instrument, devlce, machine or equipment which is designed to transmit and/or receive telephonic, electronic, digital, cellular or radlo signals or communications or any part of such instrument, device, machine or equipment as well as any type of instrument designed to have sound, or image recording abilities and shall include, but not be limited to, a cellular or digital phone, a pager, a two-way radio text message or modem device (including a modem equipment device), a camera. a video recorder and a tape or digital recording device, or any other device that has such capabilities (Radios sold in commissary are excluded from this prohibition.) Inmates shall not possess any type of device or any part of such instrument designed to have sound and/or image recording or capturing capabilities. Such devices shall include, but not be limited to cameras (digital film), video recorders, and tape or digital recording device Inmates are also prohibited from possessing any type of phone or battery charger, or *AJC* adapter for any electronic device prohibited by this rule

103.12.6: Inmates shall not possess any contraband with intent to sell or distribute such contraband.

103.12.7: An inmate is guilty of the offense of Possession of Contraband Grade I when such inmate possesses money whose value exceeds twenty {20) dollars in cash or check. Money confiscated as contraband will be deposited in the City's treasury and will not be returned to the inmate.

Grade U·

103.13 Inmates shall not sell or exchange prescription drugs or non-prescription drugs. Inmates shall not possess prescription drugs that they are not authorized by medical staff to possess. Inmates shall not possess prescription or non-prescription drugs in quantities in excess of that authorized by medical staff. Inmates are not authorized to possess any drug that by prescription, or by medical order, must be ingested in view of Department and/or medical staff.

103.14: Inmates shall not make, possess, sell, exchange, use or display any item that identifies the inmate *as* a member or associate of a Security Risk Group or of a gang. Articles of religious significance that are Security Risk Group identifiers shall only be considered contraband if they are displayed.

Grade III

103.15 Inmates shall not possess unauthorized hobby materials, art supplies or tattooing equipment or implements.

103.17 Inmates shall not possess unauthorized amounts of jewelry, clothing, or food.

(5)   *Count Procedures*

Grade II

Inmates shall not intentionally cause a miscount.

104.11 Inmates shall not intentionally delay the count.

(6) *Creating a Fire, Health or Safety Hazard*

Grade II.

~~Inmates shall not create a fire~~ hazard, health hazard, or other safety hazard

!05.11: Inmates shall not tamper with any fire safety equipment.

105.12 Inmates shall not cause any false alarms about a fire, health emergency, or create any kind of disturbance or security problem. Inmates shall not flood any living area or other area in the facility.

Grade II:

Inmates shall not store food in their housing area or any work place, except food items bought in the commissary, which must be stored in the food container provided.

105.15 Inmates shall not litter, spit, or throw garbage or any kind of waste or substance.

105.17 Inmates shall clean their cell or living area, toilet bowl, sink and all other furnishings every day. They must keep their cells and beds neatly arranged before leaving their cells or living areas for any purpose, they must clean their cells or areas and make their bed.

105.19 Inmates shall not obscure, block, obstruct, mark up, write on, or post any pictures or place any other articles on Department property, including any walls, windows, cells, or lighting fixtures.

105.20 Inmates shall not cook in any living area, including any cell.

105.22 Inmates must keep themselves and their clothes clean.

(7) *Demonstrations*

Grade I

Inmates shall not participate in, lead, attempt to lead or encourage others to participate in boycotts, work stoppages, or other demonstrations that interrupt the routine of the facility.

(8) *Disorderly Conduct*

Grade III

108.10 Inmates shall not shout out to, curse, use abusive language, or make obscene gestures towards any person.

108.11 Inmates shall not behave m a loud and noisy manner.

(9) *Disrespect of Staff*

Grade I

109.10 Inmates shall not physically resist staff members

109.11 Inmates shall not harass or annoy staff members by touching or rubbing against them.

109.12 Inmates shall not verbally abuse or harass staff members, or make obscene gestures towards any staff members

(10) *Hostage Taking*

Grade I

114.10; Inmates shall not take or hold any person hostage.

(11) *Sex Offenses*

Grade I

122.10 Inmates shall not force or in any way coerce any person to engage in sexual activities.

Grade II

122.11 Inmates shall not voluntarily engage in sexual activity with any other person.

122.12 Inmates shall not expose the private parts of their bodies in a lewd manner.

Grade III

122.13: Inmates shall not request, solicit, or otherwise encourage any person to engage in sexual activity.

(12) *Escape*

Grade I

Inmates shall not escape or aid others to escape, attempt to escape or aid others to attempt to escape. Exiting Department property, a Department facility, or vehicle without permission from Department staff is an escape. (emphasis added)

And that is a fitting place to stop. Because the way some people live in the past to better cope with the present, Nuno lives in the future. In the future he's set on creating, he leaves that island without anyone's consent, weighed down by an object of minimal physical force but outsize metaphoric and monetary. Leaves and just keeps on leaving, leaves until nothing around him is familiar and no one knows his name.

76

||||||||||

The past is fixed and without potential. A child doesn't question its setting and, hear this out, growing up the child of an NFL owner isn't all that different from growing up under a janitor if we constrict the relevant space-time slice enough.

The Gill home housed little evidence of football's relevance, that's what team facilities were for. But the way a toddler Wayne Gretzky would stare raptly whenever hockey appeared on the television screen, Nina Gill never allowed televised football to go unnoticed. And, even at age seven, she often had opinions on what she saw. Opinions she'd use a ridiculous wooden pointer (successfully requested Christmas present) to help elucidate.

NINA

See, Pop? The league is becoming more pass-oriented. I say we go with only three defensive linemen and use four linebackers. One of the four would come on every passing down giving you your four pass rushers but all four would also be available to drop into pass coverage depending on the play call and formation.

Also, I call this the shotgun. The quarterback doesn't have to be right under center like this. Let's drop him about three yards behind the center and have the center pitch it to him between his legs, like on punts. It's perfectly legal and would give the QB a far better view of the field, see?

And their father would laugh but also occasionally jot down some notes.

Or when nine-year-old Nina carefully perused her neighborhood's innocent child-operated lemonade stand then set about systematically crippling it until a victorious Nina is sitting at a bar in her driveway below a humongous fake lemon; the one with the giant hose protruding to end in a beverage gun that Daniel and three other employees are forced to operate beneath a neon sign indicating cups of the all-natural lemonade will set you back a dollar apiece. The line stretches well into the street.

Or the time in that horrific courtroom: their father, Worthington, is seated at one table with his attorneys and at the other table is their mother with hers; Nina appears to be of neither side, but instead appears to have fashioned a makeshift counsel table between them, where she sits in a serious if slightly ludicrous business suit while sternly holding a briefcase.

JUDGE
Come to order. In the matter of *Gill versus Gill* the only outstanding issue remains primary custody of the two children, let's see, Daniel and Nina Gill. Having reviewed all of the submissions and heard all of the testimony, I rule that primary custody of the two children will reside with Laura Gill, their mother. Furthermore—

NINA
I object! You have not ruled on my petition for complete emancipation, I refuse to reside with either of these cretins!

JUDGE
Young lady, I have been exceedingly tolerant of your constant interruptions and pro se filings but you are eleven years old and there is simply no precedent for—

NINA

I didn't ask you how old I was. I asked you to rule on my application to be declared an emancipated minor. A marriage is a fairly simple thing and these two screwed it up. I no longer trust them to properly water our plants let alone raise someone like me! Surely even you can see the logic in that.

JUDGE

I've had just about enough disrespect out of you. One more word and you'll be in contempt.

NINA

How about three more? Screw you, meathead!

JUDGE
(*enraged*)
Officers, take charge, remove her immediately!

The court officers take hold of Nina as her parents beg her to behave. Brother Daniel watches from the front row in shock as she intentionally goes limp and the officers begin to pull her out of the courtroom, her heels dragging on the floor.

NINA

Unhand me, you troglodytes! This isn't over!

As they approach the door with their charge and open it Nina has time for one last outburst at the judge.

NINA

I'll have your seat on the bench, you corrupt meatball!

. . .

In a mind, thirty years are susceptible to subsecond traversal. Daniel Gill has semi-intentionally recalled these events (alone in the reception area to the fourth floor of NFL headquarters at 345 Park Avenue) because he will soon have to try to explain a rather famous person to uninitiates, where fame creates the illusion of understanding and where he's not particularly artistic or effective when it comes to that sort of thing.

Surroundings don't always register their full impact the first time, or even the first few times, they're displayed. Daniel has been in that precise room many times before but only now is the maybe silliness inherent to that room emerging. The receptionist across from him is inexplicably seated atop a platform of some sort. This has the effect of raising this woman significantly and it just seems weird that the league would purposely create this dynamic. Probably just an oversight.

Also weird, you could argue, is the rather large sculpture of the Vince Lombardi Trophy erected in front of her desk. Who does that? Or the odd displays, a cube per team, positioned at eye level all along the walls containing what can only be termed that team's memorabilia with the team ring as focal point but one that can only be sufficiently discerned through use of the magnifier attached to the track railing that it may slide from display to display. What? Then there are the great many television screens arrayed on a wall to look like a giant sudoku board and each one creates an image that standing alone lacks full meaning but that combine to form a larger all-encompassing image but somehow all this is done in service of airing a meaningless preseason game from the year before, huh?

All these things are creating a novel unease in Daniel Gill and this unease feeds on itself to grow by virtue of Daniel's complete inability to name or even describe it. This inability is not curable by time or effort; it is more like saying that Daniel Gill cannot dunk a basketball. Luckily, overriding truth is not dependent on individual ability and the truth here is that all these ostentatious exhibitions designed to create the illusion of inevitability and permanence have had the opposite effect and made Daniel feel as if he were wading in a pool of contingency.

The receptionist puts her hand to her ear before nodding then tells Daniel, Mr. Gill to her, that all parties are now present and in the conference room. In response, he walks the narrow hall then, after pausing, enters the conference room to find five of his fellow NFL owners, the other members of the negotiating committee. Each has two or three acolytes with him. The commissioner has been asked not to attend but more by omission than directly.

DANIEL

Gentlemen, thank you for agreeing to meet on such short notice.

OWNER # 1

An offer from the union, Daniel? Are they desperate already?

They all laugh, all except Daniel.

DANIEL

Nothing like that, but I do feel I owe you gentlemen an apology. I trust you all saw my sister yesterday.

OWNER # 2

Yes, that sure was something, entertaining at least.

More laughter.

OWNER # 1

Think nothing of it, Daniel. We all have family members we're, shall we say, less than proud of (*knowing, supportive murmurs from the others*). Doesn't change in the slightest what we're going to accomplish here.

DANIEL

No, you misunderstand. I apologize because during a recent interview I called my sister's contributions to the Cowboys something like overrated, then there was something else, and the upshot is I believe we've made an enemy of her. You understand that she's essentially formed this rival league now, right?

OWNER # 3

And? Really, Daniel, what business is that of ours?

DANIEL

Well, they're going to be playing this fall, on Sundays.

OWNER # 2

Again, what's the relevance?

DANIEL

The relevance, if I may speak freely, is that, as I understand it, we intend to continue to engage in, quote, *good faith* negotiations, before ultimately canceling the upcoming season.

OWNER # 1

That's right, all our studies indicate that the players, unlike us, literally cannot afford a lost season and that this is the quickest way to essentially bust the union and get a real CBA. One that doesn't give damn near sixty percent of our money to the players, which we can all agree is an outrage (*all emit agreement sounds*).

DANIEL

This, I believe, changes all that. If we cancel the season and the IFL becomes the only game in town, Nina will make serious headway.

OWNER # 4

Wait, are we still talking about the IFL here? Are you being serious? My money people tell me the entire league is worth five million. I spent that on dry cleaning last year.

DANIEL

That was before Nina took over.

OWNER # 2

They have no television.

DANIEL

She'll get that.

OWNER # 3

No significant players or coaches.

DANIEL

Yet.

OWNER # 1

And no resources with which to get them.

DANIEL

She has resources.

OWNER # 4

You're saying what? She would use her own money? (*universal derision; well, if the universe consisted of everyone in that conference room but Daniel*)

DANIEL

I'm saying precisely that. And I'm saying we underestimate this threat at our own peril. I recommend we continue the lockout only insofar as it results in the best possible deal, then we make a deal. We make a deal with enough time to play a full, high-level NFL season. Only in that way can we fully defang the IFL before it even gets started.

OWNER # 1

I must be missing something. We abandon a plan we've had for two years because some *woman* has a pathetic new toy piggy? Is that what you're saying?

DANIEL

No, we would be doing it because *Nina Gill* has a rival league positioned to replace us.

The other owners guffaw and look at each other in disbelief at what they're hearing.

DANIEL

Okay, I can sense deaf ears as well as anyone so let me leave you with a little story. When Nina was ready to go to college at fifteen or so we caught wind that she planned to take the SATs with a pen and with full knowledge that the computer could only read number two pencils.

We all begged her at one time or another to reconsider but she refused, saying only that the mechanized aspect of the process offended her. Sure enough she did it and she got a zero. Well my father was enraged, of course, as he would now have to start pulling all sorts of strings. But before he could even commence, Nina began with the letters. Personal customized letters from a fifteen-year-old to all the relevant parties asking them to disregard decades of precedent and grade her test by hand. They ultimately did of course, everyone always does, and eventually she received a handwritten letter in the mail apologizing and informing her of her perfect score.

That was Nina Gill at fifteen. She has no interest in money, but if she started a company selling icemakers to Eskimos today, I'd invest heavily tomorrow.

OWNER # 2

Please, you talk about her as if she were a superhero, or superheroine.

OWNER # 1

That's not a thing.

OWNER # 2

I'm sorry she trounced you at chess or something growing up, but this is a multibillion-dollar issue not a daytime show on sibling rivalry.

DANIEL

There was no rivalry.

OWNER # 1

He's right, Daniel. We all admire the work you've done so far as the point person, but this changes nothing.

The rest all seem to be in agreement that Daniel is needlessly worried, but one owner does then rise to speak.

OWNER # 5

I'm not so sure. I saw that press conference yesterday and I also recall Ms. Gill from some league dealings a few years back. I think Daniel is right to be concerned. Let's adjust our expectations downward and make a deal. No one says we can't go to the eleventh hour.

OWNER # 1

Of course that's easy for you to say since you've never been in favor of cancellation anyway. And that's fine but there's thirty-two of us and I see a more united front on this issue than on anything else that's come up in my thirty years. Sorry, Daniel. (*rises to leave and others join him*) But check your stomach, man! After all, this is the National Football League! We're supposed to fear a woman?

DANIEL

Suit yourself, gentlemen, but understand that this woman will run a first-class operation.

75

||||||||||

Concurrent with that utterance, Dia is driving Nina in what is essentially a giant pink pig, the Paterson Pork company car. The horn is a loud double oink. The car radio is blasting what is, to Nina's ears, the most egregious death (not really, *thrash*) metal possible (Pantera's "Mouth for War").

MUSIC

Revenge!

NINA

This is very relaxing, thank you. Was an audio recording of a dentist's drill unavailable?

DIA

Tell me where we're going and I'll change it.

NINA

We need a coach.

DIA
(*excitedly killing the radio*)
Ooh, you mean like a life coach to help us get in position to achieve our goals?

NINA

No, like a football coach to help us get in the end zone.

                    DIA

Don't the Pork already have a coach?

                    NINA

No, he resigned in the off-season so he could take a more lucrative
offer.

                    DIA

Coaching in the NFL?

                    NINA

Delivering water for Poland Spring.

                    DIA

So who do you have your sights set on?

                    NINA

Please don't speak like that. Remember the first prong of your training program.

                    DIA

Who do you want?

                    NINA

Make this left. Buford Elkins, probably the only coach I ever inter-
acted with whose skull wasn't completely numb.

                    DIA

So why isn't he still in the NFL?

                    NINA

He washed out.

                    DIA

You mean (*mimes drinking motion*)?

NINA

I do.

DIA

Wow, this is great! You're saying he's like a recovering alcoholic with one last chance at redemption?

NINA

He ain't recovering from shit. He's an *active* alcoholic with one last chance at a paycheck.

DIA

My God, almost forgot. *Song to a Seagull* is great.

NINA

Uh-huh.

DIA

No, I mean it, it's a great album.

NINA

Okay.

The hesitation here is that Nina's not sure how deep she wants to get into this, especially given some of the freaky intuitions she's beginning to have. Is *Song to a Seagull* great? If you define *great* as strictly as we're going to, probably not. That it derives from a great source is not open to debate though. On the other hand, it's probably more accurate to say that *Song to a Seagull* and the two other early works are *merely* great. Someone like Dia, listening to *Song* for the first time, and in isolation, would think they've happened upon a highly skilled California (actually Canadian-born but that's the least of the burgeoning misconceptions) folkie beginning to create transcendent music. Nobody could have predicted what would transpire over the next decade, but one clue might be the fact that someone like Carole King or Rickie Lee Jones would have been beyond thrilled with *Song* whereas its creator was essentially just clearing her throat before beginning in earnest. Nina decides she's going to leave it at that, Dia is a girl.

DIA

So I definitely want more, what songs should I download?

NINA

Songs? Did I miss a conversational shift? Are we talking about some fucking idiot like James Taylor or something? This is about albums, first of all.

DIA

So then *Blue?*

NINA

Lord, no. You're nowhere near ready. I'll let you get *Clouds* and *Ladies of the Canyon* then we'll talk.

DIA

Okay, geez, I didn't know it was so serious.

NINA

I know you didn't, that's why you're only being allowed the next two.

DIA

I like the way she sings.

NINA

And it's about the eighth most impressive thing about her. But still important, don't get me wrong. She has no true comparables but the ones that are constantly offered up tend to be merely competent singers. But listen to her on something like "Nathan La Franeer." That's the kind of singer who would be enlisted to sing someone else's song, a common occurrence back then, at least before she essentially invented her position.

DIA

Yes! Agree! So I'm in for some fun you're saying.

NINA

Not exactly fun, but I do admit to some envy for your immediate future in this area.

DIA

Great, soon as I get home I'll download—

NINA

Stop. You'll do no such thing, you'll go and purchase the CDs, only because I'm assuming you can't do vinyl.

DIA

Okay, is that how you listen to them?

NINA

Am I an ape? I have the goddamn master tapes. I can hear the fingers of a revolutionary guitar player when they briefly stick to the strings.

DIA

How is that possible?

NINA

How? Human activities seem that impenetrable to you? If you want something enough you first have to identify who can procure it, easier today than ever before, then you do something that looks like asking, but a special asking that I admit can become costly.

DIA

But why?

NINA

I guess that's a better question. Humanity's best unnecessary invention is art. The term itself is of course a value judgment, but even within the category, there are definable gradations tied to quality. Most purported art is ephemeral crap, so when timeless stuff gets made in your presence, I don't think there's any such thing as an overreaction.

DIA

But—

NINA

Here!

They stop in front of the charred remains of a house that doesn't appear to have been all that impressive preconflagration either.

NINA

Damn, this is where he lived last I heard.

DIA

It's okay, we'll find him.

NINA

No chance, this guy's more reclusive than Salinger. He's obsessed with privacy.

As Nina speaks, Dia has pulled out her phone, on which she thumb-types away furiously.

NINA

He's like a cipher. You'd have better luck finding a needle in a haystack, or an intelligent psychiatrist, or a manly French guy or—

DIA

Here he is, Buford Elkins. I have his phone number, address, e-mail, credit history, you name it. Want to see the results of his latest colonoscopy (*bringing the device near Nina's face as Nina demurs violently*)?

They arrive at another house that at least appears to be close to code. Nina and Dia maneuver through depressing obstacles on a front lawn only to reach an even more depressing front door. Nina rings the bell, which makes a malfunctioning, dwindling sound culminating in a spark.

COACH ELKINS
(*gruffly and slurred*)

Who in the holy hell?

Dia is scared and starts backing away down the stairs.

NINA

Ace Doorbell Repair! We'll ring your bell or the next knock's on us.

Elkins comes to the door seemingly bent on violence, recognizes Nina, and almost manages a smile.

ELKINS

Come in I guess.

NINA

Yes, thank you for inviting us into your squalid abode.

ELKINS

Don't start, Nina. I'm not dropping the lawsuit no matter what you say. I can't believe I let you in, by the time you're done talking I'll probably be giving *you* money.

NINA

Easy, I'm not with the Cowboys anymore, keep your lawsuit. I'm here to offer you a job, head coach.

ELKINS

Not with the Cowboys but offering me a job?

NINA

I own the New York area franchise now.

ELKINS

What?

DIA

And she's the commissioner.

ELKINS

How's that?

NINA

Never mind her. I spoil my employees, they talk when they should be listening.

ELKINS

What does she mean? I know you're not the commissioner.

NINA

It's complicated, it's a job, football, head coach. Yes or no?

ELKINS

It's no unless I know what I'm agreeing to.

NINA

It's the IFL, a historic league for five and a quarter seasons.

ELKINS

A quarter season?

NINA AND DIA
(*in unison*)

Don't ask.

DIA

The Pork.

ELKINS

The what?

NINA

What do you say?

ELKINS

I say I'm not nearly that desperate.

NINA
(*turning to Dia*)

I guess you win, young lady. You were right, Dawkins is better for this anyway.

DIA

Told you.

ELKINS

Nina, I'm a drunk, not an idiot. You don't think I see what you're trying to do? As if Dawkins would ever.

NINA

Guess we'll have to find out.

Nina signals to Dia and they head to the door, but not before Nina takes one more dramatically exaggerated look around Elkins's home.

NINA

You're right, Buford. You're obviously doing quite well for yourself. You don't need the seven figures I was going to offer you. I'm sure your lawsuit will work out great. I remember your lawyer, the guy with his ad on the matches, right?

ELKINS

I didn't say no.

NINA

Oh? What did you say?

ELKINS
(*resigned*)
I said yes. Well, yes pending our negotiation.

NINA

No drinking on the job, Buford.

ELKINS

During the games.

NINA

At the facility.

ELKINS

On game day.

NINA

Before six.

ELKINS

Five?

NINA

Deal, welcome aboard.

ELKINS

And as coincidence would have it, I was just about to call my
attorney—a fine litigator whom you so casually disparaged—about
a friend's bankruptcy proceeding. Now I can have him review my
contract instead!

NINA

I'm sure he's available.

74

||||||||||

What is coincidence anyway? The sensation of its sudden appearance depends on the unspoken assumption that the individual, event or person, is essentially isolated from all but its most immediate causal links. Assuming the opposite, that the seeming outsize complexity and plenitude of the world is just an illusory mask obscuring an underlying to the point of all-encompassing and ineluctably enmeshed interdependence, can greatly defuse the sensation.

Can but, as I say, it requires reliance on this assumption, one that's never remotely occurred to Emergency Medical Technician Larry Brown. Instead he ascribes all sorts of mystical import to the fact that there are eight hundred million 911 operators (an estimate) serving the largest EMS system in the world and of all those possibilities he happened to get connected to Sharon Seaborg on what would easily prove the most unsettling night of his life. Simply stated, this connection has to *mean* something.

She was an earwitness to what happened and all he wants is . . . who knows, really, what he wants. His life is one big *want* and right now that manifests itself in what he admits is, objectively, strange behavior.

He is driving, uninvited, to a house in Paterson, New Jersey. Guided somewhat by fleeting memory but mostly by a disembodied voice that only blurts into existence at the last possible millisecond its directives can be safely followed.

When he arrives, he parks at a distance. He can see the front door. The place looks a bit worse for wear; say what you want about Hugh, he was definitely handy. Not just that though, it's as if you can see suffering being emitted by the structure.

MECHANICS' INSTITUTE LIBRARY
57 Post Street
San Francisco, CA 94104
(415) 393-0101

And Paterson is bipolar, man; maybe even tripolar. Parts look post-apocalyptic but others, like this one, manage a shabby representational vibration, like a movie set that was never quite completed because funding dried up.

A small man crosses in front of the car Larry sits in. The man's limp causes his upper body to sway in intermittent counterpoint. Swinging side to side like an upside-down pendulum. Hypnotic and dispirited in a way that makes Larry rethink the whole thing.

73

〡〡〡〡〡〡〡〡〡

On that block in Paterson there'd lived an amputee. An amputee and her son in a tilting green house not easily visible from the street. For a decade it was the amputee's only space.

The son was a different story. He would leave the house. Two times a day every day, at nine a.m. then again at four p.m. Those were the times Elsie Heredia would drink her two cups of coffee and, because she insisted on imbibing only *fresh* milk, those were the two times Feniz Heredia would walk to the supermarket that was more like a convenience store. On the corner across from the vacant lot.

Don't think Feniz Heredia didn't know that Two Aces Food received precisely zero milk deliveries between nine in the morning and four in the afternoon because he did know. But living with just one person for a long time can grow odd, and there were times he found himself almost adopting his mother's less paranoiac inclinations and starting to think there might be a difference between the two pints. But mostly he just thought of it as something harmless he could do that didn't require a great deal of effort and that, while it could not be said to make her happy, served a significant purpose in the area of what we'll call anxiety abatement.

She was the rare octogenarian who slept late. Her entire preceding life she'd done the opposite. In Puerto Rico, for example, she was, almost without fail, the first in her house to rise in the morning (describing here the behavior of even eight-year-old Elsie). This, she said, was a way to miss nothing.

And maybe it worked. At age sixteen a husband, then a husband and son, then just a son. But such an entirety of a son was Feniz, that when he and his so-called wife decided the NYC area exceeded the San Juan area as a living destination, Elsie in turn decided that this new distance was a profound betrayal. One she would make complete by wielding a perfect retaliatory silence.

And this lasted years, how many no one could say, until a distant cousin managed to communicate to Elsie some relevant Feniz facts. New York, yes, but also single now with multiplying unrestrained nerves and pills and erratic behavior until psychiatric hospital. Elsie left Puerto Rico to sit in plastic chairs with rounded edges in Bellevue Hospital's relevant rooms. Sixteen hundred miles traversed where her previous high had been sixty.

And when they were free of that place, life's undulations and fitful starts landed them together in Paterson, NJ, in the kind of apartment even two people with extravagantly minimal income could afford. And it was on Paterson's Market Street, mere months later, that Elsie was pinned under a collapsing construction scaffold that, when finished devolving, looked like it had swallowed her up to the waist.

Lots of surgeries and rehab follow. Then in what feels like a sordid transaction, with a lawyer she speaks to maybe once, she loses a leg and gains a check. Nothing outlandish but enough to buy the small house across town that would then hold her and her son for thirty-five painfully uneventful years.

Following the amputation, or maybe it was after Bellevue, Feniz never really worked again. Instead, life consisted mostly of tending to his mother. It was a small house, sure, but he had his own room. He had friends, you could say; not always the same ones, different people would emerge then fade at different times. He read a lot. She needed him, truly. A wheelchair is heavy and cumbersome, difficult to operate. The house was never really made accessible to it, nothing was ever really done to that house and if something fell into disrepair, well, there it stayed, fallen.

And there was usually something needed to be done—a doctor to be visited, an agency's line to be stood on. Back then, she would leave the house. He would get her on the bus, they might get something to eat, provided Elsie's very restrictive price limits were not breached, and at the end of a day like that she might even express something like satisfaction with the day's events.

The last ten years even that changed. The change was gradual enough before becoming sudden that it took a while for Feniz to realize his mother was no longer leaving their house, as in *at all*. The doctors' appointments were ignored until they were no longer even made. Any necessary errands, and these declined in number daily, were addressed solely by him without her presence. Her isolation was like a wave that just submerged their house as the new normalcy so that one day Feniz could mentally answer in the affirmative his shocking question: *Has my mother not left the house in a decade?*

Routine has a way of blurring the passage of time so that what actually elapses far exceeds the sensation. Truth is, Elsie's voluntary immobilization didn't greatly alter daily life in the Heredia residence. Feniz would wake at seven and read for an hour. Classics or nonfiction, mostly history. At eight in the morning he would get in the shower. The knob that told water to stop coming out of the tub spout and exit the showerhead wasn't even a memory anymore, so he kept an adjustable wrench on the radiator for that purpose.

Then he would go down to the kitchen to make the coffee, purposely making enough noise to wake Elsie in the adjoining bedroom, but not so much it would get harsh for her. This would allow her to pretend she was already long awake when Feniz would come in to put her in the chair. He would then express love along with a kiss and Elsie, her cheek still wet, would complain about the noise outside her window and the impossibility of someone sleeping soundly through it and the fact that it almost certainly emanated from criminals even if, she conceded, they may not necessarily have been engaged in criminal activity at the time.

Feniz would then tell her the coffee was ready and he was going to get the milk. This was always where he was going but still he told her. He knew she wanted to see him leave so as to eliminate the possibility of subterfuge with respect to the milk she would soon drink and he knew that making sure she saw him leave couldn't even conceivably be considered a sacrifice. He also had to make a big display of how little money he was taking out of the red envelope in the hollow book so as to stamp out any accusation of profligacy before it could even begin to form.

At the store the clerk changed often; it sometimes seemed as if the name of the store was Under New Ownership. But new or not, the clerk soon learned the base of Feniz's morning order because that never changed. Of course the pint of milk, but also the buttered roll in plastic shrink wrap and, most crucially, the *New York Post* and *Daily News.*

Back at the house, they would breakfast in the kitchen. It was there that Feniz would dutifully inform his mother of the world's events. Regardless of the nature of the information, Elsie's reaction was consistent in kind. If the news was inherently grim, she'd signal her assent: *Yes, that's how life is.* If it was neutral or even positive, she would seek to uncover its underlying grimness. This kind of thing he would laugh off but truth is, over time, he began to share more and more of her view.

After breakfast, Elsie would bathe. Feniz would have to help her into the shower because the early few times she objected she would end up enduring bitterly cold water or else burning herself, nasty singes that never fully healed. She needed to be dressed by noon because that was when good television started. The television was in the kitchen for optimal reception.

If something needed to be done outside, this is the time of day when Feniz would go. Often he would pick up Burger King on the way back, McDonald's if it was time for a change. Or he could quickly fry something up if money was tighter (the further you got from the first or the fifteenth). Prime Elsie had taken pride in her cooking but that was a long time ago. At four he'd go back to the store for the afternoon milk. Dinner was something very light, as insubstantial as buttered toast. And because to Elsie the quality of TV programming dropped off precipitously at this hour, Feniz could usually interest her in a game or two of checkers (the Great Chess Experiment I and II having failed miserably). Then Elsie would fall asleep in her chair, no amount of warnings could prevent it, and Feniz would have to roll it into her bedroom and negotiate her into her bed. Then he would watch some more TV before going up to read in his twin bed and close another day.

This pattern brooked little deviation but, as always, time's passage would shape the details. So help getting into the shower grew to encompass help bathing, getting on the toilet, changing her diaper; even, at the very end, feeding her like an infant.

Today it's a very rare thing to witness the complete, unadulterated, and prolonged shutdown of a human body; gradual death is now almost invariably managed through a chemical fog. But to the end, Feniz stuck to his promise, no medical intervention. What was doing it to her was impossible to tell, so general the pain. Looked to him as if Elsie's body was consuming itself from within, and from where screams of pain would not have surprised, what emanated instead was accusatory strife. Each day seemed to produce its own special bile: *I never loved you. You were an accident I lacked the physical courage to remedy. You need to move out today, you are a financial drain on me. You have done nothing of value, an entire lifetime of nothing.*

Feniz could *see* intuitively that these ravings were a form of mania, but he also *heard* every last syllable and, far from lacking the ability to ever hurt, hurting is one of the things words are best at. Because if you think the bad drunk is just revealing his true rotten nature due to a compromised filter, then was he not justified in suspecting that these were Elsie's true thoughts finally free to escape because of the fever currently coursing through her brain?

But he withstood the assault and said nice things in return and kept his promise that no one would enter their home and when she refused to eat he kept trying and he lit candles and cleaned up messes and tried to remind her of past events and there was no one who needed to be called and told about her state and this was so because it truly was just the two of them and then she adamantly would eat nothing nor would she watch anything on television and then she wouldn't even get in her chair anymore just lying on the bed, eyes open then closed, open then closed, her voice a whisper and the content insensible. Then not even that, just an exaggerated heave and two emptied eyes that would never refill.

Only this last development truly bested Feniz. There was nothing that needed to be done in response. Everything else had an answer. Hunger you filled, dirt you cleaned, language you responded to with more language. But the ultimate negation just levels everything. At first he felt nothing. Nothing begets nothing. Then he felt something. Then, finally, *everything*. But *everything* all at once, so scarcely bearable.

He couldn't say how long he sat there because, sitting there, he didn't feel subject to time. But he did eventually make the necessary phone calls.

The man to arrange the funeral wore makeup, light but discernible, and that fact prevented Feniz from effectively focusing on anything else.

There were options, but that wasn't the usual good thing because Feniz struggled mightily with asserting decisions. He went to the bank: $1,289.38 exactly.

The next day (was it really only that?) he had ashes, Elsie, in a container.

There *was* one woman. A friend of Elsie's dating all the way back to Puerto Rico. Now in Hoboken? Haworth? Ho-Ho Kus? Somebody besides him should be made aware, should have a reaction. There was no way to find that phone number, buried somewhere within the stacked boxes of unruly paper. He went to the library. A woman helped him in a whisper (placed her hand on top of the back of his) but he wasn't strong on the spelling of the surname and the confusion seemed to spiral unrestrainedly outward until he felt better just standing up and walking away. Besides, successful contact would have meant the responsibility to create some kind of ceremony and he wouldn't really know where to begin with something like that.

The next day (maybe) he is walking with a purpose. His Paterson is almost perfectly devoid of significant natural manifestations like trees or grass. Everywhere he looks is something made by man and, like all such matter, lifelessly imbued with decay. *That* he's had his fill of, so he's walking instead to one of the primordial basins of our world.

From far enough away, the earth is a tiny blue speck. That's not what it looks like, that's what it is. Only closer does it become a gas-

eous sphere. Then past the inert stone circling it. Past the cotton reb-
els clashing in air. To reach the inverted bowl of mostly aqueous blue.

And about halfway down one of the landmasses, what initially looks
like a shaggy carpet made of trees makes way to reveal copious criss-
crossing wires and abandoned warehouses, amidst which the only
thing that moves is a lone hunched figure clutching his brass infant
to his chest.

Too bad a procession requires more than one moving part because
that's what this most resembles. And if the movement looks disorderly
look closer because, no, it's funereal, and it orients inexorably to run
alongside the Passaic River as this river runs unimpeded towards a
fissure.

It can easily happen if you let it. Stare intently enough at stasis and
the overriding suggestion is death.

So instead, Feniz's intent, the profluent flow of water is supposed to
engender the sensation of rejuvenating transcendence.

But it's actually grade school geometry controlling his thoughts now
to the point of fixation: the culpable geodesic of the sudden straight-
line fall. Metaphoric truth can hit you with greater force than more
obvious instantiations of that element. He looks closely enough at the
orderly sluice of liquid atoms and he can delude himself into thinking
the movement is cyclic and without end. He *could* but for the sound.
The sound swells and insists as you approach it and it is the sound of
a violent interregnum.

All that lives in ordered coherence is just serving time until its
grave descent. He sees this in the way the water becomes a fall. Paterson Great Falls. The earth wants everything that once trod upon
it to be swallowed into its core. People like his mother, for instance,
spend their latter lifetimes burrowing closer to that inert center like
sedated moles. Some get buried piecemeal, the way her leg became
refuse before the rest of her did. But those are just the details. The
paths change but the destination remains, will always remain, the
same. Everything attracting itself into collapse. Everything, no matter
its complexity, ultimately interred. The water he stares at reflects that
reality. He can feel the force pulling that water in, converting life and

its many components into a null set. The River Styx may not be visible to us but it needs constant refilling and no matter your guide you will someday be swept up in its current like Elsie Heredia and all the Elsies before. And that's the body of water this relentless flow is causing to swell.

We, mankind, have nothing to counter this. Closest thing we have is like a special language and if you stop using it the result can be a kind of sudden-onset illiteracy at a time when casual eloquence would have great utility. He should've cheated. The book was among her papers. An artifact in the truest sense. An emblem revealing how life was once lived, but in the present, obsolete. Still, if you're standing with your mother's ashen remains near roaring fluid infinity you crave ceremonial predictability. So he feels he should have searched that Bible, found something to say. Words don't turn to dust. Their invisibility. They're invisible. Intangibility. Therein their permanence.

The beating frigid spray can give a human face. The kind of thing doesn't need to be analyzed. Lot of things like that. From now on, life as just a body.

Every step must be a careful one. This mist makes it like walking on a waterslide. But he has to get close. The ashes have to make it all the way down to the waterfall's bottom, is there a name for that? Can't have them just land on the surrounding area. Has to keep his feet too, falling would be bad. Flat there on the ground, people noticing, coming over, imagine?

Should've got the cane where the bottom spiders out into four legs but it was more and always have to get the one that's less. Always the damned one that's less. No, the real worst thing would be dropping the urn.

Ode to a mother's urn? Is that a thing?

The wind has to die down. Would have to be the coldest day of the year too.

Has to say something as he spills her out. There is no one else there. Is that always the case, that no one comes here? Or is it the time? The time. People work.

Being very careful not to fall is a good way to feel like you are falling. Like noticing one's breathing then trying to return to not.

At the end it was only her breathing that told him it wasn't over and when it stopped it wasn't like what he'd imagined. Not at all. But what does he mean? He never imagined or tried to imagine what it would be like so why think something like that? That it wasn't what he imagined. Just that, looking back later, it wasn't like anything he'd ever felt before or even imagined feeling. It was entirely different than anything in his past and how many things can you truly say that about?

This is the best spot to do it. No one anywhere. But not even to see these falls?

This cold hurts. Everything hurts. Emptiness hurts. If you say you miss someone that implies something is missing. So what should make sense would be feeling something like desire, right? Like hunger when food is missing. But this is more like pain. More like an injury.

Can he open this alone or is it sealed too tight? Is it giving? Maybe. Yes. But he won't open it all the way yet. The wind has to die down a bit. He should've checked that book. Have to say something. For I am that I am. Then took the rib of Adam and filled it around with woman and called it woman and Yahweh said call it woman and she will have dominion over you and the rest of the animals until that which is ash will return into ash. Dust to dust.

"From dust to dust. Ashes to ashes, dust to dust," he says.

He should say more than that. Doesn't even know what that means. Is that supposed to be a good thing that at the end all that's left of her is these ashes? As was, will be, and forever shall be. World without end.

"World without end," he says.

Stupid. Again with the not making sense. If by *endless world* they mean things like this waterfall, who does that console? He's looking at the waterfall and can almost agree that it feels pretty endless. The ashes in his hand, though, those have an end. They're nothing but ending.

What happened to life as just a body? Stop thinking and just do what you came to do.

Could be the ashes and the waterfall are part of the same thing and that thing has no end so the ashes have no end so his mother has no end. Begotten not made, one in being with the other—

"Begotten not made," he says.

He must act quickly before the wind returns. His hands are numb. The numbness makes it so there's a delay between the urn dropping out of his hand and his realization it has happened.

"Damn it!" he yells.

Everything is fucking like this, he thinks. Everything. Decide to save the urn and maybe half the ashes and it will assuredly slip out of your hands to land on jagged rocks. Then all the way down to where the falls land before the river continues. He watches the empty urn float away and when he tries to follow he falls facefirst into the rocky ground. Her ashes, the cloud that escaped before it all went crashing down, land on his neck and face, and he stays there on his hands and knees like a supplicant with no hope of success.

The walk home is consumed with horror that everyone can see the ash on his face when in truth no one does because there's no one to look.

He thinks how he could be made the ruler of infinite space right now and would feel like a peanut in its shell. How he can do no right. He wants to be like that urn. Falling and falling until just gone. He can taste ash.

He is home. His stairs are crumbling. He doesn't know how to fix them. How much does a thing like that even cost? Doesn't matter. One of the benefits of what he's going to do is the way it just erases the future. Frees one from a lot of the thinking and planning that becomes a human life.

Once inside he feels liberated from a surveillance that in truth never existed. On his face his tears mix with his mother and he gets in the shower to rid himself of both. Most of his mother had dispersed into the air as the urn fell incrementally, creating desolate sounds that oddly didn't include a climactic splash. Still, some of her must have stayed in the urn as it wobbled away. Away from Paterson and its people, through towns never referenced. To end in Newark Bay, where by then enough water has seeped in to turn Elsie into mud and begin propelling the hundred-dollar urn to the bottom.

The sinking descent of this vessel is shrouded in secrecy. The water is dirty. The sun has gone down.

Although, we now know, that's just a manner of speaking. There's no down or up for the sun. It's just that this part of our world has turned away from it, away from that orb's effluent light and into indurate shadow.

72

|||||||||

When Sharon finally emerges, Larry pounces with preplanned eloquence.

"Hey!" he says but she is confused and can't place him. "Sharon!" he adds unhelpfully.

"Hello . . ."

"Larry, Hugh's friend."

"Oh. Right."

"And from that night."

"Yeah."

"That was insane wasn't it? The way we slowly came to realize who we each were, you know?"

"What's going on? Why you here?"

"No, oh, nothing's wrong. I just . . ."

They only stand there in silence.

"Yeah?" She breaks it because she has to get to work but truth is even standing there in awkward silence is preferable to her job.

"I just had to come here about a thing and I remembered that Hugh, you and Hugh, I was sorry to hear, and then that night, or I guess that morning."

"I have to get to my bus, late again and I'll catch the next level of hell."

"Yeah, definitely. But I have my car, I can give you a ride."

"It's just a few blocks."

"No, I mean ride all the way. I'm going into the city anyways."

"It's okay."

"It's no trouble."

"No. Thanks."

"This weather."

"You're going in anyway?"

"Yeah, it's no trouble."

She looks at the sky then her watch.

"Okay then," she says.

The brief walk to the car's no better but it's a long ride and Larry's thinking the social lubricant of time spent together in close quarters will do most of the work for him. But she can't get into the car.

"That door sticks, let me get it."

He does get it but not without difficulty, and when she's safely in he spends the time walking around back to his side contemplating what would be the most brilliant opening conversational salvo. But ultimately all he comes up with is

"Eighty east to the bridge, right?"

"Right."

"I didn't even know about you guys and what happened until I called Hugh the other day to ask him if he was still going to play on our softball team, ex-EMTs are welcome and I know the Rikers league sucks. Ask me, I think he should've stayed with us. So close to finishing his twenty, you know?"

"On second thought you can drop me right up there, there's a better bus stops there."

"You sure?"

"Yeah, that one gets to use the bus lane so it will actually get me there quicker. Thanks."

"Well, at least stay out of the weather until it comes."

"Should be soon."

But she does stay put.

"That call, at the bus stop. What are the chances it would be routed to you?"

"Ø"

"Right, Sharon?"

"It happens."

"I guess."

"Ø"

"Such a bad call too."

"They're all bad, most of them anyways."

"It was more than that though."

"Hugh used to come home, we'd compete over who'd seen worse. Or in my case, I guess *heard* worse."

"Really?"

"Yup."

"How do you mean?"

"I mean what I just said, Larry. Christ, you know the job."

"No, I know."

"He'd say, *We got there too late and a four-year-old choked—*"

"I remember that."

"And I'd say, *I heard her last breaths, with her boy crying in the background.*"

"Oh, man."

"Hmm, there it is, thanks again."

"You see some shit, no question, but that night—"

"It's stuck."

"You just have to jiggle. Let me. There you go."

"Point is, that's the job. You don't want to do it, they'll find someone else."

"I hear you, but I still say Hugh should've—"

"Yeah I'm done worrying about Hugh should'ves, sorry."

"Right. But something like that night. Alls I'm saying is it makes you think."

"Good luck with that. While you're thinking them deep thoughts, Socrates, I'll be getting in and out of buses so's my kid can eat. Take care, Larry."

"Okay."

She rushes out, her shoulders hunched up by her ears. An alien observer would think humans must protect the backs of their necks from water at all costs. He lowers the passenger side window.

"I will!" he adds.

71

||||||||||

Nuno's Rikers cell is vile in every respect but maybe most currently offensive is its criminal paucity of reading material. He's read the shit he took from Seaborg at least thrice in a manner suggestive of memorization. In desperation he has closely read things like shampoo bottles. But he *has* managed to get ahold of pencil and paper somehow. So what he'll do is write. Write principally so that he can later read it. *Notes from Inside* by Nuno DeAngeles. From inside a cage.

2015's February 13 (Friday) from JATC in Rikers Island—
Queens, NY

I am an angry man. Angry and wrathful and savage and none of it can be traced to a source. Because I don't mean to suggest, when I say this to you, that something has happened and in response I am angry. There's no retributory element here, just anger. I feel it, this anger, even now. Not because it has suddenly arisen, but rather because I now choose to attend to it if that makes any sense. I attend to it and when I do I become aware that it is always there. Always is and always was and maybe always will be. Past, present, preterit, pluperfect, and any other fucking tense you can invent to conjugate what seethes in me.

Let me put this in terms even you can understand. You traffic fundamentally in effete leisure. You mainly stare at screens. Mostly listen to language explaining why this particular screen is a necessary advancement, even if you thought you'd advanced enough. And here's the ratio at work that you never pay attention to: what you paid for the screen is like the yearly salary of the people who put it together for you.

Don't let that fact just flit through your skull, attend to it the way I do my anger. Because this is one of those situations where the rationalization is more damning than the fucking thing being rationalized. So the maker of the screen says, *Hey, I'm paying them more than their friends are getting and more than their laws require, not my fault where they live.* Now, of course, it's entirely illegitimate to fault the maker for some asinine stupidity like *sending jobs overseas* because what the fuck does that even mean? That you value a human being more if they achieve the accident of birth of being born here instead of Amerignorance, Indochina?

I'm going to, without any basis, assume you're not that stupid. And since you're not that stupid I trust you'll see the egregious problem with the rationalization, at least where it concerns wildly successful screen makers. In the interest of brevity, I'll just say that the problem with paying someone a dollar a day to make an item that goes for a thousand times that is that you are paying someone a dollar a day to make an item that goes for a thousand times that.

And you know this but you smile, change the channel, then line up the night before to buy the latest example of this ratio. And I don't bring this up to judge, though I am judgmental to the fucking teeth, but rather because, as implicitly promised, I am going to propose an analogue. I said something like *You're awash in decadent luxury* and I think I'm done marshaling the evidence. You can casually spend what would elsewhere be a lifesaving sum to improve your life's recreational and entertainment quotient by maybe .0001 percent; in other words, you are such royalty that untold people, flesh and bone like you, across the globe must essentially donate their daily toil to the goal of making it easier for you to update your Facebook status. I know you don't think about this often, if ever, but it informs your every act, volition notwithstanding. So, to finally bring this around, the subtle role that luxurious apathy plays in your daily existence, anger plays in mine.

Which brings me to where these words are being written. I come to you from one of this country's foremost repositories of Anger. My cell's thirty square feet pulsate with the stuff. It bubbles up out of the approximately twenty-year cauldron I've been brewing since birth and everyone trapped in here with me should give thanks for the comically small window that looks out onto the surrounding waters and serves as cooling rod for the fissile material threatening to cohere into runaway violence within.

And that's *now*, if my extensive reading of this place's procedures is accurate, and experience is any guide re: my ability to meekly conform to rules, it won't be long before I am *in the hole*, where everything that now festers in this cell probably undergoes something akin to cancerous growth.

2015's February 13 (Later Friday) from JATC in Rikers Island— Queens, NY

Although maybe not. Because, readers, what if your diarist is growing up, evolving even? See, far as this place is concerned, I'm eighteen, and that means, my rabidly antisocial act notwithstanding, I am someone institutions like this have to at least pretend to ascribe hope to. Hopeful scams like LIT (Literature for Incarcerated Teens) and Religion for the Immersed Penally, I think it's called. Consistent with that, I have met two notable people since beginning my temporary stay here and I now inform you, with justified pride, that I somehow resisted the temptation to put both their lights out.

First was this twee fucker in a vest, the kind of douche who corrects someone calling him a writer by specifying he's a novelist. Really, fuck? Where can I pick up your intergenerational saga spanning the great panoplic expanse of the world from Connecticut all the way to Wall Street? Or your other one. You know, where the narrator's marriage dissolves over that one fateful summer in Martha's Vineyard while her daughter burgeons into womanhood? Fuck off's what I'm saying. This fuck's reaction to the majesty of literature is to buy a fedora and make sure everyone knows he lives in Brooklyn. But, again, your diarist held his tongue, man. Held it when he said he lived in Brooklyn like me. Held it when he told me to write what I know, and, most difficultly, held it when he referred to his MFA from Brown—an institution only slightly less contemptible than this island. That's where these pussies invariably come from, man.

What I should have done was confess, confess that we'd met. Remember when you did that group interview with those other soft douches? And you were all blowing each other about the importance of your work and how, where, and when you get together for regular poker games? Remember how the next time you all got together two guys burst in and relieved the assembled puny literati of all winnings and potential stakes? Yeah, I was the one without the heater, the one relying just on the force of his presence, which to no great surprise was more than enough. Sorry, I don't much believe in civilian victims, but I confess I gave in to the urge to display a bit of the true 718. Besides, if it interfered with any future work from that putrid assemblage, one could almost deem it public service.

Give me a Russian any day's what I'm saying. A Russian writes like the world is about to be violently split in half and his words will determine which half he'll inhabit. College is over and you don't know what to do? Which prescription to fill first? Fuck you, how's that? Don't get me started, man.

Far as the rest-in-peace chaplain, it was hate at first sight when I saw this prick. Because if sweater-vest produces ineffectual garbage it's, in some sense, not his fault and, more importantly, no skin off anyone's apple. The chaplain, on the other hand, is a tool, no different than this fucking sea of corrections officers currently undulating around me. But whereas they convince through firepower and restraints (in other words, the proper way of the world [Force]), the chaplain seeks to succeed through the relative silver content of his tongue, and that's a goddamn perversion. Language is no less his stock-in-trade but now it's in service of subjugation—and the worst kind, voluntary. These pricks, and I know them well, want you to accept barbaric injustice as long as you're its victim. Well, you know who profits when you stop trying to gain the world? Who else? The most fucking unjust, that's who. So I don't accept acceptance, sorry. Yet that's what these fuckers preach. Chaplains need to stop chaplaining.

Here's the thing though. Different activities have different standards of proof: see the production of an element like hate-at-first-sight versus the creation of enduring hatred. So while his costume was initially enough for me to hate the chaplain, to move beyond that I needed greater proof. And try as your diarist might, I could find none. No fucking brimstony quotes from goddamn Leviticus or some shit about layingeth with unclean animals. No fake empathy that's really sleazy fascination with what all I've done. No judgment really. Also he was very round without even threatening sloppy fat, which is quite pleasing to the eye I must say if you can ignore the man bun. And soft-spoken too, which also accrued to his benefit as I don't really countenance hard-spoken. The chaplain. Ventipony maybe? Yes, leading his flock from the prison of the soul to Mount Immurare.

Anyway, did I say *temporary* before in characterizing my stay here? That was no slip. Like a deity willingly made incarnate, I'll stay here not a minute longer than necessary. Problem is, that'll be months. And months like this is the kind of weight can drop a pen out of your hand.

2015's February 13 (Even Later Friday) from JATC in Rikers Island—Queens, NY

You only think you've heard loud noise. Measuring decibels can give you a putatively objective quantification of loudness but it wholly ignores things like timbre and orchestration. So before now worst noise I'd heard was of this dude Red (where I'm from, get one hair that fucking hints at red and, forget it, you're Red forever) losing half his ear to a snub .38 that reported literally inches from my ear. And Red was all right but it was really anger at the invasion of that noise, not his mutilation, that led me to snatch that still-hot number from its owner and make him eat one of its slugs. This is not me euphemistically saying I shot him; no, I literally took one out of the chamber and made him swallow it.

Well, but, so, that noise was technically the loudest, true, but there's a recurring sound here that has it beat to a messy pulp when it comes to eliciting horror. The constant, unremitting plaint of metal ramming into metal. The sound of implacable coercion. But like everything else there is no underlying rhythm or pattern, just the universe's drunken drummer sloppily asserting his role whenever you might forget about him.

And the worst is becoming a kind of connoisseur on a subject you detest. So there's nuances to the sounds that I would rather unlearn. The obvious difference between the locking or unlocking of a gate and the collision of gate against frame, sure, but I fear I've actually gotten to where I can differentiate between a locking and an unlocking. Fuck me, in other words. What does it matter the relative richness of the universe if my sole function in it is to cower in a darkened closet? There it is, these fuckers don't miss a cue.

2015's February 13 (Latest Friday) from JATC in Rikers Island— Queens, NY

Just saying that hearing is an underrated sense. Everyone talks about what they've seen and how that can come flooding back. Proust, of course, brilliantly covered taste. I say what I've heard and keep hearing is what's going to be hardest to erase. These sights? I can probably avoid resonances.

Although, even before landing here guess I'd seen some shit. A killer poet once asked his son what his blue eyes had seen. No one asks after my green ones, but understand I stare often at clouds as if through catatonia.

I saw armadas of cotton sink to the ocean
I saw cast-iron fingers grasp at the open
I seen amputee buildings yawn at their sickness
I seen marionette lines bow into saggy parallel

Been down where the earth resolves into nothing
Been out where the sighs of the seas fall on deaf land
Seen empty swords in the arms of the hopeless
Seen emptier eyes center bleeding graffiti

Seen slaves worship chains in the tongue of the needy
Seen masters ascend to . . .

Ah, never mind. Even then, your sirens' lyrics lack the ring of *my* truth, and you've done nothing to merit me writing you more apposite ones.

70

|||||||||

Dia is again driving Nina in the company car, *Clouds* on the CD player. Dia thinks she must be looking particularly good today because every time a fellow motorist passes they stare at her intently. Nina's seat is partially reclined and, although she's awake, her eyes are closed—a position they retain throughout.

DIA

I must be looking particularly good today. Every time one of our fellow motorists passes, they stare at me . . . intently.

NINA

You're driving a giant pig.

DIA

Oh shit, that's right. Thanks for killing the vibe.

NINA

And we appear to be traveling at about twenty percent the speed limit. You do realize said number is supposed to function more like a statutory minimum, right?

DIA
(*flooring the accelerator to little result*)
Not my fault, this pig has like no pickup.

                              NINA

Uh-huh.

                               DIA

So where to now?

                              NINA

We need a quarterback on whom a disproportionate amount of our
success will depend so that our three hundred fans can spend all their
time complaining about him.

                               DIA

Who though?

                              NINA

Dinner first.

                               DIA

Ooh, yum. I'm thinking Thai, maybe Ethiopian.

                              NINA

And yet funny how neither of those has the slightest chance of happening; we're having steak.

                               DIA

I'm vegetarian.

                              NINA

Major Steak to be precise, midtown Manhattan.

                               DIA

I don't eat meat.

                              NINA

Don't worry, hippie. This is meatless steak.

                              DIA

Fine, we'll do what you want just this once. But if I'm going to have
poor cow you're going to answer a few questions in return.

                              NINA

No.

                              DIA

Why'd you leave the Cowboys? I mean, your father's team. Must've
been ugly. Answer?

                              NINA

It's complicated.

                              DIA

I have time.

                              NINA

It's complicated was the answer.

                              DIA

No, not good enough.

                              NINA

Can't I just give you another promotion instead?

                              DIA

No, my curiosity overrules even my ambition.

                              NINA

Let's just say the last couple years my pop's not the same and my
brother's taken advantage of that to take the whole thing in a direction I hate.

Also I was the only woman in football, the sexual harassment was
extreme.

DIA
(*offended*)
That's terrible, why didn't you get a lawyer?

NINA
What for? Most of it was on video, I couldn't deny I'd done it.

DIA
Oh. But—

NINA
That's enough, Nancy Drew. I've got a contact inebriation from Elkins's breath to sleep off. Wake me when we get to the steak.

A labyrinthine later because Dia is a horrific vehicular navigator, the giant pig pulls up in front of the Major's valet area. The several valets there have nothing to do in their red vests except make derisive pig sounds, at least until the two ladies emerge and their jaws drop.

DIA
(*handing keys to dumbfounded valet*)
And don't get any mud on him, he's fanatical about cleanliness.

The two enter the decidedly not bustling restaurant and are seated at a prime table. A waitress approaches solicitously.

NINA
Two almost criminally voluminous tequilas and a medium-rare porterhouse for two; (*turning to Dia*) what're you having?

While we're on the topic, and she decides, I see the owner over there loitering by the bar. Will you inform him that I demand to speak to him about his anemic vegetarian offerings?

DIA

Nina, really, I can have—

NINA
(*to waitress*)

Run along, missy. It's urgent.

The waitress leaves and approaches an athletic well-dressed man. He looks at the table but Nina has raised her menu to obstruct her face. He goes over.

MAJOR HARRIS

Listen, ladies, the word *steak* is right in the name of the goddamn place.

NINA
(*lowering the menu*)

Goodness, the language.

MAJOR

Oh man, I thought I sensed the NYPD on high alert.

NINA

They'll never get me alive. This is Dia. Dia, Major Harris is the man standing there.

DIA

Oh! I know Major Harris. I mean I know *you*, I mean I don't know you, but I know *of* you, and I know that you played, and that that commercial with the—

Harris has not taken his eyes off Nina. Now he is putting his finger to Dia's lips to stop her noise then kind of softly pushing her face aside as he sits across from Nina practically in Dia's lap. Dia tries to slide out of the way into the adjoining chair but loses her balance and flies back, her legs cartwheeling in retreat until she is splayed on the carpet to much attention.

NINA

Can't take you anywhere, can I? What a spectacle.

DIA

But—

NINA

Listen, I know how much you enjoy beef but I just remembered that, for some reason, you promised the American public Radiohead. Here's the company credit card, treat yourself to a lavish meal on the Pork at one of Mr. Harris's many more successful competitors while maybe getting started on that.

DIA

But if I take the pig . . .

NINA

I'll find my way home, kind strangers and all that, thanks for the concern.

DIA

Okay. Nice to meet you, Mr. Harris.

He smiles and nods without looking at her and she starts to walk away.

NINA

Oh, and Dia?

DIA

Yes?

NINA

You're a killer deputy so far.

DIA

Really? I am, right?

Dia is walking away and Nina and Major are doing that thing where they say nothing until she is completely out of sight. Why do people do that? Except, once she's out of sight they still say nothing. It's been many years.

"Nice kid," Major says. "I almost feel sorry for her."

"Don't, she's having the time of her brief life."

"It can't last, and she looked none too pleased when you handed that press conference off to her."

"Caught that, huh? Jesus, stop stalking me."

"You're hard to miss."

"You mean you miss me and it's been hard?"

"It's always hard, but that has nothing to do with missing you."

"Always? How uncomfortable."

"So is it official, the losing your mind thing?"

"Because I think you've missed me?"

"No, because you're taking on the NFL."

"You mean the IFL is taking them on."

"Same thing, who you kidding?"

"Maybe, but why out of my mind? Everyone knows they're canceling their season."

"So they cancel, but the IFL?"

"Why not? It's football on Sunday. Football! I don't have to tell you. An addictive combination of beauty, violence, intellect, and cooperative balance. Where else they getting that?"

"You can't give them that."

"I can and will."

"Maybe you're right, what do I know? If anyone could it's probably you."

The food arrives and Harris is able to see it as if through Nina's eyes, but after a second of insecurity, he is pleased.

"You have TV?" he asks.

"Not yet."

"That's important."

"Thanks, you're like an ancient seer in your vast wisdom."

"Fine, resume your suicide mission, see if I care."

"Speaking of that box by and for imbeciles, saw you on it a week ago. Hawaii, I think. Sponsored by Gillette, fancy moving targets with varying point totals, good grief."

"Hoping that'd escaped your attention but guess I should've known better."

"Did notice you still have that rifle arm though."

"Probably have it on my deathbed, it's everything else that's gone."

"I don't know, didn't look that way to me."

"Listen, God knows you know what you're talking about, but you wouldn't say that if you could feel what I feel in the morning. You know, before all the moving parts get going."

"You went out there for a reason, you never used to do those."

"Free Hawaii, big deal."

"*Free* matters now?"

"Not really."

"You sure? Because this looks like a nice quiet place to get some thinking done."

"Well, that it is." He laughs and it hurts (*it* is his entire body). "I guess you don't try to cash in on a defunct athletic name in the city of your most hated rival. But I never really fully warmed to Texas you know? I'm New York, man."

They look around, it's like a private dinner.

"But, yes, I get what you're driving at and, no, it's not an issue. Even though I did miss out on the really crazy green those dudes are getting now."

"So it wasn't free Hawaii, it was what?"

"I don't know, I guess it was a little bit of the tragedy of every athlete. For a long time you can do things with your body others can only

152 Sergio de la Pava

pretend to do, so what happens? You take it for granted, man. You do it without thinking. Then later you start thinking and your first thought is *Oh man, wait until I get back out there with this brain operating that body*, only by then it's no longer *that* body right? My last year in the NFL I was thirty-nine and, I swear, I knew what defensive players I'd never seen before were going to do before they did. You know what it did for me? Very little. I would see it better than ever, throw it as hard as I could, as accurate as I could, and some twenty-two-year-old wearing the wrong color would catch it. There's that split second in the NFL, man, and it's one of the cruelest time increments in life."

"I agree, but I can give you that split second back."

"Is that so? You've perfected time travel and waited until this late stage of the conversation to reveal that fact?"

"Quarterback the Pork. Be our quarterpork, if you will."

"That's your solution? Dress up like a pig and play against guys who were bagging groceries the week before?"

"Pork is just the name of the team, we might change it, you don't have to actually dress like a pig. There's no actual pig involved. Well, the mascot's a pig . . . and there's . . . a little pig on the helmet . . . the car . . . it'll be legitimate football!"

"First of all, I'm forty-four and feel a decade more. And even if I wasn't—"

"You can still play and the league will be legitimate, Buford Elkins is our coach."

"Really? He was drunk when he agreed to that shit."

"Yes and no."

"As in I know it was yes."

"And besides the aging NFL free agents we'll pilfer and our draft, you know as well as anyone that there's a ton of people who can play this game but for that split second. And when those people play each other without elite NFLers involved, guess what? You have football. I need TV, you're right. You sign with us, we get that. I want a championship. You sign, we get that too."

"An *IFL* championship?"

"Yes! If they're going to the trouble of giving out a trophy I want it, you know that."

"Okay, well there's about five, no ten, other guys who get you the same thing. Get you the television and get you your championship. Start going down that list, but only after crossing me off."

"I want to win a championship with you."

"That's nice but we had our shot."

"And it bugs me. You got caught between championship eras and I blame myself for not putting the guys around you. To this day you're my father's favorite."

"Only because you prejudiced him in my favor."

"No, because he's a real man and therefore recognizes the breed. He's won three in a row, great, but it's not the same when you do it with a guy who models in the off-season and shrinks from contact during it. I can't tell you how many meetings I was in where the sole focus was how to keep this guy from getting hit because we knew he would go in the tank otherwise."

"Seems like a foregone conclusion with that line."

"With you we always kind of suspected you were working out some type of self-loathing the way you kept getting up."

"Nice."

"Point is you'd have won four or five with those guys they have now and don't insult my intelligence by saying you haven't thought about that. I think that's why you were in Hawaii. I think you were pissed three weeks ago when you didn't get in first ballot."

"Come on."

"And I think you know that what I'm saying about the split second is true. Damn, man, Sunday and the stadium's full—"

"Arena."

"The two middle linebackers cross and come on a fire blitz up the middle. Your dim-witted center picks up neither. You're looking downfield but you sense it, the air right in front of you is displaced and violence is coming. You can roll right or left but that means disrupting the timing to your primary, who you know will be open for six. You've been waiting for this call all game so you plant. You plant your feet and deliver just as some two-hundred-and-sixty-pound maniac launches the crown of his helmet into and through your chin. Now all you see is his face as he lays on top of you but you hear it, right?

You hear the crowd and you know. The pass was true and true because you planted those feet and took that hit and that was the only way to get that six. You did what your father started teaching you to do at age seven and what you can do better than all but a handful of people on the entire globe, and as a result ninety people succeeded and five million or so people you don't know are just a little bit happier the next day. You don't want that rush again?"

Silence.

"Okay, Major, I'm a big girl and if pop music has taught us anything it's that big girls don't cry."

"It's not—"

"But remember what Terry Bradshaw said when he was inducted. Here's a guy with the best post-playing career possible and what did he say? He'd trade it all to stick his hands under his center Webby's ass one more time."

"Can't, Nina, you're great fun but I can't."

"Will you quarterback the Pork? Be our quarterpork, as I said earlier to no credit?"

"I just said, I—"

"Don't answer. The IFL doesn't play preseason games, so camps open August first. The quarterback's the leader of the team so if you're our quarterback I expect on that morning you'll show up in a modicum of shape, looking for a playbook, and flashing that crooked smile for the press."

Major Harris is marveling at the ability of the past to suddenly inject itself into the present but Nina Gill is not one to allow reflective quietude.

"This steak kicks by the way; maybe you can cater training camp as well."

They eat for a while in silence.

"Enough football, how's your art collection these days?"

"It's brilliant, Harris. And soon to improve."

69

||||||||||

Salvador Dalí died on January 23, 1989, at age eighty-four. When he was exhumed decades later, to resolve a paternity question, his mustache was still intact.

Prior to that, Salvador Dalí attempted suicide, with varying degrees of failure, multiple times.

Dalí spent considerable time on a glass floor he'd had installed near his studio.

Nina Gill is rabidly pro-Dalí.

In 1965 Dalí donated a work to Rikers Island. Took about an hour and created a four-by-five-foot crucifixion out of charcoal and watercolor. The donation, like maybe all donations, was guilt-inspired after Dalí took ill and was unable to make a scheduled appearance on the island to give inmates an art lesson. It was hung in the jail.

Almost forty years later the painting was stolen. A ludicrously performed inside job by four corrections officers. Witnesses were flipped, convictions secured, and jail sentences served.

The painting was never recovered.

Another famous heist of a Dalí work occurred in 1984, when thieves tunneled into California's Signature Gallery and stole eighteen of his paintings, including the magistral 1941 work *Adolescence*.

There've been others (*Two Balconies*, *Woman with Drawers* [sculpture] et cetera).*

In 1940, Dalí painted *Old Age, Adolescence, Infancy (The Three Ages)*.

Dali met Sigmund Freud on July 19, 1938, and sketched his portrait.

At age five, Salvador was informed by his parents that he was the reincarnation of his brother who had died before he was born. This happened at that brother's grave site.

Salvador Dalí was born on May 11, 1904.

*In 1969, at the request of a friend and that friend's money, Salvador Dalí designed the famous logo of the Spanish confectioner Chupa Chups. To tell the truth, it's nothing all that special, the big insight was having the logo run on the top of the lollipop so as to remain undisturbed; also that company name can loosely be translated as Sucky Suck. They make other candy besides lollipops.

68

|||||||||

Travis Mena, MD, is quickly running through the established symptoms in his head, a diagnosis has to emerge, no? Let's see, elevated heart rate, shortness of breath, extreme anxiety. Whatever he has it's pretty obviously fatal and susceptible only to palliative end-stage treatment.

But then he sees the cause and it's not at all mysterious. Not only is Chief of Medicine Lenahan in the area but one could even say he is pointedly walking directly at Travis with the intent of addressing him. One would be right.

"We're having M and Ms tomorrow morning. You'll be first."

Travis laughs hesitantly.

"Glad I could amuse you, be prepared."

"Ø"

"I must confess, I don't understand the grin. It was only out of esteem for your father that I steered it into being about that GPO instead of a thirteen-year-old girl with nothing more . . . never mind. Be at the morning one, promptly."

The confusion is decreasing, but with Travis there's always a healthy delay between mental state and corresponding facial evidence of same.

"You'll be first" repeated sternly as if an entire cycle of friendship to enmity has revolved between those two mirrored utterances, then the chief walks away and through one of those swinging doors.

Travis stares. The chief's shrinking image somehow manages to intimidate him even further. The doors swing in steadily decreasing horizontal arcs and he notices their windows need cleaning—incredibly, not an ambient rarity despite the pervasive odor of cleaning solvents.

A nearby observer, dressed like a colleague, comes over. She seems bathed in delight.

"The hell, man. You must be new, or else have bowling balls between your spindly legs. Either way, I think you've vastly overestimated Lenahan's sense of humor."

"I wasn't trying to . . . my God, I swear, I was thinking of the candy!"

"Ah, confusion not concrescence. So the rumors are true."

"Rumors? What—"

"And you now know what the chief was referring to?"

"What is it, that Morbesity and Morality thing?"

"What did you just say?"

"Moribundity and Mentality?"

"Morbidity and Mortality, and I will *definitely* be attending this one."

"But don't they have to give me formal warning of one?"

"What do you think that was? Idle chit, or chat?"

"Oh."

"Listen, don't get offended, but where did you come from? Meaning, graduate from."

"Just thought it would be more formal is all. What case, for example? Which patient?"

"Well, that mystery should clarify rather easily. How many big sleeps did you preside over that infamous night?"

"Huh?"

"Christ, how many terminal patients that night you were alone?"

"Only two, but I assure you neither one—"

"Okay, so it'll be about the one that wasn't the tragic conclusion of a girl's life before it even gained proper momentum."

"So . . ."

"No, I'm eating, come with."

"My break's not till—"

"Nonsense, and I get the feeling your life's been nothing but a series of them."

"Hey—"

"Don't sweat it, same is true of me and pretty much everyone else around here barking orders."

They walk, mainly in silence though she does almost imperceptibly shake her head a few times. They're in a section of the hospital Travis has never been in and they arrive at their destination.

"Burger King? In a hospital?"

"You have something against the king? Who do you think paid for Lenahan's boat? Or is it you have something against boating?"

"So if Lenahan's not talking about her, then what does the GOP have to do with anything?"

"The other one was pretty hopeless right from admission, right?"

"Yeah, there was severe—"

"A real GPO, good for parts only."

"Ohhh."

"See the break now, detective? God, this place is so corrupt. Or wait, maybe the world at large is orders of magnitude worse and this is where we come to get a respite. After all, what do I know about that larger place? I spend a hundred and twenty hours a week here."

"In neither case. Both patients."

"You really think they want to grill you about the girl? Creating a hard record of fitful inefficiencies and imprecisions that accumulated into—"

"She was very sick—"

"Ah, I see you've got *that* lingo down at least."

"I've never—"

"Softballs, as if from a batting cage machine."

"—been the focus."

"Doubt they'll even listen to your responses."

"But I have seen them conducted."

"You gonna eat those?"

"No, I don't even know why I ordered them. Did it seem to you like she put undue pressure on me to add fries to my—"

"So this program was in the US? Of A?"

"Of course, where else?"

"True, you're definitely an all-American."

"Thank you."

"No offense."

"Uh."

"Listen, you'll be fine. I have to round, take that *to go* as you accompany."

"But I already indicated I was *dining in* so to speak. The necessary implements—"

"Here, squeeze this together like so. Now open your hand, there, let's go."

"Okay . . . but . . . hold up!"

Ever seen someone juggle poorly yet *just* pull it off? He tries to keep up as she practically trots away. He loses sight but is able to feel his way to a reunion.

"There you are," she says, annoyed. "Where'd you go? You know, our custodial staff has better to do than clean up after your fast-food discards."

"I told you—"

"Actually, they probably don't."

She kicks debris away with her rubber sole.

"It's a setup's what I'm saying, Mena. At this point, the Lenahan persona is far harsher than Lenahan himself and it'll be an odd mixture of the two leading the questioning. Once you understand that, then it just becomes a question of playing these two entities off each other, I'm sure you understand."

"I don't."

"Then don't."

"But what about?"

"Yes?"

"The girl? Because—"

"The girl . . . the patient . . . what about the girl he says." Breathed with an almost ruminative wonder. She turns to a woman whose presence he hadn't even noticed. "Forty cc's was right, Nurse. Thanks."

"So . . ." Travis is desperate for closure but she's moved on to yet another interloper.

"Where's the chart on this guy? Did I do this one already? Will you page Clarkson for me? I can't master that damn thing, I end up yelling into some patient's bad ear. Come this way, Mena. I did this one already. Tell you, if my damn head wasn't attached."

"You mentioned the girl, what about the girl?"

"Right. What if, *about the girl*, I told you that you, and everyone else involved, were both completely blameless and, collectively, entirely at fault? That the two things were simultaneously true."

"I don't understand."

"Look, Mena, where are we?"

"Uh, outside Labor and Delivery I guess."

"No, more generally."

"Bellevue Hospital."

"And generaller still, a famous hospital in insane New York City, an institution famous for its treatment of the mentally ill and for its truly diasporic volume of infirm."

"Okay."

"My point is that even here, where Death permeates the very walls—although I admit he behaves discreetly here for the most part—even here, that steep a decline of a thirteen-year-old girl like that? All the way to the basement? Even here that resonates loudly, man, like a scream."

"No, I know, that's why—"

"Thing is, it's all perception, kid."

"I think you're younger than me. You look younger."

"First thing a magician learns is to wave that wand."

"Almost certain you are."

"We're all *science* and *technology* and *cutting edge* and *state of the art* but really it's just a bunch of people standing around guessing."

"I know."

"I mean, you know the gap between what people think and the reality of a place like this. Take the tests we order. A machine takes us a picture, then what? How many times, show the same picture to three of us, get three different interpretations, debate it long enough and that can double. Half the time I'm debating someone who started practicing when we were still bleeding people with leeches, calls me missy, can't believe I have the same title as him. And you know what? He could be as right as anyone, that's how slippery a concept *right* is. Think about it, how many people come in here on a one-way because of an infection they get here? They get it here! Let me think, what could we possibly do about that? Oh, I know! What if everyone here washed their hands a hell of a lot more! I know, radical technology. Yet, what's the general perception? That we spend more time cleaning our hands than talking. Whatever, who has the time? It's like, who's in a better position than us to know the deleterious effects of human sleep deprivation? So what do we do? Make sure the people making critical instantaneous decisions, exercising complex judgment, and attempting fine motor tasks are impaired to an extent inconceivable in any other industry."

"Well, it's not an industry, right?"

"Oh?"

"Medicine, I mean. Not an industry really."

"Is that so? Don't scare me, I owe about half a million dollars so it damn well better be. Let's just say I'm not worried, because it most certainly is. Kid, if the answer isn't money, it's only because you're asking the wrong questions. What do you think explains everything I've just said? You think the people in a position to effect change don't know what I know after about thirteen days here? Trust me, the only changes that get implemented are the ones that promise to turn red numbers black. Numbers. Look close enough and you'll see that the bodies being wheeled around here are actually mere conveyances of insurance and social security numbers, the prime numbers for this place's pump."

"No, I reject that. You're talking about human beings."

"And? So? What's a human being? Why do you say it like that? Was I supposed to experience some kind of awe just then? Of course I know what you mean on some level. But it's more like I *remember* what you mean, the way I can remember believing in Santa Claus. You did a neuro rotation, otherwise you wouldn't be here. No one can pay attention during that rotation and maintain anything resembling a lofty view of humanity."

"I found something like the opposite."

"You're putting me on, right? Hi, I need the pictures of this guy's kidney. I know he posed for them yesterday. We'll wait here." Eye roll. "Found the opposite, huh? Let me tell you about my rotation in that field. Hideous car accident. The guy on the donorcycle has the good sense to check out on impact, brain stem. The female driver, forty-five, not as lucky. She ends in a tree, a sharp portion of which goes through the windshield then through her eye socket to hit cerebral pay dirt. Yeah. Now, she's going to survive this, rather handily actually, it's just a question of how much function can be restored. My first night coincides with her first out of ICU. Her daughter—passenger, unscathed—is her only visitor.

"Listen carefully. I'm at the foot of the bed with her chart, the daughter sitting next to the bed. The patient opens her eye, sees her daughter, and smiles an apologetic smile that causes her left upper lip to quiver. She then tilts her chin slightly up and to the right, opens her eye wide, and says *Johnny?* She is asking about her grandson, the visitor's son. After a little bit of confused interplay, the daughter reminds the patient that Johnny wasn't in the car. At this point, the patient does exactly this: she exhales in an exaggerated way, looks up at the ceiling, and says *Thank God.* Then she looks to her left and, after exactly two seconds, adds, *for that at least.*

"Now, around now you're wondering why I've told you this woman's actions in such sharp detail. And you're probably thinking that this level of detail is just a mildly compelling storytelling tool I've chosen to employ for enhanced memorability or something. But I assure you that what I just described is precisely what she did, down to the slightest infinitesimal gesture. How can I be so confident in my account? Believe me when I tell you that I personally watched this woman take these exact actions, speak those exact words, upwards of fifty times.

"Understand, I'm not giving you a particularly vivid example then saying that her conduct generally conformed to it fifty times. I'm saying that she did the exact same thing fifty goddamn times. Every single time, she would start with that exact smile. And I mean *exact*, as if they were copies run off by a printer. Then the *Johnny* with the exact same inflections et cetera. Every. Single. Time. Likewise, with everything else I've described.

"It got to the point where the daughter would see the smile and just try to cut to the chase by telling her that Johnny wasn't in the car. You know what would happen then? The patient would just skip ahead to that part of her rigmarole, with the exhale and the *Thank God* and all the rest."

"Her brain damage prevented her from forming the memory. She was condemned to live that moment of relief over and over."

"Thanks, Watson. But that's not quite the point is it? What *is* the point is the perfect, mind-numbing consistency of her reaction."

"Ow! What the hell? Why'd you do that? You pinched me, hard!"

"What just happened?"

"What just happened? You pinched me just happened, hard!"

"Then what?"

"What do you mean?"

"After I pinched you, *softly*, what did you do? Exactly do."

"After your hard pinch I said *ow* then rubbed the spot."

"What made you decide to do that?"

"I didn't *decide* anything, it was an instantaneous reaction."

"Okay, after that reaction what did you do?"

"Let me think, I inquired after your motivation, of which I'm still very curious by the way."

"Another instant reaction?"

"No, in that case I decided what to say before saying it."

"Wrong. That implies that you could've had a different reaction than saying, *What the hell* et cetera."

"Of course I *could* have."

"No, see. That's the terrible lesson of this patient. Whereas you had a soft pinch, the inciting stimulus for the patient was the healthful sight of her daughter. You would say her version of your *ow* was the smile. But why would a smile *always* be her reaction."

"Because she was happy."

"And, worse, why should it be the exact same smile every time?"

"Because she's not choosing to smile that way."

"That's precisely my point. If the smiles are identical because they are in a sense automatic and not a product of will, then the fact that all that ensues is identical as well means it too is automatic!"

"No."

"No? Over and over the patient did the exact same thing. Tilted her head the exact same way, said the exact same words in the exact same order. Fifty out of fifty times she had the exact same reaction to what was, to her, novel stimuli!"

"But—"

"Look at it from her perspective, pretend we could. What is it we think is happening in her mind?"

"She sees her daughter."

"She sees her daughter."

"And sees that she's safe."

"She knows she and her daughter were in an accident and she has just established that her daughter is safe, she's relieved."

"So she smiles."

"She decides to smile?"

"Of course not."

"Okay, she smiles automatically. Then what, Mena?"

"Then she gets worried again, thinks the grandson may have been in the car as well, she's doing a kind of inventory."

"I agree. Then what?"

"She asks about him, nothing weird about that."

"Generally not, but what about the fact that she *chooses* to do so precisely the same way every time, with the expanding eye and the one-word question?"

"A little odd maybe, but—"

"But let's go back in her head. Specifically, to the later moment when she discovers that her grandson was not in the car."

"More relief."

"Right, let's pretend someone only witnessed this once, what would such an observer guess had gone on in the patient's head?"

"In her head? She felt great relief and thanked God for it."

"More than that though, right? Remember she looked up, thanked God, then said *for that at least*, all in a matter of seconds. So a reasonable interpretation is something like this. She felt great relief, then gratitude, then engaged in what looks like a little bit of logical reasoning."

"I don't see that."

"Sure, she thanks God but then thinks something like If I thank God for Johnny not being in the car, I have to also accept that he allowed me to lose my eye."

"Okay, I see that."

"Well, that's what it *looks* like. But I now know, fifty times later, that here appearance doesn't correspond with reality."

"I get it."

"The patient wasn't actually *doing* much of anything, any more than an infant does something when it closes its hand in response to you poking its palm. We like to think we're these idiosyncratic, highly complex beings constantly responding to novelty from an infinite universe of possible responses. Hell, the patient thought that, the fiftieth time as well as the first!"

"It is strange, I admit."

"But it's only strange if you still believe in Santa Claus, and I don't. These are the wrong pictures. Nurse? These are wrong."

That's what they gave her, the nurse objects.

"See what I mean, Mena?" Looking up, eyes only, then back at the nurse. "When you're done there, take me directly to the person who gave you this. Because that is the individual I'm going to drag here by the ear to tell this patient he has to pose again in that machine because they photographed the wrong slice."

"I better go so you can handle this."

"Wait, Mena. My point is there's nothing lofty about this place, the human body, or *human beings* as you breathlessly pronounce them. There are no ghosts leaving machines here, just machines running out of battery power. There are no minds in Neuro, only brains. Brains that skip like faulty records. Faulty blips asking and asking after Johnny, but only using preprogrammed settings."

"But that's not what you feel you're doing when you ask after someone, that's only your impression from the outside looking in."

"Of course, you're right, but that's the worst part! What's worst is not that we're soulless automata set loose to kinetically enact complex-seeming behavior. No, the special twist of the knife is that as we so behave we're also actively being fooled into thinking we're so much more than that. In other words, our evil brains don't content themselves with being all there is, they also have to somehow magically create the illusion of sentient control. There it is then. Don't trouble yourself with questions of what constitutes consciousness or how it arises out of purely physical processes, just know that what we call consciousness is illusory misperception."

"If that's true—"

"There's no *if*, it's true. They wheel a malfunctioning collection of atoms in here and we try to restore them to functionality. If we fail, it happens, plenty of other collections keep humming along and the ones we failed will organize therein."

"Except when our failures create agonized screams in the hallways."

"Even then, still don't see?"

"I just—"

"Ready, Nurse? Okay, give me a second and we'll go."

"With the girl, it was like . . . You have to go, right?"

"Yes, one last thing, and I'm not trying to be mean."

"Uh-oh."

"Well, customarily this might end with some indication from me that I'm ready to take you under my wing."

"I still think you're younger than me."

"So I don't want you to get the wrong idea. I'm not the mentoring type. I'm not here for the hospital, or medicine, or the patients. I'm here for one person and I'll let you guess who that is. Truth is, if I viewed you as any sort of threat we never would've shared whatever this was, no offense."

"How could I possibly fail to be—"

"It's not personal, kid. I'm just a madwoman who has to finish first. Just thought I'd take a slight break from that to casually toss a lifesaver at a boy just before he drowns."

"Boy? And thanks but if you're madly bent on finishing first, then everything you just said could be—"

"Gotta go, be good."

There'd been a lot unsettling about that exchange. Start with the fact that only about halfway through had he noticed the DR. SINCLAIR affixed to her chest and then only because, with considerable difficulty, he had finally gotten over his fear that a stare in that direction would be misinterpreted. Sin-clair were already magical syllables in those parts. Travis had once heard someone casually declare that he'd never encountered anyone who seemed appreciably more intelligent. Travis had then reflected that he didn't think he'd ever had the opposite experience, encountered someone noticeably less endowed.

Either way, if those were the only two choices, Sinclair was probably safely placeable in the former category. And here she was, making ludicrous assertions that, given the source, couldn't be ludicrous and, worse, about three quarters of the way through, he kind of, and don't read too much into this because we're talking about an absurdly low-level form of this, maybe, slightly, just a little bit, started to sort of fall in love with her.

That ended abruptly when she left but it also still kind of lingered. So it was through a bit of confusion that he remembered he could leave the hospital and did. But really he should have stayed and reviewed the records to prep for the next day but he could also come in extra early tomorrow because he really needed to be home just then. Although you could argue that going home and depressurizing could maybe prove to be the wrong move as he was highly skilled in that area so would then have to restart his medical engine in a panic to immediately take it onto their version of the autobahn with the opposite of a closed course.

And all this breeds sufficient indecision in Travis that he is doing that thing where he's shifting back and forth on alternating feet while debating which way to go and therefore not paying great attention when he bumps into a nearby girl. Significance of this is that the girl was holding, immediately prebump, a rather outsize raised-relief-globe balloon. She loses her grip and the balloon rises. A perfect scale model, accurately colored and rendered, with a helium core in place of magma.

67

|||||||||

A slight bump, that's all it takes, and now the world's come loose. It rises, slowly at first then accelerating. Travis, very tall, reaches up nonchalantly. He can still be the hero. Then a jump, not a big Travis strength. But no. Then another with an empty swat and gone.

Now Travis turns his attention to the girl, whose mouth's corners are sinking precipitously. If he can just quickly charm her out of the tears option maybe parental involvement can be avoided altogether. And this becomes the first Travis success in about a week, greatly aided by the inexplicable fact that Dr. Mena is a very thin man who somehow possesses a remarkably chubby face that tends to disarm every recipient, but especially recipients like pets, youngsters, and anything else not prone to excessive critical thinking.

Lost, true, but the world keeps spinning. And rising.

And the white satin ribbon trailing it resembles nothing more than the jet-stream tail pop culture depicts whenever a body hurtles through outer space. That this is no ordinary body but rather Earth entire only makes it all the more poignant. Also the spin is countervailing human progress. It is westward spin and sci-fi tells us that the result of such spin will be a traveling back into the past. In such a way can human history ascend and devolve simultaneously.

The toy rises, Brazil drifts left and is replaced by Angola then, because a change in the wind has tilted the balloon's earthly axis, upper Australia.

It's a fake rubber ball of a world but damn if it doesn't float and spin convincingly. And if it were explained that the ball's not really shrinking, it's just the increasing distance between observers and the object that makes it seem so, well, this is a concept familiar to preschoolers. But what explains that this world seems instead to be growing in size and scope the farther away it gets? Maybe it's the arrival of a replacement world, that would explain the swelling.

The counterspin? Could be the world apologizing for the whole thing just not working out.

After all, that landmass is where human gathered up fellow human to make them chattel. As if they were indiscriminately picking wildflowers. Over there? Rape the women, kill any infants that result, maim and mutilate anyone who dissents. Here? Take power by killing then kill to keep it. Someone speaks disruptive truth? Cut out their tongue. A rule obstructs? Change it, blot it from the records. See something shiny? Cut a throat open for it. The resulting sound of bubbling blood is the soundtrack of acquisition. My landmass is better than yours. My skin, my God, this pretty flag, our sacred text, this hallowed ground; bunch of fucking apes.

Given that open and notorious a failure, with its unremitting and unrepentant propagation, would it be any wonder if the world essentially exhausted all forward momentum and sought its own undoing? What would such a reversal in the flow of time look like?

First to come undone would be a network of toys really. With no true utility beyond distraction, proceeding pastward means the toys would oddly grow in size and slow in velocity until fading all the way to disappearance. This would leave mainly a sea of pouting children in adult bodies with the universe of significance left largely undisturbed. And this would be an odd cataclysm that would drive people not indoors to shelter but rather outside to engage with largeness and interconnectivity.

But let the great leftward spin continue and instead of mere toys disappearing, the world would lose tools and the necessities they unearth and ideas and rights and rules and leisure and freedom and choice until people were driven literally closer to the ground in violent and oppressive subjugation to crawl like anteaters. No, to bray and beat their chests like apes. And hurl their feces at the other apes until they all just melted into paramecia-like creatures that ooze into the water to merge with the ocean floor back into a great nullity.

The earth is smug and would pretend this was always the intent. That the plan was for a certain evolutionary peak to be reached then for the archer that oversees everything to fire Time's arrow in the opposite direction that Man might retrace its steps like a doddering grandfather looking for lost keys.

Or maybe a never-ending cycle. One where the ocean would then once again spit out building-block organisms that culminate in animals who willingly carry little boxes at all times and these boxes reveal the animals' precise locations on the globe.

Boxes that fill the air with invisible inchoate data that even thirteen-year-old fingertips can conjure into reality in what would look to eighteenth-century eyeballs like a wizard plying his trade.

66

|||||||||

—¿Qué hora es?

"It's six-twenty."

—¿Porque tan oscuro?

"Sunrise at six-fifty-one."

—¿Pero *tan* oscuro?

"It happens fast, it's not gradual, faster than people think. Moonrise is two hours later."

—¿A caso eso es algo?

"It most certainly is something."

—No te creo ni cinco. ¿Que mas se inventaran?

"It's not invented, it's what the moon does."

—¿Casi seis y media? ¿Y tu Papa?

"I was going to ask you that. Is he working late?"

—No dijo nada. ¡Ay, happy san vallantie!

"He's not answering his phone."

—¿Que buscas?

"I can track his phone's location online from here."

—Que rarisimo.

"I've actually been up a couple hours and the whole time the phone has been there."

This is when she first notices that her son looks mildly harried and only because he is expending effort to keep it at that level.

—¿Y?

"It's just a street, I think it's a bus stop. See? That looks like a bus stop, right?"

—No se ve el teléfono.

"It's not a current picture. But it's recent, and I think it's a bus stop, see the booth thing?"

—¿Entonces?

"The phone's been there since like midnight, six hours."

—Ah, no faltaba. Una semana y ya perdió el teléfono. Le dije que no lo compre, pero tu papa siempre tiene que tener lo último.

"A bus stops there that comes within a block of here."

—¿Asi que perdido?

"Yeah, he probably just lost it there." He looks up from the screen, at her face.

—¿Que?

"So where is he? Why hasn't he called?"

Moments in a life bleed into each other, group into throng, then disappear. But not all of them. Some are so magnified by their content, usually negative, that they sear into your mental life and it becomes difficult to imagine that burn ever healing fully. An example of this is the events incited by the phone call that will come three minutes later.

As for the moments just before that, the ones described above, those are only retrospectively charged and, moreover, this charge differs in quality. Instead of paralytic horror, what permeates these moments, when recalled, is a wistful sense of prologue.

Nelson de Cervantes would intentionally recall this exchange with his mother and, not inaccurately, remember a rising tidal sense of foreboding. Still, he would also greatly envy the lost-forever ability to exist in that world.

That's what it is. The horrific moment is marked by an oversaturation of the senses. Moments like the above, the opposite. The surrounding details fade into indefinition until the moment seems less than real. That such placidity could have ever existed. That you could pinpoint the exact moment it was stolen by the suddenly-clear-to-you unfeeling universe.

Couple hours earlier, an anxious thirteen-year-old insomniac and his amazement that his school would even cradle the Pandora's box that is the classroom dissemination of valentines. It was not going to go well for him and, weirdly, it was his lack of confidence in that area that made him confident in his prediction. Early teens handing out shiny red cardboard hearts, website postings of updated class rankings, strangers wearing your favorite laundry placed on injured reserve, ambiguous declarations from pulse-raising female peers that are open to a multitude of interpretations with wildly variant implications, all wiped clean as if some unseen force just capriciously decided to shake its Etch-A-Sketch—your life.

Maybe it was this lack of gradation that most offended. That and its irrevocability. Ever wake up after misfortune and into momentary ignorance of or at least ontological doubt re: the misfortune? Then that moment when the realization washes over you and you feel that interior blackness. Nelson realized that for a long future time the best he could realistically hope for would be those confused moments where the blackness is there but is invisible background and not in close-up.

Like so many things, a form of imprisonment; so it was perfectly natural to envy not just those moments before incarceration but even more so the time when it (Time) flowed without even consideration of that possibility—the subtle freedom a repetitive lack of incident engenders. Envy it all you wish, you cannot re-create it, cannot meaningfully exist in it. Memory may be more powerful than pure imagination but both are muffled rumor when compared to our experience of the urgent *present*.

The way a skilled singer can give birth to a syllable then via melisma guide it in and out of various notes, so can a single scream cycle through a series of emotions, almost assertions, that span all it means to be human. Celia de Cervantes, mother of Nelson and Gisella and until then wife of Jorge, let out precisely such a scream not long after the almost-passé sound of the landline phone ringing. It was an anguished acoustic nightmare that somehow expressed disbelief, fear, shock, outrage, devastation, catatonia, surrender, resignation, and, finally, immeasurable loss all at once and it so permeated all the surrounding inanimate objects that the space became haunted, at least in the literal nonsupernatural sense of the term. Existing in that ruined space thereafter became a chore.

65

||||||||||

Of all the things the term *right* can be extended to encompass for humans, the right to a space where mere existence commonly borders on the effortlessly pleasurable would seem to be near the top and very generally the universe complies.

Sharon Seaborg (she wasn't quite yet ready to lose the pleasing alliteration) is one of those people who inexplicably approaches orgasm at the presence of natural light, and the only location in her apartment where she can sometimes experience this sensation is her little breakfast nook off to the side of the grim kitchen, where she has, post-Hugh, removed the wobbly card table used for base dining and there placed an actually rather interesting chair and footstool combo, thereby fashioning a genuine reading corner (hat tip to various low-rated interior-design reality shows), where Sharon would sit with tea that claimed calming properties and try to dull whatever the previous night's telephonic horrors had been.

Across the street, Feniz Heredia has forsworn reading (no more gods that fail) in favor of being on hold; the plan is still the same but his dwindling time will be primarily spent with a phone to his ear waiting to opine on one of the various Spanish-language radio-television entities he monitors closely, ready to pounce should one of the many topics he's informed on suddenly emerge, and because his phone is not cordless the only place to engage in this activity is the kitchen, which consequently becomes the one bearable spot in his suddenly cavernous house.

Travis Mena's Lower Manhattan kitchen technically belongs to his father, who for alleged tax reasons is rather fervent about rent collection and far less so about interior-design trends so that this kitchen has a distinct eighties feel that drives the rare visitor to adjoining rooms, including Travis's favorite, the office, where the rather ludicrous level of compubility can give the impression that Travis has some form of responsibility for nothing less than the continued operation of the world itself.

And directly below that office, in an illegal sublet of one room, Dia Nouveau, despite her youth, is surprisingly intolerant of noise and has a special stick she keeps by her bed to express that via taps at the feet of the offending party.

In Queens, Hugh Seaborg only enters his kitchen to procure the appropriate utensil whenever the delivering establishment neglects to include plastic spoon, fork, or spork. Otherwise, it's a lumpy sofa that CO with the Fu Manchu no longer needed. The flyer's only condition that the donee pick it up.

Hugh did, to drop it in front of the immense television he was finally able to purchase, incrementally, now that there were no high-pitched protestations to contend with. No protests. Just a morgue silence that only that manic slab might properly combat.

64

IIIIIIIIII

Rikers Island is technically in the Bronx and only reachable via Queens, but nobody really knows or believes that, that it's truly part of anything else. And, yes, even there the above principle applies whereby people will stake out a safer spot, so *human* is this need. In fact, it's not uncommon that among the always twelve thousand or so inmates, little pockets of almost community will emerge in what can only be termed restorative—

"Fuck you looking at, fuckface?"

"Easy there, better get used to it."

Nuno, who really can go zero to sixty faster than anyone in these situations, rises and walks at this fuck to say, "What is it exactly I'm getting used to?" with far more menace than those words could seem to support.

"Whoa, just saying that famous people tend to get longer-than-usual looks, so now that you're one of them you might have to be a bit more tolerant of eye contact's all I'm saying."

"If you know me then you know *why* you know me and you should also know that it's better to stay out of my way, unless you're so desperate to get off this island that a body bag'll do."

"Man."

"Exactly." And he walks away. Usually this settles something like that but here's this guy getting up and walking *towards*, not away from, Nuno.

"We were supposed to be having this conversation in ARDC."

"What?"

"Adolescent Reception and Detention Center. Did you know New

York is one of only two states that sets the age of adult criminal responsibility at fucking sixteen?"

"Stop."

"Yo, while fronting as some kind of liberal circle jerk."

"Stop talking to me."

"I mean, about fifty thousand sixteen- and seventeen-year-olds in adult criminal courts year after year."

"I said stop."

"I think that's where I went wrong, yo. You know? Sixteen, they got the bracelets on you, what chance did I have, Your Honors? Ha, ha! My right?"

"You are wrong."

"But I am right that you were supposed to be a youth and this conversation was supposed to occur in ARDC, or the Robert N. Davoren Complex if you want to be a stickler. Do you?"

"I am a youth, see for yourself." Nuno subtly displays his ID, which he kind of immediately regrets but truth is the fucker's disarming in a way.

"Yes, I see. Of course, you can pretend to as much youth as you want, if what you do is insane enough it's Otis Bantum or, here, James A. Thomas instead of good old Bobby."

"What's your point?"

"We said ARDC."

"*We* said nothing. I've never seen you before in my life and keep this up very few are going to see you from here on out."

"Okay, is that what I should say to The Absence?"

This mention slows even Nuno. He says nothing. Just is obviously thinking.

"The plan required you to land in ARDC, no?"

"I have no idea what you're talking about," Nuno says, but half-hearted. "You're confused. I don't blame you, you don't look too smart."

"I'm Solomon," extending his hand.

"What kind of fucking name is that? You kidding with that shit?"

"Hey, what's in a name?"

"In your case? The strong implication that its owner is a weak pussy."

"Or wise, motherfucker, the wisdom of Solomon. So you're Nuno. I told them, man. I said, Don't let's use someone coming in here for the first time. There's a shock to being put in for the first time that you can't prepare for, man. Right? It's like no matter how bad you had it out there you still *had*, dig? There was something about which you could say *it* is miserable, deprived, whatever. Here, you can't talk like that, there are no souls here, only empty shells being moved around. Understand, doesn't bother *me*, I'm old pro at this shit by now. It's just that, with someone like you."

"Slow your roll, bro."

"Just that the adjustment period's not the best time to be making critical decisions. Also, I mean, *remand*? No offense, but what you did to get in here? That's extreme shit, man."

"I don't know what you mean, I'm innocent."

"Oh, okay. I didn't realize. Of course. But that doesn't change the remand, does it?"

"Not my concern."

"And let me tell you, remand status, no bail, complicates everything. No work detail, enhanced supervision, wrong area."

"There are areas that are less wrong on this island?"

"For what we're trying to do? Most definitely."

"See, I'm not trying to do anything, and *we* are definitely not trying to do anything. I told you, I'm innocent. The system will vindicate me. Until then, I may as well be a lifer for the amount of trouble I'll be stirring up."

"I see, go along to get along."

"Right, so so long."

"I must have the wrong guy then."

"You must."

"But, hypothetically."

"Keep your hypothesis."

"Hypothetically, if a small group of people of the inmate variety were tasked with executing a highly complicated operation while under

close supervision, the inexplicable no-bail status of one of the participants would represent a significant hurdle. And what would make it
worse would be the fact that that individual basically chose that status
given the great many other ways there are to be placed in here."

"Hypothetically, because I'm innocent, if I had done what they say,
it would be because it was fucking necessary. And since, hypothetically, I had to get my ass in here anyway, then I may as well make it
count is all. Any problems I create, I fix myself. You don't see me coming to you crying for anything, do you? I'll deal with the remand like
I do everything else."

"I want to help."

"So help, start with answering a few questions."

"Shoot."

"Yeah, be careful I don't. The thing you said about the sixteen- and
seventeen-year-olds being charged as adults and that shit, where'd
you get that?"

"Law library."

"Yeah, that. They can't restrict my access to it, right?"

"They can't deny it, not entirely. But you ain't gonna get what we
all get, yo. This is the problem with remand."

"Enough about that, and there's like a motion bank and shit?"

"Sure, but the quality is fucking grim, man."

"That's fine, but they got McKinney's and Richardson and shit."

"Holy fuck, what the hell, Counselor?"

"Not as dumb as you look."

"Yeah, they got that shit."

"Good, how are you on procedure?"

"Cold, man."

"I got a court date in two days."

"Part F?"

"Yeah."

"So they got you four days ago and Wednesday's your 180.80?"

"Right. The lawyer served cross just to fuck with them, not ready
to do the grand jury yet."

"Yet? Unless you're going to waive time, Wednesday's your only chance if you want to testify. Not that I can imagine in any way that that's a good idea. But like I said, if you don't waive they are definitely presenting that day, they ain't doing no fucking preliminary hearing and giving your lawyer a preview of their case and shit. Who's your lawyer, anyway?"

"Doesn't matter."

"You understand what I'm saying, though. Wednesday's it. Hope you're not counting on some successful 190.50 motion letting you testify later."

"No, I know. I got something else, we'll see."

"Listen, yo."

"So we don't waive and I get indicted, what then?"

"I don't know, a month? A month for arraignment on the indictment in whatever supreme court part's gonna have the case."

"That's just it, which one?"

"Impossible to know until Wednesday. If you knew the trial bureau of the DA's office—"

"Fifty."

"Damn. All right, so a part starting with fifty, which of those has a calendar? I guess only fifty-one or fifty-two? Fifty-two probably as he's also the administrative judge and this case certainly . . ."

"A month, huh? What's a month, right?"

"It's a fucking lifetime in here."

"What's a lifetime?"

"Out there? Out there, a lifetime feels like a month."

"Such a philosopher."

"Damn straight, yo. Philosophize this for me, how much of suffering is actual suffering and how much of it is just the pain that comes from the recognition that one is suffering?"

"Not sure, how bout I punch you in the mouth to help you examine the question?"

"No thanks, let's keep this theoretical."

"I can do a fucking month."

"Well, you won't have me to kick around."

"What the hell?"

"Told you, I'm in and out of here at will. Boost something clumsily at a pharmacy to get in then take time served whenever I've had enough of this torture."

"So?"

"So this thing's gonna take time, seems to me. No use me suffering in here in the meantime."

"Thought suffering's all in your head?"

"Yeah, but turns out in-your-head is a big fucking deal. I'll talk to the law library dude, you won't have any problem. What do you say I come back around your arraignment on the indictment date and we'll take stock and shit then?"

"Suit yourself, who needs your sorry ass?"

"Shit, the count's in five minutes. Oh, last thing, safety. This is a delicate question, yo. I'm as politely correct as the next guy. You know . . ."

"Spit it the fuck out, you fuck."

"Do you, like, have a race?"

"A race to what?"

"No, man, like, what are you?"

"The hell you talking about? I'm a soulless inmate according to you, remember?"

"Yeah, but what kind?"

"Currently? Angry."

"You know what I mean. Like that creed, religion, or color thing."

"What are you a fucking census taker?"

"Like I said, it's a safety issue, bro. In here, you need to group yourself with your kind."

"I'm unkind."

"To decrease the possibility of people fucking with you."

"People tend to not fuck with me."

"I can definitely believe that. But still, only a lunatic would reject identifying with their race."

"I reject it."

"Okay, what race do you reject?"

"No, I reject race itself."

"You can't do that."

"I reject it and anything like it."

"Like it?"

"All that other shit you mentioned, nationality, creed—whatever the fuck that is—color, all that shit."

"What's with you, you don't want to be part of a group?"

"Yes, very astute."

"Safety in numbers, yo."

"And death in platitudes, so shove your fucking census up your ass."

"Have it your way."

"I always do, no one else's really suits me."

"Obviously you wouldn't dream of name-dropping The Absence for protection, right?" Solomon puts his hand to his mouth. The realization that he has said those two words out loud, maybe even for the second time. He looks around. No visible reaction. But that's also exactly what one would expect whether he just signed his own death warrant or not. He whispers, "Right?"

"Fuck them too" is the answer and Solomon visibly recoils. He's thinking how the latest rumor is The Absence skinned a guy alive for some unspecified offense. Probably untrue but who cares about probability in this context?

"You've got issues, bro. If it weren't for the obscene amount of cheddar at stake this would be your last Solomon sighting."

"Don't go away angry, Sol dear. But do go away."

And damn if the count didn't start just then so that they, Nuno and Solomon, shared nothing more in that initial interaction.

63

|||||||||

There's a holding cell they put inmates in during the count, and in the interests of mass appeasement there's a nearby elevated television that, shit you not, almost always displays a bootlegged version of a movie then in theaters. This time, however, the television is tuned to ESPN and that bullshit entity is replaying a recent bizarre press conference tangentially related to the NFL.

At times of crisis the inherent stupidity of organized sports reveals itself with crystalline rapidity. So Nuno, who normally could be numbered among fans of the stupidity, is consummately unimpressed by the above goings-on. Well, unimpressed until he looks up at the screen at the precise moment the new deputy commissioner of whatever the fuck the IFL is is being pressed into duty behind the microphone.

She is stunning. Literally, meaning he is stunned. It's just that she looks exactly like. So much like.

Just as Nuno reaches the apex of his confusion, some rather odd-looking letters appear below the deputy commissioner but above a scrolling crawl designed to make you feel you're not missing anything. They are magical letters too:

What a world. Can't be. A name like that. Not susceptible to repetition. But don't really even need to debate the name or its prevalence.

It's that face. There it is. There it is again. Years. The permagrin, the plump hint-of-rose cheeks that manage to exist under cheekbones on a shock of white under barely restrained and lustrous black coils. Oh man, a face to get lost in.

Now it feels like a damn cage all right. Nothing brings out the desolation of a situation quite like evocation of an even-if-only-retrospectively-idyllic past.

Back in his cell after the count. Suddenly there are no tools sufficient to the task, which can be distilled thusly: pretending extreme happenings aren't happening through a near self-hypnosis where necessary.

Writing, for example, in that stupid diary, like some stupid middle school girl, what the fuck is, or even *was*, the point? Yet

2015's February 14 (Saturday) from JATC in Rikers Island—Queens, NY

It's okay, anything temporary is tolerable.

And I was wrong before when I said there's nothing in the universe for me, because I can read and that universe, for any single individual, is limitless.

Also, Everything is still out there, I'd just stopped thinking of her.

2015's February 15 (Sunday) from JATC in Rikers Island—Queens, NY

This can definitely be done, I can break out.

But to do it right I first have to experience this place in all its various permutations.

Except for cherub up there before, not sure I've ever felt great warmth from someone who wasn't in some sense obligated.

2015's February 16 (Monday) from JATC in Rikers Island—Queens, NY

Solomon can help, because now I *need* to get out.

Why is the memory of something so pleasant, at base, painful?

The pain of regret is, unlike other injuries assigned to memory, perfectly and inexhaustibly renewable.

Nuno tosses the notebook and it lands somewhat under the bed that dominates his space, his world, his very fucking life.

He sits on that bed. There's never any place he has to be or thing he has to do. He stares out the window.

Right now there's some motherfucker in a flowing robe claiming to have completely emptied his skull. And not even Nuno thinks everyone's full of shit *all* the time so maybe it's not only truly a thing but one that Nuno can do as well.

A vacuum wants to be filled but that's not to say that what rushes in to fill it will be benevolent or even benign.

More than anything Nuno's memory is a memory for language.

Dia Nouveau. *Dia, Dee-ah.* The way no one gave in to the temptation to shorten that name to one syllable, as if it would somehow diminish the dignity of that electric utterance. The rise and fall of it, its supple energy, like when previewing an imminent spectacle.

Her voice comes to him, past utterances restored. And with the clarity of a professional recording:

> *we're friends now*
> *no, I wasn't asking, I was stating a fact*
> *you could probably stay at our place, want me to check?*
> *aww, I'll miss you so much*
> *you're gonna miss me something terrible too, mister*
> *you know we're friends till we die*
> *don't think that's accurate, you got me for example*
> *disagree, I say yes, and I'm the foremost authority on the subject*
> *xoxo, wait, can you say it or does it have to be written?*

guess that makes me the girl of your dreams
would you say I have one of those megawatt smiles?

Then yet another loud clash and when he tries to hear Dia again he finds he can't. Just like he can't get that visual out of his head either:

DIA NOUVEAU
DEPUTY COMMISSIONER?

He has much critical thought to engage in if he's going to get out of that hell. He will *will* her out of those thoughts because he has a vicious will. But really he knows the truth. That it will be a long time before he's close to the same.

62

||||||||||

In Dia's parallel existence, she does not think of Nuno DeAngeles. Truth is she thinks of no one other than Nina Gill and of nothing other than the various permutations of football knowledge that woman is essentially compelling her to acquire. She ingests no entertainment, partakes of only survival levels of food (really gruel), sleeps little, falls into no casual conversations, and even her reading consists of nothing that isn't peppered with ludicrous terms like *the gridiron* or *the pigskin*.

As a result, considerable IFL progress is made. The facility in Paterson is markedly upgraded and whereas before it was only Nina and Dia, now bustling others are present at said facility. This includes a full staff of assistant coaches for Coach Elkins and loads of otherwise unemployables performing clerical duties that require no football knowledge and may even be favored by actual antipathy towards its acquisition.

Dia sits in the open area Nina must pass to enter her corner office and the initial pass always feels like the arrival of a weather front—the kind that inspires local news directors to assign their most junior member to inexplicably brave it in front of a camera that the viewer might learn to reappreciate the indoors.

"Good morning, Nina."

"What are we mourning? The death of my professional reputation?"

"I beg your pardon. Things are going quite well, I'll have you know. Well, except for one devastating turn of events, but first the good news."

She sees Nina's face for the first time.

"Goodness, are you all right?"

"I'm fine, rough night. Some people can't hold their liquor, start flinging fists."

"Oh my, was anybody hurt?"

"Two guys, but my pettifogger says they're not pressing charges so I should be all right."

"Oh. Anyway, the good news is the Canton Claws just signed running back Michael Turner!"

"Really?"

"That's a big deal, he won the NFC rushing title two years ago!"

"No such thing."

"You know what I mean, he led the NFC in rushing. He may be a Hall of Famer!"

"Not in a million years."

"Fine, not first ballot."

"No ballot, you nut. But look at you."

"I know, call me Georgia Halas."

"I will not."

"But this stuff is fascinating if you delve into it."

"I'll keep that in mind."

"It's just like you predicted, Nina. That's ten guys who were significant players in the NFL last year!"

"Well, it's a bit misleading. All ten had one year left at most and the lockout threatened to erase their last paycheck, but we'll take it. And you're right, Turner is a big deal, still a big name, and more importantly a totally class act."

"He's only thirty-one."

"Yeah, but an old thirty-one. Want to know what it feels like to play an NFL game at running back? One of them once put it best. Climb to the top of a twelve-foot ladder, he said, then tip it over and have it fall on you. Now get up and repeat about twenty more times."

"It's getting a lot of press though. And that other thing you predicted would happen is in fact happening. The other owners are starting to get into it and spending money."

"Only after I indemnified the pricks against any financial loss."

"Boy, you're just Nancy Negative today aren't you?"

"Sorry, you're right. Good day for the league." Nina sits at her desk and instantly her feet appear on it. Dia at the door with more.

"For the league, but Coach Elkins is very testy about the Pork."

"Told you not to interact with him before five."

"Where's *our* major acquisition? That kind of thing."

"I'll talk to him. That's the devastating turn? You're going to have to toughen up a bit. Thing about Elkins is—"

"No, (sad face) the pig's in the shop. It was heartrending, really. He kept trying, but he couldn't even get up hills anymore."

"You realize it's not an actual pig, right? It's an automobile in pig costume."

"I know but . . ." She can't continue.

"Okay, it looks like you have everything well under control."

"I e-mailed Major Harris the links to this latest development and everything else so far like you said." This changes the tenor.

"And?"

"No response yet, but he definitely got everything."

"Well done."

"Also . . ."

"Yes?"

"Well, this guy stopped by, said he had something you'd definitely want to see."

"So now we know one of his beliefs, do we know the name of its holder?"

"That's just it, he wouldn't divulge, despite considerable and skillful prodding by me."

"I guess some mysteries are just never meant to be solved."

"I could describe him, physically."

"Nice to know."

"Ready?"

"If you insist."

"I do, he was a Michael Jackson impersonator."

"Oh."

"Yeah, the King of Pop."

"Wrong."

"I'm sorry, were you here?"

"I was not, but I know who you're talking about and it's Marlon Jackson that he loves slash impersonates, not Michael."

"What?"

"That."

"Who the, who's Marlon Jackson?"

"I hope you didn't say anything like that around him."

"You mean Michael's brother? One of the five?"

"Correct."

"That's impossible."

"It's so possible it's actual."

"Marlon Jackson has no fans."

"Really? You have more?"

"I mean, he has no fans independent of Michael, or the five."

"Well, Dick Dickens, PI, makes at least one. And he's such a one that he firmly believes that Michael and the rest essentially rode Marlon's coattails."

"That's insane."

"Maybe, but he has a whole convoluted and diatribic explanation that is oddly persuasive if you let it be but which I cannot do justice to even in summary."

"And he's a private investigator?"

"Well, the private part of that could seemingly use some work considering he came here but—"

"Why do we need a private investigator?"

"We?"

"And how good could he be—"

"He's elite."

"—given that getup."

"Though I'm probably the only one who feels that way."

"If he's doing work for the IFL, it should go through me."

"Through you? The only thing that's going to go through you is my fist if you don't drop this."

"Dropped."

"Good."

"Lastly . . ."

"No."

"I haven't said anything."

"To my ears, all you've done is *say*."

"I mean, on this subject."

"Which is?"

"Clouds."

"Clouds?"

"Do you have time to talk about Clouds?"

"The fuck do I know about clouds? Do I look like some kind of meteorologist to you?"

"No, Joni. Joni's *Clouds*."

"Later, kid."

Nina walks almost *through* Dia then down a flight towards Elkins and the coaches' area.

61

||||||||||

Clouds, released in 1969, was Joni Mitchell's second album and along with the following year's *Ladies of the Canyon*, which Dia is only now beginning to dip a mental toe into, represents the first of several significant steps heavenward by this consummate artist. The experience of listening to these two albums is, for Dia, startling. To begin with, she listens to little else during that time. More than that really, all other music seems oddly inappropriate; almost as if it were mere simulation.

The two albums are, above all, genuine. Their authenticity emerges from the speakers with hypnotic grace.

Dia has not heretofore been a connoisseur of notes, mostly just listened to whatever the radio deemed worthy of audition. Only now is it beginning to dawn on her what a grave error this has been. Not that she's engaged in a clinical dissection of keys and modes and theory, just her almost reptilian response to visceral pleasure. A response that pretty quickly developed an anticipatory element; which element only enhances the pleasure whenever that anticipation is musically sated.

That relates to enjoying the purely musical elements. The next level of appreciation involves the language. With this kind of music, closer inspection of lyrics is almost uniformly where a listener's enjoyment starts to decrease precipitously with the realization that the actual content and shadings of the words being employed are often atrociously inane, if not sheer doggerel. But with Joni, even this early, the opposite happens. Here, examination of the lyrics only deepens the awe. The melodious words have worked their way into Dia with seamless significance and with a weight that's almost shaped, or at least reshaped, her actions.

Dia is twenty-one but maybe she should stop allowing other people to determine the significance of that fact. A mind has no age, only periods and levels of activation. Nothing is one-sided really. But active propulsion is required to behold the entire multidimensional geometry of an examined shape. Because one way to acquire wisdom is through the osmotic accumulation of what many years bring but one can also just will oneself into it in a sense. So a twenty-one-year-old can mentally posit what it will be like to experience the relentless revolution of the wheel of life as it cycles you in and out of focus. Contemplate what obligations arise or don't out of the various ways people connect with each other, intentionally or otherwise. Try to pin down exactly what it is about material reward that complicates, maybe even enervates, otherwise salutary pursuits. In short, in this body of work, Dia is not so much learning or discovering something novel as she is experiencing the sensation of a preexisting phenomenon being aptly named.

And all that's happening contemporaneously with a frantic immersion in the world of professional football, about which Dia knew next to nothing previously, creating a weird mental stew that feels like a rebirth during those rare moments when she can reflect a bit, like when she's lying in bed and the nameless faceless prick upstairs deigns to suffer a respite in his constant percussive treading on her ceiling.

60

||||||||||

On Nina's way to Elkins's office she passes the film room, wherefrom a loud yell. While Elkins is undoubtedly top-notch, save for his major issue, filling out the rest of the staff has been more challenging as no one of conceivable worth has been eager to burn bridges with the NFL. Still, the passion emanating from there must bode well, right?

"Are you nuts, Wince *Lame*-bardi? You don't send a corner blitz from there. It takes too long and leaves a gaping hole!"

"There's no hole, Barely Bryant, gaping or otherwise. I roll the coverage that way, like so, and tackles invariably react to coming corners in a way that frees my DE to the QB!"

"Except my hot read is a swing pass to the shifty halfback in that exact area, Knute Rockhead."

Nina enters to find the two young assistants furiously activating video game controllers against each other.

"Then why's *this* happening? Oh yeah!"

They notice Nina, their boss after all, and scramble to hide the evidence, only to end up bound to each other in a tangled mess of cords and underperforming humanity. Nina steps over them to pour water on the console, resulting in a tie, then again to exit, without a single utterance. She enters Elkins's office without a knock.

"Is it five yet?" he wonders.

"Almost, it's about eleven . . . a.m."

"Has everything always been this bright?"

"I understand our fearless coach is concerned about personnel."

"That's just it, what personnel? I mean, I like my staff."

"Yeah, the two out there are very impressive."

"Happy with the playbook."

"Better be."

"But where are the players?"

"Camp opens August first."

"You're saying no off-season player presence at all?"

"This is the IFL, Buford. Ninety-nine percent of them have real jobs. The kind where they don't keep score and you have to attend day after relentless day."

"Our roster's awful, never won more than three games."

"Not true, the three games part is, but not the awful part."

"Every day someone signs an NFL player or at least someone I've heard of and we've done nothing."

"We've done plenty, relax. Besides kickers, you need twenty-two guys. Of those twenty-two, fourteen can get by on heart and that's exactly what I made sure we have, bighearted guys. If you read my reports and saw the film you know we have a running back in Sims. Runs low to the ground with serious burst and never goes down on first contact."

"And puts the ball on the ground, led the league in fumbles."

"I'll fix that. As for the two receivers, don't even pretend they're not NFL quality. Only that league's obsession with height at the position has kept them out."

"They're good."

"In the secondary, where you can't fake it, you're going to love this corner we drafted. He slept with the coach's daughter in college so got no PT then he gets the stomach flu the night before the combine and blows all his measurables. He's a complete cover beast, you'll see. The kind of guy who gets picked by the NFL in the third round then goes to Hawaii ten times."

"Maybe so, but . . ."

"The free safety got a fifty on his Wonderlic, studies like he's running for president, loves contact, has a crazy nose for the ball and just enough speed."

"I'm sure these guys are all as great as you say but they're in the IFL for a reason."

"Don't be a snob, Buford."

"So what is this, then? On paper, I'm guessing West Coast offense."

"Ugh."

"Don't get me wrong. *On paper,* these guys are suited to selling insurance. Provided they agree not to play on the company flag football team."

"You better have balls, Buford, and throw the fucking thing down the field."

"Using who?"

"We'll get to that."

"On D, I need a nose tackle who will eat up—"

"You need a what to eat what?"

"A nose tackle, where's mine?"

"As in a zero?"

"Yes, as in."

"You don't have a zero-tech nose because you don't need one because we ain't playing no goddamn 3-4."

"Hell you say, I'm a 3-4 coach."

"No, you're a coach. What that means is that you analyze things like available personnel and trends in the sport before deciding your defensive alignment, right?"

"So, Tampa 2?"

"God, no. Since when does 4-3 necessarily mean Tampa 2, for shit's sake? We're gonna have real corners, why waste them? Plus, where am I supposed to get a middle linebacker with that kind of range?"

"I've grown to hate the 4-3. What the 3-4 does, it allows you to—"

"Please, Buford. I know what the 3-4 *does*, I fucking literally invented it. And, yes, I'm using literally *literally*. What I'm saying is that it's outlived its usefulness and is currently a pussy defense. Are you a pussy, then? Because you probably didn't read it closely but there's a pussy clause in your contract that allows me to terminate your employment at first signs."

"Fine, convince me."

"Aw, just like the old days."

"Feels old, all right."

"Two major shifts provoked my 3-4 insight all those years ago. A change in rules and one in the character of available personnel. First, the league outlawed defensive contact with receivers past five yards with an unsurprising explosion in the forward pass. More passes meant a need for more lighter guys who could move and defend those passes. Exchanging a beef mountain for a two-twentyish guy just made sense. The other thing was that around this time these freaky 3-4 OLBs just started appearing and OCs had no answers for them. So if we take like 1980 as a starting point, over the next decade or so you could employ a 3-4 and make one of these nuts your primary pass rusher. I mean, guys like Lawrence Taylor, Rickey Jackson, Pat Swilling, Greg Lloyd, Kevin Greene, Derrick Thomas! What do you do with those guys if there's no such thing as a 3-4? They're too light to get in a three-point stance. You want to send them after the quarterback anytime there's a pass but if they're a 4-3 OLB that means you're blitzing on every pass. Notice how outdated everything I'm saying sounds, Buford. My point is it served its purpose back then and worked okay. It was certainly a more athletic defense than you could field running a 4-3 and the alignment had the added bonus of sowing indecision on the part of the opposing offensive line regarding which four guys were coming."

"Still does, and we both know it's all about personnel anyway. We can debate this all day but if you have Reggie White you run a 4-3 and vice versey, Nina. Some of the greatest defenses have been 3-4, proving my point."

"Ah, see, only two."

"The hell are you talking about? Only two effective 3-4s? *Ever?*"

"First off, you said great. Let's define a great defense as one that carries the team to a championship."

"Agreed."

"At a minimum, right?"

"Well, not sure."

"Look, if a defense was great and the team didn't win the championship then we can safely ignore it since our goal is the championship not some nebulous *great* designation."

"Fine."

"Super Bowl era, counting the fourteen or so played before the 3-4 even existed, let's say there've been, and I'll be extremely generous, ten or twelve great defenses? A grand total of *two* have been 3-4s."

"The Giants."

"The 'eighty-six Giants and the 2008 Steelers, that's it. A remarkably poor record for my brainchild. Think of all the other signature defenses. The seventies' Steel Curtain, the 'eighty-five Bears, 2000 Ravens, the 2002 Bucs. All 4-3s, my friend. Want to expand to nonchampionship-yet-arguably-great defenses? The Purple People Eaters? The Deacon Jones Rams? The Reggie White–Jerome Brown Eagles? You get the point."

"I look at it the other way, it can be done. The Giants and Steelers have shown that, so let's us do it."

"That's silly, why would we purposely increase the degree of difficulty? A mere two defenses? Twenty-two years apart? Know what those two defenses had in common, besides alignment? They both had a transcendent, once-in-a-generation player at right outside linebacker. LT was probably the greatest defensive player ever, his backside pursuit alone was probably enough to get him that designation. James Harrison? Late bloomer, so he didn't do it nearly as long, but for five years or so he was easily the best since Taylor."

"I agree, he threw left tackles around like rag dolls, best I've ever seen against the run."

"While being an elite pass rusher, you're making my point. The only way for the defense to work at the highest level is to have a Hall of Famer at the most critical position, that's the definition of a flawed system."

"I like that element of surprise, I must say."

"Surprise? Who's surprised? What's next? You going to sing me the praises of the zone blitz. This stuff is so passé now. The offensive linemen are too good, too well coached. Who cares which of the four LBs is rushing if the linemen across from them are employing zone-blocking principles anyway?"

"I don't know."

"You don't? How about this? When coaches first began replacing DLs with linebackers those linebackers would give up maybe forty pounds to the guy blocking them. Today, these left tackles are what, three twenty average? That means even the biggest OLBs are giving away seventy, even ninety pounds! Then you watch the film on Monday and wonder why the poor fuck couldn't seal the edge or do anything on a pass rush besides run around the tackle and right out of the play. And don't get me started on the nice unfettered running start the guards get at my inside linebackers. It's lunacy to concede the line of scrimmage like that. That's why I maintain it's now a pussy defense. Find four real men, stick them across from the other team's line, and let's find out who's better at football in a fair fight."

"Maybe you're right, *about the NFL.* Are you suggesting I'll have three-hundred-and-twenty-pound tackles? Who can move? Nothing you just said has any relevance to this lunatic place."

"Well, I have my eyes on this guy who—"

"God, how did I end up here?"

"Relax, the Claws just signed Michael Turner."

"The *what*?"

"Never mind."

"These people are not quality, Nina. You know that."

"*These people* are playing against other people in the IFL, Buford. Have you somehow forgotten that critical fact?"

"Still."

"Tomorrow, Dia and I are going to get you a free safety who has enough range to sell hot dogs in the stands in between plays. And the other corner, who we'll also be acquiring tomorrow, is truly great and will satisfy your criterion of being someone you know. Our corners have to be beyond elite if we're going to beat . . . if we're going to have a great season."

"I notice you didn't mention the most important member of any squad."

"You'll have the best QB in the league."

"Who's that?"

"Can't say yet."

"And it's definite?"

"Feel better, right?"

"Is it definite?"

"No."

"Then we need a fallback. The guy now is terrible."

"No fallback. I don't fall and the rare times I do it's forward not back."

Cognizant and reluctantly respectful of the power of the jinx, as ample empirical evidence has dictated she must be, Nina very carefully steps out into the dull Paterson air.

59

|||||||||

What the hell is Paterson, New Jersey, anyway? That the Pork are based there is close to happenstance. Their original owner, Mario Bent, a highly respected mobster who was dogged by constant rumors that he had ties to legitimate business, had essentially exhausted what little community goodwill there was for his Edison Emperors. One night, or early morning, under the cloak of darkness (a cloak that was entirely unnecessary as no one really cared), he loaded all Emperor chattel, most of which had already been heavily liened on, into several company trucks whose acquisition involved more broken thumbs than Bent's nearby Littlest League Catchers' Camp and transported everything north into the welcoming arms of the then-mayor of Paterson, who was eager to distract the voting part of his populace from the recently announced, eighty-count indictment named after him.

The move was allowed to stand only under condition that the team name be changed to protect the royal bloodline. And following a rushed sale to a local butcher conglomerate with a thousand bucks to spare, precipitated when someone actually bothered to read the indictment and discovered that Mario Bent was featured almost as prominently as the mayor, the Paterson Pork were born. How the Gills ultimately become involved is when Worthington Gill overreacts to a particularly tasty sausage-and-peppers hero on San Gennaro by buying the conglomerate minimally responsible and, of course, all its holdings.

At first blush an odd choice, Paterson was actually ideally suited to mass gatherings convened to watch humans interact with each other through violence.

Originally conceived (late eighteenth century) as an industrial hub whose manufacturing would be powered by harnessing the energy of the Falls—which intent was actually marvelously realized for a time so that, for instance, silk production eventually reached such a level that the city was nicknamed Silk City—I'll let you deduce how that changed over time.

Fact is, except for the crushing density of American humanity, which only New York City exceeds, what Nina sees when she looks around today from the sidewalk in front of Pork Headquarters on Market Street bears little resemblance to any concept as orderly as a city. Market Street, for example, does constitute a concentration of commercial activity but it is the oddest lawful commerce around. As an initial matter, it is often quite difficult to ascertain exactly what good/service is being offered. Part of this is the complete absence of any nationally recognized commercial entities. This then is exacerbated by those proprietors who do exist evincing an almost palpable desire to sow confusion. So nothing's a grocery store or supermarket, it's a FOOD CENTER. Other signs are either so basic they seem designed to insult or else they just seem to pick a word at random from the dictionary; so you will find two gas stations across the street from each other with one saying only GAS and the other inexplicably CUSTOM. Also there's the almost comic prevalence of proper names in the titles of businesses that don't normally lend themselves to their inclusion, like CARLOTTA'S INSURANCE or NORBERTO CHECK CASHING.

Then there's the nature of those businesses. For one, there's an unhealthy fascination with deflated tires, with seemingly every other storefront just vaguely and unhelpfully identifying the problem as FLAT TIRES. Getting your check cashed is a big deal. Being in the LOTTO to thereby potentially win it is a constant reminder. Also, there are a lot of yards that unmistakably cater to what is quite obviously JUNK.

There's garbage too, goddamn everywhere. Nina has been staring at that same fucking half-faced toy dog with the remote-control noose for what feels like weeks; but an earlier attempt to investigate, then maybe even remedy, revealed the presence of a nebulous substance so vile in its particulars it took all the steam out of any further inquiry.

Still, that was part of the fascination. How is it that the most basic social reassurances that she had taken for granted her entire life, the way one expects say, breathable air, or processes like the collection of one's refuse, had faded out of view in an East Coast American city? The curiosity nagged and nagged at her until she just went up to the highly paid intern who seemed less dim than the rest and gave him an assignment he had no power to decline. What the hell is up with Paterson? That's all the guidance he got.

Highly Paid Intern, whose name never materialized, responded to this assignment as if he were in mortal danger and that was certainly the implication. And one of the many fascinating things he unearthed, in one case literally, was a surprisingly coordinated attempt by the city to *rebrand* itself, as more than one eagerly put it. This culminated in a decision to stage a contest whereby an official slogan for the troubled city would emerge and this slogan would be of such subliminally persuasive force that the troubles would remain but its audience would be powerless to process their import in the face of such rhetorical splendor.

So proposals emerged that veered wildly among the following: the verifiably untrue, the unintentionally insulting/intentionally uninsulting, the so vague that sense fails to be created, the rhyme or alliteration for its own sake, and the technically true but not even conceivably relevant; pretty much such a sea of inappropriateness that the committee was ultimately forced to retreat into the abject defeat of *Welcome to Patterson*—another fiasco for the city, and engineered at such exorbitant cost, after the corruption tax was factored in, that a planned playground had to be quietly canceled. Still, Patersonites weren't even all that upset given what they'd avoided:

Paterson, Come Home Again (if you're from here)
Paterson, Home Is Where the Hard Is
Paterson, Home in on Us
Paterson, The Seat of a New Jersey
Paterson, Take a Seat
Paterson, It Happened
Paterson, What Happened?

Paterson, Where Happenings Happen
Paterson, You Bet
Paterson, Bet on Us
Paterson, Wanna Bet?

(These last three after someone proposed legalizing gambling, under the theory that all the usual attendant ills were already present anyway.)

Paterson, Where the Passaic River Goes to Party
Paterson, A City
Paterson, There, We Said It
Paterson, What You Looking At?
Paterson, Enough Said
Paterson, We're History
Paterson, Rejuvenation Through Resignation
Paterson, O Paterson
Paterson, Who Knew?
Paterson, Who Knows?
Paterson, You Never Know!
Paterson, Son of Pater, Cousin of Progress
Paterson, We Don't Stand Pat
Paterson, Nice and Pat
Paterson, Who Said That?
Paterson, It's Really No One Else's Business
Paterson, Giving You the Business
Paterson, We Mind Your Business
Paterson, No Retreat, or Surrender
Paterson, Never Give Up
Paterson, We Give Up
Paterson, At Least We're Not Camden

Truth is, there was something to that last one. Camden, another city devolving into a state of nature from within one of the richest states (NJ) in the country, was undeniably worse off than even Paterson. There, the citizens have essentially been left to govern themselves after the governor, who himself has a security detail that can play a softball game against itself, showed how much he valued the security of others by basically defunding the police force. He did this while under no illusions what that would mean. Well, it meant what everyone knew it would mean, and when Camden's descent was almost total the governor naturally wanted to make sure he got all the credit. Accordingly, podiums were set up from behind which he would do just that and, more importantly, because you can only truly defenestrate the same city of undesirables once, new targets ripe for the same treatment were searched for.

Paterson looked around then stared at the other two likeliest candidates. Newark was rising (new arena, transportation hub that wasn't going anywhere, decreasing homicides) so even they wouldn't dare. Trenton, the state's capital after all, has all sorts of symbolic value and that tends to complicate things.

That leaves . . . hey! Paterson may be all sorts of dysfunctional but it's also like that guy you know who's constantly inventing ways to be a mess but underneath it all is actually pretty sharp, so the city knows what's likely coming and an exponentially increasing portion of the official-yet-quiet memoranda dug up by the intern reflects this anxiety; and the way Nina read the stack, in chronological order and with the services of an imaginary yet omniscient Tolstoyan narrator, it was like a dramatic tale that somehow grew in import as it gained predictability. Indifference swelling into actionable animosity.

But the intern also thinks he senses something resilient about Paterson that nothing on paper can accurately reflect. He lets this spill during his oral report, under the mistaken belief that Nina somehow values his opinion. Yet while Nina sat stone-faced during the entirety of this report, damn it all if this twerp didn't have a point. There *is* something. It may not be as apparent as the uncollected garbage or the dangling and/or fizzling traffic lights but it still hovers there and can be picked up on even if you're just standing there absently as Nina currently is.

What it is is maybe the memory of relevance. Everywhere you turn you see the residue of what was once productive human activity and, in turn, that creates a feeling that a latent potential is merely resting in expectant anticipation waiting to be activated. This is aided and abetted by what is undeniable natural prominence. Because the Passaic River is a legitimate body of water with all that implies and the portion of it used for the Paterson Falls achieves a pulchritudinous grandeur that is not subject to the whim of opinion or manipulation by the powerful. And this, the thinking goes, will keep Paterson from becoming Camden. All that is true, but still Nina makes a mental note to again remind Dia not to leave headquarters at night without one of the sketchy black-opsy security escorts Nina hired.

58

‖‖‖‖‖‖‖‖

Maybe there's a flip side to everything. One Paterson business that never has a customer shortage is Fernandez Funeral Home. The impeccable house sticks out from its surroundings as if it were the only finished part of a painting. And one of the several weird things FFH does is feature a movie-theater-like marquee that announces the day's *mournful event.* So today is

Jorge de Cervantes (1967–2015)

The person placing the plastic letters on the marquee always does the math to properly anticipate what the day's going to be like, what the tenor will be.

And on the third day he died again.

This is the thought crosses the mind of Nelson de Cervantes at the terribly significant moment he didn't know would be either.

Those three days contained just a slew of odd sights, sounds, even smells. One element not really present for someone ingesting reactions was surprise. On the contrary, there was a sameness to those reactions, with the only varying aspect their levels of intensity.

The news being reacted to was simple, it was only the sense of it that was lacking. A forty-seven-year-old man. He works all the time. When he's one of the people in the room, his intelligence is piercing, man. His heart too. He works all the time not because he's some emotionally stunted fuck only truly comfortable within the confines of a work environment. No, he works all the time because it's the only way up and up is the only direction he'll accept for his family. He's basically a Poindexter but with an edge. In other words, the Coke-bottle glasses and fancy words, but also Colombian so look out. He is all those things.

No. Was. He's gone. None of it is true anymore.

He was standing in an enclosed bus stop. After work, what else? He was standing there and it was that time of day where whatever happens will take hours to implant itself in the world's consciousness. Some garbage was driving a car while high as the clouds. His head in the clouds, the feather canyons and ice cream castles, but his hands and chin on a wheel that suddenly veered right at the exact moment his body weight shifted onto the accelerator, gunning the car forward and into the glass-enclosed bus stop.

The details take time to emerge. There's a prescription for what elevated the driver. See, it's all on the up and up. Someone somewhere got paid. A sunny destination was chosen to talk about dopamine reuptake inhibitors and the like. There, everyone agreed that the best brand for inhibiting said uptake happened to be the very same brand that's on all the pens, pads, and shiny iCcessories flowing freely from their host, who has generously sponsored this conference where no one confers as well as the various *surprising* studies being repeatedly cited to audible respiration.

The result is a spike in prescriptions for the *medicine* and commercials shot in open fields urging consumers to "ask your doctor," who in truth doesn't really need all that much prodding. So the flow grows and regenerates without end as checks that never bounce keep getting cut. The extensive preceding use of the passive voice means no one specific is at fault. Or does it mean everyone is?

What is undeniable is the suddenness of it all. Because, as a great artist once wrote, it's not a small world, it's a sudden one. So those receiving the news get no grace period. They must go from a world where this person was an invaluable contributor, to a world not much different from one where he'd never existed.

So while nothing really eclipsed the initial scream of his mother, a scream whose echoes might never dissipate fully, those days Nelson was subjected to grievous sounds in seemingly all their multiplicity. And *subjected to* doesn't mean he wasn't often the source.

The worst was when the relevant room would quiet. Because he grew to learn what would happen next. Quiet silence conducts thought. And because the room invariably contained numerous people, many extremely familiar faces but also others he had not gazed upon for a long time, that meant a lot of people engaged in thought. And that meant at least one consciousness would descend anew onto the grim realization that Jorge de Cervantes had been killed leaving a wife widowed and two young children fatherless. And this realization, its finality, would somehow attain its initial force and result in another dolorous exclamation that pierced the silence and retained its power to startle.

For example, Jorge's older sister thought how they would wade into Colombian rivers and it would be her responsibility to ensure he didn't attempt nautical tasks beyond whatever his swimming ability was at the time. How he took great delight in torturing out those very limits in her full view. She thought how that very same person grew into extreme spiritual and physical fullness only to now empty entirely and without warning. She screamed.

It was three days of that and Nelson is not the type who's keen on talking things out in these kinds of situations. Problem is decades of pop and pap have conditioned everyone into the unexamined belief that the silent person is stewing and that the resulting stew is harmful. So, many have approached him and, using altered voices, attempted to compel reciprocating speech from him. And he's not a maniac so he answers, but he speaks out of a sense of obligation not out of any real desire to move beyond a superficial level of discourse. This means that someone already under considerable duress is being asked to expend significant psychic energy to make others more comfortable. Because Nelson understands fully that if he doesn't in essence play a role, a thirteen-year-old drawing comfort from the words of others, he will cause others distress and this will in turn, he knows from experience, cause *him* distress in a never-ending recursive loop of dysfunction that accomplishes nothing but precisely what it seeks to avoid.

The emptiness of language. Turns out the only thing that truly helps is the occasional unexpected charge of physical contact. Sometimes inside a hug it never happened. But then the hug ends and it did.

He fantasizes primarily not about it not having happened but rather about somehow being the only one implicated in the suffering. The sheer plenitude of people sharing the pain is not dissipating the pain, it is growing it.

His mother and sister for example. He cannot join them. He feels that otherness now more than ever. He wants it not to have happened to them more than he wants it not to have happened to him. What happens to him stays contained within the shell that is him, he makes sure of it. What happens to others is not only not susceptible to that process, but in a cruel twist is almost no less painful for it. This thus becomes the principal stressor. That there is something vicious and irrevocable that has happened to two other people and the pain that is currently emanating and will continue to emanate from them will so poison the atmosphere that nothing unequivocally beautiful will be able to flower there for the foreseeable future.

And this is true no matter what actions he takes. Regardless of whatever new reality he creates out of his impenetrable will it will still be only his reality and, as such, will aid no one else. Still, Nelson understands his responsibility, which is to not make matters worse by melting down like some little girl.

Man, there's an appeal to that too. Saying to the universe, to existence itself, that there is nothing it can throw at me that will truly end me. Because if before he felt invincible owing to the fact that it seemed nothing truly terrible could ever happen, it's now the opposite realization that makes him so. He's seen the worst, seen that you don't even have to get a goodbye. That a particular past guarantees no particular present or future. That every phone call can carry whatever nihilistic darkness it wants, every elevation of the sun like the parting of curtains to a play written by an unmedicated schizophrenic and the last thing we have is any assurances, because this playwright cares not the slightest fuck for our notions of appropriate storytelling.

So? So he's seen what the world's got. It can't fool him anymore is the thing. Go on fooling everyone else. They're fooled, he sees it on their faces. But he knows more and wonders if that's all it's got. This is the worst thing can happen, he can sense that from the behavior of those around him. And a substantial portion of them lived the majority of their lives in Colombia, where the definition of bad is a lot less restrictive than here. But point is there's freedom in that *worst*. If he's suffered the worst that means he *suffered* it, past tense. It happened so it can no longer threaten to happen and a whole hell of a lot of other things have also lost their power to threaten. We say things like *I would die* or *I would not be able to deal* but then the kind of thing we say that about happens and guess what? We don't really *do* anything in response. We just absorb it in a way that's independent of volition; the way an object will either float or sink in water.

Nelson absorbed it and three days passed and a black suit appeared on his body as if magically and he moved through space, and time elapsed, and soon he was in a well-designed room sitting in a folding chair across from a casket. And all that would have been bearable in its way except that *on the third day he died again* was what he would end up thinking.

The morning had been full of the language of faith even if there was nothing left to believe in. But if someone doesn't think religion consoles then they're not doing it right because that's precisely what it does. People say the things that durability of the soul would inspire and by just assuming the veracity of the major premise in that way they hope to profit from the resulting mood. Secularly, people glance at a refurbished representation of what housed the departed and it somehow works to maintain the illusion of presence.

Nelson learned that this was at least part of what the refurbished body does through involuntary yet minute observation, the default resting state of his mind. See, the room with the body contained the occasional sound of laughter or at least bemusement and of course the point of that is it creates something like solace. The incidence of this was aided by the fact that Jorge de Cervantes had been—by virtue of his sustained intensity, restlessly theorizing mind, endless fostering of baseless quirks designed to maximize the enjoyment of physical life, and a pronounced susceptibility to superstitious-to-the-point-of-mystical thinking among still other elements—a considerably, if unintentionally, comic figure. This allowed for the recollection of considerable comic moments. But that portion of the thing ends at some point and what happens then is everyone heads to the cemetery.

The cemetery is nearby. Fitting, as all of Paterson is like a cemetery now. But the vehicular procession to it is so haphazard and disjointed that Nelson is quickly losing what little faith he had in the competence of Fernandez Funeral Home. And it's that thing where everything looks so ugly, even though you know its appearance is same as it ever was and it never offended you greatly before. Once parked, the cars look like the kind of Matchbox set you might find offered at an octogenarian's garage sale. The walk to the actual plot is like trudging on grass turned rock, so cold is it. The speaker's lips struggle to form sense from within a vast arctic void. The trees may someday fill and cover but today they cower in skeletal impotence. What we call *people* is just the universe's bit parts, here attracting, there repelling. We're all extras. Matter is the star.

Why on the third day Jorge de Cervantes died again is that after everyone who wished to do so had placed a flower on the casket, the damn thing was then actually lowered in their presence. And one might not think there would be any great metaphoric force to this, the parties present had had three days to process what would be an absence in perpetuity, but that would be so wrong. The moment it becomes apparent what's happening (the flowers on top of the casket stir as their platform jerks into a slow descent and the surrounding soil encroaches on the air above it), a severe desolation sets in and the evidence is a multilayered polyvocal wail that seems to gather then reissue the collective pain of that moment.

That enervating sound was when Nelson realized his father had just died for the final time. Seems there had been an imperceptible irreality to all the preceding. Meaning the depth of understanding hadn't really been all that great. First, there were all these details to attend to. Everything had been upended, everything but commerce. The funeral home spoke in hushed tones but the underlying message and push-pull were the same ones we experience every day. Not even criticizing either, because the illusion of necessary decision making is part of what gets you through it. But that moment when the thing goes down punctures all that. There's nothing left to decide, nothing with which to distract. Every last consolation is gone. Drew comfort from the presence of his lifeless body? Too bad, we're going to drop it in a hole and cover it with dirt. The organization of this complex event filled the mind with coveted bland busywork? Well, the sinking of that box into its final hole terminates the need for any further related action.

The greatest power the dead have is their power to multiply apace. It's all a journey to the globe's central cauldron and the gravitational pull from that destination is irresistible in the strictest sense. The visual of a coffin dragging what was a prized receptacle of love down into that journey drives that point home, but in a way that is completely unhealthy. Competent funeral homes, inapplicable here, have largely come to this realization and therefore tend to omit this final step by just having everyone place their flower on the casket then split, with the rest occurring offscreen.

And on the third day he died again.

Afterward, there's little need for orchestrated precision in the exodus. Many cars are simply returning whence they came and the ones that aren't know the way to Nelson's uncle's without need of following anyone.

One of the cars is Larry Brown's Ford Fiesta, whose factory-installed GPS has sent him on a rudderless and dispiriting quest, owing to equal parts user error and the Ford Motor Company's decision not to recognize the continued U.S. sovereignty of Paterson, a decision manifested in the deletion of all relevant satellitic markers from its otherwise *state-of-the-art* system.

The intent had been to be a kind of laconic hero. He'd wanted to tentatively approach the wife, widow he supposes, of Jorge de Cervantes as she sat in the front row of that room with the casket. He would lower his eyes and declare that he was sorry for her loss. Then he would do what he came to do. He would say he was with the New York Fire Department. New York's Bravest. But not a firefighter, no. He's an EMT or emergency medical technician. In New York it's all merged under the FDNY, but that's not really important.

He just wanted to say that he was there at the end. There when it happened. In a *professional* capacity. It would be important to clarify. Emotions would be running high and Larry's identity as part of the blameless, even benevolent, framework must be established as soon as possible if the heroic part of this was going to take shape.

He would say he did everything he could. Some distancing technical jargon might come in useful here. Then the payoff, which how could it fail to console?

As far as plans like this went, it wasn't terrible. Technology had made it possible. The full name of his decedent was easy. Hell, he'd be talking about him the next day at Bellevue for one of them M & Ms. Privacy's no longer a thing so a quick search landed Larry on perhaps the world's only funeral home that is excessively proud of its social media footprint. And they used every bit of that prowess to ejaculate news of the service's when and where.

Armed with that information, the above plan was hatched. Only to result in Larry impotently traversing seemingly every square inch of Paterson before arriving at Fernandez Funeral Home. There he is directed to the nearby cemetery but arrives just as a spasmodic wave of cars is leaving.

He rides among them for a while until he concedes the opportunity is lost. He's already in Paterson. He decides he'll visit Sharon again and immediately starts planning that interaction.

57

||||||||||

Nelson's Uncle Leonides is his mother's brother. Jorge de Cervantes's brother is in Colombia and, along with a great many interested others, unable to navigate the U.S. visa labyrinth in time to attend.

They go to Leo's after the funeral because Leo has the most space. The most space and three daughters and one of those wives, especially prevalent in the Latin American community, who seems almost superhuman in her ability to nurture at the highest level without even slightly diminishing her tensile strength.

Nelson's sitting there but he's not really sure what this is. There's food and conversation and comfortable seating but also more crying and not all that much to say that isn't either wildly inconsequential and banal or else potentially constitutes a charged trigger to metaphysical musings; neither of which elements is exactly welcome at the moment. What is it, then? It emerges over time, not a lot, that what they have there is a loosely choreographed evasion. Nelson senses it almost immediately. No one says it outright but their home is contaminated now. Poisoned by absence. The idea is clearly that the three of them, but especially the widowed Celia, must be kept at all costs from what will now pass for normalcy. If their moments are full of enough noisy distraction, then the enemy, silence (enemy because its temporary form is like an emissary from the vast, eternal, and inexorable Silence we're all trying to ignore), can be kept at bay.

Even the positioning of the people in the room is a statement whose truth value can be determined no different than that of verbal ones. *No somos muchos pero somos machos* is a favorite of his aunt. That one is verifiably false. Not the toughness part. Just that if there's one attribute that collection of people has it's its extraordinary number of active members. This *is* a consolation actually. It does feel at times like there's so much kinetic *living* around that even death might be tamed, but Nelson rightly reasons that this feeling is only temporary.

Nelson has two cousins. Well, he has a lot more than that but the two now most relevant are approaching him in tandem. These two are themselves cousins and are sufficiently older than thirteen-year-old Nelson that they have always inspired in him an awe not greatly distinguishable from fear. It's not just their ages though. There's a hardness there that you don't even have to be Nelson to notice. The whispered stories about them that trail off into generalities only confirming the intuition.

"'Sappening, son?"

"You serious?" Nelson manages.

"What?"

"The hell, man. Some sensitivity, yo."

"It's okay, really. I know there's a limited number of ways to start these conversations," Nelson says.

"Shit, check out Egbert. Besides, man, dude was my uncle and I had mad respect for him. Shit's not gonna stand's what I'm getting at."

"So get at it then already."

"The hell, you got someplace to be?"

Their tone is all conspiratorial and such so Nelson's mentally running through various exit strategies until alighting on just plain old . . .

"You going, little man? We trying to talk to you!"

"Easy, he's a kid."

"Yo, he's fifteen."

"I'm thirteen."

"When I was fifteen, shit."

"Shit."

"What I'm saying is this wasn't some fucking act of God's what I'm saying."

"No."

"Some motherfucker *did* this."

"Okay," Nelson says, not sure where this is going.

"No, there's nothing *okay* about it, it's retribution time."

"Recrimination and shit."

"I got a friend in that precinct. Well, technically he's just a filler in a lot of their lineups, ten bucks a pop."

"Fuck you talking about?"

"Ain't you been listening? I'm talking about revisceration—"

"Pretty sure that's not a word," Nelson objects.

"—of the highest order, yo."

"No, what are you talking about *specifically*? Spell that shit out, man."

"You need me to? What are we, a bunch of fucking Connecticut WASPs here? Sitting around talking about a hot stock? Some fuck drove his fucking car into my uncle!"

"Easy, yo."

"What do you suggest we do? Litigate that shit? Every day above ground for that fuck is an insult to every de Cervantes."

"You right."

"Now, technically, this shit falls on Nelson."

"He's a kid, man. Get a grip."

"That's why I said *technically*, bro. I'm not a savage. I'm talking old school. Old school it would be on him, even if he had to wait to grow up and shit."

"That's some Shaolin shit right there."

"Exactly, schools don't be getting any older than that neither. Point is, the kid's got to direct this shit right here. Even if he can't physically do it himself it's being done in his name and whatnot."

"My name?" Nelson asks.

"Agreed. So what do you say, kid?"

"About what?" asks Nelson.

"About a guy killed your father and now you gotta tell us what to do about it."

"I don't understand," he says.

"It's simple, what do you wish would happen to this guy?"

Now here was an interesting question. So interesting it jolts Nelson into something like a state of supersensitivity. Because one of the few unambiguous and easily classifiable feelings he's been enduring the last three days is seething anger.

Any event can be viewed through varying lenses, and the sudden death of Jorge de Cervantes was no different. So a person could, for example, pull way back and say something like *The universe houses an unending cycle of life into death then rebirth and the unavoidability of that fact transforms it into something almost salutary.* This is the best lens. There's still obsession about things like the moment just before the accident and the strictly enforced, one-way linearity of time. Still feel trapped within a tidal disruption that makes it difficult to anchor everything again (this sensation manifested itself quite literally the day before when Nelson lay on his bed and suddenly his entire room seemed to unmoor from his field of vision and began to violently shake, the hell was that?) but it's still the best lens because its lack of specificity serves to reduce emotion.

Closer in is the tragic death of a father of two well before his time and closer still is the sudden death of *his* father without any kind of preparatory prologue. This lens is far more troubling but nonetheless provides a view people are at least familiar with and somehow feel capable of addressing.

Not so, closer still. At the micro level, there's an extreme focus on the reason for all of the above. At this level, a fixation on an individual person can be excused. Because this didn't randomly happen, a person *did* this. Who is this person? Nelson feels an electric connection to him, whoever he is. All Nelson's understandable theorizing on the cruel nature of time. His silent musings on chance. The nature of absence. All combine and distill into just plain unintellectual anger, and its concentrate lands fully on this contemptible prick.

When Nelson imagines him he always imagines him unrepentant. Unrepentant and callous as a stone. Truth is, Nelson's not all that big on human connection and all that. He has, for example, an extremely high tolerance for solitude and the resulting silence; no, he prefers it. His favorite music and poetry only minimally disturb its atmosphere so as to leave room for him to fill in the rest. When forced by circumstance into a gathering, his strong inclination is to stand apart and observe—a thoroughly enjoyable activity for him that is often prematurely terminated when someone comes up to him with readily apparent pity to ask, *What's wrong?*

Point is, his need to feel like a component of something larger is severely lacking. Wait, it's worse. Whenever Nelson starts to get the inkling he's supposed to function as some kind of minor organ in a larger, more important organism, he kind of starts to panic. And at work here, it seems to him, is a related concept. The idea or realization that someone, anyone from that vast featureless sea of humanity, can suddenly, without his consent, create and enforce a new connection to him and said connection can be as toxic as they wish. This intrusion, that suddenly he's meant to care that a specific stranger exists and draws from the same store of breath that he does, is maybe what's most offensive and, standing alone, is enough to make him want to excise that stranger from existence.

And that's the offer, make no mistake. Would it actually be carried out? Does he truly want it to be? Fuck, man. His father's in a fucking hole, his *father*. Who the fuck is he if he doesn't want to see that remedied? His mother and sister doing that crying that's like hyperventilating. Who is he? His *father*. People get one, that's it. He got the spectral suggestion of one. A tease that ended the wrong way.

And let's be honest here, Nelson spent the majority of that period steeped in resentment at the fact that he was not considered a fully formed human, and Jorge de Cervantes the foremost symbol of that. So? So Nelson's sensation of having been more discovered than created then raised more accurately matches reality now. Does that mean he hasn't received a mortal wound? And if he absorbs it does that make its source any less culpable? So there's the whole question of what should happen to someone like that. Not in any conventional crime and punishment way, talking about on the primal level where actions blindly beget reactions.

Of course, this goes beyond any clinical assessment of what is just. What is being asserted is that he, Nelson, has a newfound responsibility that goes beyond skillful mourning. It's all so base; but baseness doesn't preclude truth. Maybe it does fall on him. But to do what exactly?

A man got high, a man Nelson knows nothing else about. Does he care? It's none of his business who chooses to alter their brain and how. Seems stupid to him, but so what? He's sure he does things that seem stupid to others. Then the man stayed high though. All the way into the driver's seat of a car. And that car all the way into an innocent bystander, which also wouldn't be any of Nelson's business except . . .

Getting high is an intentional act, the rest not. Let the punishment fit the crime is a thing, right? But with so many blameless people being punished, and severely, worrying about proportionality for this guy seems dumb. The worst things imaginable can happen to this guy for no reason at all without violating any natural law. What then is allowable where such ample justification exists? Why then not allow the universe to dispassionately handle this question of justice? That's what it does and it'll do it with or without Nelson's input.

Unless it's not really about justice at all, and it isn't. Everywhere he looks from now on will be life. Forever and again, Life everywhere. The lowliest slug will inch forward to gravely insult all that's inert. Every intake of air or pump of a heart will smugly declare its superiority. The contrast will create a pallor and this pallor wants to lead to victimhood someone who's nobody's victim. Better to be the aggressor. Any argument that he's overblown the injury death carries only militates in favor of sending this guy off to discover for himself rather than letting him continue to share in what the slug enjoys.

This is not one of those things he needs to think and think and think about. Everything's been ruined. Either upended or terminated. That means any course of conduct is acceptable, only feeling matters, not logical thought. Pain abatement, anything that relieves pain is permissible so long as it works. It feels better to act, defy, assert, than it does to deliberate and reason so let's go with those. Someone hits you, you hit back. Anything else is the work of fiction. Only by lashing out can you pierce such a malignant, adhesive stupor.

Then again . . .

"So we're in agreeance? Nelson?"

"He's just a kid, told you, leave him out of it."

"That's his choice, yo. What do you say, kid?"

"Okay," Nelson says.

"Whoa! There it is! Told your ass this guy's not as soft as he looks."

"Wait, what?" Nelson asks.

"So you're gonna handle it?"

"Uh" from Nelson.

"This fucker wasn't even paying attention!"

"Of course I was, I just want to make sure we're on the same page," says Nelson.

"The page we're on is you hitting the guy up since you knew him best."

"Yeah."

"Okay . . . the guy?" wonders Nelson.

"The hell we been talking about?"

"What've we been saying?"

"You gotta hit him up with this news, the rest takes care of itself."

"Who?" Nelson asks.

"The who we been talking about, that's who!"

"Your cousin."

"My cousin?" Nelson asks.

"Nuno."

"Nuno?" Nelson asks.

"Your cousin."

"Nuno?" Nelson asks.

"Your cousin Nuno."

"What about . . . Nuno?" Nelson asks.

"Nuno your cousin."

"Your cousin Nuno."

"Okay, I know who you're talking about. I don't think he was actually my cousin, we just called him that. What about him?" Nelson says.

"Shit, you don't know?"

"Know?" Nelson asks.

"No?"

"No, know what?" Nelson asks.

"He doesn't know."

"No."

"You need to watch the news, yo."

"Yeah, man. Staying informed is like a citizen's obligation."

"You may have noticed I've had stuff going on," Nelson says.

"Good point."

"As we said before—"

"I wasn't paying attention," Nelson admits.

"—Nuno's being held in Rikers."

"The very same Rikers this motherfucker killed your dad's in."

"Why?" Nelson says.

"Who knows, fate I guess."

"No, why's Nuno there?" Nelson asks.

"So you see the beauty of our idea."

"No." Nelson doesn't.

"Beauty."

"I don't," Nelson says.

"You know what that dude's like."

"Shit, the whole world knows now."

"Wouldn't take much."

"For that fucker to represent."

"You were closest to him."

"Don't think I ever said five words to the guy," Nelson says.

"Scary guy."

"Plus you got the most sympathy angle and shit. With him being your dad, I'm saying."

These two don't need much to keep going and that's just what they do, but without Nelson, who is now purposely trying to call up the relevant mental images. The name Nuno was still a magical sound to him but it wouldn't be all that easy to delineate why. The cousin thing was pretty clearly untrue on a strictly factual level. And if he sat down and added the amount of time spent in that nut's presence it might not exceed the hours in a day. But maybe that's not the right way to measure these things. Regardless, it was strange to have this presence suddenly reinserted into his consciousness, even if only in this manner. Something had happened, something bad, and now Nuno was in jail, which is a form of death, and so constitutes more garbage to heap on these garbage days, don't want to learn the specifics from these two, not sure the capacity exists for more harm anyway.

He walks away.

"Told you he's just a kid."

56

||||||||||

Larry Brown is thinking that his funeral home plan failed miserably but this is not a bad audible. The original plan involved him delivering a dying man's particularly significant final words to his widow and children and doing so at the man's funeral no less, which would certainly have lent the utmost cinematic gravity to the whole thing. That failed.

This new plan calls for him to again *run into* Sharon but before she can even begin to misinterpret a stalker vibe, blurt that he is in Paterson for a funeral and remembered she lived in Paterson and also that she knew what had happened and the coincidence of it all so . . . oh God no, he couldn't impose that way, wouldn't dream of it, let me take you out for coffee instead. Dinner? Even better. Oh, here? I guess if you already started, but only if you swear it's not a pain.

Why does he make these weird plans like this all the time, anyway? Well, Larry has become big on trying to preplan his way into satisfying social interactions. This is a practice born of necessity, at least that's the conclusion he comes to following extensive analysis of all the variables.

He'd needed to explain to himself not only the often-enunciated big markers applicable to his life (thirty-nine, lives alone, very few to no close friends) but also why he almost always looked back on those human interpenetrations he did participate in with such dissatisfaction. He wasn't quick enough, he'd decided. In other words, he very often said the perfect thing. Problem is he said it hours later back at his apartment. In addition to those omissions were the times when he actively said the wrong thing, usually because his statement was either too true or else subject to multiple interpretations and the intended favorable one was simultaneously the one least likely to be adopted by an independent auditor.

What about those people who always say the right thing as a reflex? Even though, truth be told, they don't seem to be saying anything of great substance. Or, worse, those who say really apparently funny things, the kind of stuff Larry's not even capable of coming up with hours later, and do it on the spot. The room fills with laughter and he forces a smile, not sure if his inability to sense the humor means he is its butt.

Work is different. For one thing there are clearly defined roles that stem from well-established labels. These labels do a lot of the work that would otherwise have to emerge organically from social alchemy and people like Larry are extremely grateful for this.

For example, there's no denying that Larry is very good at his job. Not surprisingly, the place where this fact acquires the most prominence is work. So there he has a certain status that he can replicate nowhere else in his life. This status in turn breeds an ease to his interactions that frustratingly seems to disappear whenever the EMT uniform comes off. At a scene or in an ambulance or an ER he has what is prized, skill and knowledge. Elsewhere, he's not even sure what it is that's prized, he just knows he doesn't have it. This realization often results in him trying to create a loose bridge between the two worlds by either injecting medical parlance and procedure where they distinctly don't belong or by treating the nonmedical sphere as if it were nothing more than a giant press conference convened to discuss recent EMT-flavored events. Both tacks just make things worse.

Also interesting is why he's such a good EMT. It's not out of an excess of intellect, something like the opposite. Fact is that being as good an EMT as he is, and a viable argument could be made that he is among the very best, is *just* beyond Larry Brown's native intellectual weaponry, and this turns out to be a positive. There is no condescension whatsoever in his approach to the job. He still, seventeen years later, finds it astounding that he is who you call when someone is dying. One way of looking at it is that the job still generates a healthy but manageable amount of fear in him.

It's a job with true stakes, and from what he sees when he looks around, that seems rare. That also means you can mess up though. No question you can mess up, man. He's seen it, he's *done* it, though thank God not for a long time. When it happens it's not like a downpour of negativity lands on the responsible individual, it all tends to dissipate too fast for that. In that sense, the job almost proceeds from the notion that the main thing humans are meant to do is die, and all available evidence speaks in favor of that premise. But while particularized harm may not come to the offender, it seems something like the universe is still offended by these errors and the result is a kind of generalized malaise. And people tended to respond to this malaise by silently judging harshly the party responsible. So even though the opposite is also true—those who consistently avoid errors breed palpable goodwill—the end result is that this arena of human activity creates significant pressures beyond those inherent in keeping fellow human beings alive while battling everyone's greatest nemesis, Time. Meaning that in addition to the pressure to be good at keeping others alive comes the pressure to identify those who are so skilled and the concomitant pressure to be thought of as one of the skilled, which is of course distinguishable, though not mutually exclusive, from actually being one of the skilled.

To this reality there are only two reactions worthy of respect. The far more common one is plain abdication. There's no better way to term it. A good number of those who thought they wanted to be the person you call when someone's body seriously betrays them and threatens to assault them all the way to even death, flame out in a hurry and quickly undecide they want to be that person.

Why this is worthy of respect is that some admissions so serve the greater good that they acquire the characteristics of a solemn responsibility. If anyone doubts this, let them imagine someone calling 911 because their infant daughter is turning blue or the left side of their mother's face is drooping and she's not making sense. What kind of person does the caller want showing up to likely not move fast enough for anyone's taste? Thought so. Hence the respect due someone who realizes they're not that type of person and does the only honorable thing, without regard to relative bullshit like job security or benefits.

Then there are the Larry Browns of that world, who sense the pressure as much as anyone yet react not with avoidance but with immersion. Seventeen years of honing that peculiar mix of mastery of a body of knowledge that seems to evolve daily and the perfecting of techniques designed to optimize crucial physical tasks. For example, he is definitely who should show up for the blue infant. All EMTs technically *know* what's supposed to be done. Difference is (a) they don't know it as well as he does; haven't investigated the underlying biology at all, let alone to the extent he has, and (b) they haven't worked on the applicable physical techniques the way a pro golfer works on his swing until it can accurately be said that he is an expert in the tactile identification of the relevant nuances of a particular infant's breastbone so that his infant CPR is just plain more effective. None of which guarantees anything really, but still.

Yet this is the same person who has taken to preplanning his social interactions. Why is Sharon his current focus? See, another good thing about the job is this whole concept of partners. More than anything, a partner is a ready-made friend. So chance may throw you together initially but then you ride the same ambulance, see and hear the same things, have your personal system of rewards and demerits inextricably linked with this person. Predictably, what happens then is that the usual system by which friendship is established, the great many little variables that can go either way, is accelerated if not altogether bypassed.

For a big part of his seventeen years, Larry's partner was Hugh Seaborg. This meant that, because of the above, he was present at Hugh's wedding to Sharon. In fact, pretty much any milestone event that ensued in the life of Sharon and Hugh Seaborg, like the birth of Donald Seaborg III or the purchase of their first home, bore at least a slight Larry Brown imprint—usually in the form of an overly generous gift, which he would try to explain away by referring to the fact that without a family of his own to support he had an excess of disposable income and it pleased him to spend some of it this way, so it's not a big deal, trust him.

There were casual get-togethers too. These were best because their underlying motivation couldn't fail to be the desire of the guests' company and because he was one of the invited guests that meant his company. At these, Sharon would often seek him out, at least it felt that way to him. They'd had real conversations, lots more than once. It sure seemed there was more to it than just *This is my husband's partner, I should make an effort to bond.* Not what you're thinking either, just the genuine affection of friendship.

But one weird day, Hugh just kind of perfunctorily announced he was leaving. A corrections officer at Rikers? Where did that come from?

In retrospect, maybe a distance had formed. One-word responses had replaced Hugh's mini-essays on the various aspects of life. References to Sharon, even Donnie, had grown muted then ceased altogether. Still, a little warning would've maybe been appropriate.

Since then, contact never even rose to the level of sporadic until Larry heard thirdhand that there was no more Hugh and Sharon or Sharon and Hugh, just each now alone. By then it was like hearing it about characters on a television show you'd stopped watching.

That likely would have been the end of it except Larry incredibly heard Sharon's voice again on that 911 call for Jorge de Cervantes and the brutality at that bus stop. Heard her voice and it was as if a hole he didn't even know was forming started to fill. Maybe it was just the lacerating setting. Whatever the explanation, when Sharon comes out to retrieve her mail, Larry walks slowly to her. He is whisper-rehearsing his opening line.

Before he can reach her there's a thrilling millisecond when Sharon looks up at him and does this thing with her face expressing that she'd been meaning to talk to him, which expression doesn't make the greatest sense until Larry realizes she's not looking at him at all, more like *through* him. Through him to the man obliviously hobbling towards her from behind him. Larry has stupidly worn a hat, the most effective means of subtle disguise, but in this case it is unintentional subterfuge. Realizing his mistake, he'd done that thing where you begin to interact then try to play it off in horror, he is nearly jogging away now;

that quickly having moved from near elation to potential mortification should she now recognize him.

She does not. He is going to circle around, go home, try to forget this day. Bellevue tomorrow morning, need to rest. Tonight maybe pizza, maybe Chinese. He'd heard only the beginning of their conversation but that was enough, so effortless:

"Hi."

This is for the guy in front of him, right? thinks Feniz. Almost certainly. But what if it isn't? Isn't he then being impossibly rude?

"Hi?" Feniz asks cautiously.

"I was thinking of you," Sharon says.

What?

"I saw the ambulance the other day, everything okay?" she continues.

This isn't normally Sharon either. She's not the biggest talker, Hugh used to fill that role mostly. And when you're talking about strangers, well, usually pretty tight-lipped. But weird thing about being that way is that every once in a while you can get this sudden urge to blab. Stranger still is that this urge cannot really be satisfied by talking to someone you're already tight with. What you need to do then is be one of those people who's always ready to make with a quick word to a stranger, in what amounts to little more than an invitation to a rote exchange. The recipient then decides what happens next and this loss of control may explain why Sharon so rarely sends up these kinds of conversational flares for the unknown general public.

But also, was he really a stranger, this recipient? Certainly she's seen him a lot in her brief time in that area. Working nights as she did was a bit like being a neighborhood spy and this was true no matter your level of disinterest. You saw the same things at the same time in the same way, the only thing that changed was you. That mailman, this school bus, that delivery. Feniz's labored afternoon walk to the corner store was like that. Still, she was sure she'd never directly addressed him or vice versa. So what does that make him, *stranger*?

"Oh . . . the ambulance," said the stranger.

"You look fine, you all right?"

"No, it wasn't for me," says Feniz.

"The green house is yours, no?"

"Oh, yeah . . . that's me . . . but . . . for my mother."

"Oh, I didn't know anyone else lived there. She okay?"

"She passed."

"Oh no, I'm sorry."

"It's okay."

"I never saw her, I don't think."

"She didn't really leave the house anymore."

"Sorry for your loss. What was it? I mean . . . she must have been very . . . was she . . . was it sudden?"

"I don't think it was sudden."

"Oh."

"But it felt sudden, so maybe."

"Glad I have you here too. I been meaning to go around to all the local houses, do you get your mail?"

"I think so, did you send me something?"

"No, I mean in general. Do you get your mail every day?"

"Every day?"

"See? I knew it, we have the worst mailman alive."

"Tom?"

"It's as if he delivers only when he feels like it."

"Yeah, Tom."

"It's not right. How long you think something like that would fly in some rich town like Alpine? Hm-hmm. It's always screw the bitch-ass poor. They probably won't even notice and if they do, who cares? What are they going to do about it, right?"

"I know what you mean. I feel like, with my mother, I called for help and it was like they didn't care. They came to pick her up, it was like they were picking up a fridgerator I didn't need anymore. I feel like a lot more could have been did, you know?"

"That's terrible."

"I hear they can tell from your caller identification ID when you call Emergency, what insurance you're having, if you have insurance. Probably they hook it up through the phone company, they're all together."

"See what I mean? The only thing the broke have going for them is there's so many of us. It's like with this mail thing, the only way we're going to be heard is if we speak with one voice."

"I'm not gonna lie, I don't get a lot of mail. Nobody really writes me letters."

"Don't worry, ain't nobody writing anybody letters anymore. Shit, that's what e-mail's for."

"Oh yeah, I'm meaning to get that, is it expensive?"

"I'll let you know when we're ready to complain so you can be part of it."

"I don't know, what if he got in trouble from us complaining on him?"

"That's the idea."

"Oh."

"That and getting our mail in a timely fashion."

"I see, but what if he has a good reason and, you know, I just feel like we can never really know his reasons. If he has any, you know? And then complaining when I don't even really get a lot of mail even. I feel like if Tom could get all the mail done every day he would, know what I mean? I don't even know why I feel that really, it's not like I know him all that much, other than to say hi once in a while. It's more like I feel that it's better to feel that way."

"Um."

"And I just don't get many mails, *much mail* I mean. You get a lot?"

"Too much. Come to think of it, the hell am I complaining about? It's all bills I can barely pay anyway. It was more the principle of the thing, you know?"

"Yeah, we deserve our mail."

"Exactly, *deserve.* That's the perfect word for it."

"We deserve it, it's deserved."

"Take care. Oh, I'm Sharon by the way, weird to only introduce myself now."

"Feniz."

"How do you say that?"

"*Feniz.*"

"Feniz?"

"No, *Feniz.*"

"That's what I said, *Feniz*."

"*Feniz*, right."

"Okay, Feniz, see you around. I lost my mother recently too, so . . ."

She didn't really say anything more about it than that, so how was it that this final utterance was so helpful?

Feniz went up his crumbling stairs then, after struggling with a front door key that was becoming problematic, entered his empty house without a sense of desolation washing over him and it was the first time for that in a while. The interaction had helped him, there was no denying it. For days he'd felt hollowed out but now there was less of that. He didn't pick up the phone so a radio station could put him on hold then let him explain a conspiracy only he was fully aware of. He didn't seek out his book on forms of suicide; actually, the sight of it kind of offended him a bit. He just sat there. After a while he realized he was smiling. He put on the radio but this time music.

It had helped. All of it but especially the last thing she said. She'd lost her mother too. Recently. So silly that something like that should help. After all, he knows full well, on an intellectual level, that mothers plural, *very plural*, die all the time. What's more, a clear majority of those deaths would appear more objectively tragic than the death of his mother—a very old woman reduced to increasingly creative displays of meanness. Still, there's something about a tangible fellow human looking you directly in the eyes to say they've experienced the same harm as you that no amount of impersonal data can replicate. But it's fundamentally silly.

Only problem with the interaction is that time starts to pass again. Not referring to just the fact that the beneficial effects of the inter-action fade as time elapses the way every such thing fades, with us furiously grasping for a stronghold as it all just evanesces through the between of our fingers. No, something worse.

Further he gets from the conversation the more a suspicion begins to form until it solidifies into near certainty. The doubt that creeps in is that the thing ever even happened at all if that makes any sense. Looking back, it had been an odd interaction, not least of all in how abruptly it began and ended. With distance, the whole thing takes on a hallucinatory quality. He literally feels he could have imagined the entire thing.

He daydreams a lot. Nightdreams too. Thing that's occurred to him about dreams is that the dreamer supplies all the dialogue. Might seem obvious, but even so this has all sorts of odd implications. For example, ever laugh at something someone else says in a dream? Given the role the element of surprise plays in most comedy, doesn't seem possible does it?

In fact, why any surprise at *anything* anyone says to you in a dream? It's not just that everyone's there for your benefit, they are literally only given the power of speech through you. And, more than that, this power extends only over content that you alone generate and determine. If it's all just coming from you anyway, what the hell is it? More importantly, had Sharon said anything that couldn't have come from him? If so, that would nicely terminate the debate in favor of the concrete and away from the mysterious.

Though probably no great mystery to what a dream is either. Safe bet that like everything else the explanation will end up disappointing. So it won't be anything like a provisional gateway to an alternate reality or a manifestation of unrealized possibilia. Instead it'll just end up being a purely physical process and this area of the brain and these cells or neurotransmitters and all that exists is what you can see and touch and smell and it's all just billiard balls of matter bouncing off each other in a way that creates confusion as to its true nature and nothing to see here basically.

Of course none of that will adequately explain the sensation of being inside an aggressively vivid dream. And isn't that always the problem with these kinds of explanations? That they only acquire logical force retrospectively or from a distance? So, for example, we cling to the purported qualitative differences between dream and reality and ignore how difficult it can be to separate the two when they adopt or blend each other's characteristics.

Feniz has no such difficulty. He knows intimately how porous is the partition between mundanity, dream, imagination, and everything else that comes our way. Point is he knows from dreams, and what happened there with Sharon (if that's even her actual name) had to be dream or imagination, anything but true real. How else could you explain its ease? Who was that idealized version of him constantly and confidently volleying back effective answers? Forget that, what about the very existence of the interaction? How was it possible? Naturally, he'd seen her before. For what seemed like forever but was actually just months he'd see her almost daily. She must work nights, because that's the way to the bus stop, and at the same time every day. But while he'd seen her often they'd never exchanged so much as a syllable. What little eye contact there'd been had possessed a distinct accidental quality to it; and though he more than once began to open his mouth on those occasions, in what is universally interpreted as compulsion to maintain the contact so that communication can occur, she'd always rejected this with extreme prejudice. Yet there was this same woman now talking to him as a friend. Either that had to be fiction or else everything that surrounded it, the large impersonal infrastructure whereby they and pretty much everyone around them share mainly estrangement, was fictitious. A vivid imagining he decides and somehow this is consoling.

He is inside now and executing an innocent-seeming series of physical maneuvers. The maneuvers have undergone two main lines of development. One is the solidification from contingency to necessity. So he's always taken the garbage out, boiled water for tea, swept and mopped the kitchen floor. But now it's every day, then every day at the same time, then every time in the *exact* same way.

That exactitude is the other line of development. What were once general tasks susceptible to vague denotations like *making tea* have grown and grown in specificity until their component actions now seem only tangentially related to the purported activity. So the flame must emerge from always the left burner to contact the teakettle at the precise location where its faded burn mark terminates. Then the instant that plaintive whistle begins to form the kettle must be violently removed from atop the source. Those are just the preliminaries too. The rate of fill over the tea bag is a precise constant as is the subsequent amount of honey (0.60 tsp.) and the spoon used to stir it.

There's much much more, and a similar level of detail attaches to the cleaning of the floor and expulsion of the garbage.

At least with the tea a tangible, unrelated-to-a-psyche *need* is being met. If someone wants tea to end up in their stomach, some variation of this highly choreographed performance is going to have to occur. But the thing about the floor and the garbage is that very often there simply is no *need* to address. The floor for example is almost always clean enough, sometimes spotless. Yet he cleans it.

Of course with a concept like *clean* you can always get cleaner if you're insane enough. But what do we say about an undeniably empty garbage can? Feniz generates very little garbage and even a twenty-four-hour period bereft of any is not uncommon. Yet, his response to this emptiness is almost painful. He still uses the same foot and pedal pressure multiple unjustified times a day to activate the raising of the kitchen garbage can lid and form a yawning gap. Still doesn't trust his eyes when he sees nothing therein. Still uses both hands to remove the liner receptacle. Then out the side door to invert and *empty* it into the larger aluminum can that goes to the curb once a week so a robotic man in crossing-guard colors can make it vomit into a sanitation truck. It's all empty reflex but just how much of a charade it is is best evident when no actual garbage is involved.

What's going on here? How did it come to this? It all started with a kind of increase in his freedom. Knowing he wasn't being observed allowed him to give in more and more to only the precise details that pleased him while engaging in some of his preestablished activities. It then pretty quickly became about chasing more of that pleasure by repeatedly honing and perfecting the particulars. And the increase in newly requisite particulars was itself a form of pleasure so that the whole thing grew in complexity until it all became so demanding. Which probably marked the turning point where suddenly even just the threatened absence of something that had formerly only provided pleasure would result in genuine anxiety. So now it was relief more than anything when, at precisely 5:55, after whatever dinner he'd prepared and eaten, he could start the tea water and begin his highly specific work on the floor. Relief because he'd spent the preceding minutes inventing scenarios whereby he would be prevented from turning that knob, manipulating his broom, emptying the garbage.

But while relief is a positive emotion it is only the dominant emotion at the outset. Almost immediately, every time, the relief gave way to a form of joylessness. A joylessness that grew successively more pronounced each time he engaged in these activities, which had like lightning gone from desirable to painfully necessary. It started to feel as if the activities were performing *him* is what's being asserted.

The other strange thing is the effect that breaking an activity down into highly specific component parts has on one's experience and interpretation of that activity. You might think it would make the activity seem senseless, as if the truth were being cast into relief. Actually, the opposite. Whatever its true significance, the attachment of highly predictable ritual seemed to generate a genuine, if slight, transcendence to the event. Suddenly he wasn't just making tea, it was more like he was honoring those ancestors of ours who first harnessed the power of fire as well as those who first cured tea leaves to pour boiling water over the result. Cleaning the floor becomes tending to the earth and the removal of garbage a form of expunging the pain of the past that one might be liberated in the present.

What is this like? There's an analogue but it's evading him at the moment.

He used to go to church and it's like that. More than that, it was probably the very reason he stopped going. The repetition of the same phrases, kneelings, and gestures at the same times started to feel like an empty exercise. To say nothing of the central event. Consume a tasteless wafer and God enters you?

Now he fears he may have been wrong. Ritual and symbolism may create, true, but they may also indirectly point. The repetitive specifics may serve truth and it may be that potent entity that once powered and now continues to power them into prominence. In that scenario, the transcendence is already there and the communal actions just a nod. But, of course, the two situations are indistinguishable, at least in the present. Even that is assuming you ever felt the transcendence in the first place. Ever overcame the illogic of a tripartite yet singular entity, ever experienced forgiveness via conduit, or ever gave in to the notion of ingesting something like pure love. Feniz once had, but he'd been a small child then, and later all mysticism stopped attaching to the actions until he just quit going to the place where those things were done. Just saying that his ministrations with the tea and the floor et cetera reminded him of those times.

He does it all like a metronome is the point and this night is no different; except tonight it was as if he was also simultaneously observing himself do it and that was disconcerting. To be more outside seeing than inside doing. Afterward, the anxiety is gone and he can retreat into the purely mental.

Soon we lose the light, he thinks. It'll get so dark too. Everything will worsen. He sits to read but finds he can't. Music he can listen to. Majestic. Three hundred years old and look where it finds itself. Not some Viennese castle, here. The same twelve notes everyone uses but what an ever-expanding universe it is. Doesn't seem sensical really (is that a word even? he thinks) if you step back. Key is to never step back.

He looks up. The ceiling. From flat on his bed. Its constant struggle with gravity and the stalactitic plaster evidence of this struggle. A kind of testimony against his failed stewardship. His reaction to his current state is what most interests him now and what most interests him about it is how alien it feels. A realization is taking hold and it is prospectively charging everything that surrounds him. It's not so much the novelty of his state either, just that he doesn't think he's ever done the work of identifying and descriptively naming it. What makes him think he can do so now? What kind of talent would that even be? We misuse *can* and *can't* in these areas. Of course he *can* do it; it would just then become a question of whether or not he did so well.

So, finally, this is what he comes up with: he is in a state that can best be described as the perfect absence of physical need.

55

|||||||||

That's the sun going down now but not the way most think. What's happening is more like what physicists call *spooky action at a distance*, in the sense that the sun never appeared in Paterson that day that it might later disappear. That day's light had seemed to have no source. The sky a perfect gray as if that's what our primary star emits. So, sure, the sun had made things visible but only in a manner that made it seem as if the slight illumination were coming from within the objects and not anything external.

Now we have that phenomenon where you can best detect something, maybe only retroactively, by the effects of its absence. For example, it turns out there'd been some warmth, only no one knew why. It was the sun, stupid. Just because it wasn't visible?

And as it leaves, all beneath it desaturates into indefinition. Everything chills too, until what emanates from objects pierces human shells to frigidly annex what's inside. Incrementally, like a spill. A premonitory silence emerges. Then the rebirth of sound but this time the sounds of attrition.

Because Paterson without photonic surveillance is a scary entity. The buildings and homes shut in on themselves in what feels like willful avoidance. The dark is blacker than elsewhere. Any natural sounds extant now dissipate instantly, leaving only the artifice of man and its primary suggestion of violence. Police cars patrol but only in the loosest sense of the word and those being patrolled know the cars will never release emissaries, so lost is the cause. The predominant feeling is of a threat.

Something vital about the universal is being portrayed, no, *enacted,* on those fractured slabs of Paterson concrete. After all, at the universe's extremely macro level there is a complete absence of volition. Unthinking galaxies repel and attract each other. Stellar fuels ignite and extinguish. Orbits fulfilled with the consistency of an atomic clock. But none of it *means* anything. The only things being expressed are the ineluctable qualities of inanimate matter and how that matter necessarily interacts with itself.

Closer in, we at least begin to perceive processes that foment life. Still, no truer judgment can properly attach to these events. They differ in kind from the collision of cosmic material primarily in the proximity of their result not the nature of their cause. The particular hothouse this ozonosphere creates may indirectly result in the infinitely variegated complexity that is humanity but stripped to its essence there's still no sentience there.

Contrariwise, street-level Paterson is all sentience. At this level, objects are animate and less the captives of unsympathetic physical laws. This proves fertile ground for the growth of charming elements like resentment, avarice, callousness, enmity, and intolerance. Which, in turn, create highly directed physical acts that seek malevolent results. It is here that we can for the first time meaningfully say of something—an action, a collection of movements—that it is good/bad, right/wrong, moral/im- or a-moral; though generally that kind of utterance has come to be avoided. Yet that's what gives sense to statements like our assertion that a Paterson night like this one is mainly shot through with human malice.

Precisely the kind of statement that will again lose all sense as we continue our trajectory from the colossally macro to the miniscular micro. Go far enough out and we lose the ability to explain exhaustively, but the under-understood truth is that the same applies in the opposite direction, and not just at the quantum level either. Because even at the relatively gargantuan size of the cellular level you'll find no volition.

So there is no satisfying explanation for the earlier instance where that human cell escaped senescence. Cells just do that and there's no more use looking for a deeper explanation than there is asking *why* light travels at the speed it constantly does. Thing is, what started as one rogue cell has, through that cell's manic recruitment, bulged into a teeming army of cellular soldiers. And the way ancient armies were aided by the flow of natural water, this one grows apace on the strength of the swollen profluence of nearby blood flow. In that way is a process that is life-generative to its core, circulation, co-opted and used to spread maleficent decay.

Also, the fact that we are talking about an enclosed space—glioblastomas don't really look to venture outside their brain—means the warfare takes on a guerrilla quality. So where usually cancerous cells will, through exponential growth, crowd out their healthy counterparts, these cells take a more actively devious approach on the issue. With space at such a premium, two tacks emerge. One is just open assault on the healthy because maybe envy but also just to make room that death may properly thrive. The other is a form of camouflage where the sick seamlessly hide, through integration, within the healthy; making it impossible, for example, to resect them without the collateral destruction of wildly valuable cerebral real estate.

Whatever the methodology, it is a war without true suspense. Sickness will overrun health. Vital processes will be disrupted. Functions marred then forever lost. Gathered under the large umbrella of death everything will cohere enough to turn a complex something into that final nothing that resists all distinction.

But not yet. At the moment what is happening is primarily invisible, just know it is happening. The extent of current evidence is a maybe greater incidence of headaches like the one he's feeling now.

And now Paterson is completely dark.

54

||||||||||

The next morning is just as dark, so early did everyone have to rise. Travis Mena, MD, and EMT Larry Brown have a first-thing-in-the-morning M & M to attend while Dia Nouveau's predicament is more directly attributable to individual and personal caprice (not hers).

The way they dealt with the temporal injury differed as well. Larry Brown dealt with it prospectively by getting in bed earlier than usual the night before. He'd wanted to be freshly alert for the opportunity to do something he enjoyed and do it well. And it worked, with him rising the picture of alacrity before the alarm had even had the chance to declare. Travis woke into alertness faster than anyone around out of the environmental conditioning being a young doctor entailed. Dia, by contrast, had to be truly alarmed out of sleep and usually her day's first hour or so was spent lamenting the emotional separation from her bed.

Why Dia had to wake so early was strict Nina instructions to pick her up for an undisclosed road trip. And remember the pig has passed so this picking up was to be done using Nina's personal car. This had started okay, with Nina exiting her car at the front door of her building while Dia moved into the driver's seat as increasingly complex instructions for the following morning were being delivered into her ear by its owner, who also handed her a fifty with instructions to park it safely overnight near her (Dia) and be back at such and such time, which couldn't possibly be right so she said:

"So . . . a.m.?"

"Yeah *a*. What other *m* could it be? Long drive, you know. See you then."

Which led to more questions that were ignored not so much out of active rudeness as out of absence since Nina had already entered her building after slipping the doorman a twenty and thumb-gesturing at flummoxed Dia parked in front.

"I don't know, there's *p* for example."

The drive home was fun, no question. It was at least suggestive of power, to have something so audibly strong respond so solicitously to the slightest movement of her feet and hands. The fifty she thought a lot about, aided by the leisure of abysmal traffic. On the surface it wouldn't seem susceptible to much critical thought. Nina had handed her a fifty and, contemporaneous with that handing, told her to make sure the car was parked safely overnight. Someone not under severe economic pressure would easily spot the connection between the two events: the fifty is meant to be used to procure the insulated parking spot in a city that doesn't feature almost any free ones.

But Dia is the polar opposite of someone not under severe economic pressure; precisely this kind of pressure is what powers the pump of her lungs. To someone like that, the two events can grow to seem distinct. After all, no explicit connection between the two had been made, right? Someone gave Dia money, always fun, then asked her to execute a task. *Must* the money be used to execute the task? What if, instead, the money were the compensation *for* executing the task? Isn't that the usual run of things anyway? Someone pays you to do something and you do it all quid-pro-quo-like? Clearly the definition of *safely parked* was being left to her discretion. She could exercise that discretion, at which point the fifty would transform into payment properly earned for that exercise.

Several purely mental objections emerged at this point, damn traffic. She is employed by the person who gave her the fifty. Further, her brief employment history under this person would seem to indicate that almost any action Dia undertakes while sharing the globe with her employer, Nina, even those that consist of little more than mere existence, falls under the rubric of said employment. Consequently, a convincing argument could be made, though she is not now making it, that the recompense for actions like safely parking the wildly lavish car of her employer is that portion of her salary that attaches to the action's space-time. That would slide the fifty pretty effortlessly into the area of Expense, where you're expected to keep receipts and the rest.

Why was all this so critical anyway? Put simply, Dia was destitute. She was employed, true, full-time and everything. Man, more than that. What comes after full-time the way full comes after part? All-time employment? Either way, what was missing was the gainfully part. It wasn't truly missing the way it was for most of her peers, hypereducated impotents reduced to defiantly unpaid internships that shamefully dangle experience and the hint of future salaried employment.

That wasn't the issue. Dia knew she had a salary, she just didn't know what it was exactly. Her ascension, at least in terms of titles, had certainly been spectacular. It's just that at every ascension of a step she had failed to raise this rather critical issue. She certainly couldn't raise it at this late a stage while still preserving the illusion rich people demand that money (well, only yours) is meaningless. She'd decided to just wait until she got paid initially but even that had grown complicated. Something about payroll and a computer and a bug and was it okay that this first paycheck would be a little delayed? This is what's meant by the illusion. Dia had wanted to scream with the entirety of her soul that she needed money the way a fish needs water, only worse because if denied water the only thing that happens to the fish is he or she dies.

But she didn't. It was embarrassing. She owed Brown University the equivalent of a front-page bank heist. Her degree was in mental masturbation and that was surprisingly not in demand. The deli she'd worked at paid wages that would've insulted a chain gang and each paycheck (there was nothing so formal as an actual check involved) was immediately swallowed whole into her maw of debt. That was her position when she commenced her stint at Nina Gill Enterprises and the empty weeks that followed were only the latest jag poking at her financial wounds.

So imagine what that fifty looked like to her. It looked like ten dinners is what it looked like. A fiver was the rock bottom she'd been able to negotiate herself down to when budgeting what she could spend each night dining. The challenges of that—dispiriting repetition in an area where human obsession has resulted in what seems like an hourly increase in compelling variety, and this exacerbated by having to constantly repeat from within the very apex of this activity—spread beyond her eating life to at least somewhat deaden all her existence.

Still, it's the rare problem with such an unambiguous solution and in her hand is like a lowly representative of that grand solution, sent to mollify and placate her that the unnatural order may remain undisturbed. Fine, there's right and wrong, but there are also exigencies. Her cell phone service is going to be cut, how's that for exigent? The plus side is her many creditors would have no way of contacting her.

So she parked the car on the street and pocketed the fifty and it resulted in a fitful night of what can only generously be called sleep. At first there was generalized anxiety about having parked the car on the street. That ceased but not because it disappeared; instead it just morphed into anxiety about the clock's relentless ticks in consumption of what was already a severely truncated time period and what if as a result she failed to react appropriately to her alarm and so Nina would be just standing there waiting fruitlessly and when she went to call sleeping Dia to yell at her just then Heartless & Wireless Phone Conglomerate would have picked that precise second to suspend all telecommunicative privileges for lack of payment so Dia's slumber would continue and when she finally awoke into terror she'd rush out to see the car she'd been entrusted with and whose worth is of the type generally associated with real property and find it in a debased-by-criminality state and have to drive it in that condition into the eye of what would have to be an epic Nina storm.

This anxiety eventually faded as well.

But not entirely.

And this residual anxiety was enough to keep her still and still awake.

Also enough to generate its own ancillary anxiety about the presence of the underlying anxiety and the fact that both were keeping her awake at a time when falling asleep was critical and became more critical with each tick of what had to be the loudest clock in existence, which loudness made no sense because it wasn't that kind of clock it was a goddamn digital and she thinks the ticks are meant to be like fucking hipster ironic and that easily she was again caught in one of these evil loops where the anxiety has to decrease to fall asleep but the failure to be asleep creates anxiety so it's not going to happen unless Dia can get out of her head for at least a second and then . . .

Point is, Dia is nearly vegetative as she walks towards Nina's recklessly imperiled car that dark morning where the soothing relief of averted disaster washes over her in a way that almost electrifies her into wakefulness. But only *almost* because truth is Dia's drive to Nina's had definite dreamlike qualities, all of which were only accentuated when an impossibly not-fresh-but-prime-seeming Nina dropped into the passenger seat without salutary preamble and growled, "Ossining or bust."

The effect of this declaration was no effect because, to Dia, it didn't even seem like human speech.

"Gas is the one on the right. What's the delay, weirdo?"

"Just that . . . where to?"

"To the Ossining in *Ossining or bust*, you got a better destination?"

"I don't know what that means."

"Sing Sing then, does that help?"

"The jail?"

"No, the prison."

"We're going to Sing Sing?"

"As I made clear to you last night, Dia."

"You most certainly did not."

"What a memory."

"I don't want to go to jail."

"Said everyone who's ever gone."

"So why are we going?"

"To pick up a cornerback, can we move?"

"Touchy."

"Sorry, past my bedtime."

"You're really going to recline like that, is that even safe?"

"Guess that depends on you."

"What time did you get to bed?"

"You're looking at it."

"You went straight through? Why?"

"Good night, Dia, morning."

"Wait a minute, starting to think you had me come this early so you could seamlessly . . . and this car is like your bed . . . that way you could avoid the unpleasantness of . . . says here Sing Sing's not all that far away either . . . Nina? Care to defend yourself? Nina?"

Dia had hoped to talk on the ride. She would talk and in a way that would compel Nina to talk and they would build on that until some hard-won-but-kind-of-cute insights would emerge to draw them closer in a way that would signal the onset of a new phase of their relationship and at the end Nina might even make a declaration that starts with something like the clause *If I had a daughter.*

But none of that happened because Nina, asleep in a manner highly suggestive of death, wouldn't be saying much of anything coherent let alone anything epiphanic. Which left Dia to defeatedly insert *Ladies of the Canyon* and just mentally talk to herself. Or maybe it was a form of conversation; but conversing, track by track, with Joni Mitchell, not her comatose passenger:

These little towns you pass while driving upstate. Ah, those were the days. Well, as long as you weren't a woman. Or black. Or Hispanic. Or foreign-born. Or gay. Or armed with any sense of social justice and impatience.

Why is it our mental illustration of this thing "morning" doesn't include at all that portion before the sun appears?

"Rainbow fashion" sounds nice but the undeniable link between money and wardrobe can drain the color out of that and real quick like.

"I don't object at all when a singer stretches the limits of pronunciation to create a hard rhyme. You, Nina? Hearing nothing, your consent is deemed."

Although twice in the first minute might be pushing it. Putting on a harmony would probably have been a great idea, a way to close that divide that was maybe artificial but which she was definitely omnisensing. And I don't even like harmonies.

We're keenly aware when we're doing something solely for compensation and it's maybe aggravating when someone who isn't subject to this worries needlessly that they are. Or not.

Not sure conversation is even really a thing anymore, you know? Love is *a story. And, like all stories, illusory, something our brains try to fashion out of uncooperative material. If someone's primary interest in another one was that one's words and thoughts what would that mean with respect to considerations like selfishness and those other negatives? What if the interest were entirely mutual with both parties swooning over the Austenian mental liveliness of the other?*

Don't get it really and the fact it's the title track only bewilders more. How much of my life consists of deferring to the centrality of these epochal types even if it's just the energy spent defying them? I'm going to start saying things like "epochal types" out loud more and see if it spurs more conversations or just aborts them.

I don't want to be simultaneously mother, child, and lady, whatever that means, to someone. I don't want to be anything to anyone, I just want to "be" and I don't even really want to even "be" all that much actually.

The fact that everything can be more takes all the consolation out of the fact that everything could be less.

The piano is the most arrogant instrument. It knows it needs nothing and no one else. Were I Nina presently I would fall into a dream that I was a piano. A tan piano.

What's-her-chops was the daughter of a priest. Or a minister, reverend, whatever. She would say Religion worked best if you had developed your ear at an early age, like Music or Poetry, and that my complete absence of training to this point boded less than well. Maybe I can still get me to a nunnery. I'd adapt the habit greatly to make it excessively sexy. Those motherfuckers wouldn't know what hit them. No matter what, no ear at all for something can't be good. Of course, that chick was also the single crummiest person I've ever known.

The once a week someone calls me "girl." And the one time I retaliated with "boy" it would have to be the stealthiest bla . . . frican American ever.

Yes! The way you only truly value something retrospectively. But that may have less to do with merit than with the inherent pain of loss, whatever form it takes.

Something turns and you're a necessary cog in it. A revolution that's reliant on you. Seems near impossible. This thing, humanity, is just carved up into so many separate pieces. More likely you're a part of the turning but not strictly necessary and question is whether that's enough or at least preferable to observing the turn from without. She doesn't know who in the world she might be or is.

Confused carbon, that's the problem. Carbon misthinking it's more than that. But wait, that can't be right. Mere carbon can't achieve even confusion. And that's what's so confusing about the whole thing of course, confusion arising somehow out of carbon. Even so, why do I have to know who I am, or who anyone else is for that matter?

Like with the two-sided clouds before, this is someone in their early twenties? The hell's that about? Holy shit. What if the message of the seasons is exactly that? Constant and repetitive regeneration. For everything but us. Our noses pressed to the glass excluding us from the party we can't attend. Up and down, up and down, and circular, starts not to feel so bad after all when contrasted with our straight drop.

"Here we are, Miss Bosswoman Nina Gill. Thanks to what I must say was rather expert driving of what is after all a rather unfamiliar vehicle. Which vehicle I skillfully—"

"Hell's this?" Nina says, literally rubbing her eyes like in a cartoon.

"This is hell, of the maximum-security variety, or Sing Sing if you prefer."

"Interesting."

"Did you know that in many ways this is the first real New York prison ever built?"

"Wow, did *you* know you took us to the wrong prison? Jesus, get catatonic for a mere hour and the whole operation falls apart."

"You said Ossining!"

"I made no such sounds."

"You said it was there or bust!"

"Well, you busted all right. You think I would have us leave this early to go forty miles? Where's your head at? And now look at you, sitting there with that befuddled expression instead of heading towards our true destination."

"Which is?"

"The other one, where else?"

"That's not a thing, *other one*; they name these places."

"You know what I mean, the one with the chant."

"Chant?"

"Yeah, inmate unrest? Fomented revolution. With the *This Here Place, This Here Place*!"

"Attica?"

"Ding, ding, ding. Wake me when we're there and not a millisecond before."

"But—"

"Leave your butt out of it."

"Fine, here."

"What's this, a tip? No need, the satisfaction of teaching is its own reward."

"It's the fifty you gave me yesterday to park. I parked freely on the street hence—"

"I barely understand this language you're speaking right now, just never hand me money is all. The fundamental relationship is you work, or whatever you call this, and I give you money. More than that, you work *because* I give you money. You start giving me money and next thing we know you'll be expecting me to work. And I, who have never worked a day in my life, am not about to start now for the likes of you."

"Speaking of, with the giving me money, the thing with payroll, I hate to be pushy—"

The audible harrumph that dead-stopped Dia there turned out to be no sign of disapproval, thank heavens, but rather the sound of its source's resubmergence into apathetic slumber. Dia wondered if Nina would even remember this Sing-Sing interaction. If not, would she have to reoffer the fifty?

53

|||||||||||

Knowledge of the tempestuously unpredictable nature of memory was something Travis relied on often to soothe his troubled mind when the trouble was anxiety. He would say to himself, and I mean out loud, that whatever was currently emitting wave after wave of tense misery would not only pass but also likely prove highly delible. In other words, years would pass and the laughable insignificance of the erstwhile stressor would emerge. Not actively. Older Travis would not look back on the event and retrospectively grant it little importance. No, the whole thing would just fail to register as if elegant proof of the consoling postulate whereby *in twenty years you won't even remember this.*

Problem is Travis has been employing this tactic long enough that he has taken notice of its decreasing merit. So while it was true that his third-grade oral report on the evolution of the corn dog would conform perfectly with the above, it was likewise true that certain ensuing events would not be so easily dismissible. In those instances, it really was as if the past were superior to the flow of time and thus had the power to injure with only slightly reduced force in the immediate present. For example, sitting down to take the MCATs you couldn't say that you wouldn't even remember it in twenty years. Well, you could say whatever you wanted, it just would never become true is all. The result is he didn't even contemplate saying it now, the morning of his first ever M & M.

There were times, man. Times of great envy. Even walking into Bellevue's main entrance that morning. Someone is cleaning those glass doors that magically slide open as you approach. Travis looks at him—the sponge emerging from the bucket to paint soap spheres on the glass then rotating 180 degrees so the rubber blade can squeak out harsh descending rectangles—looks at him and purely wants to be him.

There are people, maybe the vast majority of them, who have no genuine relationship with the concept of performance or the anxiety it can generate. The sponge moves up and down then again and what was dirty becomes cleaner. The finger mindlessly depresses the pump's trigger and the penetrated tank fills with gas. Most critically, in neither case, nor in the countless others like it, is any value judgment made about the quality of the action.

And because Travises generally have no true conception of what it means to be someone like the window washer or gas pumper, Travis was capable of genuinely envying precisely the very mechanistic quality of such a life that should most engender horror. Remember that of all the toxic emotions, Envy is the least dependent on foundational logic. Meaning that often the envious person is more fabulist than sober judge. So just then Travis was able to look at the window washer, whose name was Goran by the way, and envy just that slice of Goran's life that was relevant to Travis's current predicament while lending not a thought to the balance.

Here's a partial list of the many Goran-slices Travis could never envy but which were necessarily intertwined with the attractive one: Goran spent a substantial portion of his time nodding yes to signal comprehension where in fact there was little of same. This behavior was conditioned response, conditioned by the many descents into morasses that seemed to hint at imminent unemployment on those early occasions where the nodding was absent or slow to appear in the presence of his employer, really his employer's human avatar (Goran could nod this way and get away with it because truth was there are only so many ways to clean a window or take out giant contractor bags of garbage). Goran's salary was not lower only because of federally mandated minimums. Goran received two weeks of paid vacation per year; these two weeks could not be taken consecutively. Goran smelled, and smelled like, various simultaneously no-frills yet genocidally powerful cleaning agents even when those agents were definitively absent. Goran's uniform did not account for the change of seasons in any way despite being worn in one of the spots on the globe where those changes were most pronounced. And also this uniform was really one garment that sought to subsume normally discrete concepts like shirt and pants. Last fact, Goran's mind or, if you prefer, brain, was, by every possible measurable—think rapidity, retention, creativity, depth—vastly superior to Travis's.

So, really, Travis only wants one thing Goran has. What he really wants is for being a doctor to be like being a window washer in every respect except salary, vacation time, prestige (the ambient reaction when he says the word), setting, co-workers, opportunities for advancement, parking spots. It's kind of his goal to eventually make it that way, which is why things like this imminent M & M feel so stridently out of tune.

The M & M itself is in one of those amphitheater-mimicking classrooms. So he can be sat at a surprisingly flimsy table at the bottom with his sad supporting documentation while the empowered materialize arhythmically as if shot through a membrane to fill the ascending rows. These people have yet to pay Travis even slight attention and the paradoxical effect is that, despite being the purported focus of this meeting, he is also temporarily in the best position to stand apart from the proceedings, as it were, and from his geographically privileged vantage point collect the unique species of data that all human gatherings necessarily emit.

His ability to do this is surprisingly aided, not hindered, by his temperament. So whereas one might think that someone under stress is less able to attend to the physical details of their environment, what is applicable here is what arises beyond that point. For example, someone suffering from Parkinson's may suffer from visible physical tremors. Quite intuitively, as the disease progresses so do the tremors worsen. However, further along that progression a seemingly odd thing happens. What happens is something like the tremors become so bad they disappear. A shaking so violently disordered that it in effect cancels itself out like a messy equation on whiteboard that ultimately signifies nothing, with the result being a kind of purely physical catatonia.

Similarly, Travis has allowed his anxiety to reach such exorbitant levels that it can no longer even be truly said that he is anxious at all. In its place an extreme dissociation that leaves him feeling like not just a dispassionate observer but one who practically exists on a different spatiotemporal plane from the events unfolding before him, events he is unable to influence in any way. In this context, his powers of observation grow exponentially and he's almost able to sit back and enjoy the performance; even if the acting, it had to be said, was rather insipid.

The performers, save a very few, definitely attempt a monochrome. Looking at them you might even be tempted to conclude that people who *don't* wear a light blue dress shirt with a shockingly white collar are the ridiculous ones, not the other way around. These people talk about golf, way out of proportion to its global incidence. Also, someone talking about golf always seems to be saying so much more than is strictly conveyed semantically. More accurately, the speaker seems to think that's the case. So someone talking about the specifics of their golf game is at least as much saying to everyone in earshot that they are able to play golf. Not that they are able to play golf *well*, just that they are literally *able* to play, with all that implies.

These implications are many but they're dependent on a tiny bit of specialized knowledge on the part of the listeners. The ideal listener would know that golf equipment and instruction are susceptible to great expense. Would know that you can't just decide to play golf the way you can decide to play basketball, say, or to bowl. You make a reservation first, for example. That is, you ensure that you'll have access to a vast area that humans have carefully beautified and tended, and not to sustain but to amuse. Before that, if you're serious, you join a country club and pay six annual figures to do so, which means you're the kind of person who can do that and, further, the kind of person who is positioned to justify that expense with respect to the other pertinent resource of leisure time. All that is the not so subtle subtext of golf discussions like the ones sprouting above and to the left of Travis.

Truth is, the only thing *not* being discussed is medicine, no medicine in any form. This is highly comforting, of course. Travis is starting to realize that it doesn't matter that his father's not in the room, his father's world is in the room. The room is his father's. More than that, the room *is* his father. That makes him literally *of* the room. How then can the room harm him? Would it harm its own child? It would not, and now he is genuinely relaxed not just delusional.

Also his sudden ease dovetails nicely with a realization he's come to have regarding hospitals. The realization is that life means less in a hospital than it does elsewhere. On the surface this seems wrong. Everything in a hospital seems designed to sustain life. Yet a hospital is not full of life the way a lavish garden or an ecstatic river is. What a hospital is full of is death. Everything but the maternity ward is infused with the stuff. Working in one you catch on pretty quickly that all you're collectively doing is arguing against death but as in one of those feeble protests everyone knows can never lead to actual victory, yet still you want to make the point.

And one of the things about battling an undefeated opponent daily is that a certain defeatism can't help but set in. Because you're never vanquishing death, you're at best delaying it. There are two major reactions to this. One is to recoil and run from the horror. The other is to just mentally assert that there's simply no horror to run from. This second one is what people who work in hospitals do. There, death is treated as just one of several possible outcomes and probably, all things told, the least interesting one at that; certainly the one that requires the least amount of future decision making.

What that means is that even though everything presently occurring around him is in direct response to the death of forty-seven-year-old Jorge de Cervantes and is further designed to ascertain what role Travis may or may not have played in it, this does not lend to the event anywhere near the gravity the medically untrained would expect. The actual death is secondary, maybe even tertiary. This is a teaching hospital, this room a teaching tool full of teachers, and if there's one thing true of all intellectual exercises it's their lack of tangible real-world effects. Besides, de Cervantes had been the epitome of a lost cause. Any search for a cause of death didn't need to extend beyond the blitzed idiot behind the wheel. Travis need only keep remembering that to get through the next forty-two minutes.

So point is everything just seems so much less serious now than when Travis first walked into the room. True, some other doctors have just entered and maybe messed the vibe a bit. These few don't remind him of his father. They are mostly women and have difficult-to-pronounce names and don't really look like they have much use for golf. Still, they cannot change the true nature of the room, can they? That's why it's called a minority. The thing has started without his input and now he must scramble to catch up without betraying his previous inattention. His natural facial expression aids this.

"Doctor? Dr. Mena?"

"The patient presented with a severe abominable—" Travis starts.

"Abominable?"

"Sorry, *abdominal*, uh, distress."

"Distress?"

"Yes, uh, basically everything that was supposed to be inside was outside, um . . ."

"Doctor, when do we get to the part where you give an account consonant with the fact that you have received extensive medical training?"

"Easy, Joan, give him a chance."

"It's Dr. Nguyen, and I'm getting the distinct impression that's all this individual's ever gotten."

"You know as well as anyone that it's not customary to interrupt this portion. I'm sure in your day you were extended the same courtesies."

"Doctors, please. Doctor?"

"Thank you, Doctor." Travis is heartened.

"Please continue your account, Dr. Mena."

"Right. The patient presented with severe apocryphal, um, abummable, um, severe injuries to the stomach area of his torso."

"Yes."

"EMT Brown, not sure of the pronunciation, reported that a vehicle had struck the patient at a bus stop. Apparently the impact of the vehicle dislodged a structural metal beam that then became embedded in the car's front grille, where it was driven into the patient's . . . *abdomen*, yes! The location of the entry wound was the *abdomen*. The abdomen received a severe *abdominal* laceration or almost vivisection as a result. The exit wound was located in the patient's dorsal area but without impacting the spine, so at an angle. As I said, the result was almost a complete, an almost complete vivisection."

"Ø"

"So . . . the patient was terminal . . . the patient was going to terminal . . ."

"Vital signs?"

"Vital signs were . . . quite bad. Blood pressure . . . let me see . . . blood pressure was—"

"Doctor, we can read the chart for ourselves. We're interested in what you can independently recall."

"Blood pressure, heart rate, were virtually nonexistent. This was, additionally, consistent with my ocular observations of the patient and his prospects. Here's a slide of the impalement. And I'll here add that while this slide is of the highest possible quality, definition simply doesn't come any higher than this, it still falls short of what it was like to actually—"

"What did you do, Doctor?"

"Doctor, I, attempts were made to locate the attending physician. All attempts were unsuccessful. These attempts were numerous and various, they varied in number and methodology."

"We get it, you were unable to contact the attending. What did you *do*?"

"We tried his cell, an e-mail chain—"

"What did you do *about the patient*, Doctor?"

"Oh. As I've said, vital signs were very faint. EMT Brown advised that—"

"Who?"

"Um, a medical conclusion was drawn that removal of the foreign agent would result in immediate . . . that the metal oblong was essentially performing a skeletal function and that the impacted organs were continuing to perform not in spite of it but in reliance on it. Our focus then shifted to contacting next of kin with our energies centering on the patient's cellular phone, which we were ultimately unable to locate. Later we lost all vital signs and when all attempts to resuscitate failed I called it and pronounced the patient dead at . . . let me see . . ."

"At a full twenty-two minutes after the patient arrived at the ER."

"I don't think we have a precise time for the patient's arrival at the ER."

"Larry Brown, of the ambulance that transported Mr. de Cervantes to our hospital, earlier today fixed a very precise time."

"Highly precise."

"Okay, then everything I said happened in those minutes," Travis said.

"That's just it, Doctor. You haven't *said*. What precise measures were taken?"

"There were no appropriate palliative measures given that the patient—"

"Forget palliative. What measures, if any, did you take or order be taken to further treatment goals? What such goals did you have for that matter?"

"You don't understand."

"Make us understand, Doctor."

"I can't. *You weren't there.*"

"I'm sorry, what?"

"You weren't there."

"I'll concede that, Doctor. But I don't understand. Are you saying that because we weren't there you cannot convey to us what happened in your ER that morning from a medical standpoint?"

"He's not saying that, Doctor. You're not saying that, Doctor."

"So, what are you saying?"

"It doesn't matter, Dr. Nguyen. You know full well there was nothing that could be done. The purpose of this exercise is purely—"

"You weren't there."

"That's enough, Dr. Mena."

"No, Fred, let's hear this. Because if Dr. Mena is right this promises to upend lifetimes of medical practice."

"You weren't there."

"What?"

"The result was not going to differ irregardless."

"Oh, is that the new standard?"

"You weren't there."

"His father is . . ."

"Go ahead, finish that sentence, I'm so uncurious."

"You weren't there."

"Okay, that's enough, I'm calling a halt to this."

"You can't do that."

"I most certainly can and I just did."

"You weren't there."

"That concludes this proceeding."

And it does. The only hard evidence it all ever happened the ensuing document, which instantly sets the record for unhelpful brevity:

Transcript of Morbidity and Mortality Conference
Morbidity and Mortality
Travis Mena MD

Resident

Department of Emergency Medicine

Identifying Data

47 year old

male

Colombian

Roman Catholic

Chief Complaint: Metallic lance through abdomen, still lodged.

Medications

None

Social History

Unknown

History of Present Illness

Patient only mildly communicative at the outset. Pain scale 0/10. EMT advises patient was victim of car accident as a pedestrian. No vital organ unaffected, no prospect of recovery, no palliative measures authorized. No.

Past Surgical History

None

Allergies

None

Immunizations

Unknown

ROS:

Not necessary because no appreciable actions apparently taken, M & M abruptly aborted by acting chair of the Department of Medicine.

So stepping out of that enclosure Travis allows himself the brief thought that perhaps the M & M will be treated as if it never even occurred. Brief because the millisecond he steps out he can hear it all reignite in there. He moves quicker than he has in memory. Truth is he feels like a preteen coming upon his parents arguing over money and accordingly there is no distance too great to create.

The street has the opposite of its intended effect. Instead of burying the hospital and its atmosphere, it is emphasizing it all by bringing it into stark relief. In that outdoor nonfluorescent light, real-world consequences are easier to see. Won't be long before the vibratory words *HOLE, A.* appear on his phone and declining to **>slide to answer** will change nothing. Also, he can give him whatever contact name he wishes but no matter how cathartic that feels it likewise changes nothing.

In that state, bullied Travis gives in to the natural human inclination to try to find a target to bully in turn. But no nurses or interns where he's going, home to slide into bed like a snake. He could bully his below-stairs neighbor about the rent. She always has some reason she can't talk right then about that subject while simultaneously being so hypersensitive to noise that she's gunslinger quick with a broom handle to his floor whenever his noise exceeds monastery library levels. Yeah, right. The one time he overcame her evasive maneuvers enough to get closer than ten feet he melted down internally and barely managed to stammer out what could only generously be called coherence.

Plus there's the fact that when he pictures himself as one of the twenty or so people who faced him in that room he feels almost as sick as he did in that wobbly chair. The preceding makes him want to have no relationship to stress and that includes not being the one causing it in others. He doesn't want to exert authority over anyone either. He always says it's okay, the rent thing, then changes the subject when his father asks about the *rental income*.

Still, truth is truth, and the truth is just then he is certain that he is as miserable as any human being on Earth could possibly be.

52

||||||||||

Rikers Island inmates who have court that day are transported via bus in a large-scale mass movement operation whose oppressive visuals are now striking Nuno with the force of revelation. Nuno has court at 100 Centre Street and he is on the same bus that originally brought him to the island six days earlier. Verifiably the same bus, not just the way everything is the same now.

He's scored reading material thanks to Solomon and it's as if he now sees his world through it. Solomon also said:

"Motherfuckers be waking you up at four when you have court, B."

And he was right and as a result Nuno feels as if he's caught between dream, okay nightmare, and reality.

Solomon has taken time served and gone home. He is missed. Because he was helpful. Besides the books, he knows that island cold. That is, if you can catch him between speculating on the creative ways The Absence is going to disembowel them for not doing the job they were contracted to do. Truth is Nuno would take even that possible death over this particular certitude.

Nuno has court and knows he's not going home, but at the same time he doesn't *know* it because he doesn't want to.

He is going home, he chooses to believe. And when he does he'll need a job and he's just invented one: Supreme Global Base-Poetry Editor. Which means no language can hereafter be sung or rapped hasn't first been fixed by him. And since he's getting out, this will be his last ever diary entry.

2015's February 18 (Wednesday) en route from JATC in Rikers Island—
Queens, now Manhattan, NY

Truth, your rebellion needs a rebel
With a cause, who's flowing on the level
These hard-timers, and where they spread their venom in
They want silence? Y'all need to yell like Munch's Scream

I'll say it, but then you gotta hear it
Y'all move to music, while deaf to all the lyrics
None are left that are angry and def
The sound of silly brags, in every putrid breath

I guess I'm dumb, I guess I'm just a criminal
But I'm methodical, defiant until lyrical
All em players on the sideline wondering what they should do
Just listen hard for the play from a rebel to you

∞

Law, suckers wanna cage me
Like a zoo, but one that stays unseen
Coming to go then going till you come again
An in and out outing, until they tell you when

Score? We're getting shut out
Flip the field, to start another rout
Diverse as this verse rest their heads on this word guillotine
Read the charges, the crimes, the scene

Guilty, and I'm a tell you how
Forced segregation of the nation how we living now
Round em up and tag em then you put em in
Fore you say it, willful blindness same as intent

∞

The world is Technicolor but up in here it's a blackout
I gotta tell you all about it in the time before I break out
You got enough for a country inside in case you don't know
Unlock the doors and they'll be charging like a rhino

Dalí rhinos bleeding out to curb-stomp your ass
POs dropping guns to run away and cower with the brass
You wonder why now? You wonder how, son?
Same toxic shit called out by Baldwin and Ellison

But there's a limit and you're boiling up to reach it
The virus spread like a profit-motive racket
Problem is we're going to breach the quarantine
An outbreak of righteous anger the likes you've never seen

He stops because the bus arrives at the indoor garage of 100 Centre Street and spills its waste, including Nuno, into the court building's many holding cells.

51

||||||||||

The buses at Attica Correctional Facility are certainly imbued with a higher degree of finality than the ones on Centre Street. Reason is these buses have less a utilitarian purpose and more a punitive one. These don't do round trips. They're more in the area of waste disposal. So twice a month they come from places like Rikers Island to that parking area to excrete dwindling orange pellets. Deadened penitents that will kinetically bounce off each other like cellular components but never breach their membrane.

Dia is watching this from where she sits, not knowing the above explicitly but still sensing it intuitively because she's good like that. The result is anxiety to go with her confusion.

"Okay, now what?" is how she expresses this to Nina, who is staring at a gate and had frankly forgotten she wasn't alone.

"Oh, you. Now we wait."

"But for what?"

"What do you think is the most important position on our sad team?"

"Long snapper."

"Close, cornerback. *What?*"

"I was going to say corner."

"No you weren't."

"But the answer seemed so obvious I thought it must be a trick question."

"Cornerback."

"Agree."

"The reason is—"

"Then long snapper."

"That a true shutdown corner is the hardest thing to find. The hardest, let me tell you. But if you find one it changes everything, lets you really get nutty on D. There's also just something about someone who plays cornerback, don't you think?"

"How do you mean?"

"I mean that in a league of insane athletes they're the insanest."

"I saw that, their forty times are off the charts."

"They have to be. Remember that when they line up across from a wide receiver, it's anything but a fair fight. Start with the fact that the receiver knows where he's going. Obviously it takes a lot more athleticism to react instantaneously than to act according to a predetermined plan. Throw in the new rules that don't let them so much as breathe on the receiver and you get an idea of the degree of difficulty."

"Everybody calls it a new rule but wasn't it really just a reemphasis on a rule that's always been on the books?"

"Wow, you really have hit those books."

"And the film, thank you very much."

"Anyway, you're right and wrong. Right that it was already a rule but wrong that it was always one. Before 'seventy-eight defensive backs could hit receivers with impunity all the way down the field provided the ball hadn't been thrown. Mel Blount for one used to destroy guys, take away their will to even compete. Limiting that to within five yards of the line of scrimmage is a huge part of what developed the forward pass to what it is today, starting with guys like Coryell."

"So it was a good thing."

"Profitable thing anyway. In that league there's no distinction. Point is, I love cornerbacks."

"Because they're the most athletic players on the field."

"More than that though. There's almost something admirable about wanting to play corner. Think of a little kid playing organized ball for the first time. Try convincing him not to be the guy calling the plays or prancing into the end zone to dance. It takes character's my point."

"That's kind of my thing with long snappers."

"Will you stop with the long snappers? Goodness, I'm trying to share with you."

"Really?"

"Really. I'm trying to tell you I have this Ahabian thing going when it comes to the cornerback position and all you can say is *long snapper this, long snapper that.*"

"All you said is you like them."

"Way more than that, I've been on a search for the perfect one since I was fourteen. I don't just mean for my team either. I'm talking about just getting to see the fucker's play is all."

"See who play?"

"That's just it, there is no *who.* Just once before I die I want it to not be a false alarm. I want to look down and see this flawless specimen. Huge but with loose hips, impeccable technique, and intelligence. And most importantly? The will. The will to do it play after goddamn play. Because it's such a thankless position. Shut a guy down for fifty-nine minutes but give up the winner and everyone labels you a loser."

"Not sure what you mean. I'm looking at a list of Hall of Fame corners. Surely one of them—"

"Let me see. Forget anyone before 'seventy-eight; as I said, they were playing a different sport. Darrell Green, too small. Mike Haynes, perfect technique but not physical enough for what I'm talking about. Deion had the best combination of hips and speed I've ever seen but he tackled as if Justin Bieber suddenly found himself on a professional football field. Rod Woodson was probably the closest to it I ever saw. Physically he was a beast and his straight-line speed insane. But, his hips were maybe a little tighter than I need to diagnose perfection. He couldn't change direction like Deion and was just slightly less dangerous if he got his hands on the ball. Also, temperamentally, he'd get bored to the point that he'd go for the occasional double move."

"I have to say, sounds like you're nitpicking."

"Of course I am. That's precisely the point. Just once I want to watch a guy play corner and see no nits to pick."

"Fine, but what does any of this have to do with my question?"

"I'd have to know what your question was, which I don't."

"Why are we here? In this place that is so over-the-top penal?"

"We're here for two reasons. Because released prisoners come out that gate and because Dylan Reeves once chewed off my leg, leaving me only with this stump."

"Oh boy."

"Six two, two ten, with twenty-five reps. Easily the strongest to ever play the position. Forty in the 4.3s, but my God, the hips. Fastest three-cone time ever, by eight percent."

"Never heard of him."

"I know."

"Why?"

"Well, he had his issues."

"Obviously, look where we are. And, given that, why would we possibly want someone coming out of *there* to be on the team? I thought you were interested in high-character people?"

"Exclusively, and I didn't realize you were a judge now, Your Dishonor. And at all of, what, twenty-two?"

"Point taken."

"Not everyone gets to prance around the Brown campus looking for the next kegger."

"I believe I essentially withdrew the comment."

"While you were slinging ice skates over your shoulder and going to practice, Dylan Reeves was dodging extension cords at home."

"Oh my . . . so sorry."

"Just kidding, I made that extension cord thing up."

"Weird thing is I did skate as a kid."

"You don't say."

"I do. And I also say that we're opening ourselves up to criticism. They'll say we're employing, you know, the *t* word."

"Tyrants?"

"Thugs."

"Ah, right. Read and watch about players long enough and you'll eventually hear one referred to as a thug or lazy. Here's what I say to that: the chances that an NFL player, which Reeves was for years, is actually a bona fide thug or lazy are exceedingly slim. Reeves comes from a place where every guy in his position would give his left arm to play in the NFL. You know what the difference is between him and them? He actually gave the arm. From a purely quantifiable stand-point, the amount of extreme physical effort that is required to become a premier NFL cornerback is far beyond the abilities of even ardent workers let alone *lazy* people or *thugs*. Those are loaded terms that are bull! Lazy thugs get out of bed at eleven, grab a brown paper bag, and hang on the corner complaining. While they did that, Reeves starting at age ten would subject himself to what can only be called voluntary physical torture. That's the physical part. Mentally, let me say that Reeves wasn't the strongest reader, yet he would watch so much film of upcoming receivers that the machine would malfunction. Then he would make these little logbook entries with shaky spelling. Sound like any lazy thugs you know?"

"Okay, but this goes beyond that, doesn't it? I mean he's coming out of jail!"

"Prison."

"For a reason, no?"

"So young, so credulous. He's currently incarcerated, true, though not for long, or even short. The question is, what can we reliably draw from that fact?"

"A great deal."

"Very little. To interpret the fact we first have to orient ourselves geographically."

"New York?"

"No, the land of the free. People still speak of things like criminal records and time in jail in hushed tones as if they were wildly extraor-dinary events worthy of great embarrassment. Problem is they're hushing in a place that looks at incarceration the way a fat kid eyes cake. Forget fame, in the future everyone will do at least fifteen hours of jail time."

"I, no."

"I'm glad you know, now we just have to get everyone else to know."

"No, I mean, I don't—"

"Exactly."

"But what did he do?"

"What business is that of ours?"

"Just curious."

"He did what almost everybody else does, save for doing it on a much larger scale."

"Here he is, right?" Dia raises a screen to Nina's eyes, first time she's taken them off that gate:

 NEW YORK STATE   Services   News   Government   Local

Department of Corrections and Community Supervision

About SOCCS   Board of Parole   Offenders   Visitors   Resources   Legal   News and Media   Submit a FOIL

Inmate Information

Inmate Information Data Definitions are provided for most of the elements listed below. When a detailed definition is available for a specific element, you may click on the element's label to view it.

Identifying and Location Information As of 02/18/15	
DIN (Department Identification number)	13B2370
Inmate Name	REEVES, DYLAN
Sex	MALE
Date of Birth	02/05/1986
Race/Ethnicity	BLACK
Custody Status	RELEASED
Housing/Releasing Facility	ATTICA
Date Received (Original)	06/29/2013
Admission Type	NEW COMMITMENT
County of Commitment	WYOMING
Latest Release Date/Type (Released	02/18/15 PAROLE – COND REL
Inmates Only)	TO PAROLE

Crimes of Conviction If all 4 crime fields contain data, there may be additional crimes not shown here. In this case, the crimes shown here are those with the longest sentences. As of 02/18/15	
Crime	Class
CRIM POSS CONTR SUBSTANCE 3RD	B

Sentence Terms and Release Dates Under certain circumstances, an inmate may be released prior to serving his or her minimum term and before the earliest release date shown for the inmate. As of 02/18/15	
Aggregate Minimum Sentence	0000 Years, 00 Months, 00 Days
Aggregate Maximum Sentence	0002 Years, 00 Months, 00 Days
Earliest Release Date	02/18/2015
Earliest Release Type	PAROLE ELIGIBILITY DATE
Parole Hearing Date	01/02/2015
Parole Hearing Type	RELEASE CONDITION
Parole Eligibility Date	02/18/2015
Conditional Release Date	02/18/2016
Maximum Expiration Date	08/18/2017
Maximum Expiration Date for Parole Supervision	08/18/2017
Post Release Supervision Maximum Expiration Date	08/18/2017
Parole Board Discharge Date	08/18/2017

"That's him."

"So drugs then."

"He maybe likes that stuff more than most."

"Not everyone uses drugs."

"Just an overwhelming majority, including you."

"Well, I only claimed not everyone. So, he's banned from the league?"

"He is. Which, of course, is a weird fact in and of itself."

"How do you mean?"

"I mean that somewhere along the line the league got this notion that it had a right to regulate its players' private use of recreational drugs and astonishingly the players went along. This is a stupefying fact if you think about it. Let's face it, these guys aren't exactly driving buses full of schoolchildren. Society at large isn't really being put at risk here if the fullback is high as a kite when he crashes his brain into another guy's brain."

"I never really thought of that."

"Yeah, you and whoever the union chief was at the time. Point is, he's banned because of that sheer stupidity."

"But has he ever been violent? Because violence and that seedy underworld go hand in hand." Nina takes her eyes off again to shoot Dia an incredulous look, to which Dia quickly responds with "If highly acclaimed television shows are to be believed."

"To my knowledge Reeves has never harmed woman, child, or non-lethal animal. Now, fully grown male? Look out. Because he's an angry guy, no doubt. Still, he never lit into anyone didn't have it coming and couldn't defend himself. Throw in the fact that this dude once told our general manager to go fuck himself while they debated, I shit you not, what would constitute an appropriate minimum wage, and I'd say character's exactly what we'll be getting. But the larger point is none of this matters. I care about football. I want to win football games. I want, at longest last, my perfect cornerback. If Reeves can help me get those things, we're friends for life. If not, maybe in the next one."

"Not sure I approve. But also, what makes you so sure he can help? It *has* been almost two years."

"I'm not so sure at all, I need to see his eyes."

"Riiight, to make sure he's off the smack."

"The only smack will be to your face if you don't reform. I'm talking about something else entirely. His eyes are going to tell me if he's the same guy who offered to have his finger amputated rather than miss a critical game or if this place stole that from him."

"What? That's insane."

"I take it back, there's no way he's the *same* guy. I just want to look at his eyes and see whether that guy is still dormant in there somewhere, that's all. The physical can be trained up, it's that other thing you can't manufacture. Once that thing goes out you can't relight it. It's like a pilot, it has to be producing at least the slightest flame. His eyes will tell me that. The hell's taking so long? Let me see that hideous website again."

Dia is pulling it up when an absurdly athletic man appears from behind the gate wearing a white sleeveless undershirt above orange pants and holding a big brown paper bag with his possessions.

"Most importantly, he sure is fun to look at, huh? That's the only good part about prison, they come out even yummier."

Dylan Reeves's first few free steps are not what he expected, is anything ever? What he thought would be pure elation is more like anxiety really. Thing is, routines bolster and strengthen their relevant neural pathways until they become more like deep grooves. These grooves then in turn strengthen the routine in a system of reciprocal reward that can feel like constraint.

And that's run-of-the-mill routine. Now take the extreme routine that is long-term incarceration. Because every millisecond of the inmate's day is in some sense planned. That and there is very little variation from one day to the next. Start with the fact that everyone dresses the same way every day or that the exact same sounds are heard at the exact same times with zero variation. Exactly. What happens, of course, is that the inmate can become a kind of OCD-riddled mess, only that fact won't really be apparent in the context of such an unchallenging setting; like trying to judge how well someone would handle success when they're living in a homeless shelter. Upend that, however, say by releasing the subject, and the principal dynamic at play is the confirmation of a suspicion.

So Reeves is experiencing that thing where your legs feel like their own separate entity and that just adds to the uncertainty, the sensation that he is watching himself exist instead of existing. Also he's having trouble with the brightness of the sun and doesn't appear to have the strongest sense of where he should go next. He gave no thought to this question and now it feels like the only question. This is a problem because if he can just get out of that parking lot, if he can, for the first time in almost twenty months, just not be on Attica Correctional Facility property, then *he* will not be Attica property and he can maybe start to figure out a life whose primary selling point might very well be that at least he is not said property.

Those two over there staring at him aren't helping matters. He'll walk towards them and when he gets close enough they'll walk away, always works. But these two don't and he starts thinking they're with DOCS and are going to put him back in as they explain *a regrettable mistake.*

The sound of his first name shocks, he's been just *Reeves!* for so long. What is this? Even a familiar face actually relies a lot on context for its familiarity so he knows he knows this one but how and from where not a chance. Then:

"Ms. Gill?"

"You mean Nina."

"Nina. So?"

"So, ready to blanket some prima donnas?"

"What you talking about?"

"No, what are *you* talking about? Still a cornerback by trade are you not?"

"No."

"Time to line up across from some guy who won't shut up then can't find himself on the stat sheet at the end of the game."

"Thought I was banned for life."

"That's the NFL. That league doesn't exist anymore, where *you* been?"

"So?"

"So you're a lockdown corner for the Paterson Pork of the prestigious IFL. How's that sound?"

"Um." He hasn't made the greatest of eye contact during all this.

"Actually it doesn't really matter how it sounds. Playing corner for me is the way you got out."

(Not true.)

"Then I guess it sounds great."

"Good, it's settled then. Follow me if you want to live."

He does.

"Here, let me." Nina snatches Reeves's paper bag then absently shoves it into Dia's face as they near the car. Once there, Reeves maybe starts to relax a bit. The car he stands in front of is the kind of enclosure he wouldn't terribly mind living in. He will get in it, close his eyes, the world will be vastly different. A car ride and Attica is expunged from the world.

Is someone saying *the world* always just necessarily saying *my world*—those events, places, and people they're aware of and that have at least *some* effect on them? Doesn't matter, because that's what Dylan Reeves means.

And just as he's had no significant concept of anything happening outside that facility for almost two years, he now intends to create the same dynamic, but in the other direction. He can sense it happening too. How he sees it is, every free step, every similar breath and thought, moves him down the birth canal (still the worst thing he's ever seen) to start life as if nothing before counts.

That parking lot is like a state of being between these two points: life and prebirth. Fitting that in this state of disgrace no sensory input registers. Just an emptied mannequin man staring at an expanse of sky you could convince him didn't exist until just then.

The weight of human stares is unlike anything else inanimate.

"Huh?"

"I said, this is Deputy Commissioner Nouveau. She can answer any questions you might have on the ride as I'll be sleeping off my long night working with underprivileged youth."

"Oh, okay."

"She'll be giving you a clothing allowance too, you look terrible in orange."

50

||||||||||

The vast majority of human events leave no lasting record. A man fries an egg, a woman replaces a lightbulb, a boy packs a snowball. The egg is consumed. The light resumes and is indistinguishable from before the brief interregnum. The snow melts. The only evidence these events even occurred resides in human memory and in just a solitary one at that. And it's a limited residence too. A memory must constantly crowd out individual memories, and ones like the above are the first to go. So a memory is no place for memories but with something like the snowball a memory of it is almost all that ever existed of it and there's nowhere for that memory to go and it has to go because it's not compelling enough so then it becomes, in a very real sense, as if the snowball never existed. And a snowball never having existed is decidedly not a big deal but what if ultimately the same can be said about a human being?

Now, there *are* exceptions, and they can be instructive. For example, almost any time the police are called is a memorable event in the above sense of the word. More than that. In New York, every one of these calls is recorded in its entirety. What happens next depends principally on the substance of that call. Most of these calls are erased after ninety (90) days, whereupon they join the fried egg or the snowball in the realm of entities that technically *were* but good luck proving it.

But not all go there and this is true because of litigation and its supple demands. See, one of the most surefire ways to break through the senescent fog that cloaks most all human activity is to transgress to the point of arrest. Arrest generally means a prosecution, which always means a prosecutor, and one of the things that a prosecutor will do is direct the NYPD's One Police Plaza to preserve the relevant 911 call(s) past the ninety (90)-day death sentence then, if necessary, send said recording(s) to the District Attorney's Office of New York.

Whether and to what extent this audio recording may later properly be a part of evidence adduced at a trial is a legal question hinging on factors like the Hearsay Rule and its many exceptions. What everyone can agree on is that it's all sorts of useful to have a written transcript of the call while doing things like debating its admissibility. Only problem is that creating these transcripts is thankless and surprisingly time-consuming work. The kind of work that lands on the desk of a newbie attorney but only temporarily until it can be relocated to a law-student intern's workstation, where it will migrate into an undergrad intern's hand because that's the extent of this intern's storage system. That person looks around fruitlessly then transcribes the tape. It's an unremarkable process.

With one exception.

Around this time, in the Manhattan office, there'd emerged a DANY intern without precedent, analogue, or even scrutability. Excuse the two major preceding-sentence vagaries, *around* and *emerged*, but understand that in a supremely uptight place where every butterfly-wing flap is chronicled and catalogued, no record appears to have been made of when or where Sylvester Scarpetti began, developed, performed, or ended his internship. Likewise, there is no data trail revealing who was responsible for bringing Scarpetti in; whom to credit or alternatively blame.

What *is* known is that at some point Scarpetti joined the herd of uncredentialed twenty-somethings that at all times can be seen in that office committing the offense of Loitering for the Purpose of Experience. He was, of course, an *unpaid* intern. But he took it even a step further in that he appeared to have no other discernible reason for donating his labor. No educational entity was giving him credit. No fellowship or training program was being complied with. In fact, no unifying principle seemed to be in play at all. Scarpetti seemed to have negative interest in the prosecution of alleged criminals. Not to merely say that he did not want to one day be a prosecutor. It was more fundamental than that. He was simply wholly uninterested in the mechanics, rationales, or underlying drama of criminal prosecutions, or really the criminal justice system as a whole. He had, in short, no reason to be there.

What he did have was a high degree of roundness. Sylvester Scarpetti was a round guy. This is not a new clever expression you've been unaware of that expresses something about his personality, like saying so-and-so is *square*. No, this is straight geometry here. Reference is being made to his actual body and the fact that it was astonishingly circular. He looked like a fucking cartoon bagel created to illustrate a dietary point.

That's what he looked like. How he acted was even less pointed. He rarely spoke and when he did the resulting blandness quotient was through the roof. Nearly every syllable he uttered was designed to avoid offense. Nor was there any chance of what he said being misconstrued since it was impossible for any of it to be *construed* in the first place. No truth value was assignable; it would be like asserting that the color yellow is true or false. And this indeterminacy so bled over into his entire personality that at times it almost seemed as if he were blurring the line between human and furniture. None of which would have been of any moment whatsoever except that one time, through the accumulation of a series of minuscule imprecisions, a 911 tape was placed in his hand to the soundtrack of mumbled instructions starring the word *transcript*.

Picture the first time Rod Carew swung a bat or Joni Mitchell sat at a piano. Because Sylvester Scarpetti listened to the call one time straight through then sat at one of the community keyboards and typed down verbatim what he had heard. This all happened so fluidly and rapidly that when he went to the source assistant district attorney to return the CD she initially incorrectly surmised that he was somehow refusing the assignment and she prepared to unleash holy hell on this presumptuous fat turd. Only when he almost immediately handed her the beautifully fonted transcript did she begin to understand.

Understood, but with a high degree of skepticism. After all, you can paint a house in an hour too if all you do is fling paint at it like that brain-dead fraud Jackson Pollock. So distrustful of the speed involved was the ADA that she immediately handed it to a higher-level intern with instructions to produce a transcript and without any disclosure that one had already been produced. Two days later she placed the two side by side and it was just as expected, major discrepancies. When she was done that rotund twerp was going to wish he'd never been born. Well, he probably already wished that, but soon he'd be wishing it even more.

Except that before she could unleash her campaign of targeted and merciless destruction, she inexplicably found herself listening to the actual recording. She may have done this in an effort to exacerbate her ire just before the big game as it were. Instead it was her shock that rose. Because every single time the two transcripts disagreed it was the fat guy's one that was right. More than that, the fat one was never wrong, *period*. And remember that this superior, objectively perfect one had been produced in about half an hour to the other's two days. This fact alone was freakily astonishing but the truth is there was more to it than even that.

The ADA sat in her office and struggled to make sense of it. The rapidity was one thing but what was this other element? She crumpled and threw away the inferior transcript; Harvard Law must really be slipping. She listened to the recording again. Then she read the transcript. Then she read it again. The events depicted in the call were grim but that couldn't be it, they almost always were. No, it wasn't about the recording at all; it was about the transcript. What she realized, and she would never say this out loud in a million years, was that the transcript while being a perfectly accurate depiction of the phone call somehow also managed to achieve its own separate grandeur, one that went beyond the audio's undeniable reality.

How was this possible? Did the answer have something to do with a little-understood aspect of what we call reality? Was the fat intern revealing something? Depicting it? Discovering it? Inventing it? All while maintaining complete fidelity to the facts? If so, what were the implications? Should she talk to someone about this? Is tonight that spin class Laurie was talking about? Should she maybe even talk to *him* about it? Had she said she would meet her there?

It was and she had. She left and purposely didn't think about the transcript anymore. But you best believe the next time she needed a call transcribed she was handing it to this Scarponi-or-something-but-call-me-Sylvester and, yes, she did have the same experience minus the overwhelming shock of the new and, yes, she did respond by spreading the word but only under the guise of *this guy will get you a perfectly accurate transcript in record time*, no mention of anything remotely metaphysical.

Didn't matter because even the least perceptive person couldn't help but have a similar experience while reading a Scarpetti. His fame grew. Pretty soon it seemed he was getting all the 911 tapes, it made little sense to go anywhere else. A cardboard box with his name was set up in the corner but when that overflowed he soon had a desk, then a nook, then a cubicle, and finally an actual office and an assistant.

Even so, he had trouble keeping up. The quality threatened to suffer, only threatened. So much so that a weird process developed, albeit organically. A line would form outside his office as if to a nightclub. DAs holding CDs in those formfitting plain white envelopes with the plastic windows in the middle. See, you couldn't just drop off the CD with the expected instructions. No, you had to convince Scarpetti to take on the project, and you did this by, in essence, *pitching* its desirability. Remember, this is an artist and you are asking him to produce art, he needs to be treated as such.

So it was not uncommon to see DAs on that line consulting notes on a flash card or whispering to themselves in preparation right before entering. And it must be said that Scarpetti was not overly generous towards supplicants. He would listen, sure, but often his decision would be communicated so cryptically, and never with any underlying reasoning, that it wasn't always clear precisely what that decision was. It was absurd actually, had anyone taken a step back to see clearly, but fact is it was the only way to get a Scarpetti so nobody took that step and the situation persisted and would probably have persisted indefinitely had not a change occurred in the transcript artist himself.

The precipitating factor may have been a snippet of conversation Scarpetti overheard early one morning on his way into his office. The gist was one fifty percent of the conversation expressing mild surprise to the other fifty that Scarpetti was the author of the transcript at issue. The words nagged at him until he realized why at lunch. The realization. A great many 911 transcripts were made. He did not make all of them. It was apparently possible for an underinformed someone to believe he had authored a transcript he hadn't or, worse, mistakenly attribute some foreign work to him. From that moment forward, he decided, he would sign all his transcripts. Didn't Monet sign? Manet? Matisse? Modigliani? Mauet? All those *M* guys? Wait, did those dudes sign their work? He had no clue. But he would sign, no more Intern 8311.

Question was, what would the signature be? He started conservatively. In the lower right hand corner, in tiny script, a confident but almost respectful Sylvester Scarpetti. This was frankly justifiable. Couldn't it arise that someone might have a question about the transcript and want to contact its author? This would expedite that. That got boring though. And the truth is he had always wanted a moniker. So the above morphed into things like Sylvester "The Scarp" Scarpetti or just The Scarp or later The Scar or even less defensibly Scar Tissue. Then there were those that had a mathematical bent like "S-squared," "S to the Power of 2," and ultimately just "S^2."

All this was tolerated but not without the occasional raised eyebrow. Fact is, people put up with Scar Tissue's antics because the transcripts were that good and no one wanted to be the party responsible for their cessation if S^2 threw a fit and refused to produce any more. And everyone understood intuitively that this was a possibility too. Because *temperamental* didn't do it justice whenever anyone dared comment on one of his transcripts even if the comment seemed objectively laudatory. Same thing if you asked when one might be ready as the astonishingly speedy turnaround of the early transcripts was increasingly replaced by more deliberative exertion. Still, it was widely acknowledged that the work being produced was extraordinary and that tends to dispel most all objections.

But *most* all is not the same as *all* all and what critics of The Scarp there were tended to fall into three major groups. The first group just bluntly denied his greatness. To them he was a glorified Dictaphone. He listened to what people had said and he reproduced it in written form. This was not a big deal. True, he did it faster and more accurately than most and the resulting transcript was often compelling, but he was still nothing more than a tool. To the extent the work had any value, he was merely mimicking those who had come before and he was a poor substitute at that. Most crucially, he was not responsible for the substance of his work, whatever the relevant people had said. Hell, given their usual circumstances, these people themselves were barely responsible for it. Accounting for that truth, the claims being made on his behalf were wildly unwarranted. This, it must be said, was the majority opinion among his critics.

The second group took an almost wistful position. According to this group it was undeniable that Sly had produced great work in the form of those early transcripts. That work was superb and transcendent in precisely the way people claimed. But that was the past, this is the present. Somewhere along the way things turned. Likely it was the praise done it. Whatever the cause, what was at the outset genuinely, almost transgressively, *new*, had now devolved into self-parody and affectation. No likely about it, it was definitely the praise. Because there was an undeniable exclusivity in those early days, when only a select few were even aware of what The Scar was up to and how he was revolutionizing what had heretofore been a rather dull process. As that changed, as his exposure grew, well, at first it was exciting, but there was no denying that, eventually anyway, quite a bit of the thrill was lost and the loss appeared to be a permanent one. Significantly, this group allowed, the widespread popularity had less disrupted the creation of Sylvester Scarpetti's work than it had the reception of it. Either way, what mattered, and what both these two groups could damningly agree on, was that what Scarpetti was currently doing when he made a transcript was unworthy of notice and was easily replicable by any number of other interns.

The third and last group's critique was simultaneously the most deferential and the most devastating. It could not be effectively countered. This group not only conceded that S-squared was once great but asserted unequivocally that he *remained* great; a supreme artist in peak control of his gift who was sharing that gift right here in the present. More than that, they said. His work continues to grow in both richness and innovative execution.

That said, their position boiled down to, *So what?* So what that Scarpetti exhibited extreme artistry in his transcripts? That he seemed expert in human truth and impervious to cliché or shallow thought. Has everyone forgotten that we are in a DA's office? 911 transcripts are made for one highly utilitarian purpose only. Scarpetti transcripts served that purpose no better than any others. He was a luxury and, worse, a luxury in a place where three or four law degrees routinely shared an office.

For a long time this objection just lay there inertly. There was nothing that could really be said against it in the sphere of logic, but the world has amply proved that this sphere rarely controls. During this time the objection had roughly the status of Einstein's theory of relativity prior to Sir Arthur Lord Conan Eddington the Third or whatever's observation of that solar eclipse in 1919. You'll recall that when Eddington confirmed that light had indeed bent around the sun in precisely the way the theory would have predicted, theoretical physics exploded in intellectual delight at the realization that this theory that had been around in some form for about fourteen years was actually verifiably true and this all rocketed Einstein into superstardom.

Similarly, though in the converse, a natural experiment would ultimately undo Scarpetti. What happened was a rush job materialized suddenly at a time when Scarpetti was out getting a massage. Everyone agreed this was cataclysmic but the massage was deep tissue in nature so there was nothing to do but hand it to a hack who delivered the way only hacks can.

What developed next is what proved revelatory. In brief, the case went to trial, the hack's transcript was used, and the defendant was convicted on all counts—more rare than you think. This was, of course, the empirical support some had been waiting for. Proof that the work of Sylvester Scarpetti was full of everything but significance. Some dissented that it was precisely that *everything* (e.g., the beauty, narrative timing, psychological acuity, witty playfulness) that in and of itself most signified, but these protestations went largely uncredited. It was a bad blow. SS's popularity began to wane.

One afternoon the bureau chief no less was on the line outside Scarpetti's office and the whole thing was taking too long for his liking. Suddenly, in what many would later retrospectively label the beginning of the end, he simply walked away and dropped his CD in the wire basket of an intern whose name no one knew, though it was rumored he was a failed Ukrainian pop singer who'd stopped pop singing amid allegations of particularly egregious plagiarism. Also didn't help matters when first a trickle then a slew of inaccuracies began to come to light. Were these really faithful reproductions or were they one demented man's projection of how things should have sounded? And who signs their work in that manner, anyway?

To Scarpetti himself, these infelicities, as he called them, mattered little. He'd been asked to do a job and he'd done it. At first he'd merely done it very very well. Then he'd demonstrated unprecedented brilliance and finally a level of artistry that was unlikely to ever be matched. Was it really his fault that the whole thing had eventually gotten away from him a little bit? No one understood the price he paid to create the work. No one spoke to him and he spoke to no one outside of that work's context. Even when his mystique was most charged, when his presence in a room was enough to electrify it, it was that damn separateness above all. Still home to that one room, still that weak microwave, still that disheartening stillness. By contrast the events on the tapes were just so *alive*. That was the quality they most had, Life. But not in any complimentary way like when someone says, *Oh, so-and-so is just so full of life*. This was life as it is, not some rhetorical device. Desperate and plaintive and defeated. Halting breath, the sounds that tears make independent of crying, screams that cycle continuously between anger and fear.

At least those had the illusion of agency. Worse were the ones that were like bravura performances of denial. The ones where you could hear the voice clinging to the moments just before what precipitated the call. Where the mind has not yet caught up to the words coming out of the mouth. Hearing those was hard. Hearing all of them was hollowing, and realize that all he did was listen to them twelve hours a day every day.

So it happened. He began to serve a different kind of truth than the strict one favored by DAs and the like. How significant is it what precise words an eight-year-old boy uses to announce to the world that his mother has had her neck flayed open? Seems that what matters, the underlying lesson, is that this is what human beings do to each other. Not some human beings, not sometimes. This is what humans are. His art needed to reflect that. It needed to expand or contract like a diaphragm to breathe in the full panoply of life but mostly things like the open throat. In these situations it was best to abide no interference with respect to so much as a comma.

No one else agreed. The line outside his office grew shorter, the people on it the less-plugged-in types. The praise softened then disappeared altogether. His assistant was reassigned when she showed a talent for labeling rape kits. But instead of her moving elsewhere he was asked to vacate their office so she could have more room to work. Truth is with the dwindling number of tapes he no longer even needed a desk and so this wire basket would do. No one called him anything but Scarpetti and those three syllables often dripped with contempt. Eventually nobody called him anything.

He reminded himself that he engaged in his art solely to satisfy something within himself and therefore the opinions of others were irrelevant. He was wrong in one crucial respect. Because while other people's literary judgment may not have been of great concern to him it was other people who either gave or didn't give him 911 tapes and eventually no one was giving him tapes. Without the tapes there was no art to attempt, nothing for him to do. He had no direct access to them. He tried FOIL and FOIA requests but all he got in return was the classic runaround. He gave up. He'd stare at the empty wire basket and invent inventory he could transcribe. But invention was never his thing, he had a different, very precise skill and no others. Being that he had nothing else to offer, he did nothing. He was still an intern, but now he was testing the limits of what that means, what the implications were. He would observe strict business hours, no one could ever claim he came late or left early. It was what transpired in between those two events that lacked sense. By then he had no workstation so what he did was just kind of walk around, ostensibly looking for an assignment but in reality just walking. No one talked to him so there was never any reason to stop or even slow. The Manhattan DA's office is spread out over several floors and even two separate buildings. In other words, quite a bit of square footage for someone to operate in. He began to log some serious mileage. He knew this because he'd downloaded an app that told him precisely how much at the end of every otherwise wildly uneventful day. He quickened his pace, every day's number had to be bigger than the day before's. He started to lose weight. He worked through his lunch break and even when home he wouldn't eat for fear that it would slow him down the next day. He looked sick. People complained. Apparently there was this new skinny intern, no one knew his name, who was always practically sprinting through the office as if he were terribly late. Nobody's coffee was safe. It was a safety hazard is what it was.

One day an earlier-than-normal Sylvester Scarpetti was stopped on his way into the office by a security guard who didn't recognize him. At length he dug out his secure pass and handed it over. The ensuing delay was odd but he was sure it would soon be resolved favorably and he could commence his walking. The time lost could probably be compensated for by a minimal increase in pace. It never happened because the security guard appeared to receive some heated instructions via phone before pulling out comically large scissors he, for some reason, had ready access to and cutting said pass into multiple strips. It was over.

No one can definitively state where Scarpetti went from there. Some say he invented the circular beach towel that doesn't have to be rotated by sunbathers trying to match the sun, others that he developed an app that diagnoses skin cancer, and still others that he did both and that the lucrative symbiosis of these products made him robber baron wealthy so that he now lives on his own private island where every phone call between residents is recorded and later transcribed. An alternate path has him being evicted from several homeless shelters for insufficient net worth culminating in his arrest for raiding the One Police Plaza evidence room then when, at a press conference, the mayor, who had been misbriefed and thought he was talking about somebody else, repeatedly called him alternately a *terribly terrifying terrorist* or a *terrifyingly terrible terrorist*, receiving several concurrent at-least-life sentences in some newly formed country's vilest prison where he currently sits waiting to meet his lawyer.

Far more likely true is the rumor that he changed his name to Milton McGillicutty and found actually gainful employment with a premier closed captioning company. Those in this camp, while conceding the absence of hard proof, point to the unique yet strangely familiar trajectory of the McGillicutty career. The particulars aren't important. Just know that around this time a peculiar phenomenon arose, although you had to be paying close attention. A new TV show would premiere. Critics would declare it terrible and do so with near unanimity. Not just terrible the way every television show is necessarily terrible, terrible even within that framework. The show would quickly be canceled with nary an objection. Well, except for Internet message boards devoted to hearing-impaired television viewers. There a different kind of unanimity took hold. How could such-and-such network have canceled a show of such unmitigated brilliance? Fine, the actors were nothing special, it was photographed as if underwater, the ratings were putrid.

But, my God, the writing.

MECHANICS' INSTITUTE LIBRARY
57 Post Street
San Francisco, CA 94104
(415) 393-0101

49

∣∣∣∣∣∣∣∣∣

People v. William Boyd 911 Transcript

(Sounds of sobbing, at this early stage it is difficult to tell if there is any quality of fear in the sobs or if it is just pure misery)

911: 9-1-1, Operator Seaborg, what is your emergency? Hello?

Linda Evers: Yes, police please. Police?

911: This is 911, ma'am. What's the nature of your emergency?

LE: Oh my God.

911: Ma'am?

LE: Oh my God.

911: The emergency please.

LE: Yes, it is.

911: What is it, ma'am?

LE: It's an emergency.

911: *What's the emergency?*

LE: Oh (*this syllable is drawn out and sounds like . . . like the sound of something being emptied*).

911: Calm down, I can't dispatch help if you don't give me the information.

LE: Iguantabay (*unintelligible sobbing*) iguantabay.

911: Ma'am, I can't understand you while you're crying, okay? Please take a deep breath and tell me your location.

LE: 54, 54.

911: Fifty-fourth Street?

LE: No, 54! 54!

911: The number 54? What street?

LE: No, 54! 54!

911: What street?

LE: 54 Street, 54!

911: Okay, 54 and what?

LE: Just 54!

911: Fifty-four and what, ma'am? What are the cross streets?

LE: Hell's Kitchen, Hell's Kitchen! I'm in Hell—

911: What avenue? Ninth Avenue, Eighth Avenue?

LE: Nine, nine!

911: And, again, what is the nature of your emergency?

LE: Assault, assault. My daughter.

911: Your daughter assaulted you?

LE: Yes, my daughter.

911: Is there a weapon involved, ma'am?

LE: No, no weapon.

911: Any injuries, do you need an ambulance?

LE: Ambulance, yes, ambulance.

911: Where is your daughter now, ma'am?

LE: Ambulance, hurry!

911: Help is on its way, ma'am. This isn't slowing it down, I'm just getting more information. Where is your daughter now?

LE: She's in the apartment.

911: And what's the address?

LE: 54, West 54, I told you.

911: No, the precise address, like for mail.

LE: 315 West 54.

911: And what apartment, ma'am?

LE: 5B.

911: *B* as in boy?

LE: Yes, boy.

911: Okay, the police should be there any minute, just stay out of the apartment until they arrive.

LE: I'm in the apartment, where else am I?

911: You're inside right now? And it's that loud?

LE: I'm inside.

911: Ma'am, you just told me your daughter's still in the apartment. Why don't you step out and wait for the police in the hall or something?

LE: I can't leave her alone.

911: Why not?

LE: She's just a girl, she's too young.

911: What? How old is your daughter?

LE: She's seven (*loud scream, from daughter?*), hurry up!

911: You're not saying, are you saying she's the victim?

LE: Yes.

911: Your seven-year-old daughter was assaulted?

LE: Yes, yes.

911: By who? Who assaulted her?

LE: Her fa—, my husband.

911: Where is he right now?

LE: Milwaukee.

911: Did you see the assault?

LE: Of course not!

911: What was the nature of the assault?

LE: What do you mean?

911: Spanking? Slap?

LE: (*silence*)

911: A slap?

LE: (*silence*)

911: Sexual?

LE: Yes.

911: Aw fu, uh, *first* tell me, uh, what you know. How did you become aware of this, ma'am?

LE: The blood, blood.

911: Blood where, ma'am?

LE: Underwear blood. Blood in the underwears. I asked her how and she told me. I didn't know.

911: Okay, ma'am? Ma'am? You're going to need to save that underwear.

LE: Oh my (*unintelligible*)!

(On further reflection, this last word might be *God*. The entire phrase might be an intended invocation of him, one that goes unanswered. Whatever the case, we can now definitively resolve the question we began with: there is no quality of fear present, it is pure misery.)

911: Ma'am, listen! The police are there, you have to buzz them in. Okay? Ma'am! I hear the buzzer, that's the police.

LE: Okay, they're here. Thank you.

911: Okay.

LE: Thank you.

911: Okay.

Recording Ends

"Sly" Sylvester "The Scarp" Scarpetti

48

||||||||||

A 911 operator ending a call has no great accompanying physical gesture, so it's only when Sharon's silence persists a few seconds more that Linda Ospina feels comfortable monopolizing her attention.

"You break yet? New coffee place on Hester, half off all week, and without it I'm not getting through these last two hours."

"Linda."

"C'mon, check out."

"Linda."

"Yeah, me Linda, you Sharon, now let's go get that fitty-off coffee."

Linda is tilting her body away from their pod (the calls are fielded from within a large open area with many cubicles with four operators per *pod*, making these two longtime podmates along with two other operators who are not herein relevant) and towards the hallway that leads out, but the tilting, no matter how acute it gets, is eliciting no reaction.

"Sharon, dear?"

"Linda, that was it, I can't do any more. I just can't."

"What's wrong? Do you need to dispatch?"

"No, they're there. I was supposed to ask her to put them on, I'm just off today. No, I'm just done, no more."

"Come on, let's go. Bad calls are part of it. That's what coffee was invented for, especially after I sneak a little something-something in there for you, babe."

"Done."

"Oh, mami, here, sorry. Take them, best tissues around. Javy takes them from the hotel, one of the few things he's good for, the dog fuck."

"I'm not saying I'm done the way people be saying. I mean that I can never do another call, swear."

"Lower it, mami. We're gonna draw a crowd and that bitch Hollins is already on the war path, you know you don't need a be giving her any excuse."

"That's how I know I'm done, you know? Because this bitch who tortures us means nothing to me right now. All these fantasies of how I would quit and now I don't even care about *how* just as long as I never have to pick up again as long as I live."

"Honey, you have to pick up right now as a matter of fact. See? Hear that?"

"I will not, ever again."

"Hon?"

"I will not."

"Look out, mami. And keep it down, give here. *9-1-1, what's the nature of your emergency? Sir . . . okay, that's not an emergency . . . I understand . . . call 311 for that, to report it . . . sir? . . . has there been an accident? A fatality? Bloodshed of any kind? Then there's no pothole that means you call 911 . . . call 311 . . . or better yet shove . . . call 311, sir . . . pleasure serving you . . . thank you.* See? Just an idiot. They're mostly idiots, easy peasy lemon squeezy, right?"

"Yeah, what is? What?"

"The call. Idiot about a pothole, my God, the stupidity."

"What call?"

"Baby, I just took a call for you. What's going on, you okay?"

"I'm fine, actually. Best I've felt in a long time."

"You don't look it."

"I feel free. Free knowing I'm never going to take another call again."

"Okay, let's start there, Sharon. Why are you never going to take another call again?"

"As long as I live."

"As long as you live."

"Ever."

"Why, Sharon?"

"Why? You know better than anyone *why*. Why, she says. Why do people do what they do?"

"Oh, don't go there, girlfriend."

"Why do people cut each other's faces up?"

"I'm telling you, don't."

"Like they carving jack-o'-lanterns on Halloween."

"We're doing this, then?"

"When they're not throwing acid on each other."

"Sharon."

"Or sticking their dick in their seven-year-old daughter's ass."

"Okay, I get it now. Look, people are shit, the ones that aren't idiots like pothole guy. But . . . well?"

"Told you, I'm never taking another one."

"*Dios mio*, Sharon!"

"Don't give me that Español shit, girl. I don't know what you're saying but I know I ain't picking up anymore."

"Fine, here, now you're on break whether you like it or not. I know you're upset."

"I'm not upset at all, Lin. From now on people can stab each other in the eyes hourly for all I care, won't be any of my damn business. Live and let kill. That pot of boiling water just tipped onto a two-year-old? Good luck with that. Car on fire with two kids in mangled car seats? Sorry for your loss. Best part is, I won't even know about these things. The chaos, the tears, the pain, screaming, agony, the begging. Doesn't it all weigh on you?"

"Yes, but—"

"Don't you hear it all even when you're not here?"

"No, I don't."

"I do, but I'm not going to listen anymore is what it is. It's all going to disappear, you can't understand the joy I feel right now."

"You're still upset about Hugh, that's what this is. Maybe?"

"Oh, Linda. It's everything. Every. Thing."

"I get it, baby, but also be realistic."

"Realism? I've had my fill of the shit. Seven years old, fuck off."

"I understand."

"No you don't."

"Hey, Sharon, stop. Look at me. *I* understand, right? It's me, remember who you're talking to here."

"Then how can you try to stop me? You know when you just look at a thing and just know it's done? That's this, it is stone-cold over, girlfriend. I *cannot* take another call."

"Okay, so you'll start looking for another job. In the meantime—"

"No, it has to be right now. No more bullets, knives, razors. No more goddamn dicks."

"You know what else no more? No more paychecks. You aware of that?"

"Money is no object."

"Oh really, Mrs. Vanderbilt? I didn't realize, quit away then. Money is no object, wow."

"It's no object because I have none."

"Ah, I see. Let me ask you, honey, and no offense because you know I love you. But haven't you and I had multiple conversations where we tried to fix the exact moment our paychecks would go in so we could time the payment of one or more bills?"

"Hmm."

"Sooo?"

"So it's been a pleasure working with you."

"Yes, I'll miss you terribly. Let's definitely keep in touch, definitely let me know what homeless shelter you end up at. It'll have to be a family one, of course. You can probably hock everything you and Donnie own to get it down to a laundry bag or two, you know, make it easier to move between shelters. At least until Hugh goes to court and gets full custody. I'm not trying to be harsh—"

"Hate to hear you if you were, bitch."

"—but that's as real as realism gets. And there you go, right on time. Break over, pick up. Pick up, Sharon."

"I can't."

"Pick up, hon. You have to, I'm right here."

"I just, I can't."

"Pick up, it's a cat in a tree, a missing iPhone, no blood."

"No it isn't, those sound different. It's a sliced-off ear, a blinded eye, a missing preschooler, and I ain't even trying to hear that shit right now, Linda."

"You're wrong, it's a stupid missing hamster. And if it isn't it's those school shoes Donnie needs that you've been pretending to forget or it's a fridge that doesn't leak on your floor."

"Oh my God, do you hear that? Each ring is like a shriek from hell."

"Pick up, baby. It's okay, I'm right here. Pick up. Pick up. Pick up. Pick up. Sharon?"

47

|||||||||

People v. William Boyd 911 Transcript Continued *

* The following has been transcribed out of an excess of professionalism on the part of The Scarp as The Scarp's strong suspicion is that the
subject audio was included in error by One Police Plaza when responding to the DA Request on *People v. Boyd*.

    911: 9-1-1, Operator Seaborg, your emergency?
Caller: An ambulance, please. We need an ambulance, hurry.

    911: Sir, without telling me what happened, where do you need the
          ambulance to?
Caller: This guy, he just—

    911: The address only, please.
Caller: Oh, 100 Centre Street I guess.

    911: 100 Centre Street? The criminal court?
Caller: Yes, Part F, what is it? Oh, second floor, Part F, in the court-
          room, hurry!

    911: Sir, every courtroom is full of court officers with expedited
          access to EMS and, here, I see that it's already been called in.
Caller: Oh, they're here! Thanks, you're amazing.

911: I had nothing—

Caller: Is there a way for me to stay on and complete a survey or something about how good you were? I've never seen a quicker response.

911: The court officers—

Caller: I mean, kudos, really.

911: It was nothing.

Caller: Wow.

911: Literally. Goodbye.

Recording Ends
"Slypetti"

46

||||||||||

"What's the commotion out there, Counselor?" asks Nuno.

The commotion is that an attorney has collapsed in the well of Part F, collapsed into almost instantaneous nonexistence. But everyone in charge knew what needed doing in that situation, which was to pretend the issue was still being contested, get EMS there as quickly as possible that they may preserve that illusion, then step aside as they rush the empty body to the nearest hospital qualified to make it all (death) official.

One of the lesser effects of this collapse was that the three or four attorneys that were in the pens behind that courtroom at the time were kind of asked to stay put until EMS was done and some, like, most relevantly, Ed Coin Esq., were done discussing pertinent matters with their clients and now had to *fill*, as it were, with people who aren't generally known as superior conversationalists.

"I gather someone fainted or something," Ed Coin responds.

"Listen, if you're going to be saying things like *I gather* the whole time you represent me, let me know now so I can ask for a new attorney."

"Noted, but I can't promise anything."

"Shit, man. You're so big on my making sure I don't think you've promised anything. Not the kind of thing that breeds great confidence you know."

"That's the idea."

"Just get me off remand and all's copacetic, Counselor."

"Man, DeAngeles, uh, Nuno, that remand really offends you. What did you expect?"

"It's not about offense. Well, yeah, it does offend me, as a civil libertarian."

"As a what?"

"Shit, until recently in Jersey, remand was straight-up unconstitutional. Yet you NY jokers constantly blowing smoke up each other's asses about how liberal you are."

"So, fine, the judge sets ten million, then what? In is *in* regardless of how it comes about, right?"

"Wrong as wrong gets, Coin. First, they got all kinds of onerous rules in here for those of us oppressed by remand status. They're fucking with my library access and shit. Answer me this, what kind of fucking philistine thumbs am I under that would alienate a man's goddamn inalienable right to read?"

"I don't think that's a thing."

"Speaking of which, you get those books we talked about? That I talked about and you listened?"

"Books?"

"Musil? Sabato? In the original German and Spanish like we agreed because translations are for pussies?"

"Oh shit, I completely forgot."

"Who forgets something like that?"

"Sorry."

"No, I mean that literally, Counselor. I'm curious how something like that gets forgotten. Look where I am, man, I'm starved for illumination."

"Okay, I guess I just had no context for the request. I had never heard of either of those things."

"Whoa, hold up, walk it back a bit. You'd never heard of *Man Without Qualities* or *The Tunnel*? Or is it you'd never heard of someone so severely downing translations, or maybe an inmate asking his lawyer for novels, which is it?"

"Never heard of any of it, at all."

"Oh, fuck. Whose hands am I in? You have a law degree, at least you better, right?"

"Yeah, a law degree, not a lit doctor, uh, literature doctor, doctorate in literature."

"Except we're talking about Mu— How about this, who *do* you read?"

"No one specific, really. If a book is out that garners a bit of—"

"Fiction, novels!"

"I don't really read novels."

Nuno stares straight ahead, expressionless.

"I want you to know how dire I now think my situation is. Because a man who doesn't read novels can never be a real man."

"Godfather!"

"See what I mean? That why you don't read novels, Coin? Too busy watching fucking movies? Let me ask you a question, Counselor. Why do you suppose we say about dumb people that you need to draw them a picture?"

"Fine, you love books."

"Books?"

"Let me submit to you that my relative proficiency in the literary arts will have precious little to do with my legal representation of you and whether it is ultimately successful or not."

"All right then. I disagree completely, but pretending you're right let's review that representation thus far. It's been six days. Less time than it took your God to create this entire mess."

"My God?"

"What's the first thing I said to you when we met? All I asked, keep me off remand. Did I bother you with a bunch of illogical whining like the rest of your clients? One request, no remand."

"Given the nature of the charges—"

"We saw how that went. Then I throw in an easy request for two books any mildly educated adult should be highly conversant with and you deliver not at all. Now today I say quick get this judge to remove the remand before I'm indicted and criminal court loses jurisdiction and you hit me with this they won't bring me out and call the case until they have an answer on this indictment business. Let me say, Coin, that this is the kind of thing causes people to lose faith in our good old criminal justice system here. Because this isn't a statute or something, corrupt as that shit is already. No, you're saying this is something like standard practice no doubt invented by some august jurisprudential body like the court officers union."

"Probably right."

"Then you twist the knife a bit more with this whole there's a row of photographers out there and the judge says they can take my picture and our objection means nothing."

"I dislike it as much as you."

"So, tell me, when exactly do you start to *represent*, my man?"

"Uh."

"Easy, Coin. No need for the face. I'm a softy haven't you heard? Besides, I would harm the only friend I have?"

"Harm?"

"I know what you're thinking, we're not friends. I counter that with what else should I call an intrepid motherfucker like yourself who willingly steps between me and that evil anticolor machine out there that wants to keep me caged the balance of my natural life?"

"I guess."

"It's almost enough to make me overlook your legal inattention."

"I told you, at this stage—"

"But no more joking, man."

"I haven't joked."

"Open ears for this."

"Not once have I joked."

"First of all, I ain't going out there to get my goddamn picture taken. Good looking as I am, I don't need a bunch of fucking groupies I can't do anything about."

"Okay. I'll tell them I'm waiving your appearance when they call the case."

"No, fuck that. You do that and some of that front row of photographers will leave and move on with their day. I want those fucks wasting an entire day sitting there only to get no benefit out of it."

"And it will be all day, because you can be sure the DA is going to wait to the last minute before the part goes down to come in and grandstand by announcing you've been indicted."

"Yeah, I can almost hear the deflation now as they realize I won't be coming out to give them their agony of defeat image. Almost sad to miss it actually."

"That is funny, I must say. I approve."

"Back to the legal shit. Just to review. If I get indicted later today."

"A near certainty."

"That's not necessary. And said indictment is later dismissed with leave to re-present, then we can serve cross grand jury notice at that point and they have to allow me to testify before this new grand jury, correct?"

"Correct. But the chances—"

"Also, that there's no timeliness requirement with respect to 730 examinations."

"True, but why—"

"And lastly, that you have no lame personal policy against pro se motion practice, so that if the judge refused to accept one because I am represented by counsel you would simply adopt any such motion."

"Within reason."

"But beyond the bounds of *standard* reason."

"I never said *that*."

"You don't believe in being unreasonable?"

"I do not."

"Give it time."

"What's the point of all this, Nuno?"

"The point? Didn't know there had to be one, but okay. Point could be as simple as client relations, or *maintenance* if you prefer."

"What do you mean by that?"

"I mean that you've made it abundantly clear that you view our chances of scoring a complete and irrevocable legal victory let's say pessimistically."

"Okay."

"And I think you'll concede that that can be a grim realization to come to, especially for someone of my scant years."

"I believe we may be able to mitigate—"

"And yet you'll also agree that I have not taken out the grimness of my situation on you at all, which has had to be a pleasant surprise for you."

"Frankly, what—"

"However! Regard is a two-way street. I assume you'd rather deal extensively with a friend than an enemy but friends do favors for each other. So if, hypothetically, I were to say, *Hey man, file this motion for me.* Or maybe even *Would you mind terribly moving for a 730 examination?* That's the kind of thing friends do for each other, don't you agree?"

"Maybe, but this is several mentions now of a potential 730. I think you must mean the putting forth of a psychiatric defense and the notice it requires."

"Absolutely not, I know precisely what I'm talking about."

"So, the question of mental fitness to proceed is a very narrow one. I certainly see no reason, no evidence at all, to request such an examination. I can't just frivolously—"

"Just a second. Note that I haven't asked you to request anything. What I did was pose a hypothetical under which some time in the future I would make such a request."

"Except it's a request I've never once gotten in twenty years. Why would a defendant calculatingly ask his lawyer to request such an examination? The truly unfit, in my experience, are the last to know it. What you're describing smacks of strategy and it would be improper of me to participate in such—"

"Easy, Clarence Darrow. I'm not asking you to do anything that goes against your delicate constitution. I'm posing a hypothetical, nothing more. I'm speculating, in a sense, about the kinds of actions that would cause me to label someone a friend. As opposed to labeling them something else, something less desirable, understand?"

"The thing is—"

"No, look at my eyes. Understand?"

"Yes."

"See? Besides you're not saying you're qualified to make the determination regarding mental fitness yourself, are you?"

"No."

"And even in your deeply unqualified state you would have to agree that the least fit part about me is my mentality, no?"

"Least fit?"

"I agree. So you could certainly envision a situation in which you might begin to suspect that I am, or more accurately *have become*, mentally unfit."

"I think I'm far more likely to conclude that you're the most mentally fit client I've ever had. Or anyone else has ever had for that matter."

"And how's *your* mental fitness, do you think?"

"Ha, pretty good I guess."

"Congratulations, now do a little thought experiment for me will you?"

"Depends."

"But really do it, man. I want you to make a real effort to mentally experience the fiction I'm about to create."

"Okay."

"You can't currently go back into the courtroom, right?"

"Well, I guess not. Something's going on out there and I've been asked to stay put, what of it?"

"Just this. Imagine that CO came back in here and all apologetically was all *Sorry, Counselor, but this is a very serious situation and you're going to have to remain in this area for three hours. You have our sincerest apologies.*"

"Three hours?"

"What's wrong?"

"No, just, *three hours*? In this little area?"

"What's the matter, Coin? It's just three hours."

"You're right, all right. I can do that."

"What do you mean *can*? Why hesitate like that?"

"Because it's going to suck, that's why. I get your point."

"What about it will suck?"

"What about it? Everything, really. I'm hungry, looking forward to lunch right now."

"We can get you a sandwich."

"Ugh, I mean . . ."

"It's okay, I don't make them. What else? Let's say we could get you real food, why not have it here?"

"Here? No, I mean, I want fresh air."

"Isn't it raining out?"

"I know but . . . I don't . . . I want to do whatever I want to do . . . not be constrained."

"Fair enough, let's continue. That same CO comes back three hours later and apologizes because turns out it's going to have to be overnight."

"*What?*"

"Oh, now I have your attention. What if he said a month? Take your time. Every day for a month. Not here, Rikers. You been there, you know what I mean."

"Uh-huh."

"You've felt, in a small sense, the spirit of that place."

"I think . . ."

"But I want you not to imagine your temporary presence there. I want you to imagine incarceration there without a safety net if that makes any sense. So, for example, it won't do to pretend that you, Ed Coin Esquire, have somehow been induced to spend thirty days on the island in exchange for some later reward. That kind of thing negates the psychology of this place, which, let me tell you, is the truly punitive aspect of it all."

"I get it, it sucks in there. The violence, the—"

"Violence? I fucking wish. You must mean the extreme boredom, so goddamn extreme I'm this close to detonating, man."

"Oh, don't do that."

"Easy for you to say, Coin. Out there in that Garden of Eden while me and my brothers atrophy in cages, seem fair? What've we done to be treated so disparately?"

"Well, don't make me state the obvious."

"Which obvious is that?"

"What . . . you did."

"What I did? You mean being in the wrong place at the wrong time, that *did*?"

"Sorry, forgot."

"Hell of a thing to forget. And by the way don't think my situation is all that uncommon either. This place has a fucking epidemic of wrong place at the wrong time."

"I've heard."

The ensuing mutual chuckle relaxes Coin somewhat but he still damn sure wishes they would hurry up and fix whatever the fuck's going on beyond that door so he can hurry up and get the hell out of there, a location whose sheer hellishness he has only then noticed, thanks DeAngeles, not that he could call him that since he has made it scarily clear that he does not abide being called by just his last name as if he were someone's property. And even this partial relaxation proves temporary because

"Anyway, Coin, all this discussion of hypothetical future favors has put me in mind of an actual present-tense favor I need."

"Namely?"

"I know your memory's for shit but can you remember all the way back to five days ago when you had the great fortune of picking up my case in arraignments?"

"Yes."

"Another guy must have come through that night. One of those pussies who's all *boo hoo my life, I need a constant stream of foreign agents in my body.*"

"I need a lot more than that."

"I know, here's the more. This. This gentleman. Drove in that state. Drove his piece-of-shit car into my—. Into a bus stop. He's all right of course, the driver, don't worry."

"I didn't get the case."

"I know you didn't. But one of your colleagues must have. And if there's one thing you lawyers love to do it's talk. And this case being highly susceptible to that activity, I'm guessing you heard about it."

"I seem to recall something of this now, what of it?"

"Nothing much. Just, what's the name of this feckless scamp?"

"Why?"

"Is that a first or last name?"

"Why do you want to know?"

"I always want to know, so much better than ignorance."

"Why do you want to know this person's name?"

"I don't know, guess you could say I'm a fan."

"I don't know his name."

"Figured, that's why this favor is more in the arena of research."

"Wouldn't really know where to begin."

"Another frightening thought, are you actively trying to unsettle me? We know this person's arrest number will be in the general vicinity of mine. Simply run a search of those numbers for the kind of VTL charge that results in funerals. Presto, the name."

"Then what?"

"Then you run that name in the inmate locator, kindly print out the page with his book and case number and precise location and mail said page to me, favor concluded. When can I expect that?"

"I think never, a lot of what you're saying concerns me a great deal."

"Let's do this then. Lend me your cell right now for about eight minutes."

"Cell? They don't let phones in here."

"What's that outline in your suit pocket?"

"That's where my phone *was*."

"And that?"

"This? This is a business card holder."

"A what? Holy, man, you may own the last one of those ever manufactured."

The sound of obdurate steel colliding with same.

Then, only slightly less shrilly: "Counselors, all clear! You are now free to move about the cabin."

And just in time for Edward Coin, who they don't pay enough, if you ask him, to deal with nuts like that.

45

||||||||||

The weirdness of New Jersey as a state is well settled and a big part of that is the amorphous indefinition of its middle. So whereas Northern New Jersey serves primarily as a suburb of iconic New York City with the result that it features its own significant cities, and whereas Southern New Jersey has the allure of the shore points, Atlantic City, and even Philly, Central New Jersey just *is*.

One thing you will find a lot of in the center is *manufactured housing communities*, which is what everyone involved has now agreed to call mobile-home parks. Also the misconception that the *mobile* always refers to the ability to move the home at will as with the classic trailer home when, quite often, the mobility referred to concerns the one move from the factory where the dwelling is built to the site where it is ultimately dropped. The owner of this *modular* home now owns his home no different than you, with the exception that he or she has avoided the major expense of home ownership, the land the structure sits on. It all sounds okay in theory but actual practice can feature a lot of dirty clotheslines, defunct propane grills, and orphaned car parts. Certainly true of the indefensibly named Oak Plains Mobile Homes Acres in Jackson, NJ.

Still, for someone from American Samoa, where the overwhelming majority of the land is communal acreage so that the purchase of real property can be highly complicated, the underlying DNA of these parks causes no great offense. Now, American Samoa is relevant here because it is a tiny geographic entity (55,000 pop.) that has somehow produced and continues to produce a, proportionally speaking, ridiculous number of NFL players. And this already remarkable incidence seems even more exaggerated by the fact that many of these players wear their copious hair in a highly distinctive manner that positively jumps off the screen.

Now Nina and Dia are moving through this Jackson modular home park but Dia has no clue why. Nina is looking around intently but without luck until she spots a young boy wearing a Jacksonville Jaguars jersey, its faded **43** only half visible under that hairstyle we're talking about.

"There's our man," Nina blurts.

"Where?"

"Ten o'clock."

"A.m. or p.m.?"

"What?"

"Oh, isn't he a little young?"

"Very funny, that's his son."

"How can you be so sure?"

"Precisely who else would be walking around in the jersey of a guy who had a cup of coffee with the goddamn Jacksonville Jaguars?"

"Okay, let's go."

"Ø"

"Nina?"

"What?"

"Let's talk to him, no?"

"No, of course not. I'm going to talk to some infant?"

"Infant? He's like eight!"

"Yeah, an infant."

"That's not what an infant is."

"Whatever it is, I'm not addressing it directly. We're going to sit right here and observe it subtly. From the little I know of parenting it will soon lead us to its father and it'll be mission accomplished shortly thereafter."

"Jesus Christ you're weird. Can I ask why all the cloak-and-dagger? Yesterday at a penitentiary, today the middle of nowhere. Isn't it generally known who the best players are? Why aren't we just scrolling down NFL rosters and deciding who we want? It's almost like you're more interested in proving that you're smarter than everyone else than in getting the best players for the Pork. Sorry."

"Silly girl. First, I could scarcely think of anything that requires less proof. Okay, let's try it your way. We're here to get a strong safety. You say we should go back to the office and just pick a current NFLer. So who do you want?"

"I don't know, Earl Thomas, Byrd, Ward?"

"Oh really? Guys with NFL contracts that pay them half mil a game?"

"I know, but those contracts aren't currently in effect. They're in work stoppage, right? Can't we guarantee them a certain significant amount of money then just throw in a clause that if the NFL resumes our contract automatically becomes null and void and they can go back to making much more?"

"Legally, yes. Problem is contracts need to be signed in reality and in that place no one like that will sign."

"Why not, though? Is *some* money no longer better than zero money?"

"What do you think the NFL is, Dia?"

"What I think it is? A professional sports league, what else?"

"A lot else."

"Huh?"

"True enough that it's a league, but it's a league unlike any other in the world. So much so that it's more like a shadowy cabal really."

"Oh come on! What are you talking about?"

"What part?"

"All of it, start with you saying it's like no other league. What about the NBA, NHL, et cetera?"

"Okay, in terms of revenue and popularity, the NFL isn't far off from being the equal of those two *and* the MLB combined. Start with the money, which, in case you didn't know, is pretty much where you start with everything. Ten billion in yearly revenue that they'll admit to. Even more significantly, the NFL is the only game in town in a way those other leagues aren't. Realize that with the slight exception of Canada, no other place in the world has the slightest interest in playing this stupid sport. Contrast that to soccer or basketball, hockey and baseball for that matter. Think of being a human with this very specific skill set. You can execute at a high level only a very specific series of motor tasks that have relevance in exactly one country and is valued by precisely one employer."

"True of any sport, right?"

"No. If you're a basketball player you almost certainly want to play in the NBA but guess what? If it doesn't work out, you can always go play in Greece, Italy, Spain, Turkey, China! Go try and make a living playing American football in China. Japanese baseball, Russian hockey, every other sport offers global opportunities to its specialists."

"So what's the significance of that?"

"Power. Power to go with the money, power because of the money, money because of the power, who can tell anymore? Bottom line is the Earl Thomases of the world end up needing the NFL a hell of a lot more than the other way around."

"Fine, but where does the cabal come in?"

"It comes in when absolute power does what it does. Throw in an antitrust exemption, tax-exempt and nonprofit status that was granted in 1942 but now no one including the IRS can find the original application, an outsize cultural cache, mostly due to its suitability to gambling, that functions as a license to steal from local government tax bases and the NFL starts to seem almost magnanimous when all it does is something like lie about concussions for decades while backed by studies it paid good money for."

"Gross, ill."

"Believe me, there's a lot more where that came from. I know, I was there."

"That's terrible."

"Who do you think owns these teams, anyway? Better stated, how do you think you get to the point where you can afford one?"

"But what's the significance of that to us?"

"You're seeing the significance. No prominent NFL player, no agent really, is going to do anything that risks pissing off the douches who sign those heavy checks."

"But in previous work stoppages haven't players crossed the picket line and played, which is certainly worse than what we're asking them to do?"

"That was an antiunion move and their union's a joke. Remember, this is a lockout, not a strike. The players can't play in the NFL because there is currently no NFL to play in."

"Exactly, there is no NFL! They're worried about an entity that willingly closed up shop."

"Ah, but they know it's temporary and the tight control will be back in a blink."

"So what do we do?"

"We do what we're doing. Pursue players the NFL can't menace with loss of future income, either because they're all but done or because they were already out of the league for whatever reason."

"But that's a lot of star players too, right? Guys with star quality but nearing the end so maybe happy with one last score."

"Yes and no. A lot of stars want to broadcast, at least they want the paycheck that comes with it."

"That's up to the networks, though, not the league."

"Same difference."

"Too cynical."

"This prick has to be the only kid in history who stays put in one spot."

"What category is his father in? That the league can't control him?"

"Ah, Mutola. Scumbag Jacksonville cost me what would've been one of the all-time great draft picks. I had it all lined up for the 2007 fourth round, never forget it. Couple years before, another team, to their credit, had moved up in the first to draft a similar player and now this guy was revolutionizing the position. I wanted my own but also wanted to outdo them by not having to pay mine first-round money. Anyway, the guy I found was a pretty obscure American Samoan, and the more I dug the more I liked. He wasn't even invited to the combine but we worked him out privately and his change of direction was literally unprecedented. Beyond the physical he was a football savant, talking to him it was as if he were capable of coordinating an NFL defense right there at age twenty-two. Sweet guy too, with a baby boy he doted on."

"Whom I assume we're currently stalking."

"Likely."

"So what happened?"

"What happened is two picks before I can grab Manu Mutola, strong safety, out of, ugh, two picks before, Jacksonville picks him. Give me a break, a laughable organization like that? They must have had a mole in our office."

"A what?"

"Laugh all you want, I'll go to my grave thinking it."

"What did you do?"

"What could I do? I tried to trade for him but by then they had seen him play at their OTAs and knew what they had, knew what I had unearthed, the scum. Anyway, I watch their first preseason all-twenty-two, and there it was, plain as day so even your typical NFL scout couldn't miss it. A Hall of Fame safety prospect. The learned anticipation, the barbaric physicality, the kind of blurry acceleration makes you think the film's been sped up."

"Great."

"Yeah, until the next preseason game, when a three-hundred-pound oaf falls on Mutola's leg and just detonates his knee. I mean far beyond your usual torn ACL too, peroneal nerve damage, drop foot."

"Oh no."

"It was hideous. And the worst part? He hadn't been paid. Fourth round picks get shit and even that's not guaranteed."

"What did he do?"

"What I knew he would. Worked his ass off and got healthy, although it took every bit of three years since he had to do it on his own after Jacksonville predictably cut him. We sent a camp invite, he accepted but then his kid got sick. From there he connected with this lawyer who felt the Jacksonville training staff had botched Mutola's treatment then acted unscrupulously. This lawyer was absolutely correct, incidentally, but see where that gets you in life. Whatever the case, he fell off the face of the earth, at least until you found him, nice by the way."

"Wow."

"So that."

"This is going to be great then."

"This fucking kid."

"Oh joy."

"What's the smile for?"

"I'm just having so much fun watching your internal struggle. You look like you may literally combust any second."

"Talking about?"

"You clearly would rather die than talk to that child but at the same time having to actually wait for something you want is murder for you."

"It might be troubling me."

"Oh, it is!"

"So . . . do we have to, like, nap the kid?"

"As in kidnapping?"

"Should we?"

"Are you insane, Nina? Just ask him where his father is."

"So the father's location is akin to a ransom?"

"No, not at all, not akin."

"Okay, I got this. Look out, let me do all the talking."

"Just please keep it nonactionable."

Led by Nina, they walk over to the mini Mutola, who seems engrossed by mere existence. Nina recalls once reading something about matching their eye levels or some such nonsense so she kneels before this kid but taking care to suspend her knees above what has to be the dirtiest dirt ever, only the skirt she's wearing is nowhere near conducive to this activity so it rides up almost violently so that she is essentially flashing the kid now. Luckily for everyone involved the kid is about a month away from this kind of thing being the highlight of his year and the profanity goes largely unnoticed.

"You like Mutola?" Nina finally stammers out.

"He doesn't play anymore."

"I know but he was the best safety I ever saw back when he was playing."

"He's my father!"

"Really? Man, that makes you a very lucky kid."

Nina hasn't really thought through how to proceed from there and when she looks up at Dia the millennial has chosen to willfully endanger her employment if not her life by pointedly ignoring her. But reprieves are fun when they're well timed and just then a curious man appears, curious about what this astonishing woman is discussing with his son. The man has the same hairstyle but on him it looks like a wig jokingly placed atop a granite statue. He eyes Nina suspiciously. Nina notices him and is mostly just relieved she can stand.

"Mr. Mutola? Manu Mutola?"

"You're from the bank."

"God no! You would make such an accusation in this public square as it were?" Now Nina begins to speak to Mutola in Samoan while Dia is making all sorts of what-the-fuck faces. The gist of the Samoan is that Nina is aware of the bank issue and is going to make it all go away for him regardless of what his answer is to her proposal.

"What is this?" asks Mutola, who at this point frankly prefers English and whose body language signals quite skillfully not only that his wife has joined them but also that she don't know from no bank.

"I need your help, Mr. Mutola." She chin-acknowledges Mrs. M.

"Help doing what?"

"Winning a championship in the Indoor Football League with the team I own, the illustrious flagship Paterson squad."

"You're the crazy woman from TV press conference!" The wife. "Yeah, you like to pork!"

"See? What better endorsement than that? When can you start?"

"Start what?"

"Start playing football for the thing with the Paterson for the team and the championship and when can you start?"

"I can't, *don't*, play football anymore. My leg."

"Yeah, I saw that. Well, the whole country saw it and in graphic detail, but that was a long time ago, you're better now. Time to do what you do, football, better than anyone I ever saw at your position."

"I can't—"

"Or you can continue listening to your lawyers, who say not even attempting a comeback makes your case stronger for an eventual injury settlement with the NFL, what, ten years from now? Because they can tie you up for years and they will. You doubt me? You see how they blackballed you, don't you? Thirty-two teams and not one of them interested in even taking a flyer on goddamn Manu Mutola? That make any sense? Maybe not playing was the safe move but that was before. No one was going to let you play unless you settled, and if you did play and weren't the same it could cost you plenty. You had no real options. But I think you can still play and I'm a great option. See the nice smile? Seven figures *guaranteed* for one season. To do what you love and what I love to watch you do."

Now it's wife Genie Mutola's turn to display her far more fluid Samoan and Nina chooses not to try and follow but instead just fish out contract and pen from her bag, which contract Mutola stares at when Genie's finally done, but mostly he's looking at the bolded number in the center and it doesn't seem real it's so heaven-sent. The woman holding it may be the most beautiful woman in the world.

"Let's stop talking," he says even though no one was. "I need to rest."

"Rest?"

"I have work tomorrow."

44

|||||||||

All that was goddamn Northeast American February winter. No one likes that temporal stretch. People mostly just tolerate it and end up actually *living* less if that kind of thing is possible. They leave the house, true, but almost involuntarily. They have to, there's no money inside and there's at least some in the gray and cold outside. But first chance they get it's back indoors.

A form of death. Grass looks and feels like dirt on pavement. Trees like misshapen wire hangers burrowing into the monochromatic ground. The air too, doling out the bare minimum to sustain life while inertly refusing to dance. Death. And like death in all forms it drives introspection. Introspection, inspection, speculation. So little natural light to foster their enemy—mindless physical activity. It's a wonder anything mental ever gets accomplished in those places without true winter. Come to think of it, little does. Whether this is a salutary truth depends on how much you value the mental life. Because elements like isolation may better conduct a mental charge but they can also unduly wear on more vital human needs.

Given all that, the typical human reaction to spring may be, just maybe, excusable. Everyone loves it. But the thing about humans is they tend to mentally conjure up a stereotypical ideal/idealized stereotype when they hear something like *spring*. So a lot of bees hovering over blooming flowers and tall grass swaying in the warm wind beneath an inflamed sun. And color, color everywhere.

But at the same time the logical part of us recognizes that you don't go from dead gray air to *that* instantaneously. That must mean there's a kind of season between seasons. A time that's not as lifelessly gray but neither is it bursting with color. Whenever Nelson de Cervantes reasserts that he hates spring and always has, it's this nebulous time period he pictures.

So every year around this time when Nelson feels that sudden generalized anxiety and palpable distress he seeks to distill its source. Is it the weird light? The way it reflects off everything that's inevitably wet? The temperatures that won't fall firmly into any category the way he sometimes can't tell if he's grieving in Spanish or in English? The fact that everyone else seems possessed by a mounting excitement?

That last one maybe. Anything that makes his otherness seem even more pronounced. All he knows is how he feels, who cares the cause? The world is ugly with everything in it out to harm him. Looking for the cause is tacit acknowledgment that he doesn't normally feel this way but what if the way he normally feels constitutes the mistaken impression? In other words, the explanation for why he feels the world is ugly and everything in it is out to harm him is that the world is ugly and everything in it is out to harm him. A truth revealed to him only once a year at this time, the rest an admittedly useful delusion. What matters to Nelson is not how he feels or *why* but the underlying truth of it all.

Strange truth is his spring problem has never been less relevant. This time he has every right to be anxious. Yet he's fixating on the anxiety like it's all kinds of inexplicable.

Just that everything around him could maybe best be described as dissolving. His immediate physical surroundings, for example. Take his room. Someone feeling like Nelson wants distraction. Those three or four almost autonomic activities that shine enough to mask the surrounding dullness. Problem is everywhere Nelson looks he sees a transience he cannot build back into permanence.

This is not merely metaphoric, it's dispiritingly literal. Because, fact is, they were moving when it happened. A lot of stuff had been boxed up or moved out of place. This is the kind of thing that would normally have been a stressor for him but the excitement in the air, he'd often pulled up the new house on his laptop to preplan his decorative moves, was ample compensation. Excitement notwithstanding, the result in the apartment had been a kind of deflation. The fundamental truth that physical objects are inert and lifeless doesn't account for the fact that humans can essentially animate them through the mental transfer of energy.

Think of the bed or other furniture in a home. Then think of what little animalistic creatures we sometimes are, just seeking out certain specific sensory inputs we know from past experience will provide comfort. Well, once it was established that the de Cervanteses would be leaving that apartment in favor of a home they (Jorge) had purchased, from that moment forward, Nelson, for one, stopped the flow of that energy until the place started to feel more like a poor painting than his three-dimensional world.

That was all before that phone call, though. Since then it's been a progression of audibled-into defeats; including, incredibly, the news that Nelson's very elderly grandmother in Colombia, Jorge's mother, had also coincidentally died around the same time as her son.

So unbox everything because we can't move into that house. That list of prospective high schools is basically one now. Those times don't work anymore because Celia de Cervantes has a longer work schedule. Everything so debased. Is this supposed to be what *sense of loss* feels like? Because it just seems like extreme immanent anger, no real need to have created this little stock phrase.

And goddamn spring now to boot.

He should just close his eyes until summer, which he does like. Then he won't be walking into that teeming building and sensing pity, the continual recurrence of certain weirdly shallow phrases. No guidance counselors to pull him out of class with maximal drama to see how he's doing and when he says *doing what?* taking way too long to get it. By summer people may still talk about him in whispered tones as if he weren't there but chances are he won't care. Because already he feels himself caring about fewer and fewer things, things like his searchable-to-the-decimal GPA that once seemed paramount but now seems silly.

Probably everything is like that. Probably everything has only illusory importance. Today a GPA, tomorrow the whole bullshit adult edifice: your salary, your title, your country, your heritage. What *tomorrow*? He knows it *today*. These things people invent. They work, only don't look too deeply.

What's with all the self-reflection, anyway? His spring hang-up is like the color of his eyes. And if nothing matters or *means*, that includes the application on his bed and, more specifically, its request for a personal essay that will allegedly help them decide who goes from prospective student to actualized one.

But even if senseless on a molecular level, the wave of life is so powerfully unrelenting and tidal that just floating is indistinguishable from drowning and whatever it turns out life is he still intends to do it better than anyone else, if only on principle, and that would seem to exclude just passively going under. That means things like that application. Easy to say fuck it, except seven months later you're either walking into the kind of place that requires a six-page application or the kind that employs metal detectors.

So he'll write the dumb words. But it doesn't take long before the first impediment emerges and it's enough to freeze him into solid inaction: do these kinds of essays get titles?

This is what he does when he has a mental task and can't get started. He cleans or organizes. So the stuff in the boxes needs to go back whence it came and that includes the air conditioner box with the red LIBROS scrawled on it by his father.

Damn thing is packed as if it contained fissile material. What follows is an epic struggle to free its contents that would be highly mortifying were anyone else in the house but is instead just a severe personal embarrassment that only dissipates slightly once his increasingly savage set of maneuvers finally manages to dislodge a lone book from that debased conflagration of corrugated cardboard.

The initial sight of a book is always a magical thing, though. In this case Stonehenge and the *shocking* role we (the back cover) now know aliens must have played in its creation. Freeing the rest reveals a lot more newly discovered evidence in this vein. Lots of aliens paternalistically intervening in the affairs of humans but also lots of biographies of humans who, at best, just met the biography-warranting threshold.

Suddenly bobbing to the surface of that conspiratorial and hagiographical sea is yet another in the infinite-seeming line of rendered-in-support-of-literature depictions of a New England idyll. Nelson's default reaction to these is a kind of injured resentment, only this time he finds himself absently opening to a random page then sitting on the floor with a box as backrest then experiencing what seems like a non-violent yet complete extraction from space-time so that when, much later, the other residents of the apartment confront him with a request for information (what he's been up to) it feels like he's gone deaf and no one's thought enough of him to learn sign language.

Some dipshit had seen fit to organize the verse by supposed major themes like Life, Family, Renewal, that kind of nonsense. In Nelson's view this was a weakly embarrassing move that he grew to absolutely adore. So much so that he began to wish all existence came so neatly divided. An event would begin to unfold when suddenly a disembodied narrator would stentoriously announce: *the following falls under the category of Resilience.*

Categories aside, the work reminds him of something. More like it's the solution to something. See, weeks have been filled by a kind of search. Movies and music for him tended to later reduce into language, but since in both cases the language was not generally a priority, the reduction tended to expose some rather grim linguistic assertions.

This here was different. Language not as some subservient element but in its highest purity. Language indistinguishable from thought until the latter begins to seem impossible without the former. What an inversion too. Whereas before he needed to tolerate pedestrian language for the sake of compelling image and music, now the nature of the language is such (surprising vocab, heavy common meter) that it incredibly creates images and music that exceed in beauty and richness even what's found at the height of those disciplines.

That must mean that language is . . . not important right now. What *is* important is his realization that he can in some sense live inside these poems. These words arranged by a virtual shut-in, maybe he should shut himself in even more.

Days pass like this.

When he emerges from his dilatory excess the world is still there. Its call for an essay still on his bed, still unanswered.

But it's not true there's been no progress. The title question, for example. These things do indeed get titles. More like he's decided that when he writes one *he* gives it a title, which of course subsumes the determination that what controls in these situations is not standard practice so much as his individual whim. Still, because it's important to mark progress whenever made (he thinks, maybe), he decides he will sit and insert said title before sinking back into his morass of inactivity as a means of declaiming the legitimacy of such an approach. He sits and soon it's all

Emily Dickinson Is Saving My Life and I Can't Even Thank Her

Which feels good to write but also doesn't change the fact that outside his window and in the words of seemingly every corny radio personality *spring has sprung* and, ugh, spring.

43

||||||||||

On Rikers Island there are no seasons. It's called the Rock for a reason and one doesn't look for spectacular change in a rock. You could say the place is one of those spots on the globe with its own weather system.

Nuno's window doesn't open, so it becomes like a staid canvas forever displaying imperceptibly evolving variants of gray. No, gray's not right. What it is is the color of garbage. But not fresh garbage with its commerce-based soup of color. This is the color of the indefinite muck it later becomes.

This is not coincidence either. Because if you're wondering how a 90-acre island that was sold to the city in 1884 for $180,000 became today's 415-acre atrocity, the answer is garbage.

New York City's decision to build a jail on the island almost a century ago was a pivot that could have branched off in various directions. One could, for example, don't laugh, imagine a situation in which ensuing human evolution was such that the need for jails decreased drastically until this jail was closed and the island returned to its agrarian roots even to the point where it became a kind of revenue-generating botanical tourist attraction. That did not happen.

Instead, best way to look at it is through the lens of addiction. Because nothing better explains the subsequent explosion in incarceration that changed the nature of that island and so many other landmasses. But not the addiction of a human or humans to any substance. Rather the addiction of a particular segment of humanity to the capture and bondage of their fellow humans.

Main thing an addiction does is make sure it gets fed until it subtly redefines normal but the gluttonous feeding of this one required immense infrastructural support. So the one facility on the island needed to become ten separate razor-wired enclosures with the obvious question of where to put these ten and the surprising answer that you can nearly quintuple the size of an island by pouring and pouring garbage onto it so that it goes from island to giant landfill to whatever an island made primarily of landfill should be called.

People literally living on garbage. More than ten thousand of them at all times. *Garbage living on garbage* some CO says to Nuno after he casually relates this fact to him like some bullshit tour guide and it takes all Nuno's restraint to not drop him right then.

See, that's the underrated temptation of the place for someone like Nuno. It would seem his considerable violent tendencies would be easily subjugated at Rikers given the overwhelming show of CO force. But, truth is, to Nuno's thinking it's not overwhelming at all really. For example, absolutely no guns on the island. Makes sense, but also makes for an interesting contrast from his pre-Rikers life, where every other soft clown waves one around like he's posing for a movie poster, a bad movie.

Nuno's been shot, and little enough enjoyed the experience that he can be wary of only that during conflicts. Here there's none of that element. So when a CO like garbage-trivia guy purposely tests him it can be difficult to clam up. And that's all these fucks do too. Unarmed dudes who wouldn't normally dream of so much as looking at him crossly, constantly and aggressively in his face.

Part of it is they're in everyone's face, part of it is his suddenly pronounced notoriety, but *all* of it is due to the fact that, taken as a whole, corrections officers tend to really blur the line between being legitimate law enforcement and being actual criminals.

Nuno had heard this, knew it on an intellectual level; but actually living it is another matter. Living it is realizing that all of it, all the drugs, the slashings, the beatings, the gang bullshit, the pros(titution) stuff, all had a CO component to it. And there was more of that shit per square inch here than probably anywhere else in the world. He hadn't been taken off the street at all, he'd been sent to a hyper version of it.

Understand that this is not a complaint, though. Because of the many lucid islandcentric realizations relentlessly coursing through his mind, this one is actually providing comfort. Fact is, Nuno is more comfortable in a fallen world. That the COs are best viewed as simply the most successful gang around is perfectly reassuring. Humans jittering about like deprived rats in a lab in search of a productive angle? That's his element, not a problem.

What may be problematic though is another of his realizations. This is the realization that, despite all outward evidence, not every day spent on Rikers is the same. For example, his first couple days were spent in a large common room with countless beds full of other new inmates. He and these inmates were essentially being quarantined while the results of their tuberculosis and other medical tests came back. This was unpleasant, certainly, but so little resembled classic incarceration that a certain consolatory denial was able to set in. Then when he was transferred to a cell that *was* the height of incarcerative stereotype, even then he had the 180.80 court date in Part F to look forward to, which imbued those days with at least some hope.

The hope was irrational, true, but it's not like that island was some font of clinical reason. Bottom line was a procedure was in place that resulted in a substantial number of felony prisoners being released after six days, and as long as that was true those six days were always going to have a different ambient timbre than others. But the 180.80 date had come, he had not been released, and it had gone. Worse than that, the fundamental emptiness of that hope had rushed in on him with flood-like suddenness. The whole thing had disoriented him so that he'd not even asked after Dia that whole time with the nebbish lawyer.

Just as well. In his present condition, invocations of Dia cause more harm than good.

Point is since then the time's been turning hard. It is hard to abandon all questions of taste and pleasure to eat reluctantly and only for survival. It's hard to go from listening to a lot of music, and I mean *listening*, savoring notes and their combinations, having expectations mostly met but also thrilling at unexpected developments, to go from that to the habitual sound of dissonant clashing metals or, worse, the equally injurious sounds of the human voice not engaged in song or melody but in wrathful screaming or sobbing laments. Hard to accept that the air doesn't move and that it smells as if it were the noxious emission of all that poorly painted metal. Also, at the end of all that, what you lie on to sleep is so hard and narrow that the primary sensation becomes the anxious one of bouncing off and starting to fall. Visually, the backdrop to this lurching sleep is a toilet and that's one of the few things that just unproblematically fits.

Although, ultimately, it's not so much what you see as what you can't see, what you know continues to exist but are denied vision of. Start with women. There are no women on Rikers Island. No, not in a strict sense. There are female inmates of course, although they're steadfastly kept separate from the Nunos of that world at the Rose M. Singer Center. Also there are a great deal, maybe even a preponderance, of female corrections officers. What doesn't exist on the island is *women*. The way they walk. The sound of their voices. The little movements they make that are just *feminine* through and through with no other aspect or purpose.

All that had just disappeared as one moment surrendered to the next and, like always, you couldn't go back to the momentous transfer and change a solitary thing about it. And that's a component of the injury, no question. An immediacy that inappositely triggers a growing sense of intractability.

But the truest nature of this injury is of course absence and that is wholly consistent with another Nuno realization, that so much of the misery of being incarcerated is the largely mental process whereby one is coerced into recalling that one is in a state of incarceration, if that makes any sense. In other words, there's the direct, linearly derived pain of being incarcerated. This includes the abovementioned indignities like the taste of the food or the feel of the bed. Then there's this whole other category of hurt that can best be described as the pain of knowing you are in pain. It is psychological in nature so therefore invisible and as such not easily fixable in a particular location or process. It is, again, based on absence not causality so much. It is general, not specific, and as such invincible. It is by far the more problematic pain and it becomes the only one Nuno can't suppress.

So it happens over and over again while becoming no less toxic for its frequency. Because, believe it or not, there are many instances, usually while reading or near sleep, where Nuno can almost reach a state of perfectly deluded contentment of a kind indistinguishable from that of his recent past. Cruelly, this is when the metamisery most often and most severely kicks in. The sequence is not what you'd expect either. He does not suddenly remember he's in jail then feel it in his lungs. It's not that a mental image or realization forms and he then becomes physically symptomatic as a result, no. The inverse happens. Something that's like an electrified shadow almost casually darkens everything inside him and only when he looks for an explanation does he remember that he is in jail, that he has no liberty and can perhaps best be described as a kind of property.

Same with Dia memories. An infant laughs through numbing repetition at the peekaboo game because, lacking object permanence, it believes that what it has stopped seeing has ceased to exist entirely. But has Nuno been any better? Didn't he in a way come to believe that Dia had ceased to exist and his only evidence of that his failure to see her? Yet was ever anyone who passed through his tumult of a life more real? Has anyone else ever *existed* at that level? So powerful a presence that even only conjured in mere memory she seems more vivid than the great many motley assortments of fellow captives constantly posing inches from his face.

All that was true about her magnetism but also true that for years he'd given her next to no thought and this was a reality he would have found inconceivable back then. It made him feel like a savage, like he only attended to what was immediately pressing. Well, that image on the screen had certainly pressed into his mind and with utmost immediacy. Dia fucking Nouveau, fumbling at some weird lectern at an even weirder press conference. Yeah, that's what she looked like all right, how she sounded. But not past tense, man, she looks and sounds like that *now* and that fact was not only astounding in and of itself but also astounding because of some other facts it necessarily generated. Because if the world contains Dia Nouveau again this means that that part of the world is accessible to mere mortals like himself. And everyone today is constantly emitting integers and letters that fix their physical and mental location so he could probably easily locate her and work it so they would eventually gravitate into a shared space and forget it what the electricity would be like at that moment.

He could do that, yes, but this *could* refers to general principles of possibilia, it does not account for his very specific situation, in which he most certainly *cannot* do any such thing. This is the harshest reality to confront because of an underlying sameness. He cannot share a quiet room with Dia the same way he cannot impulsively decide to go to the corner Chinese where the guy knows his order the second the door chimes or drop into that Red Hook appointment-only bookstore with the tin ceiling and impossible congestion. And far worse than what he has to do and the limited number of things he can do is this infinite universe of *cannot*.

Back to Dia. There'd been no pain associated with not having seen her in maybe half a decade because he wasn't not seeing her up until the very moment he in fact saw her again and, worse, saw that she was still her. Since then is true pain, not just the theoretical sort. One of the weird things incarceration does to you, for example, is make you sad that you cannot go out and play a round of golf and this even though you have never held a golf club in your hand and always found anything related to the sport basically repulsive. This Dia thing is not that. With Dia it's superintense, hyperdetailed memories constantly detonating into little cinematic events he's compelled to witness. The past constantly intruding into the present and even though that present couldn't be darker the whole thing still manages to offend somehow. The emptier the present the more something like that happens too.

His present is empty, and he is being emptied all the way to empty to match it. He's less now. He is not the person who felt ridiculous in that *prestigious* Regis High School uniform, walked out for a quick drag, and from across the street saw Dia in her frankly obscenely alluring Marymount getup being of like mind with a burning stick in her fingers. So that he pretended not to have a light and crossed the street to request fire as if with prehistoric awe. He's also not the later guy who allowed himself to fall whole into her then said and did things that were more like referential citations to preexisting modes of human behavior in the well-trod arena of romantic love than like genuine creations (he was not then the artist he can be now and that had reduced him to mimicry).

Today he has clarity. To see Dia again but in the flesh. To recapture some of what existed before the whole elite scholarship at Regis thing predictably went to shit. This was the one good thing every life at least has. He'd sown chaos, true, but this one thing. Had watched the debasement of what little he'd held dear but still this one thing.

A purposeful goal, but lot of good that does when you need someone's permission to take a shit. So he gives in to the temptation to not think. If you're not thinking there's no Dia to pine after. The past and the future exist only in the world of thought yet they often powerfully poison the present. He can, through concerted inattention, approach existence as nothing more than a body.

He does this and at first it somewhat works. He talks to no one beyond the absolutely necessary. He focuses laser-like on just the physical components of his reality. Not its objective facts but rather its literal sensations. This goes on for days. The result is a kind of grounding of the mind so that in extremis, which he soon achieves, the mind essentially disappears and he becomes nothing more than a sensation register. First it is accurate to say that he is no longer Nuno but then it becomes more accurate to say that there is no *he* to make claims about.

As a coping strategy this is effective. It doesn't matter *where* this new kind of being exists the same way it doesn't really matter where a certain chair is located.

The escape is not total, of course. He's still compelled to in a sense *see* everything that happens to this body. But he does it without emotion or judgment. Just observations. Observation *in se* and observations about other sensations. This tack is aided by the fact that the sensations are uniformly deadening and sickeningly predictable. Woken up daily as if on a farm even though his tightening chest has already done a majority of the job. The walks where you can't fully extend your legs because of the bipedal chain that tugs on the exact same spot of the ankles with the exact same force. The same unnaturally sweet peanut butter and synthetic-tasting juice.

Where this weeks-long strategy falls apart is the day a randomly overheard piece of music pierces through all that. It's not even good music. The song is "Heart and Soul" but not one of the tolerable ones. This is the T'Pau one, whatever that means. And aesthetic judgments don't even seem applicable. Any more than it would be to ask after the specific qualities of the bell ring that made Pavlov's dog salivate. This is just sound, the specific notes and their arrangement, as mere stimulation and trigger. The *when* of the song, nothing else, is giving it primacy and suddenly yet gradually he is very much elsewhere.

It's important to note that he has not been *transported* anywhere as they say. Rather his entire surrounding world has been torn down and rebuilt.

And now he is in a yellowing apartment not all that much bigger than his current cell and his six-year-old eyes are voraciously absorbing every new detail as he's trying to figure out what went wrong with the previous place and people. That must be when he first heard that song.

Then much later (fifteen?) he has skillfully forced himself into a silver vintage Aston Martin and is driving it carefully so as not to draw attention. He takes it all the way to the extreme West Side until jumping out at the last possible second to watch those six figures drop into the Hudson River, bob a second, then pitch forward and sink like a torpedo seeking the center of the earth as a grave. The sudden proliferation of apologetic bubbles, bubbles that then start immediately and exponentially disappearing as in an extinction-level event. Almost touching, this desperate final stab at respiration from something without a soul. That song had played on the car radio.

But what had that been? What a senseless forfeit of hard-thieved money. Maybe his personal mess had suddenly seemed to him the work of inanimate privilege so that's what he'd struck out at.

Now he comes to realize it wasn't even really the T'Pau song that started his mental flight into these two pasts. It was just a snippet of it. The corny but effective intro riff had been spliced into a larger whole. This whole had innumerable such components that blended flowingly, like perfectly consonant ingredients that disappear in service of something new and greater. And the whole thing just went on and on without pause or loss of invention. It was an astonishing high-wire act that just kept working at a ridiculously high level. Just when the listener felt a dead end possibly coming on, some heretofore unsensed element of the extant music would flower without seam into another related but distinct bounty of compelling sound.

Nuno was rapt, then involuntarily analytical. The instrumentation was mostly rock, lots of pop, the vocals mostly hip-hop. It was as if the strengths of disparate mildly effective entities were being marshaled to erase all weakness. It was fun almost to the point of funny, the way all top-notch pop music is. But it was also weirdly touching in a way. If more than a thousand songs have been combined to create one inte-grated hour-plus song and that song is independently great doesn't that create a different import than usual? Here, finally, was humanity's song. The fact that, with the exception of one person, this was invol-untary and unknowing collaboration only heightened the effect. The sound of giants alongside grinders but now every barrier has dissolved and all speak with one tuneful voice. There have to be implications to something like this. If we can do this that means at least there's a *we*. This is like a soundtrack to the story of hope. Yes, Humanity's Song.

Who'd done this? But even more so, what exactly had the person done? After all, no wholly original music had been created or used. Was there even anything anywhere anyhow that was purely original? Logistically, how was it legal? Speaking of legalities, how is it exactly that they are free to listen to this right now where they were, where nothing was free, where he himself was unfree?

The jinx is a true phenomenon, don't let anyone argue otherwise. How else to explain the fact that just then the music cut abruptly off. Whatever multitudinous corrections violations had combined to fill the air with that electric noise suddenly crash-landed and the after-math was a lot of CO verbal recrimination. This was the true hidden meaning after all. It meant a human being could strive for whatever, could achieve whatever, but it will still one day all be abruptly shut down. And of course that went for humanity as a whole, which like-wise would one day cease to exist.

What did it all mean? That's just it, nothing. There was no meaning. A base animal that had a brief deluded dream of progressive knowledge. Someone said that. About people. Nietzsche? Someone should have said that. He succeeded in limiting himself to the animalistic for so long then all it took was a silly succession of notes to rip that all away. First, to take him back to an apartment he never wanted to see again then to fill his head with all sorts of underdeveloped thoughts that are more like emotions, but emotions with calculable truth value that almost suggest optimism, more of that dream of the deluded.

That's the trouble with music, its impotent power. It gives rise to all kinds of aspirational sensations but then it stops and there's nothing to show for it but inert deflation.

If you reduce yourself to a body almost anything can be borne. There's even a mechanism for it. Suffer enough physical pain and the body goes into shock, a highly effective avoidance. But where's the mental equivalent of that process?

Music temporarily snapped Nuno out of his body but his return means great suffering.

Humans create busywork, there's no progression.

He is never getting out. For the rest of his very long life he will be like an invisible master's pet. His plans (a prison break, an art heist) had more in common with fantasy or dreamy wish fulfillment than with achievable reality.

His life now has an extreme and fruitless predictability. He has miscalculated horribly and he is going to spend the rest of his natural life reliving this error. The desolation of this cannot be overstated.

There's only one way out of this infernal mess. Only one true inalienable freedom available to every human, even one as debased as him. He starts to see these potential solutions everywhere and even to spend an inordinate amount of time debating the various suicide options with a strong emphasis on the aesthetic considerations. He actually starts to put work into this.

The turning point is when he realizes that it's not really the purported goal, his death, that is ameliorating the terror so much as the moderate force being exerted towards it. That maybe it's just plain industry does the trick and if its moderate form can help what about its extreme form?

Also, the guy hasn't been born that can end him and that includes him so he'll attach that extreme industry to a more laudable goal. Here he can tie all his obsessions together with the neatest bow. He has access to the law library. He likes to research, loves to write. Loves. The weighing of each word. The music of the clauses. He will research and write a motion to dismiss that will be filed with the judge, who will then dismiss his case. He will be released. He will find Dia and unknown things will happen ever after but they will happen with her so their substance will have only secondary import.

Eventually it works. He writes and reads, thinks and reads and writes, rereading what he's written and rewriting what he's read, and the effect is a form of miracle. Because engaging in this activity is a way of losing location instead of just not caring about location. The world of the document has possibility and logical force and rhythm and cadence and his other worlds do not.

It also has an ending though. Fine, everything ends; but this one injures more than most. Because many weeks after starting he is staring and staring his hardest but still can't make dissatisfaction arise. There is nothing to add or change, at least not confidently, but whereas that would logically seem to augur a high degree of satisfaction, what instead fills Nuno is a profound feeling of loss. Part of this is just what attaches to all finality. But this effect is especially pronounced due to Nuno's special circumstances.

From the outset, the work had a genuine life-and-death quality to it. Think about a literary work undertaken in the literal pursuit of freedom, which is to say life. Because this wasn't the usual merely metaphoric death being combated, it was the actual form of death that incarceration creates. Throw in the extreme emotional resonance of creating the work on one's own and direct behalf. That said work fully taxed the abilities of the creator who was not, after all, an attorney. That Nuno had essentially eliminated any barrier between working on the motion and otherwise existing. Well, the excision of this process from his reality felt to Nuno like a complete evacuation from his body of all it meant to be human.

Crawling back to a three-dimensionally whole existence means attending to problematic entities like eternity or underlying truth or even meaning. In other words, it means collapsing into a state worse even than the one that prompted the motion in the first place, but this time without a ready lifesaver.

This is true agony. Screams not of protest or defiance, just mere markers of time and location. Silent because empty and felt only in the lungs of the screamer.

Despair births desperate acts. Someone can reject something from a position of power that they will later apologetically open themselves to in naked desperation. This is the third straight day that Nuno is staring at that list. He cups his hands then takes the pen at the end of the filthy rubber band. He has to genuflect a bit to get to the last empty line. It's all a giant game, fine, but he has calculated the outs and this is the last possible one. He prints his name on the line and it's disconcerting to him how similar his letters are to the ones in the names above him. More than that is just the humiliation of it all. He, Nuno fucking DeAngeles, has just genuinely signed up for quality time with the chaplain.

42

|||||||||

Father Simon Ventimiglia is going full rogue. Occasionally human development produces a rebel so contemptuous of convention and established practice that the very living of that rebel's life can be viewed as a form of defiant artistry. Today Ventimiglia joins their ranks. So while it is true that the breakfast bowl of oatmeal sitting in front of him on his yellow kitchen table is currently nearly indistinguishable from the five hundred or so consecutive such bowls that preceded it, all that's about to change. Because in his right hand's grasp is a viciously intense butter knife and it is time to end it. In his left is a denuded banana and it has no chance. With a trembling motion (the dissonance of what he is about to attempt is so extreme), he begins to slice away, knife repeatedly joining thumb, perfect Giotto circles that then ride gravity into the bowl and into various stages of impression on the oatmeal bed.

This adding banana to *spice up* his oatmeal is something he spotted on the YouTube but aside from the admitted thrill of reinvention he must say—mentally because there's no one else in the room—that it doesn't really add much cuisine-wise. He's just never been a big banana guy is all. Still, no one can deny that his just-consumed breakfast this morning has deviated from a strictly-adhered-to pattern and that has to have significance beyond the nutritive, right?

The explanation for the banana is just plain old dissatisfaction. Now, human dissatisfaction is of course endemic, but the problem here is that it is occurring in a context that happens to have an overwhelming expectation of satisfaction. This deepens the dissatisfaction so to speak by adding a layer of defeated surprise.

Because there is such a gap in Ventimiglia between what he knows intellectually and what he feels, it seems, unavoidably. His whole life he'd viewed *knowing* as some kind of protective seal. If he was first in his class he was also somehow least likely to suffer and he'd always had a great fear of suffering. And when he'd chosen theology at Notre Dame over so many other options that had to be a signal that he was in essence opting out of the great human game of life. If not, then his postgrad doc work in the field had definitively established that. But all that also had a certain ascensional quality to it.

Now there is no denying he is on the decline. The first sign had been how long he'd been content to remain a deacon. His whole life to then he'd always been a star but here he was almost relieved to be thought lesser. Deacons can marry he'd told himself but truth is he'd never had any great interest in the opposite sex, or the same sex, or really any form of sex for that matter. In a momentary relapse of ambition he'd taken this as a sign and successfully pursued ordination.

Of course the first thing Father Ventimiglia then noticed was women. He'd known humanity was split into these two main categories, sure, but there'd been nothing vital about that for him. Now, suddenly, he has a strong preference for one of the major categories over the other. He knows—naturally and better than most—that it's just what you can't have that becomes so alluring. Even so, has anyone else ever noticed how superior the female form is to just about anything else and certainly to the hairy, lumpy, and misshapen male one?

And is it his imagination or have women themselves changed their relationship to him since his newfound acquisition of status? To those who'd object *what status?* remember that, all questions of underlying veracity aside, a priest is still the rare person who commands something close to universal respect by mere virtue of his profession; although truth be told, today, increasingly, the admiration seems at least tinged with pity.

It's an earned emotion too. For example, he's been hearing that the numbers are *down* for so long that it's probably more accurate to not hint at fluidity anymore and just say they're low. In other words, the Catholic Church is not expecting a slew of reinforcements anytime soon. Far more likely is that he will be the last man standing, tasked with keeping the flickering light on against the invasive darkness. Pope Ventimiglia, sermonizing for his sole benefit yet still prohibited by dint of law from helping to propagate the species.

Until then, hearing *Father* et cetera was certainly good at first. At least until he started thinking about it, always with the thinking about things. Nothing was ever merely okay and then he thought about it and it became great. No, the process was like Time itself, it flowed in only one direction. The more he thought the more he lost. So he'd thought about the greater respect due a priest over a deacon and doing so had caused him to lose respect for himself as he realized how often those kinds of considerations had driven his decision making.

It was empty is what it was, this constant filling of a higher position. Just filler's precisely the way to look at it too. The positions (valedictorian, PhD, vicar) had realities that exceeded his own, then his specifics just served as the filling for these vessels. The titles themselves were in no way affected by his admission so maybe he shouldn't have been surprised when, time and again, the inertia flowed both ways and whatever title he'd been admitted into had only a minimal-at-best effect on him. He preached, literally, the fundamental illogic of concepts like prestige and authority but still any time one of these shiny candies entered his vicinity he eventually popped it into his mouth. Problem was how taste never matched appearance.

Here, appearance had promised little and delivered even less. For all the talk of a hundred and fifty years since breaking ground and landmark status the Cathedral of St. John the Baptist is still located, inextricably, in Paterson with all that entails. That Paterson meant no one clerical wanted to be stationed there and, in a wild fit of misprision, Ventimiglia thought he'd spotted consequent opportunity. His thinking was that talent rises faster in scarcity so it wouldn't be long before he was Rector Ventimiglia and with the diocese being named after Paterson and all it wouldn't be much longer before he'd ascend to . . .

The primary flaw with this thinking was the way it glossed over the significance of its first premise. Because *no one clerical wanted to be stationed in Paterson* was both premise and conclusion. More than that, it was, it turns out, an amply supported conclusion. So you had your usual blight-based reasons for not wanting to live in Paterson (these included an actual church that for all its purported historical mystique was in such disrepair that it began dropping ceiling tiles on its parishioners in 2010 and more than half a decade later had still not been reopened, so that services had to be conducted in a grim nearby gymnasium with a fifth of the capacity) but also there was a whole host of career-dead-end reasons. People have difficulty judging individual merit apart from ambient context. Paterson's atmosphere was failure and it was infectious. So if you exercised your profession therein it was assumed you yourself were a failure, one whose failings contributed to the contagion. Not for nothing did those who rose tend to come from leafy $uburban idylls and not from places where they wore out expressions like *not for nothing*.

Making matters worse was Ventimiglia's status as lowly new guy. It meant he was often subjected to a powerful new phenomenon in his life: third-party volunteering. This is where the larger entity you've been subsumed into is *invited* to expend effort on a purely voluntary basis. A dilemma then naturally arises due to the desirability of the desirable versus the nature of human effort. The solution comes when someone above you, maybe there is something to this status thing after all, volunteers *your* effort to *their* palpable credit.

This common practice had most affected Father Ventimiglia in two ways. The first was when the relevant bishop wondered aloud if a parish like St. John shouldn't offer the sacrament of confession more often than say its counterpart in Oradell. Didn't all numeric indicators imply that Paterson, for example, was like the literal seat of sin, meaning a citizenry with both a dire need of confessing and a profusion of subject matter per confession? The result was the assignation of one Simon Ventimiglia to hear confession daily at 5:30 p.m., unhappily the exact start time of the DVR-less officiant's favorite television program, *Extreme Sanitation: Another Man's Treasure*. The other occurred when the archbishop (!) this time, let slip that New York was no longer providing priests to serve as chaplains for Rikers Island because of safety concerns. What an opportunity, he casually added, for the Archdiocese of Newark to fill the void: but only, it should be said, by a priest already used to staring death down daily.

The logistics of this were onerous enough, days split between the island's various jails yet back in time to prepare to hear confessions; but far more taxing, Simon suspected, would be the psychological toll. Paterson was a mess, fine, but it was paradise compared to that Rikers inferno. The result was that by the time the latest Patersonite slid that screen over and began to vent it was often all he could do to remain awake (he'd never been a high-energy person).

And yet there *were* rewards. Not so much on Rikers, where the majority of the inmates and others he saw, even during just the preparatory stages as the official meetings hadn't yet commenced, seemed to delight in tormenting such a soft, out-of-touch target. But certainly in Paterson for Penance or Reconciliation. There he felt himself providing an actual human service and doing so daily. People needed to talk, they needed to talk to friends, but even more than that they needed to talk to themselves. Soliloquies needed to fill the air with cacophonous regret even if all that happened was those sounds merged with all the world's natural notes like dew into an ocean. Not so in his booth, which trapped the words into enough endurance that they could be overheard by their speaker—the inarguable center of any genuinely therapeutic stirrings.

Also, here his estrangement became, for once, an asset. People, strangers, spoke to him as if he were inanimate. Seemed being the new guy somehow made him less real to them and that meant a near-precipitous drop in the applicable amount of human shame. Or maybe that was just in his head and humanity had decided that there was nothing to be ashamed of after all.

Whatever the explanation, one is only *new* for so long. Over time his repeat customers made the unsettling discovery that he was in fact a person, round and full and maybe even reminiscent of them. A person they would even occasionally see outside of that booth. On Sundays, of course, but also on an inert line to buy eggs at C-Town or deciding on a stamp design at the dilapidated and lowly-vaunted William Carlos Williams/Barbara Stanwyck Postal Kiosk. The result was a decided decrease in revelation and a corresponding increase in talking-cure byplay.

Perfect example of this was the confessor Ventimiglia was expecting any minute. Can it be called a friendship? The first time Ventimiglia laid eyes on Feniz Heredia was as last-minute replacement for Elsie Heredia's funeral. This was a low-key affair. Simon and Feniz were the only two people there and neither seemed to be listening all that intently to what Simon said. It wasn't until after they'd exhausted everything ceremonial that something genuine passed between them. This man was standing there holding the kind of urn that would never be the object of an ode and there was nothing left to say really but still the man wasn't moving.

Without a script Simon hadn't known what to say. He didn't want to be duplicative of what had come before. Until then he'd never done one alone. There is no answer that will seem powerful to a neglected soul in a disintegrating body that's holding the ashen remains of its only companion.

In place of words the overmatched priest had put his hand on a Feniz shoulder in what at first seemed a successful maneuver. But only at first because Feniz then seemed to recoil and seconds later Ventimiglia was alone in the room with his sworn enemy: failure. The intervening weeks (?) contained a great deal of self-flagellation regarding things like his fitness to serve as a healer of souls when his was in constant turmoil and he was powerless to heal thyself so to speak. Death being one of the profession's bread-and-butter, his abject inability to properly traffic in it couldn't possibly augur well, could it? He began to start his morning paper with the want ads.

Then, miraculously, who would slide the screen over one night but the very dark emblem of his ignominy. Feniz was no churchgoer far as Simon could tell and unsurprisingly had very little command over the introductory verbiage. What he did have was *need*, writ large all over his face and coloring his every inflection.

Simon listened intently. Your basic catalogue but with the *sins* being maybe less charged than the norm. Then that aspect ended and it became more like a conversation. Something you might hear between two friends at a bar. Simon imagined.

The gist of this portion was that the death of Elsie Heredia had been an outsize psychic event for the speaker. Two main elements

arose during this telling. The first was surprise. Feniz Heredia seemed
like a nice, mentally unimpaired guy so what did he think was going
to happen to the body of someone as far along as Elsie? The language being used was more in line with a tragic surprise, really. The
other element had been harder to place at first. Only over time did
Simon detect and identify it. If words affect the air they're released
into, Feniz's words created a hint of finality that then grew into imma-
nence. This realization hit Simon hard and into a prolonged stammer.
He searched for words, emotions, mannerisms, anything that might
start to deflate the swelling nullity. Finally it lit. One of those pop culture truisms everyone just involuntarily stores somewhere. Get him to
commit to a future action.

Fr. Ventimiglia:	Why don't . . . in the future . . . commit . . . commit to coming again.
Mr. Heredia:	What?
Fr. Ventimiglia:	Will you come again?
Mr. Heredia:	(*shaking his head*)
Fr. Ventimiglia:	What I mean is that you've raised a lot here in our lim-ited time. Come back Friday and—
Mr. Heredia:	No.
Ventimiglia:	Come back tomorrow and we can get in deeper.
Heredia:	I don't know.
Ventimiglia:	It doesn't have to be a formal confession either; some-times it's just good to talk, like to a friend.
Heredia:	I don't have time to—
Ventimiglia:	Just tomorrow then. Just come tomorrow, you're not promising anything more than that. Just that tomorrow at five-thirty you'll be here and we'll talk about this some more, or about anything else you want to talk about.
Heredia:	Maybe.
Simon:	Okay, perfect, see you tomorrow.
Feniz:	I don't—
Simon:	Great.
Feniz:	What time?

Simon: Five-thirty tomorrow.

Feniz: Okay, but only tomorrow then that's it.

Simon: See you then.

And he did. At the next day's exact 5:37, Feniz would prove to be like a metronome, the screen slid open and their conversation resumed. And it had continued. Every Tuesday and Friday night until it became a feature of those days, no different than their positions in the week or their pronunciation.

This, finally, felt like being a priest. No, that wasn't it. This felt like something else entirely, something he hadn't even known existed. This was fulfillment in the strict sense of the word. Like the conversations had already occurred and they were engaging in a form of worship through reenactment.

It helped that there were tangible effects to their talks. The Feniz Heredia he'd originally met was like a shell but each successive meeting had seemed to flesh him out into something more and more human. That and the troublingly symbiotic nature of this effect had Ventimiglia becoming almost dependent on their meetings, to the point that anxiety would start to well up in him a bit as the relevant 5:37 approached.

Then there was the requirement of honesty, always burdensome but rarely more so than here. Not saying that Truth isn't overwhelmingly salutary. Just that there are times when it can function as a kind of deleterious stripping agent removing the exact superficial façade that was making it possible for a particular human, even humanity, to endure.

Truth here is forcing our man of the cloth to admit that maybe it's not any special ministerial skills he has brought to bear that have benefited Feniz so much as just the alchemical way the universe sometimes organizes itself to create little pockets of fleeting benevolence.

Simon sees that it is 5:39 and thinks this is odd.

Because enough speech to make him blue faced, no matter how unassailably wise that speech may be, cannot outdo even the faintest smile if the smile's source is just right. There's your truth. Even though to be fair, to himself, his gentle coaxing, teased out over several weeks, may be the only reason Feniz was in position to receive any smile at all.

5:41, is this clock right?

It is. And still is four minutes later when Ventimiglia makes the obvious realization that Feniz is actually not coming at all. He has snapped his own seemingly intractable streak the same way Simon had snapped his own that very morning with the banana. Were the two events related? Meaning causally? Almost certainly not. Still, there exist all kinds of relations. Coincidence itself is a kind of relation, which means the two events are most certainly related. But he has his thoughts on something deeper. Events are no different than numbers, for example, in their ability to be part of a set. Maybe the banana and the unexpected absence belong to the same set of proofs. The unfettered volition of consciousness let's call it. Not as moral necessity, just as physical fact. The majesty of Man located squarely in his ability to choose, you could argue. Though you'd be postulating majesty where most see none.

Before Ventimiglia can burrow any deeper, the screen slides over to violently ground his lofty inquiry with the rudeness of Now and its unknown confessor. What would have happened otherwise is he would've shortly landed on worry. Worry about Feniz and what else could be accounting for his disappearance and the way he had spoken that first confession and how it's sometimes when you most think you are out of the woods that you make the turn that seals the catastrophe. None of that enters his mind because the instant confessor fills it with more pressing matters and this effects a subtle severance of the lives of Simon Ventimiglia and Feniz Heredia that the occupied priest feels only minimally.

41

||||||||||

Feniz feels it not at all. He has forgotten the hour. Hell, he's forgotten the day, week, month, year. He is standing just outside the failing fence that somewhat encloses Sharon's home. The first time she'd told him to not stand there but come inside to the *grounds proper* with a laugh was a thrill so out of proportion to the objective facts it'd embarrassed him more than a bit. Since then he's actually been inside her home though he's not yet worked up the courage to reciprocate. This is why he's standing there right now, in fact. To invite her to a lunch meal of some kind but in his house, which he has calculated can be visit-ready in eight days if he busts it. But he also has to make sure the invitation is not viewed romantically, not for lack of intent on his part but because he then risks losing everything built to that point.

All that exists, including the relations between those things, is relative. So while to herself and maybe a vast majority of observers, Sharon seems kind of sadly beaten down, to Feniz she might as well be a Hollywood starlet for her effect on him.

Feniz is under no illusion that he has any effect on anyone. He knows, because he's marshaled and analyzed the weeks of evidence, both alone and with Father Ventimiglia's assistance, that she has more than once initiated contact with him out of the thinnest air. This means she desired said contact on some level. What that means in turn is a far thornier question. Friendship, his confessor had explained. Friendship-plus maybe, but friendship at least. Ventimiglia might as well have said *differential calculus* for all Feniz knew about the subject.

Far easier to understand is the smile Sharon forms when she sees Feniz and starts walking towards him. Truth is, it's as opaque as everything else, it's just that it seems to exist beyond any need for explication.

"Thought that was you. Why you standing all up on this dilapidated structure and shit?"

"Oh, don't say that. I could probably fix it. A long time ago . . . I could fix it."

"Get lost with that. There's only one *man* supposed to have fixed this thing longest time ago."

"I didn't mean . . . I don't . . ."

"Come on, what you on about now?"

"Who says I'm about on, that I'm about to be on something?"

"Huh?"

"That I'm *on about something*, like you say?"

"Well you here ain't you?"

"Because—"

"Well, come in, fool. You can't be standing out here in this shit, catch cold and all else."

"No, next Saturday, not this Saturday, not tomorrow, so like eight days."

"What about it?"

"Come over for lunch is what I'm saying, at my house."

"No problem, but make something good. I ain't trying to eat no bachelor toast, chump."

Feniz laughed and Sharon smiled and it wasn't nearly as bad as it sounds without inflection or context because Feniz is newly conditioned to the harsh Sharon method whereby increasing intimacy leads not to warmer language but rather to pointed barbs. Which at first seems anomalous but in fact makes great sense because, stay with this, imagine calling someone a fuckface. The utterance allows only one of two possibilities: the target is either your worst enemy or else your dearest friend, there's no middle ground. The enemy part is obvious but the other extreme is less understood. It reduces to the fact that a fuckface-type declaration generally signals a termination of not just the present one but also all future colloquies. Since intimates proceed from a base that there will be future friendliness, the declaration then somehow transforms into a solidification of that intimacy. So something like *See how tight we are that I can call you a fuckface while smiling and we both instinctively know no issues will arise as a result?*

Of course Feniz had not yet been fortunate enough to be insulted on that level by Sharon but still, in his present insecure state, it was heartening to hear even this slight invective.

Feniz is about to begin to parse it all when Sharon violently looks away as if a sci-fi tractor beam has suddenly been activated. There are a great many facial and other nonverbal cues present when talking to someone, cues that can communicate things like hierarchy, or esteem. Or, in this case, animosity. Best way to say it is that Sharon's face has become more real. Because a necessary correlate of animosity is relevance.

Of course the more relevant the person Sharon is looking at is the more irrelevant Feniz is. And this intuition of his is borne out when she speaks through her teeth at this person and comes no closer to introducing him than she would a vagrant.

"This about?" she asks.

That's no person, that's Hugh Seaborg. That's definitely him, maybe. Yeah, he looks different, older, but that's him all right. He has said something.

"Yeah, Hugh, that was two days ago," she responds.

That thing where you've been hearing a lot, tons, about a person then you see them and there's a discordance between your conception and what they're emitting.

"Sorry, my ass," she says.

He doesn't seem evil so much as pathetic.

"Don't think so," she says.

Feniz can just walk away without being rude and without causing a reaction, one of the benefits of invisibility, so he does. I guess that's the takeaway, he thinks. He is barely a presence in his own story, hard to believe he would be much of one in someone else's.

Paterson has this way of severely defamiliarizing sometimes. Like now, as Feniz slinks home defeated and feels in every way the revelation that he is not so much acting as being acted upon, constantly and negatively. True that minor pleasantries occasionally emerge but this is along the lines of a captive developing a favorite corner in his cell. And a particular day can distract however it wishes, its night will still feel like a lockdown where every isolate is perforce silenced so that you're denied even the consolation of a shared experience. If no one communes there's no community and that's as it should be since you wouldn't dream of saying something like *the community of Folsom Prison.*

Walking back, thinking that, he sees a man, not a kid, with a can of spray paint. Definitely not the man's car, no one does that to their own. Most troubling is how little concern the painter seems to pay the possibility of being seen. More evidence he and everyone around him is in a space-time elsewhere.

Feniz looks at the resulting artwork. Except for the unwilling car as canvas innovation, nothing remarkable. What's "11 over" meant to convey anyway? Everything's over, what makes eleven so special? Probably the name of some new gang or something. Their charter meeting probably had an exchange like this:

"Yo, when the clock strikes eleven it's over. Hence *11 over*!"

"All in favor say aye."

There're other possibilities, but no one can deny that the name is ominously effective whatever its source. He always leaves a light on so's to avoid coming home to pitch darkness. But this time he forgot, so when he goes in it's like walking off the design of a painting and into its surrounding black matte.

The 11 over crew could be in there to greet him violently but they aren't. Nothing is. Nothing ever does. Never. Either nothing ever will or else he is being set up for a terrible Something.

40

||||||||||

*Note: No arrest has been made in this case but I picture the perp being named as above. Mr. Javelin remains at large.

911: 9-1-1, Operator Millen, what is your emergency?
Caller: Yes, although I don't think it quite rises to the level of emergency.

911: *What?*
Caller: It's more like a situation.

911: Oh, why didn't you say so? 9-1-1, Operator Millen, what is the nature of your *situation*?
Caller: Sorry, I think somebody spray-painted my car.

911: You think? Okay, call us if anybody actually does it.
Caller: No, I mean, somebody spray-painted my car.

911: You saw this, sir?
Caller: No, ma'am. But I am staring at the incontrovertible proof, if you will.

911: If I will what?
Caller: No, it's just, my car's been vandalized.

911:   In what manner?

Caller: In a spray-paint manner. Someone has seen fit to write the word *spillover* on my car.

911:   Describe the car please.

Caller: It says *spillover* in shocking white.

911:   Okay, besides that.

Caller: It's a Honda Accord, the nineties, the parish provides it. Actually the spray paint is probably worth more than the vehicle itself.

911:   What's the issue then, mac?

Caller: Well, it's just more disconcerting than anything really. I mean, I don't know what that even means, *spillover.* I feel targeted, frankly.

911:   I'm not going to send a car, you can go to your local precinct to report this.

Caller: Actually, I'm now thinking that's a *k.* And an *e? Skellover?* That's even more troubling, isn't it? What does that even mean?

911:   It means you love skells.

Caller: Huh?

911:   It's not *skellover,* it's *skell lover,* the guy's getting all fancy doubling up that second *l.*

Caller: Forgive me but, I'm not the most culturally savvy, so what's a skell? Is that a thing?

911:   What's a skell? A skell's a lowlife, a base street criminal. Where you calling from?

Caller: Paterson.

911: Yeah, skells everywhere.

Caller: That's . . . but I don't get it . . . terrible . . . What does that have to do with me, or my innocent car?

911: What do you do?

Caller: What do you mean?

911: Do you do something? Are you gainfully employed, sir?

Caller: Not exactly.

911: Figured.

Caller: I'm a priest.

911: Oh, sorry. Let me ask you, Padre. In your capacity as a man with a cloth, do you service the skell community?

Caller: I don't . . . Can we not use that word? It just feels ugly.

911: Well, that concludes my investigation.

Caller: Come to think of it, today I do initiate the next phase of my new assignment as the prison chaplain for Rikers Island.

911: Rikers, you say?

Caller: Yes.

911: There you have it, that's skell central.

Caller: But how would anyone, oh, I did mention it during my last homily Sunday.

911: I guess at least one pious churchgoer doesn't approve.

Caller: So you think it's about that?

911: Yeah, Sherlock, I'm going to say the two things are related.

Caller: Wow. So that certainly ups the ante so to speak. Raises the seriousness quotient quite a bit, no?

911:   Oh yeah, we'll send our best detective right over. We'll pull him off that triple homicide at the nunnery.

Caller: I see your point. Still . . .

911:   Relax, Padre. In my experience almost all threats are empty. It's the people who skip the threat stage that you have to worry about.

Caller: I wasn't really thinking about it as a threat, but I guess you're right.

911:   You're welcome.

Caller: So, what should I do? What do you generally recommend in a situation like this? I'm supposed to be there in less than an hour.

911:   Simple, go have your fun on that island and when you get back stop at your precinct to file a report. That way if your body ever ends up hacked into porridge at least the guy profiling your killer will have a nice little detail to work with, it's the least you can do.

Caller: I know you're being facetious but I believe I will file a report.

911:   You should, we need to get as many skells off the street as possible.

Caller: Miss, I don't think that's appropriate really. I'm of half a mind, but I won't, to request to speak to your supervisor.

911:   I'm the supervisor, what would you like to say to me?

Caller: Nothing, I guess.

911:   Noted. Boy, if you didn't like that you're going to have a hell of a time at East Elmhurst. I mean a *heck* of a time, Your Irrelevance, uh, Reverence.

Caller: I see your point.

911: That's all it is, just trying to help. Why don't we reason this together a bit? You should make a report because it's a form of complaining. Someone violated the boundary between their life and yours. Ruined your car for no reason, where you gonna get the money to fix that? You ain't. You're going to have to drive that thing around to general population snickers. Do you deserve that? Of course you do, but that's not the point! That's what skells do, spread misery. You got off easy too, let me tell you. You want to take these calls I take? Last week I got one from a woman had trouble telling me what happened because her tongue had been cut off.

Caller: This is . . .

911: Yeah, this is. This is the group of people you're about to go chaplain is what this is.

Caller: I don't think—

911: I know you don't. You file that report instead, have a nice day.

(*dial tone*)
*Sly "Triple S" Petti***

**Transcribed by Sylvester Scarpetti for the Passaic County Prosecutor, courtesy of the Manhattan District Attorney's Office and made possible via the generosity of the Nabisco® Civil Service Exchange Program.

39

|||||||||

By the time Father Ventimiglia gets through Rikers Island's sundry institutional obstacles, erected long ago then refined not at all, his status as vandalism victim is perfectly forgotten.

The room they give him for this initial meeting is like a classroom but only the way a White Castle restaurant is like the Alhambra. What surround him are variously colored hard plastic chairs that purposely round out any edges. He has not worn his collar and feels now that was a mistake. On one of the chairs is a legal pad. He wouldn't, yes he would. He rips a white sheet off and starts to fold it horizontally, no one will be the wiser what with wisdom being in such short supply. He'll slide it under his lapels, the counterfeit will do, even if it is college ruled.

Just then large orange automatons begin to filter in, requiring that Ventimiglia subtly pretend he was reading this paper that was about to partially encircle his neck and for good measure somewhat close his eyes and activate his lips into purported prayer. It works, to a point, but this initial hiccup is something he'll never fully recover from. The half dozen are neither insultingly sparse nor intimidatingly populous so he doesn't know how to feel except that dead air is intolerably stressful.

"Thank you all for coming."

"We had free time."

"Not literally."

"Yes, well, I think if you came here this morning it's because you're searching. My name is Father Ventimiglia and my hope is that these meetings will function as a kind of spiritual oasis. You know, when the body is confined the spirit can still flourish. The education of the soul. The rehabilitation, even, of the soul. That part of us that endures beyond the ephemeral concerns of the here and now. It really is, just, in the final analysis, the greatest collection of human wisdom, and so, I think there's real nourishment here if we can in essence be reborn in a way that—"

"Aw, man, this is born-again shit? They shoulda said that shit in the pamphlet, shit."

"Shit, man, no one said born again. I'm pissed enough I was born the first time."

"No, I haven't said that."

"So who you affiliated with and shit, my man?"

"Okay, so I am a Catholic priest with the Cathedral of St. John the Baptist in Paterson, New Jersey."

"Aw, man, ain't those the baby diddlers?"

"But I envision this as a kind of journey through nondenominational belief, maybe something like what C. S. Lewis called Mere Christianity."

"Here we go, bringing that watered-down shit cuz we ain't entitled to the good stuff? Had you pegged from the get. Y'all be everything but a righteous brother, ya heard?"

"Let the man speak, your ass could benefit from even a watery word."

"Correct."

"Proceed, Father."

"Perhaps it's best if we all introduce ourselves at the outset."

"I ain't introducing shit. I ain't come here for no watered-down deity, I'm looking for Grade A brim and firestone, my man. I'm out. CO!"

He's out.

"Good, get your sorry ass out a here, firestone-seeking motherfucker."

"Yeah, he's too righteous for Venti Macklia here's brand but meanwhile he's in here for fucking his eleven-year-old stepdaughter and shit."

"For reals? Aw, hell no, he's in for a world of hurt."

"Oh yeah, I say we plan that shit right here."

"I don't think—"

"When does that motherfucker get meal, who knows? What house he in?"

"Okay, if I correctly understand what's happening here, it's literally the polar opposite of what we're trying to accomplish."

"No one said you had to help, Vespa."

"I won't stand for it is what I'll do. Or what I won't do, I guess."

"He's right, this is neither the time nor the place."

"Well it's certainly the place, no?"

"There's none better."

"True, this is where violent retribution comes to flower."

"You mean to metastasize."

"Yes! That's exactly right, thank you, your name?"

"Kiss-ass."

"Bitch."

"Why don't we settle down and get to those introductions? Who wants to go first?"

"You already went first."

"Okay, in a sense, who wants to go second? Never mind, let's just go counterclockwise."

They all look at the relevant party.

"What're you looking at me for? I'm clockwise."

"The hell you mean, you're clockwise? No one person can be clockwise, clockwise is a direction. He's looking at you because you're first, then we'll start heading in the prescribed direction, yo."

"No, if he says we're going counterclockwise then he has to start by looking in that direction, feel me?"

"Nuh-uh, he's free to start wherever he wants, thing is when that guy's done who's next will be determined by going counterclockwise from that guy."

"Fuck no."

"Once he's done."

"Why the fuck would he go to his clockwise to start when he just said we're going counter to that? *The fuck?*"

"Cuz that's his fucking prerogative, bitch."

"Well maybe it's my prerogative to shank your greasy ass!"

"Bring it, son."

"Okay, stop! Goodness gracious, we're going to proceed completely at random."

"You tell it, High Priest."

"And we're starting with you for the simple fact that you haven't yet said a word."

"I've been awed speechless. I mean, the wisdom, it's just as you promised."

"I'll admit it's been a bit of a shaky start, maybe you can get us on track."

"You want me to explain religion to this sterile group? What do you expect to reap if I sow among metal and wire that's barbed?"

"I'll settle for you introducing yourself, leave the reaping to me."

"Call me Nuno."

"Nuno?"

"Nuno DeAngeles."

"Oh shit, you're the guy who—"

"Excuse me, criminal, I believe the floor is mine."

"Criminal? The fuck you calling a criminal?"

"You. I'm sorry, you prefer *alleged*?"

"I prefer . . . man . . . I . . . just . . ."

"It's all right, criminal, I forgive you. Before I was interrupted I was about to regale you all with some rather incisive theological insights. Now you'll all have to wait until I get back in the mood."

Another orange parishioner enters.

"Am I too late?"

"Not at all. We lost one, you can take his place."

"Great, shall I introduce myself?"

"No, we're going counterclockwise."

"Not true, we're going random, remember?"

"So how would this be random when he's asking to go?"

"Because the priest would be randomly deciding to accept his request."

"But he hasn't done that."

"Yes, it's okay, please introduce yourself."

"Name's Hanes. Solomon Hanes, and I believe I'll sit next to this surly motherfucker if that's okay."

"The language, I'm going to ask that we make a concerted effort to watch that. Now, who's next?"

Solomon sits next to Nuno, who is rather stunned.

"Fucking weirdo," Nuno whispers. "Hell you doing here?"

"Shh, keep it down. I don't want people to connect us."

"These fuckers got their own problems."

"True, what's the priest's deal?"

"So you're back, how long?"

"I took fifteen days yesterday, six to go. Four days it took me to find you, the hell?"

"Find me for what purpose?"

"What's this about anyway? What's the angle here with this Jesus freak shit? I mean, don't get me wrong, it's the only way I was able to track you down, I just don't see how it fits."

That last part was too loud.

"Is this something you two want to share with the rest of us?"

"Sorry, we're old friends, Your Sanctimony. Just catching up briefly before rejoining the discussion."

They continue.

"Smooth, Sol."

"So what's the answer, Nuno? Why'd you sign up for the chaplain?"

"When did this start? You asking me questions and expecting answers? Why exactly?"

"No, but if we're working together on something aren't I entitled to know about this new angle?"

"First, this has nothing to do with anything about that. Second, even if it did, I report to you now?"

"In a way."

"Like an underling?"

"No, more like to a messenger. You'll admit even we have people we answer to, right? The whole world is answering and answerers. The Absence ring a fucking bell?"

"What about them?"

"Would you really blame them if they went in a different direction at this point? And I think you know the full extent of what that would mean. Blame them?"

"Yes, and let them know I mean that quite literally, I would *blame* them with extreme prejudice."

"Understood, insane but understood. Look, we're on this and we'll be staying on it thanks to me. But I had to do some fancy oratorical footwork, let me tell you. The remand, the media, none of this was the plan."

"I'll get out, man. I'll get out *with* the prize for The Absence, who better then have my money in full because I'm going to need every last cent to disappear forever with Dia Nouveau."

"But how, man? What do I tell them? *Who?*"

"Tell them it's none of their business. Just have my money ready and we'll inform them of anything we need."

"All I know is it better be soon."

"Because?"

"Because they're trying to close this place."

"Who's they?"

"Organizations, yo. That's who."

"Talking about?"

"The New School, for one, is all over this movement to close Rikers. Human rights, man, suddenly people care about that shit. Listen, I don't want to speak poorly of your home but this place is a cesspool."

"So dry this one up, what relevance to us?"

"Relevance is that if they close this place that seven-figure matzo ball stays right where it is. Maybe you'll be allowed to look up an image of it from whatever holistic facility you'll be caged in instead."

"Man, where's your head at, Sol? Couple professors write a law review article and you see revolution?"

"Nah, man, it's more than that. Mass incarceration, there's even a name for it now."

"Exactly. They only name the intractable. Once they're convinced something is unrelenting they make it a referent, that's how the sun got its name."

"Nothing lasts forever."

"Correction, nothing good does that. Let's just say I'm not worried about this place. We're going to extract its precisely one good thing then watch it sink from the weight of the loss."

"Enough said."

"More than."

"So?"

"So in a couple days I file a motion on my case and we'll go from there with specific dates."

"Okay."

"In the meantime I may need your help to get into the same room with a particular inmate."

"What he do?"

"Aw, gee, I really want to help you there but you see there's all sorts of confidentiality considerations and, though you're in the minority, you probably like your face the way it's currently arranged."

"I see, I'll shut up. Who is it?"

"You tell me, vehicular manslaughter, how many can there be? I know for a fact there's only one that manslaughtered my somewhat uncle Jorge de Cervantes."

"Oh, fuck."

"Yeah."

"Shh."

They look up in concert.

"Okay, introductions out of the way, I think we can finally get started substantively," says the chaplain.

"*Count!*"

"What does that mean?"

"Means your wisdom gon have to wait till next time because we need to be counted."

"Like livestock."

"Don't complain, it's the only time we count."

"In that case, I think this worked well and I'll see you all next time, which I don't yet know when that will be. Also please prepare Matthew fifteen, verses one through twenty for our next meeting. Mr. DeAngeles, might I have a word on your way out?"

"You might, but that's already two so I guess it'll have to be next time."

"Mr. Hanes, is it? Would you kindly excuse us?"

"I love this guy, a truly spiritual type. Thinks we're like old friends at a pub free to improv into whatever activity we wish. Let's go, Nuno. Good day, sir."

"No, it's okay," says Nuno. "I'd just as soon not be counted. Let me hear this sinner's confession first."

"Dude, you're going to risk the Bing for this?"

"The Lord is my shepherd."

"You're a sheep now?"

"I only don wolves' clothing to evade him."

"Where we at then?"

"I'll update you before you leave, after I've filed that motion."

"Fine, but don't let this guy in your head, it could be hazardous to your health."

"What health?"

"I was talking to the priest. At any rate, adios, which I only now realize translates as 'to God' and therefore sound like the kind of badass thing a hard guy would say to someone right before dispatching them for good."

"To God, Solomon."

"Yes, to him."

Solomon leaves to be counted.

"What can I do for you, Simon? What does Simon say?"

"How do you know my first name?"

"Oh, wow, this is not an auspicious start. How does someone this far into the twenty-first century's calendar acquire easily accessible information?"

"I see. To that point, I guess, I was certainly intrigued by your history."

"How so?"

"For one I can't imagine there are many other Regis High School alumni in here."

"I'm not alum."

"Okay, still."

"Yeah, well, you see the value of that education and where it got me. Don't think I'll be making the next alumni newsletter."

"Harng!"

"What's that? That how you laugh?"

"No, not making light, I know you must be suffering."

"Oh, boo fucking hoo, rarely better."

"Yet you signed up. After all, this isn't compulsory."

"Is there a point to this?"

"You bring a base of knowledge to this that perhaps the group could benefit from."

"I won't be bringing anything anywhere because you can take me off your list. This appearance was both first and last for me."

"I'm curious, why?"

"It seems harmless enough, I know. And, let's face it, the bar for entertainment is set as low in this place as anywhere in the world."

"So you'll come again?"

"No, because at some point what will happen is these other clowns are going to raise their hands and start asking questions."

"What's wrong with that?"

"What's wrong is that, although I am currently doing my best to hide this fact, I am an intensely impatient and violent man. One who can't stand dim uninteresting questions, which these will undoubtedly be."

"You'd be surprised."

"Shocked. Complicating things further is that I would like to avoid solitary during the brief time I'm here and that just happens to be the penalty for cracking thick inmate heads that confuse and delay."

"Perhaps I should offer one-on-one tutelage."

"Offer whatever you wish, just not to me."

"But if—"

"Apathy at first sight."

"What's that?"

"The first time Nuno saw the chaplain, he felt deeply apathetic."

"Ooh . . . that's a . . . reference!"

Which is neither confirmed nor denied because the only person in position to do so has created surprising distance from the priest and seamlessly inserted himself into the count. Nuno is counted and the numbers agree and at three p.m. he remembers how there was some kind of rending of some garment or other, millennia ago when Jesus died at that exact time. And truth is there'd been no apathy, just Nuno being intentionally mean.

38

The great question of intent. *Hugh slept over last night* is a fact, but standing alone it is one with limited significance. What signifies is what was in his head just before those dead eyes closed. Sharon had let him in, not sure why even as she did so.

Outwardly at least, he seemed humbled, and Sharon had spent the most significant portion of her life constantly lowering expectations when it came to Hugh Seaborg so next thing she knew that was him sitting on her sofa, a new piece she'd thought would never be contaminated by him. The whole thing bowing under giant him like a toy. It was all so offensive. Save for one element: six-years-old Donnie Seaborg had come home unexpectedly to find that bag of guts on that sofa and you'd have thought Han Solo had stopped by from her son's nonverbal reaction.

This was primal shit. No matter what she did she couldn't create that right there.

She cooked, he had his weapons she had hers. They sat at the jittery table and wasn't this the greatest food ever? And while the scene was unlike anything Sharon had ever before experienced, to Donnie it was indistinguishable from everything being in its right place at the right time.

Afterward, men had convened for the zillionth time to have a formal dispute over a ball and this was deemed important enough to televise. Hugh had stared at that screen, technically *with* Donnie, alternating between muted delight and almost existential despair, and Sharon quickly came to view him as almost a harmless prop. And later when he closed his eyes on that sofa, his beefy hand resting on the defeated carton of a six-pack, it was mostly true that she just didn't have the energy to expel him.

This morning his presence is more grating, maybe it's just the effect harsh morning light has on everything. But again Donnie seems more whole than before. She cleans, cleans and listens.

Sharon is not an illusions person. She knows the reason Hugh is currently in the same room with Donnie is not humanity or even obligation, it's defeat. Hugh had a conception of what his future life's tenor would be but it was, at bottom, a vague one. Like most such conceptions of a potential life it transported, whole and unmolested, that which the conceiver was already happy with while repairing through reform the rest. Reality's not like that. Reality may fix what was wrong but it will only do so by withdrawing from the account of what was right, and these transactions are almost uniformly irreversible.

So with someone like Hugh there'd been no genuine weighing of the relative merits of being married versus being divorced. Instead there'd been only dissatisfaction at some of the ways being married differed from being single or at least from being recently married. A dissatisfaction that grew so pervasive that by the end he no longer cared what Sharon discovered or suspected or knew or how she acted in response to it all. It was that, the unmerited contempt really, that had so greatly aided Sharon's adjustment.

Hugh didn't have that advantage and his maladjustment sat on his face like a mustache from a vandal's pen. Doubtless a third party's illusions had intervened, she thought, and once that woman had been left with daily relentless Hugh Seaborg minus any thrill of marital transgression the grim severity of it all must have set in rather quickly. He hadn't learned anything or grown in any way, he just lacked stimuli, and the search for it had driven him to her home to pretend it was at least partially his.

Sharon susses this all out so quickly and suddenly that it takes considerable self-restraint to keep from smashing his stupid fat face with that Flintstone glass she turns over in her hand to fantasies of that motherfucker having to pluck pieces of glass Rubble out of his cheek. The extremity of that leads to such a pronounced correction that she pretty quickly settles into complete apathy.

He's talking. The way people say *mistake* as if they'd messed up the tip on a check instead of having done something fucked up. He is talking and talking and one of the few words she recognizes more than once is *Donnie*, and also *father*.

She knows what she is going to do but it still hurts. Actually this knowledge is what makes it hurt but she won't see that connection until later. He knows too, knows he is getting a do-over.

What burns worst is knowing what category she'll now be in. She'll be in the women-who-take-shit-from-dogs category when she has spent the last couple months investing heavily in an aggressively opposite self-conception. And it doesn't matter what you feel internally when a label is that strong.

It's not about love or anything similar, it's just simple math really. If you don't dig too deep you see that it's easier to double-team an attention-deficit kid than it is to single-cover him. That it's easier when that kid isn't angry at you without knowing it. Easier when you can pick up your phone without first looking at your checkbook. When you don't have to wait for a particular date on the calendar to buy groceries.

She can't help but dig deeper though, at least lately. Life is cruel. Not what her particular one has become, the thing in general. It's imposed on you without your say then its most important features determined completely at random like a tiny silver ball hopping on and off numbered divots. She knows their evil sphere can deal out a lot worse than what she got and that's terrifying in its own right. Even scarier is the notion that it might never deal out anything all that better than what she got. Everything in life seems open to attack except what she experiences in relation to Donnie. That nameless what? Substance? Ideal? Invention?

What else is there? She intuits that it would be better for Donnie to at night sleep in the same location as the two people biologically responsible for his existence but does she *know* this? Not directly she can't. What she once directly experienced or continues to experience becomes a kind of knowledge but the rest is better characterized as propaganda.

Before she really even knew what was going on, when she was like

Donnie, was the sensation of being an afterthought. That and a con-frontational household anxiety that was always ready to light. Forever, it seemed, there was a cap to how happy she could really get, as if she were attending a funeral that just wouldn't fucking end.

And it didn't end and it never really varied either. School was a chore and that alarmed no one at all really. Not a chore in the usual way though, imagine all day every day being talked down to like an idiot or just ignored because there's always something more pressing. No matter because when you couldn't go to school for free anymore that just meant you didn't go to school. Then jobs, then Hugh.

Hugh was more than just Hugh though. Hugh was like the mascot for everything wrong with everything. A guy you literally couldn't talk to. I mean, you could get information. Was it hungry? What time would it get home? What you couldn't do was *talk*. By the end Hugh wasn't all that evolved past animal really. He had a grand total of two distinct states of being: he was either in physical need or not. This led Sharon to realize how comparatively little physical appetites drove her existence yet how fixated her immediate environment was on all that shit. Lots of talking with plenty of *how* or *when* but no one else ever asking *why*. They'd have these get-togethers. The men forming a wall across from the televised ball, the women never all that far from ingre-dients discussing only news so local you had to double-check who was in the room before you could really let loose. It was all like her job, it started as something then felt like nothing and finally became so hurtful she had to just run the other way, so little could it be tolerated.

But, of course, it could be. And, worse, she'd maybe decided it would be. Occurs to her that if she does endure, if she does, then Hugh's job couldn't be more fitting. He watches prisoners, she would just be one more. One more wretch doing time. *Doing time* is syntac-tically perfect and a diluted version of this realization jumps into her head just then. Time is much less gift than burden, doing it is exactly what we do, at least the people in there have the good sense to call it what it is.

She can do this. She's forty. Looking at life spans, she figures worst case she just has to do what she's already done one more time. But isn't it in a way a waste of a life? You get only one and this is what hers will be. Maybe not, because she'd pinpointed this one thing, a sure path to meaning. There's a spiral that has to stop. A person formed by shit parents becomes a shit person and by extension another shit parent who forms a shit person until you just end up with shit everywhere. A life spent accomplishing only one thing can maybe be justified if that one thing is significant enough.

She could therefore literally decide that the sole purpose of her breathing was terminating that spiral currently pulling Donnie towards its diminishing circles. She could speak certain lines, wouldn't even have to invest all that much in them, and their environment would change into something that was at least on the surface better. This would be a form of accomplishment. Her son wouldn't know her suffering but he would profit the world from it. She was going to suffer whatever path she took, difference was this path had a benefit.

If she protected Donnie, this was animal kingdom shit, a mother protects her young, then he would grow, not physically, they all do that, really grow. Grow like those people she sees but never knows well. People who give orders instead of just being scheduled, who have time to reason and gain insight, wise people who always know what everyone has decided is the right thing to do. It was like a secret society, as if they'd attended a hush-hush meeting in Vail or some shit that taught them the kinds of things you say and don't say.

It wasn't race, black-white, Spanish-English, none of all that that everybody thinks. It was education and all its ingredients and Donnie was going to get that shit if she had to steal it at fucking gunpoint. He wasn't even going to have to work particularly hard for it, it was just going to happen to him the way it just happens for the secret society fucks. It would just happen, but only if she controlled the laboratory conditions just so to make sure there were no excuses. And once she fixed it so it would just happen then guess what? It was just going to happen to every Seaborg from Donnie on. Seaborg was a shit name on Hugh and shit on every other male Seaborg she'd met but that was more because of what males are than the actual name. Fine, Donnie could keep the name, we'll just have to change what that name is and means.

Sharon was forty and drank and smoked and ate primarily at least partially invented food. With any luck she would quietly die the second the job was done. No one would know what she'd done but maybe no one ever knows what anyone's ever done yet there everything ever done stood, no less true for it.

She could do that, in essence forfeit her life. But it would take a strange kind of courage. People aren't often forced to make this kind of decision, the permanence of it. It didn't strictly have to be permanent but it had to be permanent to work. She was smart, obviously, she knew this wasn't a question of overlooking an incident. This wouldn't be a stint in the can, it would be a life sentence. She would have to ignore this, true, but also she would have to just keep ignoring all the way into a kind of reduced humanity. She would be accepting that the resting state of life is a kind of dull pain.

"A life of pain," she says out loud and human brains are so weird because it's almost impossible to predict those stimuli that are going to brand themselves onto your store of experiences; but she instantly identifies this event, her saying this out loud, as one of those searing things, with the way the light was coming through that dirty window, in particular the crack that somehow hadn't really worsened, the orange tile floor, her alone but talking out loud like that, this would be one of those things.

37

|||||||||

Don't look for an area of the brain where this happens because that is wrongheaded and superficial. Instead ask why the whole structure can't be more sturdy, why it has to be made up of such flimsy material, why everything has to be so perishable. Above all, why the astrocyte from earlier couldn't just be *incapable*, as a matter of biology, from dividing over and over so quickly into a tumor.

As a glioblastoma tumor grows it's not like there's primary pain at the location or anything. What there is though is rapid growth owing to the plenitude of available blood vessels and the nature of the cells being fed. Only once this putrid mass grows to a size where it interferes with normal processes, so, bigger than you'd think, would its owner even begin to suspect. Since the tumor our astrocyte birthed is now a black, gangrenous golf ball it is almost ready to debut as it were and like a cosmic vortex suck in the massive attention it's due.

Now is still before that so it's more like a general malaise. Slight impairments that can be hard to notice given the tumult of daily existence in our sensory-input maelstrom. But like animals with a storm it's like you know something's wrong before it even technically is.

36

|||||||||

"What's wrong?" asks Dia. They're alone, our two, at IFL headquarters. "Nina?"

"Who says something's wrong?"

"Your face says."

"Yeah, well, from now on just worry about what my mouth says."

"Every time that cockamamie investigator comes by you get some version of this."

"Huh?"

"Weirded out, basically. Is there something wrong with the league that I'm missing, because where I'm sitting all appears to be going quite swimmingly. Moreover, as deputy commissioner our charter dictates that—"

"Not everything's the league you know."

"It is for me, I have *literally* nothing else going on. Wait, did I just make you laugh?"

"Let's not belabor it, shall we?"

"I did! What a feather in my cap, don't you agree?"

"You're so needy."

"I am, is that bad?"

"Tell me about your childhood."

"Oh, God no. Anyway, about the league and the swimmingly, it's true that we don't yet have a TV contract but there are definite nibbles now. In the meantime how do you feel about broadcasting all our games via Skype?"

"What did you just say to me?"

"I said . . . vacation, you know, what our vacation policy is? Just that I think I may need a couple days to recover and, after all, it is your fault in a manner of speaking."

"Recover? From what?"

"From Joni, what else?"

"Hell you talking about? Who's Joni?"

"Joni Mitchell? Remember?"

"What? Why would you bring her up at this exact moment? You messing with me?"

"You gave me all her albums? Told me I had to listen to them in order? Any of this ringing any bells?"

"Fuck, that's right . . . so?"

"So you're responsible for my psychic breakdown occasioned by listening to only *Blue* for the last few days."

"Ah."

"I'm only half-joking, I'm a bit lost. I mean it, what is that thing? It just feels like . . . I don't know, the emptying of a soul? Listening to it is unnerving and elevating at the same time. I don't know what to do in response."

"Do?"

"It has to represent another level of artistic flowering in that arena, no?"

"You're not expected to *do* anything. Joni Mitchell is not a person in this world of ours."

"That's just it, she feels like the most important person in the world right now."

"Believe me, the people you know are far more important. Especially since one of them is about to punch you in the face."

"It feels like an interaction, Joni."

"It isn't."

"Why so defensive? You're the one insisted I had to listen to it all like it was some religious calling."

"I can't be wrong once a decade?"

"Funny part is I've never really been a big lyrics person but she has this way of compressing so much into such few words."

"Poetry."

"Yes, that! I'm thinking of one thing in particular. I should start by describing my romantic slash sexual life first."

"You most definitely should not."

"Okay then, I'll just summarize that it has not been a rosy picture. Naturally, with such a decided trend one looks for explanatory theorems."

"Naturally."

"So there's the moment where Joni wonders to a potential lover whether he will have her as she is. Of course the brilliantly hilarious follow-up is that *how she is* is strung out on another man. Kind of weird, right? We laugh that no one would ever really agree to that, but why? Say I'm with someone and that's what they want, why should they care if I'm maybe not entirely into it because of someone else? Well, they do, and I realize that maybe the reason I'm not all that into anything is that I'm still kind of hung up elsewhere, you know? There's this guy I've never really been able to get out of my head. He was crazy, really he was everything and at the highest level all the time if that makes any sense. The ending was too abrupt and so I've always felt like it just lingers. Years too, but still, you know? Even now, just talking about it out loud like this, it's like my heart rate is speeding up."

"Oh, brother."

"Wonder what became of him."

"Likely dead."

"Nuno DeAngeles," says Dia, slowly savoring each syllable.

"Fuck . . . off."

"What?"

"Come here, look me in the eye." They stare at each other for seconds.

"What?"

"Nothing, just that the name sounds made up is all."

"I know, funny how people with spectacularly memorable names are always at the ready to be recalled in our minds."

"Said Dia Nouveau."

"Naming's weird, like with Joni again and 'Little Green'—"

"Enough, please. I'm knocking off early today."

"To do what?"

"To stare at one of my walls and assess my life."

"Seriously?"

"No. Well, the wall part's true. You know why?"

"No."

"Because that wall's full of Dalí works and that's what I like to look at when in need. Add the fact that my failure to add to this collection is currently exacerbating my malaise and I think I have ample justification for my planned afternoon."

"If you say so."

"And here's the thing, Dia. I'm going to do that staring with maximal intensity but I'm not going to then expect the clocks in our real world to start melting or rhinos to start materializing, understand? These people are guideposts, you can't turn over anything tangible about your life to them. The same way they didn't turn anything over to anyone but just launched out in their own direction."

"I don't know."

Silent pause.

"I know I do things. I've done things, it wasn't like now." Nina's face is in her hands. "It just wasn't."

"Huh?"

"You're a happy person, anyone looking at you would say so."

"You want me to teach you how to be happy?"

Nina laughs.

"That's twice in one day!"

"Two feathers?"

"Yes, two!"

"I'm going to go now, you're in charge in my absence."

"I know, that's what *deputy commissioner* means."

"That's what I'm saying."

"I know, but there's no need to say it, it's just who I am."

"Fine, you're *not* in charge, activate the autopilot."

"There was one work-related thing I was hoping to convey to you before you left."

"Convey away."

"We got the armory! All hurdles have been cleared for the IFL's

Pork to play all their home games beginning in September at this historic location. Want to hear the press release?"

"No."

"Ahem. *Professional sports returns to the Paterson Armory! All hurdles have been cleared for the IFL's flagship franchise, the Pork, to play all their home games beginning in September at this historic location.*"

"Sounds familiar."

"*Originally built as an installation for the Second Regiment of the New Jersey National Guard, the armory has a long history of hosting athletic feats in addition to its role as cog in the violent machine by which man hones his ability to kill his fellow man.*"

"I'm not sure—"

"*As example, the armory was once home to the Paterson Crescents of the American Basketball League, a team whose major contribution to round ball was its employment in 1948 of Larry Doby. Yes, that Larry Doby, the Patersonite who a year earlier had been the first player to integrate baseball's American League and now found himself playing a similar role for professional basketball.*"

"I feel you may be veering too wildly into social—"

"*Which makes him some kind of American hero for sparing us the sight of too many Caucasians playing basketball.*"

"Yeah, definitely you've strayed a bit afield, so—"

"*Likewise, Joe Louis, who it is rumored may occasionally have been the target of at least mild racism, graced the armory with his magnetic presence that same year.*"

"What in the—"

"*Now the Pork are proud to announce that they will add to this noble tradition of commercial corporeal contests by bringing their finely tuned athletic battalion to the armory, where it will ably prosecute its gridiron war with peerless pigskin pulchritude. For tickets . . .* and then everything about how you get tickets."

"That's truly insane."

"What should I change?"

"Who said change anything, you hearing voices now?"

"Oh."

"Lock up when you leave. And as you do remember and abide by our security protocols."

"I'm not aware of any such protocols."

"This place is a goddamn war zone."

"Oh, don't talk that way about poor Paterson."

"I was referring to Earth."

35

|||||||||

For undeclared yet open warfare on American soil maybe the only place that rivals Rikers Island is the Tombs. Truth is, even saying *the Tombs* is almost as much concept as it is specific location. The concept, centuries old, is finite incarceration in Lower Manhattan and the current incarnation of this is the Manhattan Detention Center at 125 White Street. This is really two structures, one of which is like a fourth art deco tower of 100 Centre Street, where the vast majority of Manhattan criminal litigation occurs.

This proximity to court may lead to a lesser sense of isolation for its sometime double the capacity (nine hundred) of prisoners (highly relevant stuff is happening next door!) but it also fosters a certain anxious desperation that can ignite into violent unrest, like the time inmates basically took the place over for eight hours in 1970.

Why any of this matters is that the day before his court date (at last) Nuno is suddenly transferred to the Tombs without, of course, any explanation or even seeming precipitating incident. Like any such change it is upsetting on a level unconcerned with logic or its factual predicates. But it also doesn't take long for Nuno to develop actual reasons for his unease. The constrained space means heightened danger. Everything and everyone is just all on top of each other, but like heated atoms colliding furiously, not in any kind of purposeful alignment or enmeshment. Also he just has nobody there. The whole place is gangs, like a convention's being held. The COs know this and protect their fragile ecosystem accordingly. And now they see this notorious Nuno DeAngeles guy who doesn't really fit anywhere. He knows it's going to be bad.

It also just sucked that the few female COs he could stomach, but more importantly Solomon and the Padre Ventimiglia, could be taken from him just like that. Because here was this development and he found that mainly he wanted to attach words to it. He wanted to talk about it, angrily to Solomon or loftily to the chaplain, but above all speaking to discover what he felt about it. His diary might be even better but he'd lost access to it in transit and his new captors had already denied him pen and paper, perfect example.

He lay in bed and spoke aloud to just himself, his drive to language-as-thought wasn't suppressible.

He knew now, with revelatory force, that his motion tomorrow would not work. That his lawyer was nothing special, at least not special enough. That he had in all likelihood dealt a fatal blow to nothing less than his life. He spoke long into the night, into a darkness so complete it almost hurt his eyes.

The next day is court so they pull him from his cell early and walk him across that internal bridge to the court pens on the twelfth floor of 100 Centre. He's put in the cell that feeds Part 52, where he'll appear later.

In there are probably thirty others. Nuno sits in a corner, where no one can get behind him, and tries to determine if he can safely disassociate. He cannot. He's always had some weird facial recognition deficits but even so this face is definitely troubling him.

He stares at it; but subtly, he's good at that. There are the two hollow teardrop tattoos under the left eye of course. Not the hugest deal since like most advertising it tends to be based on insecurity and in Nuno's experience they're almost uniformly located on the faces of at-their-core pussies. Still, it *is* supposed to mean two bodies so it's probably best to be alert. Beyond that is the familiarity of the face and not the good kind of familiarity. This guy is someone, he feels it. And until he figures out *who* he can't really wind down.

What he has can't really be called knowledge. It's like vague imagistic intuitions. He sees this guy in his store of mental images and he knows it's antagonistic. Problem is it's not like the average person trying to recall an enemy because Nuno has such a vast universe of these that it becomes difficult for a single one to stand out. Best he can ultimately do is that this guy's Trinitario or those DDP dudes and sworn vengeance is definitely a component and, truth is, if he's being honest he probably has it coming.

But is he really sure? To confirm, he does this thing where he pretends to accidentally make a noise that draws significant attention. Then he looks solely at this guy's face without it being at all clear that that's what he's doing. What he's looking for here is whether that face registers recognition then malice and sure enough that's exactly what it unmistakably does.

What to do? First, it may not be a problem. The guy's clear across the room with more than two dozen witnesses. The pen they're in holds inmates not just from the Tombs but from all the Rikers facilities, so the next few hours may be the only chance this fuck gets. Because what happens is as someone is pulled from the cell and taken to court they are not returned to that cell once they're done. This means any second Nuno could be pulled out to go before the judge then straight back to the Tombs, where he can reduce his worries to just third-party aggressions that would have to overcome the relative safety of his single-occupancy cell. The reverse too, his enemy could receive the same treatment and have to carry his frustration back to whatever hole he slunk out of. It would be far from over but at least a major bullet would've been dodged.

Of course neither of these happens. He just sits there with Teardrops while everyone else and their mothers keep getting called into court. Everyone talking about such and such girl and who she got with and who's doing what bids and who's got beef with who or what crew. It's truly numbing in its stupidity, but the required vigilance is nonetheless so extreme that by 2:30, when it's just them two and a half dozen others, Nuno is exhausted and almost prefers to just absorb any violence that is at least strictly physical.

At any rate the relative emptiness now means he can get better informed. What's he looking at anyway? The guy's multiple-state-bids huge, of course, with psycho dead eyes, always the worst.

These fucks love their blades but this one's definitely empty-handed. That's something at least. He presumably knows who Nuno is so he's likely not too thrilled about proceeding unarmed. Let's face it, the last thing most criminal scumbags want is a fair fight. Don't believe that then go to any boxing gym in a ravaged neighborhood and look for the area tough-guy thugs; don't worry, they're otherwise engaged.

Then again here's Teardrop standing up and walking towards Nuno while the latter does his best to pretend he doesn't notice. Although maybe there is such a thing as divine intervention because just then, the precise moment Nuno had basically decided he would just passively accept the violence because there was no blade and his mind was already too overtaxed with other concerns for him to add to it, came the CO yell for *Herrera, Elvis Herrera!*

Sensing his opponent's reaction, Nuno looks up and meets his eyes as if to say, *Fine, you know me but now I know you, Herrera.* That goes nowhere as the CO arrives at the gate to lead Herrera away.

It's over, hours of hypervigilance. Nuno actually lies down on the bench. There's considerable physical pleasure in finally releasing a dangerous concern. It might even be that he falls asleep because the next thing he experiences is one of those loud slams and it startles him into the realization that he is alone in the cell, fucking lawyer.

Teardrop Herrera is being walked down the hall to the cell, Nuno can see this. Something about the way he's walking though, two things actually. First, this prick definitely now has something in his right hand, and it's no great leap to figure what it is and its intended purpose. The other thing is related, and it's Herrera whispering to the CO, who then looks at Nuno and nods assent.

Oh fuck, this he *will* oppose. These guys go right for the face with these things and one of the very few sights in this universe that he still likes is the sight of his own face, doesn't want to see raised ropes every time he looks in the mirror. The other thing is the way the CO's in on it. This means there's no bottom. If the people who are supposed to prevent the gravest debasements instead abet them, then we may as well embrace the void of an endless fall, which can be tempting but Nuno's just not in one of those moods right now.

The gate opens. Herrera fills the opening then walks in. The CO rushes away to be sure he can't be said to have seen. Nuno has taken his outermost shirt off and tied it around his left elbow. The best defense to a punch to the face is to bend your arm at eye level then stick your face in the crook. He's wrapped the elbow because of the blade, he's willing to be cut anywhere but the face.

He'll need to land three blows but the needed precision is annoying. At least he still has the element of surprise that's how thick this other guy is.

The guy walks towards him. Nuno is sitting on the bench calmly but someone looking closely, so not this guy, would see that his right foot is slightly behind the left as in a runner's starting stance. Herrera is just about within distance when he talks for the first time all day.

"You know Trinitario, right?"

It all happens very fast. Nuno has to wait a beat until he gets close enough. At that precise moment he pretends something from behind Herrera has startled him. The millisecond Herrera can't help but begin to get distracted, Nuno hurls all his weight forward into a vicious right blast to the solar plexus. It lands perfectly, the knuckles ravaging through the soft tissue between the ribs until there's no more *in* to go. The instant Nuno had finished measuring the trajectory of the blow he had put his elbow in place and it now deflects the predictable slash harmlessly off the shirt. Now the blade is visible and still in the hand but all it does is meekly bob up and down as Herrera desperately tries in vain to recover his breath. Now Nuno's hands are perfect planes and they jab forward right into Herrera's eyes. The pain and disorientation are extreme but to this fuck's credit the blade is still in his hands and even waving somewhat, side to side. Nuno steps to an angle. Then as soon as the blade is as far from him as it will get, he pivots a brutal right hand into that motherfucker's left temple. This is not a punch, which would hurt Nuno and leave evidence, but is done with the bottom bone of his palm. Herrera is out cold and falls to the floor; there's been no real noise in any of this.

As Nuno unties the shirt and places it pillow-like under the fuck's head he raises his voice for the first time in a long while.

"CO! Seizure, CO!"

Their reaction is the typical underreaction but eventually two COs respond and one of them is the prick from before.

"He had a seizure or some shit, guess you should've listened to him, huh?"

"What?" asks the other CO.

"Yeah, he was saying to your man here that he felt like shit and needed urgent medical attention and your partner here was all *go fuck yourself*. Right, man?"

"That never happened, this skell's lying."

"Also he searched him for shit, cause when I was trying to help him I saw this. Isn't that a fucking shank in his hand? I think he's psych and was going to hurt himself, definitely the kind of thing your man here gets paid to notice."

"Shut up, you. What is this, Billings?"

"Billings, is it?" asks Nuno. "Oh look, he's waking up."

They return their focus to him just as another CO comes to bring Nuno before the court. Herrera is staring at Nuno, trying to reconstruct his past.

"Good to see you're okay, pal," Nuno says. "By the way, just before your lights went out you asked me if I knew what Trinitario was. Remember that, Billings?"

"I wasn't here."

"Right, it's just as well. I was going to tell him what I thought of Trinitario."

"Oh yeah, skell? What's that?"

"Never heard of 'em."

34

|||||||||

Nuno's has to be like the last case of the day in Part 52 because when he gets up the flight of stairs he is cuffed to the bench just beyond the courtroom and left supremely alone. He sits and stares at the radiator. He marvels at how lucky he got. Then again he always seems to get lucky in this area. He could easily lose the bracelets but then what? God, it's all *Then what?*

After a disconcertingly long time, Nuno hears, through the door, his case being called into the record. Then the entry of a court officer who uncuffs him and brings him into the courtroom. Attorney Ed Coin is already at the defense table when Nuno lands there.

"Oh, sorry, man. They didn't tell me you were back there or I would've come talk to you. Just plead not guilty."

"Mr. DeAngeles, the grand jury has filed an indictment charging you with the crime of Murder in the Second Degree. How do you plead? Guilty or not guilty?"

"Not guilty by reason of inanity."

"What?"

"That's a not guilty plea! Counselor, come up."

At the bench, the judge's face is reddening and it's almost hard for Coin to understand him at first through those clenched teeth.

"Your client is a piece of . . . work, Counselor."

"You have no idea."

"Oh, I think I have some. I trust you've seen his motion?"

"No, what motion?"

"Oh, you're in for a treat. Do we have a copy? Okay, here you go. DA?"

"Don't have it, Your Honor."

"Well then, here's *your* copy. It truly is a remarkable document. Take your time, Counselors."

"A motion to dismiss?"

"Correct."

"That's ludicrous."

"Your basic Clayton motion on a Murder Two."

"A Clayton?"

"That's right, he's moving to dismiss a murder case in the interests of justice. Twenty-eight years on the bench, I guess eventually you do see everything."

"I assume defense counsel won't be adopting this?"

"He's going to want to read it first, no?"

"Yes, Judge, if we could adjourn—"

"No, no, no, read it right now. I need to see your face as you read, this is the last case of the day and it's not very long, we're not holding anyone up."

This is what Coin then looks at:

SUPREME COURT OF THE STATE OF NEW YORK
COUNTY OF NEW YORK: PART 52

PEOPLE OF THE STATE OF NEW YORK

    -against-

NUNO DEANGELES

    DEFENDANT

    PLEASE TAKE NOTICE that upon the annexed affirmation of NUNO DEANGELES, the defendant in the above-captioned case, the undersigned will move this Court on his own behalf, in Part 52, located at 100 Centre Street, New York, New York, on the 26th day of March 2015, at 9:30 a.m. in the forenoon of that day, or as soon thereafter as counsel may be heard for an Order granting a **MOTION PURSUANT TO C.P.L. §§ 210.20(1)(I) and 210.40 TO DISMISS THE INDICT-MENT IN FURTHERANCE OF JUSTICE,** and for such other and further Relief as to this Court may seem just and proper.

Dated: New York, New York
           March 26, 2015

                      Yours, etc.,

                      Nuno DeAngeles

                    Nuno DeAngeles
                    349-15-08891
                    James A. Thomas Center
                    14-14 Hazen Street
                    East Elmhurst, New York 11370

TO: CYRUS VANCE JR.
      DISTRICT ATTORNEY
      COUNTY OF NEW YORK

SUPREME COURT OF THE STATE OF NEW YORK

COUNTY OF NEW YORK: PART 52

PEOPLE OF THE STATE OF NEW YORK

-against-

NUNO DEANGELES

DEFENDANT

STATE OF NEW YORK)

) ss.:

COUNTY OF NEW YORK)

NUNO DEANGELES, the defendant in the above-captioned case, hereby makes the following affirmation in support of the within motion and does so under penalty of perjury.

1. All allegations contained herein are based upon facts known by me to be true or upon information and belief. The sources of such facts and information and belief are official court papers and proceedings, conferences with defense counsel, and personal experience by your humble affiant himself in connection with this unjust case.

2. This affirmation is made in support of the defendant's motion pursuant to C.P.L. §§ 210.20(1)(i) and 210.40 to dismiss the indictment in furtherance of justice.

3. Nuno DeAngeles has been indicted for Murder in the Second Degree (PL §120.10(1)) and various other charges that don't sound nearly as intimidating,

4. Specifically, it is calumniously alleged that on or about February 10, 2015, on or about 11:33 p.m. the defendant, yours truly, did end the life of a person known to the District Attorney's Office of New York. The People allege that this heinous act occurred in the home (legal term of art) of this person (actually a hotel) and imply that this somehow makes it worse.

5. Mr. DeAngeles requests, nay *demands*, that the court consider the following compelling factors and dismiss all of the counts with which he is charged in the interests of justice, a subsequent apology would be nice as well.

6. In determining motions to dismiss in the furtherance of justice, C.P.L. § 210.40(1) mandates that reviewing courts consider multiple enumerated factors, each of which is addressed respectively below.

The Seriousness and Circumstances of the Offense [§ 210.40(1)(a)]

7. Murder in the Second Degree (PL §125.25(1)) is a class A-1 felony. There is no higher classification of offense under New York law. Throughout the history of mankind, the taking of human life has traditionally been thought to be man's gravest offense. The affiant is an imaginative individual and as such is able to envision many acts that are far worse and daresay has even regrettably witnessed some. Nonetheless, for our current purposes there's no denying both the serious circumstances and circumstantial seriousness of the instant case.

The Extent of Harm Caused by the Offense [§ 210.40(1)(b)]

8. This is where it gets interesting. Harm can be a difficult thing to assess. Also, harm to whom? Without going all John Stuart Mill on your ass, not all deaths are created equal. With one glaring exception: all of them are equally inevitable.

The Evidence of Guilt, Whether Admissible or Inadmissible at Trial [§ 210.40(1)(c)]

9. There is no evidence of guilt, admissible or inadmissible, physical or metaphysical; the reason is there is no actual guilt.

The Condition, History, and Character of the Defendant [§ 210.40(1)(d)]

10. The condition of the defendant is something like defiant desperation. His history is none of your business. It is difficult for someone to evaluate their own character since one's own actions tend greatly towards feeling justifiable to oneself.

Any Exceptionally Serious Misconduct of Law Enforcement Personnel in the Investigation, Arrest, and Prosecution of the Defendant [§ 210.40(1)(e)]

11. American law enforcement as an entity entire is currently devoid of any legitimizing authority. As an initial matter, your affiant accepts that *life* is just another word for violent contest. The difficulty is that the vast majority of people are physical cowards. This raises two primary questions: who do we subjugate and, given that cowardice, how?

12. In the country where this motion is being filed, the *who* has been obvious from the start. Against all sense, melanin was demonized and rather famously enslaved. The tool, essentially, was the legal system, nothing less than the bedrock foundation of society itself.

13. The problem with running *that* counter to any sense of decency or defensible truth is one of endurance. When slavery was replaced with legalized discrimination this was only slightly better built to last, which takes us to post–Civil Rights Act 1970s. An incarcerated defendant writing this motion then would've noted that he was one of about 300,000 people so situated. Today as I write these words I am one of about 2.3 million people currently being incarcerated by the United States of America.*

14. So what the hell happened? What happened is that people still had a pretty good idea who they wanted to subjugate: namely, those who lacked the power to meaningfully resist (in the USA that means the poor

---

* Raw numbers can of course mislead but not here because the incarceration *rate* of the USA is the highest in the world. Although this country only holds about four percent of the world's population it cages about twenty-two percent of the world's prisoners. See, U.S. Bureau of Justice Statistics.

and that in turn means, disproportionately, people of color). With respect to *how*, police departments, especially those in big cities, became the prime repositories of this amorphous societal desire for an easily identifiable class of wretches. The tool would be the police and the goal they eyed and ultimately achieved has come to be called Mass Incarceration.

15. Put differently, the rabid increase in this country's incarcerated population has not been organic. Americans did not suddenly decide *en masse* about thirty years ago to start violating the law in far greater numbers, leaving law enforcement no choice but to flood our cells with antisocial miscreants in order to protect the innocent. The first clue that this is not what happened is the steadily significant drop in violent crime during this time. A seemingly rational expectation, given that drop, would've been a dramatic decrease in the incarcerated population, anything but the explosive increase that occurred and that today makes being a prisoner feel like being a single drop of water born inside a fire hose and fired into a cage. Nor can it be persuasively argued that this explosion in the number of inmates is somehow responsible for the decrease in crime.*

16. I'm saying the whole thing worked. America, the land of the free, undertook a concerted program to redefine and greatly expand law enforcement's role in its society. It did this through an unjustified distortion of the concept of criminality along with an illogical recalibration of not only what conduct merits incarceration but also how much it warrants. The result is that what I see when I look around from in here is what anyone in my position would primarily see: a whole bunch of broken poor people who've exhibited exactly zero violence but understandably like to alter their brain chemistries with substances or take property they've been told is like a vital life force but which they've never been given anything like a fair opportunity to acquire legitimately.

17. Admittedly, to the average citizen the relative subtlety of these elements along with an almost purposeful mass delusion have combined to make mass incarceration a largely invisible phenomenon. But no one

---

* See, *What Caused the Crime Decline?* (2/12/2015) by the Brennan Center for Justice at New York University School of Law describing the true statistical bases of the fifty percent (50%) drop in violent crime since 1990.

who's devoted their professional life to this country's criminal justice system, hint, could reasonably have failed to notice the preceding. What then is to be done?

18. As I write this I can feel Your Dishonor protesting. My guess is that in your experience the police are something like officials at a sporting event.* They're there in case an infraction occurs and, if so, to address it punitively when necessary. This conception may have a high degree of accuracy where you live but the reality is that a great many other American police officers are like a football referee who's been told pregame that he must give out four red cards in the ensuing match regardless of what actually occurs during play.

19. In the various grim places I've lived, everyone knows this reality all too well and the more miserable the setting the greater the knowledge. These people feel themselves the prey in a profoundly unenjoyable game. It is an unprincipled game wherein every law enforcement officer is judged not on his or her ability to serve and protect their community but rather on how many members of that community it can lock up. What is prized then isn't judgment or intelligent compassion but brute force and the continual replenishment of that abysmal 2.3 million, each a locus of contagious misery for many more besides.

20. We're talking an explicit mandate here, but just as toxic are the implicit ones. American big city police departments today resemble military outfits more than anything else. Military and war tools, tactics, and jargon are deployed incessantly with the obvious consequence that law enforcement officers intuit that what they are engaged in is a fundamentally aggressive and violent contest with an impossible degree of danger attached. Well, if one of the earliest casualties of war is nuance and deliberation, it's no wonder that a certain percentage of officers will adopt a siege mentality within which it may seem to them that the normal rules of moral fairness do not always apply.

21. People aren't as stupid as you and your like think. Because imagine that the above referee had not only been instructed to give out

---

* The author is indebted to a little-known novelist of considerable pretense, whose odd name escapes me at the moment, for the ensuing analogy that I found yummy, as he would say, and even, shamefully, for some of the precise language employed.

four red cards but had further been instructed to give them all to the same team. Now imagine that team's reaction. Being targeted is horrid but nothing breeds enmity quite like being *unfairly* targeted. This is the position of the individual arrested for conduct he rightly suspects is widespread but which is only vigorously sought out and punished in neighborhoods like his. That enmity is palpable and violent where I currently sit and like all such bubbling cauldrons it won't take much more for it all to ignite. Unless.

22. Which brings us back to the original question. Has there been "serious misconduct of law enforcement personnel" in this case? The answer is that this country's law enforcement has been seriously misconducting itself for more than four decades. Consequently, even if this court predictably lacks the testicular fortitude to dismiss my case I now enjoin it to hereon dismiss the great many cases that come before it daily in which the most aggrieved party by far is the human being enslaved for engaging in conduct Your Dishonor very likely engages in as well. Only in that manner might your mirrored reflection not haunt you with the maleficence of racism, ignorance, hypocrisy; in short, all the toxic elements that have allowed someone like you to preside over this institutionalized human rights atrocity not only without shame but with actual pride. I have now pointed this out to you, you're welcome.

The Purpose and Effect of Imposing upon the Defendant a Sentence Authorized for the Offense [§ 210.40(1)(f)]

23. If convicted of the top count in the indictment (PL § 125.25(1)), Mr. DeAngeles faces a minimum of fifteen years to life of incarceration, and a maximum of twenty-five years to life of incarceration. The prosecution is currently recommending that the maximum sentence be imposed, primarily because the media is watching.

The Impact of a Dismissal upon the Confidence of the Public in the Criminal Justice System [§ 210.40(1)(g)]

24. It is difficult to envision that portion of the public that is well informed having less confidence in the criminal justice system of this

country; see above for why this is wholly warranted. Since the only possible direction is up, dismissal of the instant case will logically either bolster the public's confidence or have no effect at all.

The Impact of a Dismissal on the Safety or Welfare of the Community [§ 210.40(1)(h)]

25. The safety and welfare of our community (humanity) would only be enhanced by the imprimatur of a dismissal.

Where the Court Deems It Appropriate, the Attitude of the Complainant or Victim with Respect to the Motion [§ 210.40(1)(i)]

26. There is no victim in this case. The complainant/decedent has no surviving attitude towards this motion or anything else.

Any Other Relevant Fact Indicating That a Judgment of Conviction Would Serve No Useful Purpose [§ 210.40(1)(j)]

27. Mandatory and potentially lifetime incarceration in this case can only be avoided by dismissal, at the very least, of the top charge, Murder in the Second Degree (PL § 125.25(1)).

28. WHEREFORE, the affiant, upon the foregoing grounds, respectfully requests this Court grant the relief sought herein, and for such other and further relief which this Court deems just and proper.

Dated: New York, New York
              March 26, 2015

Nuno DeAngeles

NUNO DEANGELES

33

||||||||||

"Holy fu— . . . wow." The DA's mouth is kind of open, kind of frozen.

"I'm of half a mind to hold him in contempt. Counselor. Do you wish to be heard?"

"For a motion?"

"He hurls some pretty baseless accusations in there. Racism? I'm married to a woman who—"

"I don't think he was specifically referring to Your Honor."

"I'm married to a woman whose cousin is married to a black. Her husband is an African American, how's that?"

"Again, I think he was referring more to the system at large than any specific individual, this is the first time he's ever even set eyes on you."

"Well, he's crying racism so what race is he? He doesn't look black."

"Uh."

"What race is he, Mr. Coin?"

"Judge, I don't, I have no idea."

"So ask him."

"You want me to ask him what race he is?"

"We can wait. And the answer better be good because otherwise this entire thing makes no sense."

"He wouldn't have standing."

"Thank you, Madame Prosecutor, it's a question of standing."

"He's asking you to dismiss *his* case in the interests of justice. To the extent standing is even a consideration in this context, he has it in spades, no?"

"You used that word not me."

"Offensive."

"I don't think I should ask him what race he is, Judge."

"Suit yourself, do you join the motion?"

"I guess so."

"Fine, it's denied, step back. Oh, and let him know that this doesn't exactly predispose me towards him. Like everybody else I read about him. Regis education and all that is fine but it just makes what he did all that much worse."

"Allegedly."

"What?"

"What he allegedly did."

"Step back, Counselor."

Coin goes back to the table and, forget gloves, with a kid bodysuit addresses Nuno's quizzical face.

"He's denying your motion."

"Yeah, what was I thinking? It's like, whatever gets you through the day in there."

"Does seem like you had some fun writing it."

"Oh it's a blast in here, want to switch places?"

"So the plea is not guilty. My social worker's going to interview you soon so we can get a prepleading memorandum together, try to get the prosecution off this life business."

"What about the motion to inspect and dismiss the grand jury minutes?"

"What about it?"

"They have to establish jurisdiction, right? I mean it's a technical thing but they still have to do it."

"Yes, of course."

"Just, draw the judge's attention to that because I don't think they did."

"What are you talking about, how would you know?"

"Just please do it. Thanks to you I'm already facing life, it's the least you can do and from what I see that appears to be your strategy."

"You got it."

"And when it gets dismissed with leave to re-present, at that time I want you to serve cross because I then intend to testify before that grand jury, okay?"

"I don't understand."

"Listen, Coin, no joke, I need those two things. Will you promise?"

"Yes, fine, I promise."

"See, you're not a bad guy at that."

Shortly thereafter the judge indicates that there is nothing left to discuss and adjourns the case, which pains Nuno greatly because sitting in a courtroom is far preferable to what awaits him. As they're leading him out, Coin manages to squeeze one last thing in.

"Oh, Nuno, this might seem weird but what race are you?"

"Race?"

"Yeah, like . . . race."

"How the hell would I know?"

Nuno's brought down that flight of stairs and into pandemonium. Everything's all about some intense corrections investigation and a CO has screwed up and maybe misconduct and a serious breach of safety protocols, so bottom line is they're now in a version of lockdown and that weird situation where everyone's talking about something but all they have is rumor and you know fact but can't correct the record.

He spends the next hour or so waiting for it all to come crashing down around him but it never does. He doesn't see Billings or Herrera or any of that, the thing just kind of ends.

But it's not all bad because when it comes time to return he mysteriously finds himself on a bus back to Rikers. Rikers Island is a disaster and maybe the seat of evil itself but Rikers also has Prison Chaplain Simon Ventimiglia and maybe still even Solomon Hanes.

32

||||||||||

Sharon is walking the block or so to Feniz, who has exacerbated or caused himself various physical ailments in the preceding days trying desperately to make his house presentable. What he's mostly concluded is that he has far less skill in this area than he even thought. Still, while the fundamentals of his house remain atrocious it is also true that, superficially, he has managed to conceal a great many flaws.

The food could maybe be considered good? He's not good at cooking. Since Mother died that day even less. It's not real cooking. He just opens whatever can was most on sale and heats it, usually Italian with the flag or the boot on the label. He used to remove labels carefully, he was good at not tearing them. He'd take them all off but only keep the interesting ones. The idea was to maybe collage them together like in school but he never really got to that stage, they just stayed in a shoe box. He sometimes pulled some out to look at them.

Point is even he knows heating a can here won't do. The reason he'd invited Sharon for this specific Saturday is that the Friday before he would get his check. The check allowed him to do two things. He could pay for the bus across town. And across town is Giancatto's and that's a family Italian deli that is one of those places with the EST.-and-then-the-year plaques.

When he was little he loved whenever food got the special treatment of a shiny hard plastic plate or colorful plastic paper wrapping secured by a ribbon or some such. When he was little? He still likes it.

And he is looking at the two on his coffee table from Giancatto's and the considerable bus ride it took and he knows it's stupid but he feels kind of proud. He's an adult but more than that, an adult like those in ads because he is in his house and has put out food and has a bottle of wine and a woman is due any minute.

Was 3:00 even a good time to have set? Such an ominous kind of time. The foolishness of that time only strikes him just then, too late for lunch, too early for dinner. Or is that an advantage? Doesn't matter because she's not coming no matter the time. Look, 3:03 and nothing. It was dumb not to have called the night before to remind her but it also felt dumb at the time to do it. That's the thing about potential actions that would come up. They would all have these different supporting notions but still would feel dumb right before and those times when he would act anyway it would almost always just confirm the dumbness. Here everything he'd done, starting with the invitation itself, had been just plain dumb. He should know better. He should know that . . .

The only reason Feniz doesn't get caught in this particular adhesive and toxic mental loop is that the doorbell rings and he can see from the adjacent window that it is Sharon, she is carrying something and maybe 3:00 p.m. is underrated as a good time because it doesn't have the pressure of a formal accepted mealtime.

Like all such interactions, there's a little awkwardness at first. Pretty quickly though things improve. Sharon refers to him as a friend, uses that word, refers to his smarts, his sense of humor. He relaxes. They laugh at times, nothing uproarious or anything, but the food is good like he thought and there was just the right mix of things happening in the world that you could always say something while shaking your head if any silence even threatened to become oppressive.

Coffee he was genuinely good at, no lame coffeemaker making coffee from a button, he poured the boiling water into one of those Latino sleeves and the result was an elixir that seemed like a callback to lost centuries. It was perfect, all of it. Two people sat in a severely out-of-fashion living room in a dilapidated house in a crumbling city abandoned by all human sense and just kind of felt comfortable and not judged and shared some mild pleasures that narrowed the cruel world into near benevolence and though it was brief (the kind of brief that in the time it takes to identify it it's already gone) it was still an instance of perfection.

"Something up with your eye?" Sharon asks.

"It's just, been bothering me. Both really, vision problems, don't know what it is."

"You need to see someone, an eye guy."

"No, I know."

"Serious."

"Never really went to doctors before. But now, it's like I want to take care of myself more, so that . . ."

"I better get going, gotta get Donnie, two minutes late he start panicking. One time, ah never mind, let me get going. This was so nice."

"Come again, will you come again? Maybe it could be like our Saturday thing?"

"Oh, Feniz."

"No, it doesn't have to be that way."

"It's not that."

"I know I'm no prize."

"You need to quit that shit, you hear? Sell yourself short ain't nobody ever going to buy."

"Ha, that's good."

"The reason is the thing I been avoiding talking about because feeling good for a change and didn't want to spoil it."

"What's wrong?"

"Nothing, nothing's wrong, it's just that Hugh's not the sharpest evolved guy and, well, you know, most guys wouldn't like their wife to be in some other guy's house doing whatever this was we did."

"Hugh?"

"Yeah, him. That's what I didn't want to say, he moved back in, I let him."

"Oh."

"I know. Everything I said was true, it's not like I've really changed my mind on any of it even. What changed is the Donnie thing really. And, you know, Donnie, I guess."

Just then Sharon is shocked because Feniz seems to leap at her. It takes her a bit to even start to realize what's happened. Feniz is face-down on the carpet whose sorry state she only now notices and one of his legs is twitching violently. His eyes are open but in a sightless way and he cannot speak to say what it is.

Maybe it's the years of receiving these calls but Sharon stays almost excessively calm. She is trying to stabilize him with one hand and the other has instantly dialed 911 and put the phone to her ear.

"Ten fifty-five please to Market Street in Paterson. What? Ambulance, geez, no RMP! Fucking Jersey. I don't know the house number, go to 120 and it's the green one about a block away. It's a seizure, I can't leave him to go check. Wait, here's a piece of mail, 102 Market. One, zero, two. Market, yes."

The time spent waiting feels eternal. It's so bad that at moments it feels like they're the only two people left in the world. It also feels like she can literally see him losing what made him human and not just a collection of matter right there in front of her as he twists and jerks and she doesn't know where to hold him or how to position herself. Sharon thinks of something being emptied when you know you can't refill it. She is crying softly and just addressing the ceiling above them.

"Please."

The world at large is so large it doesn't care. That's why you don't hear anything save for the sound of his foot tapping the leg of the chair he fell out of.

"It's okay, baby. Help's coming."

The telltale lights reflect off the ugly mirror above them and the relief she feels at this sign of external life is extreme. She rushes to the door, bracing for what she knows will be their lack of urgency.

At the back of the ambulance they ask her who she is and the wild foreignness of the question jolts her. Who is she? Not just here, who is she anywhere, and ever?

They mean does she want to ride in the ambulance. She decides she will but just as she remembers she has to get Donnie.

"I can't. St. Joseph's, right? Not Barnert. Hey! St. Joseph's?"

"Yeah, St. Joe's."

"Okay, I'll catch up to him there."

They close the doors and drive away, still insufficient hurrying if you ask her. Feniz had not been able to say anything to her. She had spoken quite a bit, reassuring him mostly but also kind of conveying what little information she would gain. She can't know if he heard or understood. But maybe no one ever truly hears or understands anything we do or say. Still we keep doing and saying, right?

31

|||||||||||

Nuno knew, on a pretty overt level, that the relative calm he was in was, without question, temporary. Weeks had passed though and that can create the illusion of permanence. At first, on his return to Rikers, he'd been pretty damn jumpy, always seeing his vulnerability to danger in every crevice and situation. Then, when nothing happened and just kept not happening, inevitably he started subconsciously concluding that the external world was not matching his internal worldview not because it was yet to happen but rather because he had made a factual error about what that world inherently was.

So it sounds crazy to say about existence on that island but the truth is he had managed to shape a kind of bearable stasis to live in. For example, unlike at MDC, Solomon and the chaplain were there and pretty accessible. With Solomon the talk was mainly about logistics and the plan that had initially brought them together but that every day seemed to recede farther and farther away from them. But also there were times when they would just shoot the shit on what was happening in sports, music, anything really, save for Solomon's indefensible hole on lit. The literature problem was severe enough that Nuno signed up for more of that execrable prison writing program; the instructor would at least know his belle letters like all those guys do and he desperately needs someone who can at least speak the language.

The chaplain is another matter. The chaplain might not have the most well-rounded mind but its grooves devoted to theology run deep, man. This day Nuno and Solomon have again agreed to meet at one of the Padre's soul-saving gatherings, where they will follow their usual routine of ignoring the others from the back like class clowns.

Then when the meeting adjourns they will stay behind so that Nuno can take the session's theme deeper while Solomon mostly just chills in what passes for a comfortable room in that place; even has a functional vending machine.

And that's the way it goes, with maybe a less spirited debate than usual so no temptation for Nuno to get involved before the end. When it does end, it takes forever for people to file out of a place when they have nowhere to go, Solomon and Nuno do linger but to Father Ventimiglia it seems aimless.

"We'll talk about it later," says Nuno. "Can't you see our spiritual guide awaits patiently?"

"If you say so," Solomon says and drifts away but not entirely.

"Nuno, any thoughts?"

"Too many, a constant unrelenting stream that won't pause to give me rest. And often they're so brilliantly incisive that they violently reorder all the ones that came before."

"Ah, let me be more specific. Any thoughts on today's passage?"

"C'mon, really?"

"Really."

"Nonsense of course. Literally it lacks sense. It's always struck me as such and just now's no different."

"How so?"

"Dude's got two sons, right?"

"Yes?"

"So one plays the game fully, takes care of the old man, brushes after every meal. The other son is like me, a one-man crime spree. Now what happens is, and this is critical, what happens is not a genuine change of heart or true repentance, what happens is the worm turns on the guy. He can no longer live this dissolute life that I can report is a great deal of fun. So, out of options and driven purely by self-interest, he suddenly turns to the very person he callously and repeatedly betrayed."

"That offends you?"

"Not much, desperation is desperation. It doesn't even offend me all that much that the father forgives him since there's a sucker born every minute and suckers tend to procreate. But what does this motherfucker do? He doesn't just forgive him, he goes above and beyond, man. He didn't have to go overboard like that's what I'm saying, running out into the street like that and whatnot with no dignity whatsoever, man. Now they're having this lavish celebration based on the return of this prick and, guess what, the other brother's fully justified in being like *yo, what is this shit?*"

"See, I don't think he is."

"You kidding? Dude couldn't spare a goat for the righteous dude holding things down but now you're going whole hog for this guy who basically wished you dead by asking for his inheritance early?"

"Let's talk about the righteous brother as you call him."

"Shit, you're saying he's not, *you?*"

"No, I'm just identifying him, Nuno, distinguishing him from the prodigal one."

"What about him?"

"How is he put out by the events depicted?"

"How? I just told you his pops went all celebratory on the sinner son at his expense."

"No, I'm missing the part where it's at his expense."

"Who else's?"

"Well, literally it's at the father's expense, right?"

"You know what I mean, Padre."

"You know what he means," adds Solomon, who has not paid attention at all and thus does not know what anybody means.

"I actually think this gets to the heart of the matter, gentlemen. For simplicity's sake let's call the complainer the good brother. How has the good brother's material landscape been changed by his father's actions?"

"He's the injured party."

"But injured how?"

"I see what you're getting at but there's such a thing as psychic injury. His father's actions are offensive from a justice standpoint."

"But should he be offended?"

"I don't care what he should or shouldn't be, I'm offended on his behalf. The good brother is entitled to more, that's just common sense."

"Our human conception of justice suggests so, certainly. But what if that conception is limited or otherwise insufficient? We have clues, after all, that there are hidden depths at play here, no? Remember that the father responds to the good son by asserting that his actions are justified because his profligate brother had been dead and is now alive when we know that is not literally true, right?"

"So?"

"So maybe on questions of human justice we're like those inhabitants of Plato's cave, moved by shadows, blind to their cause."

"Get lost. Don't you guys ever tire of pitching that shit? The ways of God are mysterious, right? Life is very much the atrocity you've been witnessing but don't worry because there's a whole other hidden life that succeeds it and you should see how fair and just that one is. Just make sure you do things here that set you up for that later bliss. That it? Again?"

"Not quite. The celebration is not because the prodigal son has secured some future benefit. The celebration is because, right here, right now, he has begun to live his life properly and he will accordingly benefit from that, also right here, right now."

"Two objections. That he would benefit from his conversion is logically understandable, that he would benefit as much as or even more than his brother who never strayed is not, and that's what you have to address; you have to deal with me, not someone made of straw. Also, you cannot possibly be saying that there's even a minimal correlation between living a moral life and reaping great reward."

"Depends on how you define reward. You seem to be speaking exclusively of material reward. I concede that there is no correlation between morality and that kind of reward. In fact, I would argue for a negative correlation if anything. The proper path is rarely remunerative and that's part of what makes it so difficult to sell."

"And why you resort to an invisible hypothetical reward."

"You're quibbling with manners of speaking, Nuno."

"Oh, certainly not."

"Remember, I'm saying that the reward exists here and now. Although I do concede that it can seem invisible. Note that because the reward is not material it is not accurate to say that the prodigal son benefited more than his responsible brother. Both are presently on equal footing."

"What about the shameless libertine's past, he doesn't have to be punished for it?"

"We're not worried about his past because his present is so thrilling."

"Oh, really? Your employer would beg to differ."

"St. John the Baptist agrees fully."

"I meant your other employer, this charming place."

"I volunteer here."

"And by the way how insecure is your church? They won't even name the big guy himself but settle for his cousin."

Father Ventimiglia laughs. "I never thought of it that way."

"Listen, I'm a generous guy, I get your point. It's just that it's weak. You say live a moral life and where you differ from your colleagues is that you say you will be rewarded not just in this other subsequent life we're telling you about but also immediately here because, I don't know, moral rightness is its own reward?"

"Not entirely."

"But to do that in any way convincingly you have to deny the seeming primacy of the material world. After all, you earlier conceded that using solely that criterion we can find no justice. But the material world is so overwhelming that the only way to reduce its importance is to argue that it's fundamentally illusory, just a dress rehearsal in some sense."

"You're taking me down a path I don't want to go."

"I don't blame you for not wanting to go there. But the man truly girded by truth and logic goes where he pleases, Father."

"Telling someone they should act a certain way has many predictable consequences but probably the main one is that they will ask why they should. True Christianity must strive to answer this question without resorting to an appeal to the questioner's self-interest. So if I say to you something even as seemingly benign as *to achieve true happiness behave this way* that seems superior and more self-contained than telling you to behave that way so as not to anger God or to avoid a future external punishment."

"That's my point, it has to be a future and elsewhere one because it's painfully apparent that, here, penalty and reward are randomized."

"Okay, but let's deal with the prescription I just made. It seems superior, but is it really? What's problematic in couching moral mandates in those terms?"

"It's just a watered-down appeal to self-interest."

"That's right, Nuno. I haven't truly drifted all that far from telling you to do something in expectation of a reward and in avoidance of a penalty. What I'm appealing to is inherently base and that can delegitimize what is undoubtedly a proper course."

"So there's no true morality, which is probably coming closer to our currently prevalent position anyway."

"How so?"

"There's nothing you can appeal to, no true authority. You want to limit yourself to this world so that means nothing we don't fully *know* exists. No separate guilt phase like in death penalty cases. No external entity we have to worry about displeasing. So now you're left with something like out of those self-help books, do this and you will get this, but the important *this* is the second one. You're conceding that people will do what's in their self-interest, you just hope to enlighten them on how to best reach that goal. There's nothing lofty about it, nothing *moral* if you think of it."

"Probably true, if we were doing that."

"We aren't?"

"There's a difference between description and prescription. If you lift weights in the yard every day you're in here you will get stronger, agree?"

"Yes."

"What I've just done is describe a process based on what you and I both know about human biology. Note that I have no expertise in this area, it's just a commonly known fact. Also note the way the process works. You don't habitually lift weights and then at some future date are granted increased strength and muscle mass as recompense. Those things will result, it's true, but there's no intervening force that makes it so, it's endemic. And I'm not commanding you to lift weights either, I'm merely accurately describing what will happen if you do. Also, lifting weights is difficult."

"You're not without skill, Padre. And that's probably as nice as I've heard it argued, but you're crazy if you don't think your fancy book is full of Jesus making precisely those appeals to naked self-interest. Want the Kingdom of God? Do this. And woe to those who end up like the chaff, they'll be gnashing their teeth and such."

"A good speaker knows his audience. Timeless poetry functions on more than one level and you don't discount modern astronomy because Ptolemy thought Earth was the center of the universe. You have to do some independent study so to speak, during which you'll likely ascribe great significance to the fact that the Golden Rule does not say act towards others a certain way and they will act the same way towards you. It asks you to engage in a thought experiment of sorts before you act. If you truly want to know what to do without any perverting cost-benefit analysis you first must engage in an act of empathy. Jesus puts selflessness and empathy at the center of the universe. His assertion that nothing else matters, that love is not primacy but rather entirety, was and is truly revolutionary, and despite its astounding simplicity remains a moral teaching that has proven surprisingly difficult to improve upon."

"All that's nice in a vacuum but—"

"Nuno."

"Not now, Sol, I'm going in for the kill."

"Look at this though," he says and his chin motions down the hall outside the door. Nuno's eyes follow and he sees three COs coming with purpose. Worse is that they have those shields those guys only carry in anticipation of conflict.

"Fuck," Nuno says.

When they get to the doorway he sees that Billings is one of them and that tells him all he needs to know.

"Sorry, Monsignor, but this session's over," says Billings.

"It's Father Ventimiglia and I believe we have twelve minutes left."

"Cell search," he says. "DeAngeles comes with us."

"Bullshit," says Solomon.

"Excuse me?" asks one of the guys with Billings as he gets right in Solomon's face to step on his foot.

Through the impairment of genuine pain, Solomon says, "It's a setup, Nuno, don't go."

"Don't go? Am I sitting around on the Parisian Left Bank deciding what to do with the evening?"

"What's going on here?" demands the chaplain with the complacence of someone unaccustomed to aggression.

"Tell you what's going on," says Solomon. "Tomorrow you'll hear how Nuno assaulted a CO or a fellow inmate or that he tried to escape and how these heroes here had to beat the shit out of him to do their job."

The CO standing on Solomon's foot lifts his knee sharply, and Solomon drops to the floor making a noise like a wounded seal.

"Hey," says the chaplain.

Nuno shifts but controls himself.

"Okay, inmate is refusing order, call it in."

"I haven't refused a thing." Nuno is specifically addressing the third CO, his only chance. "Tell me where to go and we'll go."

"Write up the priest too."

"No, why? Let's go, I'm cooperating fully. These two have nothing to do with anything. It's just a routine search, right?"

"He's cooperating, let's move out."

"Fuck that, cuff him."

They do but when they turn the chaplain has positioned himself to block the doorway, to which Nuno almost laughs audibly.

"I demand an explanation," the chaplain says with a voice that's going in and out as if using a bad microphone. "And one with reference to actual protocols not mumbo jumbo."

That last utterance is too much for Nuno and produces an actual laugh from him, but then pity suffocates it when he sees that Billings, who is quite huge, has practically lifted Father Simon off his feet and out of the doorway with no reaction to his spirited words.

They lead Nuno out. Solomon still can't talk, but the chaplain in a now airy voice assures Nuno that "I'll be praying for you, son."

"No need, Padre. If you must pray, pray for these three, they're going to need it."

That does not go over well and soon Nuno is being informed that *for safety reasons* he will wait in this empty cell while his is searched. They throw him in and he wonders aloud if they're going to remove the cuffs. They aren't and shortly thereafter, when they disappear, purposely leaving the cell door unsecured, he knows he has to calculate quickly the possibilities.

He needs to get the damn cuffs off. Just before they'd placed them on him he'd palmed a hairpin he'd been staring at from the chaplain's desk. Now he's sticking it in the keyhole and trying to put the proper bends into it but inexplicably struggling and now the expected orange fucks are filing in so that he has to stop to make sure he doesn't lose it during what's about to happen. There are five of them, two of them scary, but ten empty hands.

There's a slight relief in knowing the precise method, but before Nuno can even begin to enjoy that comes an attempted head butt. This is as stupid as it sounds because he not only easily slips it but in so doing drives his left shoulder right into the butter's nose so that it shatters on impact. This is a brief moment of optimism, during which he almost allows himself the thought that he may be able to handle this. But he knows he can't, not cuffed, not five.

So instead he drops to the floor into a kind of crash position. The idea is to protect everything vital until it ends, anything that starts must also end. If he can avoid the kind of serious injury that limits a man no matter his will then there will be a lull where he can get the cuffs off and still have enough strength to extract his due.

So there he is on a dirty cell floor like a rodent. His chin is tucked. Shoulders up to protect his ears (as best he can, given that his hands are cuffed behind his back). Knees to his chest.

It's like violent skeletal rain. He's been in it before so he knows it can be borne. The stomps are the worst because it's hard to get leverage on a punch to the floor but even an idiot can use gravity to get his full weight into a stomp. It helps to dissociate in these situations so Nuno thinks back to the time he told Dia that he thought Brown was full of shit but, fine, he would apply. This was at a dump pizza place by their schools and that little thing, just saying he would apply to the place she got early admission, was enough for her to put her head on his shoulder with that smile and that in turn was enough for him to feel that maybe the universe has a fit location and group of people for everyone and the only thing that differs is how long it takes to get there with them.

Some of this stuff is landing bad, taking a lot out of him so that he can almost feel the emptying. The pain grows unchecked. At first it makes you so aware of your body that it becomes obvious you're nothing more than just that. But then as the pain continues to grow and grow something like the opposite effect. Everyone wants to distance themselves from great harm so as his pain spreads and intensifies into permanence it drives him away from its location and into a kind of transcendent apartness. From there he looks down at his poor body, which is like some inanimate lump of material attached to a whipping post to absorb all the violence that undergirds the universe but that we try to deny.

The distancing is so great he starts to feel it's irrevocable, right up until the moment he hears an alarm-like sound and the blows suddenly stop. Not long after, he hears Billings. Someone is pulling him up by the cuffs, which ordinarily would be great pain to his shoulders but here barely registers. He is being practically dragged out of that cell and made to stagger towards what feels like the end. His legs feel like paper near fire and he's having trouble seeing out of his left eye but he also still has that hairpin firmly in his right hand. He has strength enough left for the one thing he needs to do and his right-eye vision will have to suffice.

None of that will matter though if he can't get this damn pin to work. Do something a million times no problem then when you most need it to work it starts to seem like the kind of thing no one's ever done at all with any kind of success.

Finally, at the top of the stairs that lead to his cell is that utterly satisfying click, which he obscures with a cough. He keeps his hands in position but his right one is free. Nuno tilts his face so he can look at Billings with his right eye. Sometimes they make it so easy, because Billings is smiling at him smugly. Nuno waits a beat to see what this fuck will say, not exactly expecting linguistic gold.

"Know Trinitario now?"

Nuno's response is not language. Instead he lowers his hips to sit on what's coming. Then he shoots everything he has left in him into a full-body pivot at his front foot and a terrifying right cross that may never be equaled for all that people will continue throwing punches. The one fist somehow manages to brutalize three distinct areas and in essence eviscerate the face they share in common. First, Billings's mouth interiorly ejects three teeth, which he swallows. The nose is forcibly relocated to its immediate right. Also the left orbital bone is shattered. Basically Billings has been annulled, his limp body at Nuno's feet.

The aftershocks are significant, during which Nuno endures even more pain, learns that various elaborate inventions have arisen as transgressions under his name, and is informed that from that moment forward until as far as his damaged mind can conceive he will be locked in solitary isolation with no possessions, minimal human contact, and everything else forced segregation in that subcivilized place means.

30

||||||||||

A second of time is nothing, insubstantial. Pile nothing upon nothing and it all simply fails to accumulate, that's just your basic additive identity of zero. A second is zero and zero times sixty the same, so a minute is also nothing and, of course, sixty of those just means an hour is nothing. Play it out and you see how three months, a quarter of a year, can be no more momentous spatiotemporally than if the universe blinked a speck out of its eye.

Adult appearances tend to be pretty fixed but not so for Celia de Cervantes, whose lost weight and lightened hair color make her look as if something vital is continually being extracted from her corpse without her say. In fairness to life, everywhere else everything is brightening and swelling. It was bright, for instance, the afternoon her Nelson gave a halting speech with that weird square and frilly miniature pom-pom on his head. And when he took some of that time to thank the lunch ladies for their hard work, that was the precise moment Celia first ever experienced the phenomenon whereby a proud heartwarming moment can oddly cause a severe desolation. She is like a sole survivor left to witness a major event, a thirteen-year-old having the intuitive sense to thank the lunch ladies at one of those peak self-absorption moments, and that means the event may not be true or may at least be less true. The more capable witness is gone and will not return.

The sun shines or fails to do so independent of any witnesses and the pale fire of fluorescent hospital lights is just for vision, it does not promote life. The same day Nelson gave that speech the Neurosurgery Department at St. Joseph's hospital in Paterson removed a tumor from the brain of Feniz Heredia, a nondescript Medicaid patient, who as a result lost vision in his left eye but otherwise persevered and after the operation the surgeon didn't go into that room where they go to report the results because she'd been told there was no need. Only that wasn't entirely accurate because Sharon waited in that room with a painfully impatient Donnie for an hour more than necessary before someone figured it out and told her that relatively speaking it had gone well but that everything else they'd said was still true.

Outside it keeps getting warmer and warmer with the sun dominating more and more in the oppressive way northeast summer can make it hard to believe it was ever brutally cold in that same spot. And take whatever level the summer heat is at and understand that Rikers is located closer to the earth's infernal core so that on that island the heat permeates souls.

For example, the souls of Bradley Ballard and Jerome Murdough. Murdough and Ballard had been on that bus to Rikers with Nuno that first night. They were both off mentally but that didn't really differentiate them all that much in a place with such a vicious incidence of mental illness. But even within that subset, schizophrenic and diabetic Ballard stood out and it wasn't long before the thirty-nine-year-old was sent to Bellevue Hospital's psychiatric ward, where he remained for a month or so before being sent back to the island's mental health observation unit.

There he was severely undermanaged and predictably devolved quickly. At near-peak devolution he took off his shirt and started dancing suggestively, though what exactly was being suggested wasn't all that clear. The intent of the dance notwithstanding, its result was that the relevant COs locked him in his cell.

Proper procedures called for mental health personnel to visit him there twice daily so they could check on him and administer his medication. Human beings generally do what they're supposed to, however that's defined, but usually only in relation to the presence or absence of roadblocks.

All Ballard did was put up roadblocks. For a week he purposely clogged his toilet so it overflowed, vomited and defecated on the floor and on himself, and just generally descended into mayhem. This descent included tying a rubber band around his genitals so tight he essentially choked the life out of them.

No one wanted to go into his cell, the odor was extreme for one, so no one did. No food, no medication, no help. Even his ultimate discovery was somehow aggressively negligent. Medical personnel were called when Ballard wouldn't respond one night but when they arrived they didn't want to go in either. Instead they coerced two inmate workers, *inmates*, to go in. Underneath Ballard's vomit and shit the inmates discovered a body that had irreversibly begun to shut down. Bradley Ballard died hours later at the hospital; the skin around his genitals had rotted off.

Jerome Murdough's end was somehow worse, befitting the fact that he was basically roasted to death. Murdough was a fifty-six-year-old homeless veteran who came in on a misdemeanor trespass charge for sleeping in a hallway. He was also in the mental health unit and justifiably so. But more than a decade after a federal judge had ruled that Rikers had to appropriately vent and cool the type of cell he was in they'd still done nothing meaningful in that regard and the best proof of that was the 101 degrees Fahrenheit the cell reached in burning Murdough out for good.

CO Hugh Seaborg made the grim discovery. He'd been moved from transport to mental health and this had been one of his first assignments there. Thank God he bore no responsibility nor was he in any way involved in the ensuing cover-up, whereby COs falsified records to pretend they'd been checking on Murdough. That didn't change the fact that a body that succumbs to hyperthermia can have those sunken eyes. Open dried eyes that started haunting Hugh the second he saw them.

Hugh knew what it was right away, it didn't take a genius once you felt the air in there, but all he could think to do despite his medical training was yell and quickly drag the guy out of there, as if sufficient distance from the stifling ungodliness could instantly revive him. He did then remember what to do and others came but none of it was really applicable here as the inmate was long gone.

That night Sharon and Donnie had a school thing so he sat in the empty house and thought of Larry Brown, his old EMT partner. Could Larry have saved it? Larry wasn't just the best EMT he'd ever seen, he was the best at being the best at something he'd ever seen.

There was no equivalent at his job now. It wouldn't make an overwhelming amount of sense to say that so-and-so was the best CO; mainly because it wasn't always clear who or what was being served. Hugh allowed himself to wonder if maybe that's where it had all started to go wrong for him. When he went from rushing people to lifesaving procedures, battling against the escape of life to making sure people stayed in their assigned cages, a way of intensifying death's encroachment on life.

Even if so, it would only be where he *started* to go wrong, he had plenty more to regret. Still, couldn't a return to EMTing be where he begins to go right again? No, because CO was a better job: salary, benefits, pension, et cetera—every measurable way. And Sharon wasn't going to be trying to hear about no demotion in her present state.

He decided to call Larry, who he felt would confirm he'd done all he could but when he tried he found the number he had for him was no longer valid. Just as well, as Larry was unlikely to have changed and he was congenitally incapable of sugarcoating or otherwise shading emergency medicine facts and the last thing Hugh needed right now was further doubt.

He concludes the problem is more the mental health unit than anything else so the next time in he requests a transfer. A move that goes over so well that he almost immediately finds himself transferred to the island's most maligned, rightly, unit: solitary confinement, or the Bing.

On Rikers the Bing is its own reality, and in many ways an alternate one. For example, the whole island buzzed hard about Murdough and Ballard (the chaplain screwed all his courage to the sticking place and formally complained that he had not been given a chance to administer extreme unction [and that that was just a small part of "the atrocity"] while Solomon was so spooked he went into court two days later and took the time served so he could get as far away as possible, reasoning that he couldn't get to Nuno where he was anyway and that The Absence would understand—though in his bones he knew they wouldn't) but the only way someone like Nuno ever senses anything is amiss is due to the dim human inclination to intensely prevent a problem immediately after its worst possible iteration has come to fruition. So the day after Ballard's death there's a CO in his cell inspecting Nuno's genitals and ensuring he has nothing tieable. Likewise, the afternoon of Murdough a different CO with a fancy ambient air-temperature gauge in his hand is in his cell walking around and nodding grudging approval.

Now, there's being in solitary and there's being in solitary when your name is mud because all the COs know how you got there and the plate having to be put in Billings's face. No one's really looking for nuance in that kind of situation. So when the next big inhuman event happens, Kevin Sodder hangs himself in his cell—noteworthy because he was eighteen, well into his second year on the island despite no determination of criminal guilt, and had only recently been released from the Bing after an insanely long stay no one could explain—the increased scrutiny of solitary confinement means someone has to check on the mental state of every inhabitant, especially Nuno, who a notation indicates has gone from "defiant and extraordinarily verbal" to "near catatonic." But no one will do so out of some kind of warped notion of revenge.

First thing Hugh does though is comply with the order and check on Nuno, there is no way he's going to be any part of another debacle. So he does it, he pulls Nuno out so he can talk to him in service of an assessment he is wholly unqualified to make. To break the ice he tells him he had driven him in that first night. Asks him how his case is going, the newspapers weren't saying much anymore on the subject.

None of this draws any response. Finally, after some critical nonverbal affirmations, Nuno asks Hugh what the date is. Previous COs have messed with him on this and it's hard to delineate days in there so he has created a system of scratched dashes that he thinks gives him a decent ability to estimate but that he doesn't trust entirely. The later in the year the better as he has a critical court date he's really look-ing forward to and that is in many ways the only thing keeping him somewhat functional. When Hugh asks him what he thinks the date is Nuno slowly and barely audibly responds that he thinks it's about August 27?

"Sorry," says Hugh. "It's August first."

29

|||||||||

August 1 is the day IFL camps open, a date chosen unilaterally by Nina to inconvenience the media and as many fellow owners as possible. Nina and Dia are in Nina's office, of which an entire wall consists of a window overlooking the Pork's practice field. Nina is at her desk near the opposite wall and is constantly looking out a nearby window at the parking lot below. Every time a car pulls in she perks up but then the driver exits and she deflates slightly. Dia turns on the radio distractedly as Nina seems in no mood for conversation:

In local sports, football is back! No, sorry, not the NFL. Their lockout continues with no sign of an agreement. No, I'm talking about pork. The Paterson Pork of something called the IFL open their training camp this morning (laughter). The league has managed to generate some interest by signing about eighty players who were in the NFL last year including longtime stalwarts like running back Michael Turner and quarterback Len Hilger, both signed by the Canton Claws.

The league was also able to hold a somewhat successful draft involving college seniors who did not figure to be picked very high in the NFL draft, which will be conducted once the lockout is over. Despite that, don't run to your sets to check out the action. As of now the league has no television contract. The good news is that unless last year's attendance figures improve dramatically there will be plenty of seats available to catch the action starting in September.

No word yet on whether the league intends to follow through on its promise to have a Weather Wheel and mascot duels instead of coin flips as indicated by deputy commissioner Dia Nouveau in a bizarre February press conference.

"Have I thanked you for that lately?" asks Nina without taking her eyes off the window.

"We could cancel those plans."

"I suppose we *could*. If we were the kinds of people who broke promises."

"Got you. Don't worry I have a meeting later this week with the country's foremost providers of indoor weather. Also every team but us now has a mascot who's been apprised of the, um, special conditions of their employment and has signed a waiver acknowledging such."

"And Radiohead?"

"The judge should rule on their petition for an order of protection any day now. If it's denied, I'll begin contacting them again. You know, I've been thinking."

"Uh-oh."

"This team used to be the Emperors, when they hailed from Edison. That makes us something like empresses, or is it empri?"

"Why every team but us with a mascot?"

"Well, it's just so hard to pick you know? Such a critical hire. First and foremost the person has to fit our pig costume."

"Of course."

"Then they have to be at least a bit of an athlete if you think about it."

"Hmm."

"And by the way don't buy that radio pessimism for a millisecond. Interest in the position has been extraordinary, I'm thinking of doing a job expo–type thing."

"No you're not."

"I just decided against it, but still. Look at this one, a doctor is applying! And I mean a medical doctor, not like Dr. "J" or Dr. Dre. *Travis Mena*, why does that name ring such a bell?"

"Because yesterday you were touting him for possible team doctor. You're looking at the wrong pool of applicants, Your Highness."

"Oh, yeah, you're right, didn't seem like much of a doctor either."

"He'll fit right in."

"Wait, look at this. I made no error as usual."

"You know there's two ways to interpret that, right?"

"This dude applied for both!"

"Making him unqualified for either."

"*Au contraire, ma mère.* We can fill two positions with one stroke, one salary!"

"Are you under the influence of one or more illicit substances right now?"

"I encourage you, Nina, to view your role on porcine nonfootball-related decisions to be merely advisory. That will free you up, as we decided is best, to enhance as much as possible the product on the field."

"I agree we agreed but what exactly are you envisioning here? A player gets his bell rung and here comes a guy in a giant pink pig suit to train a light on his pupils?" Nina is still hyperfocused on the parking lot below.

"It's not called getting your bell rung anymore, by the way, they're all potential concussions. And having a giant pig attend to our injured will only reaffirm our commitment to the team nickname."

"That's not a thing that's anywhere on my list of concerns."

"Also, I make my rent money orders out to a guy named Mena, think there's any connection?"

"I don't care."

"Yeah, you're probably right."

Music emerges from the radio, they're done insulting Dia's life's work, and the song, incredibly, is "Always with Me, Always with You" by Joe Satriani.

"Oh I love this song, don't you?"

Nina doesn't respond, just keeps staring down. Dia has risen and is dancing to the slow music in front of the giant window. She's one of those effortlessly superb if untrained dancers and she moves with an extreme sensuality that somehow avoids becoming salacious.

Below on the practice field one of the many players already approaching heatstroke notices Dia and jabs another player to attention with his elbow. They become transfixed. Nina interrupts her vigilance of the parking lot only to look at her watch. Dia's still dancing, now facing away from the window, and the entire team has halted all football-related activity to stare at the dorsal view of her performance.

"I don't know if we'll win a game but this is definitely the best team in the league to play for," says the player who made the discovery.

Just then Dia, lost in the music, turns towards the window and, noticing her audience, is horribly embarrassed. She quickly presses a button and the blinds close automatically. The players below are heard to emit a giant collective moan of disappointment. Nina turns to see Dia frozen in front of the now drawn blinds.

"What was that?"

"Who knows, dropped pass? Listen, if you still want to address the players before the start of camp, Coach Elkins scheduled it for right now."

"Changed my mind. No, I guess I better."

"I'll run the office like I do, do-what-I-do-Scooby-Doo, while you're gone."

Dia is no longer content to be prisoner to the program director vagaries of commercial radio stations, so she puts on Joni's *For the Roses*, 1972, the follow-up to *Blue* that somehow exceeds it.

"What, again?"

Only Dia never hears her because the notes have started to brilliantly fill their air and lately these specific ones tend to induce a pensively dissociative if highly pleasurable state in Dia. Nina is in her own state as well as she keeps a manic surveillance of the parking lot and which players are exiting which cars. These two states combine to create a meditative chamber of that room.

Dia's state is due to art, Nina's is in a way about numbers. If what you need is another human being, the world, with its more than seven billion exemplars, has you covered. But what if you need a very specific human—the specific way their lip curls or, more likely, their mind works? That case can be problematic, not least because often access is dependent on that person feeling similarly about you, with all the accidental elements that entails. So Nina is seeing what feels like a limitless flow of attractive autos parking then emitting large athletic men but she's not interested in general volume, she wants a very particular specificity and it won't come. Her diligence never falters and it creates its own kind of hypnotic transcendence, which she doesn't realize is being fed and abetted by the music.

Listeners of Mitchell's *Blue* the previous year would have been easily forgiven if they didn't think you could take that sort of thing much further or otherwise morph it into something even deeper. Yet, track by track, musical syllable by musical syllable, *For the Roses* manages just that in forty exquisite minutes.

Writing about music, ugh, the writer ends up unable to include the most salient aspect: the purely aural experience. Still, here goes. "Banquet" starts the way it all started for her, with a piano. But a piano is still a toy of sorts no matter what comes out of it and the greedy still win over the needy with sufficient totality that there can be plenty to spare but it won't mean anyone's entitled to more than nothing.

Literally everything about "Cold Blue Steel and Sweet Fire" is impossibly superior. The slinkily seductive guitar riff, the singing that would be Exhibit A for anyone asserting her skills purely as a vocalist, the arrangement—basically anything that's a category. But mainly, my God, the language. Kill yourself if you must but at least leave a letter.

"Barangrill" is lighter, except for the way she sings *slave* and who she identifies as one.

Seems everyone is tautologically qualified to give at least one "Lesson in Survival" but would anyone else's be as just plain musical, and from someone self-aware enough to call herself *heavy company*?

Back to the piano without breaking and right into "Let the Wind Carry Me" with its depiction of how families can alternately free or imprison; also it's not altogether clear that someone's well served if their *faith is people*, especially if the wind can so easily dissipate any nurturing instinct they might have. Maybe the same wind Joni hears applause in in the title track but that ends in the moon's *empty spotlight*.

Looked at a certain way, everything starts out so kind and ends so heartlessly, so Joni's claim that all she wants of someone is to "See You Sometime" seems at least logically flawed.

"Electricity" has a fun organizing metaphor, more expert singing, including choral accents, and the insinuation that nothing really gets fixed easy.

Meaning arrival at the two songs most key to understanding the Joni Mitchell experience. If the universe could make one change to Mitchell's oeuvre it would place these two songs back to back when in reality they are separated by the only merely excellent "Blonde in the Bleachers."

Understanding why "You Turn Me On, I'm a Radio" and "Woman of Heart and Mind" are so central requires analysis of extramusical considerations. Joni Mitchell was an artistic genius and on the rare occasions when that occurs it is always a fact well understood by the actual genius. It also breeds a certain smugness. That and contempt for mediocrity and cynicism; to the genius all nongenius work feels like necessarily one or the other.

One day a record-executive type lamented aloud the lack of a prototypical hit single in Joni's recent work. In response, and this is important, Mitchell didn't cover a preexisting hit or bring in a hit-making collaborator. Instead, this woman who alone produced all these albums and who brooked no interference ever on anything, simply passive-aggressively dashed off "You Turn Me On, et cetera," its reference to radio not at all coincidental.

The song is sonically pure pleasure. Lyrically it's fun, showcasing Joni's underrated sense of humor, and almost completely light. Only almost because she couldn't resist informing a man that he doesn't like weak women because he's so quick to bore but he also doesn't like strong women because they're *hip to your tricks*. It was a message song but not that kind. It sent a message to everyone ostensibly doing what she was doing (this thing she and Dylan basically invented) but who was really only selling entertainment, which it turns out sells. The message was that they should not conclude that because they could not do what she does that means she could not easily do what they do. She could and chose not to. Her range, her ability to operate at different registers, needed to be pointed out so she did. She could reduce her mind temporarily and merely have fun, she just preferred not to. Above all, don't misinterpret the crude rewards that come from hitting the middlebrow sweet spot as some kind of affirmation of artistic merit.

Just how much of that merit she herself possessed is then evident during every millisecond of "Woman of Heart and Mind." The song is astounding in every way. If those same contemptible artists, to use the word loosely, want to know what it is to truly be incapable of something they can listen to this song and experience the enormous gulf between it and whatever it is they're doing. The album then ends with "Judgement of the Moon and Stars," a paean to Beethoven. Enough said.

Dia cried during "Woman of Heart and Mind" but subtly enough that Nina didn't even notice. Now, having recovered during "Moon and Stars," she fills the silence tentatively.

"I think that can be a useful way of looking at things here. Like, regardless of what people in the press and others think of our moves, one day the moon and stars will judge and that's what counts, right?"

"Wrong. She's referring to art and things like that. This is sports, one of the last bastions of the unequivocal result not susceptible to the tyranny of opinion."

"Really? Because all it does is spur opinions, you make me listen to that hideous radio station."

"Spurs them, yes, but what controls is cold hard results, facts. You think your team is better, I say mine. Well, they meet on the field and one subjugates the other. It's not so much as though you've answered the question as it is that the question just no longer makes any sense. Try doing that with two poems."

"What about a life?"

"What about it, Dia?"

"Is life a poem or a football game? Can I pass judgment on one, once it's been fully lived?"

"Maybe it's a poetic football game. Look, I get what you're driving at."

"Wasn't really driving—"

"People make mistakes. Worse, they do hideous things. Things that are arguably hideous. Then they rationalize. *Hideous* was too strong a word, some would say it was rotten at most, still others would say it was commendable, in many ways what you call hideous was actually *heroic* if you think it through. Who can judge, anyway? Poem! A life is a poem."

"Are you okay? It was really just a general conversation point."

"Oh. Hey, let's go address the players on this the first day of camp, you were supposed to remind me."

"I did, pointedly."

"Obviously anyone who's coming is here by now, fucking life."

She is walking out of the office almost aggressively so Dia rushes behind. When they get to the stairs they see what must be a player sitting at the bottom, his back to them.

"Players were due on the practice field fifteen minutes ago," Nina says. "I hope you're not trying for a position that requires intelligence."

"If this is the best facility in the IFL, I'd hate to see the worst," says Major Harris as he turns with what looks like involuntary slowness.

"Yay!" says Dia, who's nicely intuitive and has picked up on this whole drama without betraying her knowledge in any way.

"Same schedule for pretty-boy, prima-donna future Hall of Famers."

"So fine me."

"Done, but pay me in steak and tequila."

Late that night Nina and Dia are back in the office. Nina is exhausted and on the couch, Dia at her computer.

"Wow, do you ever tire of being right?" she asks. "Soon as I let it out that Major Harris was a Pork, media requests shot up tenfold. Now TV execs want to talk too."

"He's still a star."

"A major star, get it?"

"Ugh."

"You missed when he walked out on the practice field. Actual jaws dropping and desperate requests for autographs, and that was the players!"

"Big signing, he's loved. I love him . . . as a player I mean. He's tough."

"Happiest I've seen you was when he showed."

"Yeah, we need him is all. I don't want to preside over nonsense and he ensures I won't."

"No I know, football-wise. I'm just saying . . ."

"Don't *just* say, don't even say."

"Okay, touchy. Do you want me to whip up a little PowerPoint on those blitz packages you want to introduce tomorrow?"

"Actually, no. With Major and Buford here the Pork will be fine.

You and I need to leave that to them and concentrate on league matters. Visit all the cities, make sure we're not the only ones exhibiting competence. Come first Sunday in September we need full arenas. We need a TV contract, ground crews, stadium announcers." She yawns. "All that pop."

"I see what you mean. T minus one month and still a lot to do. Still, you have to be very happy with today's league developments. As for the far more critical Dia developments, I'll have you know that I have extended an offer to Travis Mena to fill both positions he applied for, look at his picture."

"You sure that's all you want him to fill?"

"Nina! He is cute though. More importantly, I have made a similarly formal decision regarding my personal life, as it were. I've decided, in essence, that my heart is *open* for business. I know what you're thinking, who talks like that? But I gots to be me, gotta *do* me, like the kids say. The universe is whatever it is, you know? It puts people in your life and that can be great but it also removes them and those decisions can be final no matter how capricious. It makes no sense to pine, pining's not good. I'm not necessarily talking about this Travis meatball either. I'm talking about a general openness—to love, life, leisure, liberty, lust, languor, even things that don't lead with the lovely letter *l*. Maybe I am a woman of heart and mind as well, how will I know? The universe saw fit to separate Nuno and I and that's that. I'm sure I'm the only idiot who even noticed. He's probably living it up as we speak, as I speak, chicks crawling all over him; he had those kind of crawl-attracting properties. God knows he was smart enough to do whatever, the prick. Living it up, I'm sure. I know what you're about to say, if it weren't for the fact they have peckers and are good at running violently into each other, there's no reason to get all worked up about what men do or don't do. Still, you'd like it to be your choice, not the stupid universe's. Maybe ours is not to question why. In a very real sense, Nuno DeAngeles is dead, when someone is fully and permanently out of your life there's no meaningful distinction. Before you ask, I refuse to do even minimal research. My decision is as final as the universe's and what I most need now is simplicity not complexity. You agree with all that, right, Nina? Nina?"

Nina has fallen asleep on the couch. Dia recognizes that this is not a terrible idea. But the room is air-conditioner freezing. She goes into a nearby closet and pulls out one of those weak airline blankets. She takes it over to Nina and extends it onto her restless body. Then, after clearing away some hair for access, kisses her on the forehead and leaves.

28

||||||||||

To Sharon it feels like she's been battling the elements her whole life but especially every fiery second of this brutal fucking summer. She's become a bit of an expert on air conditioners. Now she knows her BTUs and what she should be paying for one of them and their relationship to the amount of square footage they'll be operating in. It's true that her and Hugh's apartment grows more hideous to her daily but at least not because of the temperature.

No, this is about the house Feniz came home to and that she occasionally visits, usually at peak heat now that she's overnight shift for the extra pay. The main room they sit in is where breathable air goes to die so she says doesn't he have an air conditioner he puts in the window and it takes him maybe a little longer to answer than before but eventually he will look up, with that long scar semicircle around his bald head, and say that no, he does not.

After he quietly talks around the ability to pay for one a couple times, Sharon latches on to this as something she can unequivocally do, the way people at a funeral parlor might unnecessarily rearrange the flowers or pictures. Only it turned out there was quite a bit of equivocation. For one, although every single person she mentioned it to was quick to say that window units had become very affordable all this did was highlight how a nebulous concept like *affordable* can vary wildly depending on its user. So maybe it was cheaper than it used to be or there were favorable terms like zero interest and whatever else but that didn't change the fact that every even fractional cent of her paycheck was accounted for before it ever hit her account so she couldn't, literally, do this one simple thing.

And this, the goddamn impotence of it all, is what's derogating Sharon's soul so that all she can feel lately is variations of anger. She can't take one from her place because they're all built-ins, shitty ones too. Purchasing a new one we just covered and fans are a joke when combatting this kind of life-strangling inferno.

She's going to get a fucking unit. And someone's gonna stick it in that goddamn window for her. That's going to happen. She has a friend who sees out of one eye and doesn't hear great and maybe has a little trouble putting sentences together when he was pretty good at that before and there's nothing to be done about all that except just sit and wait; but this other problem is discernible and soluble with a solution that most people would laugh at as easily achieved, so she's going to achieve it is all. The other option, just waiting for the earth to rotate or do whatever the fuck it does so that the temperature magically drops, for once that's not going to be the type of solution she's reduced to while this fucking guy bakes in the meantime.

He'd mentioned this priest, some Vinny Miglia motherfucker or something, mentioned as some kind of friend maybe. So it's not her church but she finds this guy, tells him the situation, which seems to genuinely upset him. Could there be a collection or something? There could, but he felt he needed to warn her that the last similar collection took weeks to achieve its goal and here that would probably be the same as failure. Still, she has an ally now with a promise to call her the second he's got the funds along with a promise to see if he's physically capable of installation.

This particular instant she's coming out her front door with a lasagna and coming in, in the most inconvenient way possible, is Larry Brown. Hugh has, in the information age, overcome the faulty number he had for Larry and managed to contact him. She thinks the idea is to watch some kind of sporting event and she thinks this primarily because Hugh has put on some ludicrous jersey that says SEABORG on the back and tests the outer limits of its midsection fabric strength.

As they pass each other there's a brief conversation that's not as brief as Sharon would've wanted, during which Larry oohs and aahs at the lasagna but is informed that he and Hugh and the other esteemed guests will instead be having the wings Hugh ordered. And she's annoyed she has to do this but he then forces her to have to explain who the lasagna's for and when he says something like *lucky bastard* the devil at her shoulder forces her to describe the lucky bastard's situation to Larry Brown EMT and to do so with maximal distaste.

She gets the slack-jawed reaction you'd expect but one of the things she'd included was the fact that she could probably finish cooking the lasagna by just placing it on Feniz's sofa and that means that once Larry recovers he tells her that window air-conditioning units have become a lot more affordable of late. God, is everyone just the same but with different costumes?

Difference is that Larry is actually listening, not just to the words but to the situation. So as the conversation continues (Sharon puts down the lasagna, which has no good way of being held, and gives terse but slightly less annoyed answers) he finds himself ultimately offering to purchase a new air conditioner and to install it even. The offer is rejected and in a way that scoffs at how illogical it is; she is not going to be party to Larry going out and buying an air conditioner for someone he doesn't know, that's not the way life works. She does accept, however, his offer to carry the lasagna the block or so, just because the damn thing really is that inconvenient a package and hot and steamy.

The short walk is a useful time for Sharon to spend wondering or trying to remember what the hell this guy Larry is about anyway. In addition to everything else he's a talker, that's for sure. In their brief walk he manages to expound on the best containers for transporting hot foods, the most commonly misunderstood facts about Feniz's condition, and, out of left field, whether Sharon knew or could otherwise connect him to Celia de Cervantes, whose husband months ago was—

She knows what he's talking about, she interrupts. They'd moved, she'd heard, though not of course to the house the husband-father had slaved for; they'd moved instead to a cheaper place in Paterson, she lacked specifics. Why? He wants to speak to her about her husband's final moments, which he's only recently discovered are even more significant than he'd thought. That seems ill-advised but she says nothing.

Sharon is standing at the top of Feniz's stairs, Larry at the bottom after unmistakable body language made it clear that's as far as he goes. She can't go in yet. She doesn't know how much more she can take of what life is giving her and she means this quite literally. Lately it's like, if Donnie is not directly in front of her, then it's as if he might as well not even exist as far as things that go on life's positive ledger. And without him the best she can hope for is everything seeming empty, then moments like this, where the emptiness would be welcome over such great harm. She's a tough bitch, anyone would say this. But she feels it in her throat and there's the strong need, no matter who you are, to conform to expected human behavior and not go in there crying like some fucking needy baby. So she needs to stand there a bit and wait it out.

She thanks him, her voice cracks a bit, and when he says *what for?* she reminds him he carried the lasagna. There's a little more then he turns to leave. He gets to just the cusp of hearing distance and she stops him.

"Larry?"

"Yes, Sharon?" This so eagerly.

"Changed my, sorry, changed my mind. Could you just buy that air conditioner, I guess?"

He can and says he will. That he'll be right back with it to put it in. He resumes walking away and she watches intently. She maybe doesn't truly believe that he will, that anyone would. So when he suddenly stops short of her place and gets into his car to go and actually do what he said, at that moment she stops fighting it all, her tears fall like bluesman rain, and she mentally concedes it'll be some time before she can go in to Feniz.

27

||||||||||

Whatever crying is—and don't kid yourself because no one knows what the hell it truly is; at least not when we're talking about the shedding of uniquely human or *psychogenic* tears—Nuno has promised himself he'll be doing none of it.

In the beginning was the hardest. At some too early point in his life Nuno lost the ability to generate tears in response to personal events. Maybe it's sublimation or something worse but what's never been reduced is his susceptibility to art-induced tears. And not necessarily high art either. He's as likely to tear up over snippets of well-executed pop art where he in essence fills in the gaps to create power. But none of that matters in relation to his promise to himself to never answer isolation that way since in there he has no access to literature, music, or art of any kind or level.

The reason it was hard at first was just the obvious fact that Nuno was truly alone. No books or art of any kind was just perfectly emblematic of this, not its own separate source of pain. Still, very early on he was almost completely overcome by a profound sense of sympathy for another, the problem was the other was him. Cut off from interplay as he was, he found himself much more observing his life than actually living it. He'd look at this guy, Nuno, his body breaking down from disuse, his mind maybe doing the same, and blanch at life's indefensible treatment of him.

Out of context it all just seemed so unfair. No one spoke to him. He could do nothing. Everything around him was hard in every way. In the meantime everyone else spoke to each other, laughed, touched each other. They felt sunlight on their skin until it became uncomfortable then they felt breezes that restored them. They ate what they pleased, moved how they wished. And in the middle of all that this dying husk of a man. He'd think of this man, forget it was him, and just become unbearably sad.

That was at the beginning and it was definitely hard but he never cried about it. Why it got easier is he started feeling less, less, and less, until now he just plain doesn't feel. He still thinks though. He thinks mainly how human existence can have different levels of reality assigned to it. So a person knows instinctively that they experienced the dream, the imaginative speculation, and the punch to the face, but only one of those gets to be called real in the sense of direct correspondence with independently existing facts. The punch-to-the-face experience burrows right to the bottom of foundational reality in a way that exposes the disconnect between it and those fanciful flights.

Because what Nuno discovers in punitive isolation is that all those elements that to the superficial observer seem to complexify reality are actually just sham. Sitting in that dark square with no sound or other disturbance it all just falls away like dead skin being shed. What's left is only mere existence, what debris would fail to feel just following its geodesic in deep space. The fundamental irreality of what we call life. The compelling distractions we build and sustain to mask this truth are only powerful if armed with immediacy. Think of Dia's determination that someone completely absent, spatiotemporally and sensually speaking, may as well be dead, and multiply it by only the whole of other humanity. And the problem with being the last person on Earth is that all the burdens of the universe land on one consciousness and that's too much for it to bear so it just slowly shuts down.

He's not allowed pen and paper so he has to write solely in his head. *In the nutshell of this cell, I am God*, he writes. *God in everything large and small. Infinite doesn't only mean infinitely out, it can also mean infinitely inward. If I, in my deistic omnipotence, decide I will half the distance between me and the dark nullity at the center of all that is, then I can. Then I half that distance and the new one and I just keep halving but you know the truth. That I never reach a terminus because the distance is not only infinitesimally small it is infinitely divisible as well. The way I'm just being halved every day. Halved and halved into nothing yet something. Half of all humanity is still humanity and just endlessly repeating the process is what's got this down to me. A state where I'm the only entity consciously existing. Who said this? Or maybe I'm only saying it now. Humans are just a barely special kind of animal that delusionally invented knowledge during its brief speck of existence. So when humanity ceases so will the delusion. Everything invented, nothing discovered or learned, nothing independently true or false. Morality's like that. It's like looking for right and wrong in a shark tank. Nobody's ever done me wrong or good because no one's ever done either of those things generally so how could they do them specifically? There are no duties or obligations, only pathways and obstructions. All there is is existence or its negation and neither state is worthy of all that much speculation. I can make this come faster. I can just half my inner life and half and half but just as there's an answer to Zeno there's a reduced inner life that just amounts to nothing and that makes me something like an empty corpse subject to involuntary postmortal spasms.*

That was the last of it. No more writing, tangible or otherwise. No one spoke to Nuno and Nuno spoke to no one in return. He ate, just enough to live, but everything tasted like colored air. He lost complete track of the days, stopped with the scratches. In time it wasn't all that distinguishable from being comatose.

The day CO Hugh Seaborg comes to tell him he has court he also has to convince Nuno that this is a good thing, that this is something he has been looking forward to. Nuno is in the corner and won't move. Hugh says it's a new day and that means possibility, which puts an image in Nuno's head of Dia's face, but frustratingly from the television not from their once-shared experiences.

He stands and moves and the next time he allows in sensory input he is in the pens behind the courtroom and speaking to him incomprehensively is this Coin lawyer.

"Why do you keep saying that?" asks Nuno.

"Saying what?"

"*Thud, empty, hollow,* over and over like that, *thud, empty, hollow.*"

"I haven't said that."

434 Sergio de la Pava

"What do you even mean by it? *Thud, empty, hollow*, again and again. And how do you make it so it sounds like it's not coming from you?"

When Coin finally gets Nuno in front of the judge he's all *we need to approach* and so he and the DA do and when they return the judge is shaking his head and ordering "a 730 exam" with a court date for results.

Most in operation here are three statutes all found in the New York Criminal Procedure Law and specifically found under

---

Article 730 Mental Disease or Defect Excluding Fitness to Proceed

§ 730.10 Fitness to proceed; definitions.

As used in this article, the following terms have the following meanings:

1. "Incapacitated person" means a defendant who as a result of mental disease or defect lacks capacity to understand the proceedings against him or to assist in his own defense.

§ 730.20 Fitness to proceed; generally.

1. The appropriate director to whom a criminal court issues an order of examination must be determined in accordance with rules jointly adopted by the judicial conference and the commissioner. Upon receipt of an examination order, the director must designate two qualified psychiatric examiners, of whom he may be one, to examine the defendant to determine if he is an incapacitated person. In conducting their examination, the psychiatric examiners may employ any method which is accepted by the medical profession for the examination of persons alleged to be mentally ill or mentally defective. The court may authorize a psychiatrist or psychologist retained by the defendant to be present at such examination.

§ 730.20 Fitness to proceed; generally.

3. When the defendant is in custody at the time a court issues an order of examination, the examination must be conducted at the place where the defendant is being held in custody. If, however, the director

determines that hospital confinement of the defendant is necessary for an effective examination, the sheriff must deliver the defendant to a hospital designated by the director and hold him in custody therein, under sufficient guard, until the examination is completed.

The collection of words, nothing special about their selection or arrangement, that will most govern Nuno's existence for his immediate and lasting future.

26

||||||||||

You could make a strong argument for the very beginning of a complex process as the best phase to experience. For example, it's the Saturday night before the start of the Indoor Football League season. The NFL incredibly remains work-stoppaged so there's actually a semblance of public interest, even if it can best be characterized as a form of morbid curiosity.

The Pork are gathered in a banquet hall for their last preseason meal. Various tables have been set up. At one sit all the coaches and immediately next to it is Major Harris holding court to great laughter. Nina walks in to great attention and Harris stops talking. They catch each other's eyes and not-quite smile. Nina goes to the bar, where she's joined by Coach Elkins.

"Two double tequilas, and no well crap either," Nina says without looking at the cowed bartender.

"No, I'll have a club soda," says the coach.

"The two were for me. As for your order, certainly never known you to be a member of that club."

"Need to be sharp, we're going to have a big year."

"Really?"

"Big year, you were right about our secondary. Can't believe we have Mutola and Reeves and the rookie's all you said. Our back's a monster, runs with great lean and NFL speed, though still fumbling. The only thing . . ."

"What? Spit it out."

"Harris hasn't been sharp of all people," Elkins is whispering. "The quality of play here is a lot higher than I anticipated and forty-four years old is forty-four years old."

Nina looks at Harris, he just delivered the punch line and it lands hard. He gets up and starts walking towards them.

"I think he'll be fine, Coach. He never had good camps. Can our line keep him clean?"

"Most weeks."

"That's the priority, he'll be fine."

Elkins notices Harris approaching and, feeling prospectively third-wheeled, walks away, patting Harris on his throwing shoulder as he passes.

"What should we drink to?" Harris asks.

"Sure, two, three, whatever it takes."

"Thought you'd sold us, you've been so invisible."

"Your coach is worried you're done."

"Yeah, I noticed that."

"So?"

"Certainly a possibility," with a hint of resignation.

"Excuse me? I was prepared for you to assault me, or at least him."

"See what I mean? For a second I felt the old anger start to rise in me but then it quickly faded and I was able to look at the matter dispassionately, as in without passion. This may be a mistake."

"Your career passer rating in the preseason was like forty, don't worry. That's all it is."

"Not sure."

"You done insulting me?"

"Insulting *you*?"

"Well my primary off-season acquisition and by extension my football acumen, meaning me, yes. The beauty of sports, we start to find out tomorrow." Nina notices the Pork's primary running back walking by. "Unless this fucking meathead fumbles the season away, Sims!" She beckons him with her curling and uncurling finger.

Harris chuckles silently and walks away. Sims comes over holding a small plate of food that Nina immediately knocks out of his hand.

"I see it's not just footballs you can't hold on to, remember me?"

"Of course?" he stammers.

"I'm the person who gave you a five hundred percent raise, right? I don't understand, professional football is for workers. You led the league in fumbles last year so I can only assume that the chump who coached you while you were accomplishing *that* instructed you to work on it in the off-season, correct?"

"Actually."

"I need you to hold the football to your heart, literally. See this area?" Nina pulls her blouse down a bit and motions between her breasts as Sims gulps then opens his mouth longingly. "Squeeze it to your goddamn heart and hold it vertically like this." She demonstrates with a bottle of liquor she grabs out of the bartender's hand just before he can serve another patron. "Not stupidly like this," as she turns the bottle horizontally and extends it away from her body so that liquor starts to pour out. "Hold it to your heart and at a minimum no one will knock it out from behind. Hold it to your heart and fumble and I'll feel bad for you. Hold it otherwise and fumble and you'll be selling Amway within weeks. Anything else you can help me with?"

"Uh."

"Good."

Just then Nina spots Dia with the mascot and walks over to her.

"Dia, let's do this now. Go."

Dia motions to several people and in an astonishingly short time everyone's attention has been drawn to Nina, who stands with a microphone in her hand.

"If you don't know who I am by now you've got bigger problems than tomorrow's game." Her audience laughs. "I have a simple request."

"Anything you say!" Hard to identify the source in that crowded room but more general laughter ensues.

"Good, because I *say* win a championship. Notice I don't say do your best to win a championship. I can get anyone to do their best. I don't want your best, I want a championship and that's what you should want. You have the best coach in the league along with a Hall of Fame quarterback and I know from experience that they want a championship. They know football is a fight and a football season is a brawl. Stick together, fight until all the fight in you is gone, and prepare to the hilt. There is more than enough talent in this room to accomplish our goal, which means a failure to do so could only be attributed to a lack of will and I can't think of a worse thing to lack. Does everyone here understand what I mean by that? You are all in that position. If we gather at the end of the season and I'm not collecting your ring sizes you'll have discovered something about yourselves. The overwhelming majority of people devote their energies to endeavors that have no clear-cut winners or losers, no scores. Part of what that means is they can fool themselves if they have to. You won't have that luxury. You've all, rightly or wrongly, devoted your lives to football. This is your craft. An artist finishes a painting then has to watch as half love it, half hate it, with no way of proving either side correct. Not you. Every Sunday a score will be created and it will tell you your worth as a craftsman. At the end this team will have a record and it will tell you even more. That's why you win a championship, to know that about yourself. I know the people in this room because I put them here and I also know what a championship looks and feels like and you know what, you crazy dysfunctional dregs? There's a championship here. It's just on layaway, which I know most of you are familiar with. Go get it one week at a time starting tomorrow. Otherwise we're not friends. Thanks."

The players roar their approval as Nina starts to exit. On her way out she grabs that second tequila off the bar and downs it.

25

||||||||||

The next day, and this will be a much-discussed-because-surprising fact, a clear majority of the country's televisions are set to the football game being played in the remodeled Paterson Armory. The Pork's game against the Portland Pulverizers is the national television game as well as the inauguration of the moderately anticipated IFL season.

Viewer motivations vary. Someone like Larry Brown or Solomon Hanes tunes in out of a mixture of curiosity and the lack of available options on a September Sunday's early afternoon. Then there are the sports addicted, like Hugh Seaborg, who are incapable of changing the channel if something is being athletically contested; that is particularly true where football is involved and this is exacerbated by the simply inconceivable fact that the NFL is not currently in operation. Here the custom of fall and winter Sundays takes precedence over silly questions like quality of play or long-term viability.

For kids especially, kids like Donnie Seaborg or Nelson de Cervantes, football is football and there's the underrated fact that said activity just looks amazing on television. If anything, to young eyes the IFL even exceeds the NFL thanks to its cartoonishly garish uniforms and other elements. They tune in in droves.

Lastly, there are people like Father Ventimiglia, Feniz Heredia, and even Sharon Seaborg and Celia de Cervantes, who tune in because of their weird realization that Paterson has become, for a strange moment, something like the center of the universe and who could ever have predicted that this would happen in such an innocent non-tragic way?

Regardless, a great many eyeballs are witness as absurdly busy graphics streak across their screens launched by the league's new broadcast television partner. The network is introducing its coverage, and really the league, to the public. Two announcers in a broadcast booth overlook the field in that corny way they do to preview the upcoming contest.

"Welcome, everyone," says the significantly slighter one. "I'm Jim Sanders and this is former NFL great Slim Janders, and we're coming to you live from the Pig Pen in Paterson, New Jersey, home of the Paterson Pork and site of today's contest between that outfit and the Portland Pulverizers. Slim, it seems like just yesterday that Nina Gill, daughter of NFL founding father Worthington Gill, was announcing her presence in the IFL and her decision to move their games to the fall."

"I for one only found out yesterday, Jim."

"Great, well, elsewhere the league has managed to garner significant attention in the absence of any NFL action and a large amount of that attention has centered on Pork quarterback and former NFL great Major Harris, who most football fans never dreamed they'd ever see on a football field again. Slim?"

"That's true, Jim, and when this guy was on the field it was as if he wasn't even on the field. That's how much like butter he was, Jim, he was great."

Jim is confused but he's a pro's pro. "Okay. At any rate this should be a great matchup between two teams expected by most experts to finish near the top of the league. Also joining us today is our sideline reporter Lisa Lisa and she's with deputy commissioner of the IFL, Dia Nouveau, who would like to explain some rather interesting aspects of league play."

The production cuts to Lisa Lisa on the sideline as the players warm up on the field. "Thank you for joining us, Commissioner Nouveau."

"Deputy."

"Deputy Nouveau."

"Deputy Commissioner."

"Deputy Commissioner Nouveau."

"Call me Dia, and where's the Cult Jam?"

"I'm . . ."

"Never mind. IFL play is indistinguishable from NFL play, which no longer exists, with two major exceptions. Real football is played in the elements yet because of various recent amendments to the U.S. Constitution we are required to play indoors. Consequently, every IFL arena has been outfitted with state-of-the-art Weatherines or weather machines that are located high above the stands and are operated by rather dubious personnel. The specific weather for a particular game is determined by a pregame spin of the Weather Wheel."

"Yes, about that wheel."

"Additionally, we have the Duel Dial, which by virtue of random electrical pulses that activate a dangerously sharp needle will determine what physical contest the two relevant mascots will engage in to decide which team gets the ball first. That's all for now. That's the situation from head to toe, Lisa Lisa. Keep up the . . . work."

"But."

"Back to you, Jim, let's get this party started!"

"Um . . ."

Problem is, they cut to the booth on Dia's unauthorized command and said booth is empty. Now there's a decided amateur hour feel until someone offscreen says, *Let's go to midfield and the wheel* and they do. What it is at midfield is a giant wheel of the kind spun on beach boardwalks. Its options are Arctic Assault, Not in Kansas Anymore, Snow Problem, Liquid Laceration, and Sunny Delight. A special guest trots out onto the field to spin the wheel: Mala Mutola, son of Pork strong safety Manu Mutola. He is beaming. He spins the wheel and it lands on Arctic Assault. The arena is full to capacity with fans but their reaction is subdued as they're not sure what that result means.

They soon begin to get the idea, however, as they hear giant machines start revving high above the field and the woefully underdressed crowd (indoor game first Sunday of September) starts feeling chilly at first, then cold, then hypothermic; they've been assaulted by arctic conditions!

Next, an invisible source in the arena sends out an electric pulse that activates the needle on the Duel Dial. It lands on Fifty Yard Race and consequently the two team mascots are placed on the fifty-yard line. They will race to the goal line to determine which team gets the ball first. The crowd is wondering what the IFL's money-back policy might be.

The Pork mascot is of course Dr. Travis Mena disguised as a giant pink pig. The Pulverizers have a creature never before known to man, a strange combination of magnets and metal moving parts designed to produce maximum force. The gun goes off and surprisingly the Pork's pig is holding his own, maybe even outrunning his competitor. But as the two near the finish line he suddenly pulls up, grabbing his left hamstring with his bulbous pork paw. He's all heart however and struggles to finish before falling forward and executing a perfect somersault. After all that, the Pulverizers defer anyway and the Pork will get the ball first.

Meanwhile order has been restored in the broadcast booth, where Jim Sanders tries to pretend nothing untoward happened.

"Well, we certainly hope the Pork's pig will be all right," he says. A replay of the race airs. "Ooh, our thoughts go out to his family, especially if he has piglets."

"Looks like he pulled a ham hock, Jim," adds Slim.

"Yes, a common football injury." The game starts. "The Pork will receive and Higgins fields it at the two out to the twenty-eight on a decent return and here he is! Major Harris trots out onto the field to the roar of the crowd. Let me tell you, this crowd is very grateful to have this legendary player at quarterback for the Pork."

"I think they'd be more grateful for a sweater, Jim. They'd probably take *you* at quarterback if someone would just turn off that Weatherine."

"Yes, it's brutally cold out there, Slim. But lucky for us the Pig Pen features an enclosed broadcast booth. First and ten at the twenty-eight for the Pork and Harris will pass on first down."

Also enclosed is the nearby owner's box, where Dia has made her way up to join Nina, other Pork personnel, and some select player family members. From there they watch Harris take a deep drop with ample time to throw. He looks tentative and uncomfortable in the pocket, however. After a seeming eternity he lofts a soft pass in the left flat that is easily intercepted by a Pulverizer linebacker and returned for a touchdown as the crowd's enthusiasm abates considerably. The owner's box deflates.

"You think he's okay?" Dia asks.

"Of course, it's one play."

"I know but Travis is the type of person—"

"He'll be fine. Who the hell's Travis?"

"Travis Mena. His official title is Deputy Assistant Coordinator of Medicinal and Cosplay, the pig, he's the pig!"

"Oh, he'll be fine, we have the best team veterinarian in the league."

"Maybe I should go down there. I mean, it's a tricky situation. He obviously needs medical attention but he's our sole medical provider. If he treats himself is it like with the legal profession where he has a fool for a patient?"

"Sure sounding that way, enough please."

The Pork's offense is back on the field, first and ten at their own thirty-five. Handoff to Sims for six, he is carrying the ball the way Nina taught him. Nina has put on a headset and perks up at the next play call.

"Let's see this," she says.

Harris drops back to pass. He still looks skittish before delivering a wildly off-target pass over the middle that falls harmlessly.

"Hell's going on?" Nina mumbles.

Another pass play. Harris tries to connect with his receiver on a ten-yard out but the ball sails on him and almost hits Coach Elkins in the head. The Pork must punt.

"Goodness, could you imagine I screwed this whole thing up?" is Nina's response.

"It's early" is what Dia offers and it's not bad.

Except that a few minutes later it's not so early anymore and matters have not improved. Nina sits almost slumped in her chair and the Pulverizers have the ball at midfield up seven. Their quarterback drops back and completes a twenty-two-yard sideline pass in front of Dylan Reeves.

"Now I've got Reeves giving up twenty-yard outs to *that* guy? What's next? A ban on imported tequila and washboard abs?"

As Nina speaks, the Pulverizers' running back is running almost unencumbered into the end zone to give his team a two-touchdown lead. The crowd is silent. This is why Paterson can't have nice things.

"Let's look on the bright side, Nina. Our kick returner's getting a lot of practice."

The crowd deadens even further. Matters are not helped by the fact that the arena's overpaid public address personnel keep playing cuts from Joni Mitchell's *Court and Spark* during the many lulls in play in place of the usual ten to fifteen pump-up selections PA systems throughout the rest of the rational sports nation favor heavily. No independent musical judgment is being exercised here of course as they are under strict orders from Dia, who really has been allowed to run amok like some kind of Latin American strongwoman. The result is a lot of tanked-up *fans*, who maybe at one point could have been induced into running through brick walls but now instead seem at best puzzled as, for example, Joni describes with consummate beauty what it's like to be a true artist at events like lighthearted parties, how the drive to minute observation over experiential distraction makes it hard to keep it light but that failure doesn't really matter because laughing and crying are the same release and doesn't that have all sorts of troubling implications that ensue, then straight into a Rilkean invocation of heaven's astronauts and a lamenting of Nietzsche's death sentence. And this on an album generally considered her most commercial offering. *What the hell?* or some variation of it is the predominate response at this particular gathering of Sunday violence.

That's the state of the crowd; on the sidelines the Pork are in pure disarray. They've done nothing right and already frustration is mounting. Even Coach Elkins is having doubts and he calls up to Nina on his headset. As they speak the Pork are fielding another kickoff and taking over at their thirty-five.

"Any ideas? You own this mess."

"Not sure that's the way it works, *Coach*. But Harris is back there thinking and reflecting like it's a chess match or something, instead of fucking football. Maybe go empty-set-no-huddle with him calling his own plays so he'll get hit a few times and just start reacting."

Elkins approves and is soon shouting *no huddle, no huddle* to the offensive coordinator and really anyone who will listen. Word soon reaches the Pork huddle, where Harris's famous anger is slightly defused by the change.

"Okay, kids, you heard the man, no huddle. Get the call from me following the play and watch my hand signals up to the snap." He stares at his receivers: "And break hard out of your cuts, you worthless scum!"

Harris takes a shotgun snap as the right defensive end comes in unblocked to level him violently just as he releases a pretty pass. Complete to his receiver on a fifteen-yard in-cut. Harris rises stiffly but surely.

"Let's go, time to play, 32 Z X-ray right!"

The offense hurriedly lines up and Harris takes another shotgun snap. The pocket breaks down almost immediately and he is forced to scramble to the right. He is rolling right, rolling right, until he is almost out of room and it appears he will run out of bounds. At the last minute he spots something. Throwing the ball across his body and off the wrong foot he uncorks a frozen rope that travels fifty yards in the air into the hands of his receiver for a touchdown. The crowd erupts as do the announcers in the booth. Play-by-play man Jim Sanders is particularly joyously apoplectic.

"An amazing throw, Slim! I think the Pulverizer defensive back almost gave up on the play not thinking such a throw was even possible let alone with that accuracy."

"Jim, I think there's maybe four guys alive can make that throw. And three of them are dead!"

The Pork sideline is elated/relieved with Harris getting congratulatory head-slaps from everyone, including Travis the mascot pig, who's on crutches and uses one of the crutches to deliver the tap. In the owner's box everyone is high-fiving et cetera.

"I'm going home, I'll watch the rest on TV."

"What are you talking about, Nina, really?"

"Just make sure they cut up the game film and have it delivered to my apartment by midnight, okay? Specify that I also need the raw all-twenty-two or there will be blood. We'll do a media call on the first weekend of games tomorrow afternoon."

"Got it, threaten bloodshed."

Nina walks out of the owner's box and is making her way to the elevator as the crowd emits another roar of approval.

After the game, that night, in the team parking lot, Major Harris is slowly hobbling towards his car while being interrupted by fans congratulating him on the big win and seeking autographs. Most of these are underdressed young women. Leaning against the hood of his car is Nina. He approaches her as the women following him notice Nina and slink away in something approaching fear. When Nina talks she has the authority of a low-decibel stadium announcement.

"Excuse me, but aren't you the Thorndike's Thick-Cut-Bacon Player of the Game?"

"Not sure all the votes have been tallied yet."

"I have it on good authority."

"I prefer beef, anyway."

"Think you're in the minority there."

"What better place to be? And let me know when they start building Baconhouses to compete with Steakhouses."

"Please, it's a world of pansies, get ready for Tofuhouses. Speaking of insufficient manliness, we have at least fifteen more of these to go and I think our pig could have covered the distance between that door and this car sooner."

"I'll be ready by next Sunday. I get up, that's what I do."

"I know."

"You came here to tell me that?"

"To offer you a ride in a spacious luxury automobile, I don't know how you even get into that little thing of yours. Accepted?"

"Depends, a ride to where?"

"Anywhere in the continental U.S., where to?"

"To your place."

"What's in it for me? I mean, in your condition."

"Brilliant piano music, timeless paintings."

"That's what's in it for *you*."

"Quick conversation."

"Meh."

"How about a ravaged shoulder for your head to rest on?"

"Let's go."

24

|||||||||

Whenever the New York City criminal justice system requires that any kind of psychiatric element be formally injected into its processes this is handled by Bellevue Hospital. Bellevue as in *You're nuts, I'm calling Bellevue.*

So when Nuno receives the rather rare declaration that he is "not fit to proceed," the two psychiatrists so declaring do not wait for the next court date to announce their findings but rather specify that he should be immediately admitted to Bellevue and not return to Rikers isolation, where they feel his condition would deteriorate (with maybe no more evidentiary justification beyond the fact that deteriorate precipitously is just what things at Rikers do).

Bellevue's 19 West on the nineteenth floor is for those who are not only mentally compromised but also, for a variety of reasons, not free to leave. Nuno is sent there and while it's true that there are bars and significant restriction of motion, it is also true that what matters most with something like quality of life is not any objective level so much as trajectory. So coming from Rikers's isolation unit, simply just the bustle of people moving around in refracted sunlight and talking, at times even to him, feels, comparatively speaking, positively luxurious.

In charge is this kind of nebbish woman who had part of a wall to her office replaced by glass so she could monitor all always. This woman, just plain Dennings, secretly believes everyone there is malingering, even to some extent the staff. She's not mean or anything, though. She's more like habitually put upon and compelled by duty to announce this widely and often.

Today she believes in the efficacy of nameplates on the left breast area of the inmates and she gives a mumbo jumbo Psych 101 reason for this but the truth is she just needs to compensate for her decreasing memory and she likes the authority and control of barking to identify someone by exclusively their last name then pairing that bark with little near-nonsense commands meant to create busywork. So *Davies!* might set out a table for *McCarty!* to put Dixie cups on then once all the meds have been distributed it's up to *Collier!* or *Simmons!* to dispose of the cups and break the table down again so the whole thing can be repeated twice more daily. The overall result is a different kind of confinement but one that's no less confining for it: bars and pills and strictly appointed times and never spontaneous acts of volition.

Circumstances vary but in Nuno's case there's a clearly defined goal. Bellevue is to medicate/counsel Nuno until he magically becomes mentally fit again, at which point he will be immediately returned to Rikers and his case resuscitated so he can ultimately get the life sentence they've been preparing for him and become a complete nonentity blotted out of any meaningful human society. Currently this goal is being frustrated by silence. Nuno is not speaking, weeks, but not in the manner of someone willfully withholding something; this is more as if something has been severed and the stimuli that normally generate reactive speech are not registering.

This toxic senescence maybe first begins to dissipate with the arrival of the Theorist. This is a severely thin and gangly dude who looks like a strong wind could break him in half with, of course, impossibly thick glasses and hair that goes everywhere as if humanity had yet to invent its styling. Some tried Einstein or even Professor, but when he casually let slip that what he was describing was actually theoretical physics and not so much applied science, that was all it took for one of his less-medicated peers to dub him the Theorist and somehow that particular bit of stupidity had stuck to where no one knew what his real name was or if he even had one. Certainly in that place no one was looking too hard there for a second salient characteristic to base your name on.

Problem with the Theorist is that he seems to be suffering less than the rest and that's the kind of thing can engender animosity in a group setting. No one's ever seen him taken to task, for example. The staff treats him almost deferentially. Is that all it takes? Just throw in some Uncertainty Principle or Inflationary Universe and everyone gets out of your way out of fearful ignorance? Nuno is predictably having none of it even if it's the most appealing language he's heard being spoken in so long (theoretical physicists are like frustrated poets with the language and metaphors they continually try to employ, sometimes just discarding all pretense and cutting straight to it as in the naming of *quarks*). So what? He's not big on tangibly hearing things anyway, reading is a superior substitute and has the advantage of using his own perfectly familiar and comforting mental voice that he once long ago as a confused boy imagined into existence and which he suspects will never be fully silenced even should there be no one around to hear it.

At the moment the Theorist is on precisely one of those verbal jags in a common area where they're allowed to gather. Why is it that every mentally ill motherfucker can't shut the fuck up about being that? And one of the few things these guys like to fixate on almost as much as aliens and the government is Time.

"Some believe Time is most likely a purely human construction," says the Theorist.

And it's not that this goes over well or even poorly so much as it just doesn't go over, period. Because that's what this place is. The Theorist's statement, like the so many others similar to it and despite its significant decibels, is not a communal act. Nothing's communal here because there's no community to commune within. A facility like this is a collection of severely atomized individuals each relentlessly pursuing their own elliptical path even if they occasionally overlap orbitally with others to create the illusion of concerted union. This is such a defining characteristic, in fact, the involuntarily confined kinetically but obliviously bouncing off each other physically but mentally *in their own world*, that you can't help but strongly suspect an insuperable link. But links don't necessarily display their causal flow so who can tell whether mental illness causes you to retreat into an isolated mental state or if isolation (physical, mental, emotional) creates an ideal hothouse for cultivating insanity.

"Wait a minute, hear me out. Remember Saint Augustine? He knew exactly what time was, right up until the moment someone asked him to define it. Or Feynman, time is what happens when nothing else does. But is that true? Does something *happen?*"

None of this rhetoric is dependent on any kind of interactive byplay whatsoever.

"In other words, imagine there were no objects. Could there nonetheless be movement? Movement relative to what? Through what? Through space you'd probably say. Through something like absolute space, that substance Newton envisioned and that you don't feel qualified to doubt. But what about what most would say is the related concept of time? No one here, I hope, would dare argue for the existence of absolute time in the Newtonian sense."

The majority of people currently surrounding the speaker look like they would struggle with the concept of days of the week so his pause here couldn't serve less purpose and, truth is, with his hair and those eyes even those people seem more lucid, especially when, as here, they remain perfectly quiet.

"Good, because Einstein dispensed with that, right? Take twins and put one of them in a rocket ship. Accelerate her at a high rate of speed, accelerate her through space, and what happens if you reunite them say a decade later? We now know beyond doubt that the accelerator will be actually younger than the twin who remained at relative rest. This is another way of saying that their personal clocks will not agree. Each will have perceived the passage of time differently. No, not *perceived*, time will actually have elapsed at different rates for the twins. Seems time is relative, get it?

"A useful way of looking at it is that space and time are linked into something called space-time so that moving in space, feeding on space let's call it, means we eat less time. Incredibly weird revelation. And, more importantly, not at all consistent with what we experience sensually. It's wildly important to remember this. Here is something that is verifiably and unequivocally true yet nothing about our daily lives on this planet would've really suggested it, unless you were a timeless genius who spent all his life reflecting on something that didn't seem all that in need of refinement.

"So time and space seem less blank canvas than relational concepts, bringing me back to my original question of whether time even exists.

Of course it exists in at least some sense, otherwise we couldn't be having this vigorous exchange, could we? There's certainly something that we've all agreed to call time. And more than that, we have great agreement on how it operates, which is why it's such a useful tool, as when we agree to meet at one and be done by three. Well, it's not just that we agree, it actually functions that way as long as we avoid great speeds, cosmic distances, et cetera.

"But beyond that, what else is highly salient about this common experience we share and call time? Entropy, to start with. Look around and you'll see things like drinking glasses falling off tables to shatter into a million pieces or brick walls that if left unattended long enough will, over time, turn into piles of bricks. Know what you won't see? Ever? You'll never see those shards spontaneously organize themselves into a drinking glass or that pile of bricks just effortlessly fall into the formation of a wall. Time not only flows, it flows inexorably, and it flows inexorably in one direction. A one-way street. Past to present to future over and over, every single time without exception. The only reason this doesn't shock you is its perfect, unrelenting pervasiveness. But, of course, it didn't have to be so.

"If the most analogous substance in the universe is space, one of the first things you'll notice is how different our relationship with that substance is. Comparatively speaking, we master space. Even our three-year-olds need only think the thought and their underdeveloped legs scissor them nimbly forward through space, and if it changes its mind it just reverses course and returns whence it started.

"Contrast that to our relationship with Time. Who's the master there? Is there any question that we're the servants to the point of slavery? Do we have any true volition in this arena? Can we move about as we please? In the present I really regret that summer, out-door, all-you-can-eat raw oyster fest from eighteen hours ago. Maybe I'll just go back to nineteen hours ago and have apples instead. Not happening, buster. It's not just that shattered drinking glasses don't spontaneously reassemble, it's that once the drinking glass shatters you can't ever make it so that it didn't. That opportunity is lost for-ever, that *forever* term itself a clue to the vicious implacability of this entity we're forced to deal with and within.

"So the mandatory unidirectionality of Time is certainly offensive but wait, there's more offense. Because remember that it also never stops flowing, which is another way of saying it never stops damaging us, its victims. Right? After all, we don't care much one way or the other if that drinking glass breaks. We sweep up and buy another. Harder to deal with, by far, is how Time minces our bones, makes smiles vanish, weighs everything and every critical one down until it's all just interred into silent oblivion. That inexorability I referred to earlier, how you can't stop or even slow it meaningfully, just have to passively watch it wreak havoc on all health and vitality.

"Now, if all this were imbued with true necessity, logical or scientific or otherwise, I think we'd probably accept that them's the rules and move on. But remember that the underpinnings of the universe are mathematical and more specifically equational in nature. Specifically, at present, we can say that those underpinnings are governed by two main *theories*, we'll call them. And if you all promise not to take any great offense, I'll here speak very simply and say that we have the theory of relativity, special and general, to explain the very large and cosmic, and we have quantum theory to explain the infinitesimally small. Great, except that, to present, we have not been able to reconcile these two highly successful theories to each other.

"In the meantime, let's talk about something all the figures agree on. You've no doubt noticed that I've been writing as I speak and, there, done. See for yourselves:"

"I can see the shock on your collective faces."

This is palpably untrue, no one has so much as glanced at the sudden whiteboard.

"Well, you haven't misinterpreted. As you can plainly see, everything about the numbers and how they relate to us and each other leads to the inescapable conclusion that there's nothing on that board that requires or even describes the arrow of time we loathe so much. Newton and Einstein work equally well in either direction yet here we are. Flies stuck to flypaper spiraling down to a terminal collision. Next time I'll show how we're not quite as helpless as all that."

Through it all Nuno just doesn't talk and his eyes are empty and everyone who fills out a report with him as subject agrees there's no reason to make any change in the status section. And pills change, in color and size, increase or decrease, and you have to give them time to build up in the system. But the talking cure presumes two-way talk and if this is catatonia it's still too early to make that determination and above all maybe it's just unassailably true that the only logical response to the world, the only reaction that requires no supporting documentation or argumentation, is a kind of stunned insanity.

23

||||||||||

The regular season of the IFL's Paterson Pork almost took the form of montage. Not a comment on how it's being portrayed; montage is literally what it felt like to live it.

So in a subsequent pregame duel Travis Mena is still the Pork's pig and he is wearing boxing gloves in a boxing ring across from a similarly clad giant turtle. The pig seems almost cocky. He is dancing around, breaking out the Ali shuffle, shooting out left jabs, exhorting the crowd. Suddenly the turtle closes the distance between them and steps into a perfect straight right that catches the pig flush on his piggish jaw. Mena the pig is out instantly and pitches face forward as the ref immediately raises the turtle's arm in victory. The crowd recoils in horror, Coach Elkins shakes his head, and Dia races over, through many obstacles, to make sure the pig is okay. The Tallahassee Testudo elect to receive.

At Pork headquarters a large marquee has been erected to display the Pork's record. One early morning, Dia climbs a dilapidated ladder made treacherous by slight rain to update the record to 4–0. The numbers are made to look like contorted bacon strips.

The Pork are playing at the Sacramento Séance. The Weather Wheel has decreed Liquid Laceration, resulting in a man-made driving rainstorm that has the players sliding five, ten yards in mud during play while creating great official consternation as to where to spot the ball.

The marquee is updated to read 5–0 but now Dia has delegated the task to an elite but recently disgraced skyscraper window washer eager to prove that anyone can have the occasional bad day's reaction to an unnatural height.

. . .

Maybe it's just that the place was superprimed to cheer but Paterson responds palpably to that five and oh record. Little helmet-wearing pigs start appearing in storefronts and on automobile antennae. Now the players, and not just Major Harris, are doing things like appearing at car dealerships and supermarkets. And it's not just the informed either. Even the town's inanimate geography just seems to sense that something with the Paterson name on it is succeeding and that feeds the surrounding people, who feed it back in a continuous loop that maybe no one is explicitly aware of but which has tangible results nonetheless.

Nelson de Cervantes gets a Pork jersey for his October birthday. His mother, Celia, pulls it out of a bag, the lack of wrapping a dead giveaway it's from a male but she confirms anyway that it is from his cousin. She says he dropped it off in that bag and called special attention to the sealed envelope in the folds of the jersey, which, she makes sure to mention, he specified only Nelson has the authority to unseal.

It's a muted birthday event, maybe they all will be from now on, a twenty-five percent hole at the center. So he has something like privacy that emerges suddenly. Within it he opens the envelope then its greeting card (Hallmark here manages to be vulgar without even minimal humor created despite the clear attempt). The card has a handwritten addendum promising that

> *The wheels are in motion little cuz. The scum did this will soon be getting a visit from the Avenging Angel himself—Nuno D, muthafucka!*
>
> *Your welcome,*
> *"El Tiburón" the Shark.*

Which is all kinds of unsettling and weird and effectively ruins Nelson's birthday utterly and irrevocably; even though, truth is, he hates birthdays anyway.

That was a Major Harris "12" jersey but others sell as well. Larry gets the courage up to host a gathering for one of the games, mostly

other emergency medical personnel but also former such and current CO Hugh Seaborg, and one of the things he does is give each
of his guests a rather high-quality though affordable Pork jersey. He
even does a little research so that Donnie Seaborg gets a Mutola "43,"
which Hugh brings home and casually tosses at the kid without specifying its source. Hugh later tosses his own in the general direction of
a wastebasket while badmouthing Larry to Sharon as a guy who likes
to throw his weight around because he has money.

To Sharon this is final confirmation that Larry is a good man, whatever that is. Not that she needed much after he bought an air conditioner for a total fucking stranger but such is the perverse state of
Hugh's credibility with her; if he assures her it's perfectly sunny outside, she grabs her goddamn umbrella. This is what she's tethered to
for the remainder of her life sentence.

In the meantime she fishes the Reeves "21" out of the basket and
it feels right on time. Tomorrow is Feniz's birthday and Sharon, who
has suffered a series of financial setbacks, has been stressing the lack of
gift. She recently got a present and saved the gift bag so right in there
the jersey goes as if victim to preordination.

Later, Feniz struggles a bit to get the jersey out of the bag, tissue
paper and shaking hands, but when he does he smiles (like all his, a
genuine one).

"Wow," he says. "This . . . great . . . I saw them . . . their last game."
He raises it up slowly. "They're hot stuff, right?" Sharon doesn't know.
He puts it on in silence and is positively swimming in it. Hugh is a
fat pig and Feniz is someone who is wasting away into disappearance
because tumors are proliferating on and in his brain. It looks like a
dress. Is Porkmania now atmospheric all over Paterson, causing men
and women to question their gender?

Even Father Ventimiglia is affected, though not that way, and soon
he has worked the Pork into a sermon despite knowing less than zero
about the particulars or even generals of professional football or whatever this IFL thing is.

"In today's Gospel," he says, "we get Mark again, and I really encourage all of you to go at least a measure beyond what we read this

morning. So we did Chapter Four to verse nine and I would say go to at least verse thirty-four."

Very few are going to do this additional homework, does he know?

"If you do that I think you'll find a nice juicy piece of metafiction that's only about, oh, two thousand years old."

He giggles, alone. Why does he say things like this, who is this to? The only response is a restless collective murmur.

"Much confusion regarding Christianity in our modern world stems from Jesus's extensive use of parables as a teaching tool. Mark's Four here shows us that this confusion isn't confined to our present day but was present in equal measure not just in Jesus's own time but even among his very own apostles! The specific parable we're concerned with here is the familiar one of the Sower. A sower goes out to sow, and rather indiscriminately it seems. Jesus identifies for his audience four fates for the sower's seed, right? So some is immediately devoured by birds. Some appears to quickly bear fruit but because the ground beneath it is stony there's no genuine depth to its roots and the scalding sun makes quick work of it. Still more seed is choked out by thorns but finally there's the seed that lands on fertile soil and yields a bounty.

"Now, my knowledge of agriculture could fit in a thimble with room to spare but given the usual standard of Jesus's moral brilliance this doesn't seem all that revolutionary or powerful; it's not him instructing people who've been slapped in the face to offer up the other cheek, that's for sure. What I do think is hugely significant is what happens next and that's why I'm asking you to continue reading where we left off.

"Because what happens when he's done is that those close to him immediately start asking him what he meant by all that sower business. This part might feel familiar to those of you who've spent any appreciable time debating those who, whatever their motivation, resist anything but an extreme and thus illogical literalization of our foundational literature. At any rate, Jesus's response to them is something like *Guys, really? If you're not gonna get this one how are you gonna get any of them?*

MECHANICS' INSTITUTE LIBRARY
57 Post Street
San Francisco, CA 94104
(415) 393-0101

"Then it's almost as if he just throws his hands up in the air and is like *Fine, just this once I'll spell this one out for you.* When he does, I think at least two really interesting things happen. One is that even this supposedly plain-language explanation immediately employs metaphorical devices like Satan and the word of God; Jesus here is like an artist who can't help but create art even when he's just trying to communicate at a base level. Still, certainly his meaning is made clearer and if we substitute a concept like *moral truth* for the word of God we pretty quickly get what he's driving at and may even start to wonder: what's our state of receptivity to moral truth?

"Are we by the wayside so that even when it lands on us it fails to penetrate at all and therefore just evanesces with the wind? Are we like stone, where in the moment we're confronted by it we are persuaded, even compelled, but because there's nowhere for the roots to take hold, the slightest ensuing tribulation is enough to take us back to moral ignorance? Most likely we have a great many thorns in our life that choke the life out of this truth before it can blossom into a bounty.

"These thorns are everywhere, right? Jesus calls them the cares of this world, the deceitfulness of riches, material desires, and can anyone doubt that this has become our true religion? Aren't we perfectly willing to do what's right and true in the abstract but provided only that it doesn't unduly interfere with our love of money, power, prestige, golf, sex, food, clothes, cars, advancement, basically all those things that have no negative inherent value but which we can perversely elevate to the status of a God, and we know from elsewhere that you can't properly worship more than one of these. A way of looking at it is that the entirety of the gospels is just three years of Jesus saying the only thing that properly warrants that kind of veneration is love itself and the remarkable resistance that simple message received, although as Christians we still hold out hope it will someday be truly heard.

"Now, I said there were two particularly interesting things about Jesus's response so here's the second. Does Jesus convincingly explain why he uses parables at all? In other words why doesn't he just say something closer to his explanation right at the outset? Instead, and this is true throughout the gospels, we see Jesus as a kind of free literary artist constantly presenting and shaping his truth through stories, metaphor, symbolism. I'm reminded of my high school English class and a time when we spent about a week analyzing a poem, don't quite remember which one. Finally, on Friday one of my classmates raised his hand and since it was the only hand up the teacher kind of reluctantly pointed at it. *If that's what he wanted to say all along,* this student complained, *why couldn't he have just come right out with it and saved us a week?* And everybody laughed of course, primarily because it was true in some sense.

"The response is that some of us, and not surprisingly our English teacher was numbered among them, believe that there's added value to portraying things poetically. Is this how Jesus responds though? I would argue that Jesus defends his extensive use of poetry with more poetry! So we have this strange passage where he seems to say something like *You guys get to receive unambiguously plain moral instruction, everyone else is going to have to do work and tease out deeper meanings all while beset by doubts and other interference.* Note that this itself seems poeticized, since what Jesus seems to mean is that the apostles have to do very little moral reasoning since they are in his constant actual physical presence and its immediate effects so that their understanding is as much a question of operating their physical senses as it is any product of their moral or logical intuition.

"So what about everyone else? Put simply, everyone else is going to get metaphor and analogy and simile so they better develop their ears into the kind that can truly hear those elements. Because isn't that precisely the disconnect my fellow English student made explicit all those years back? I would say that everyone in that classroom proceeded from a bias that the poem had plenty to offer. Its failure to land in that instance I think even the student would say had more to do with his receptivity to poetry than anything else. If your eleven-year-old says he found nothing special about *Hamlet* you're unlikely to reassess your opinion of the poem as a result.

"The good news is that one's susceptibility to things like truth and beauty is not immovably fixed. Jesus's three-year ministry, his two-thousand-year ministry, heck, that English class, all proceed from the notion that human beings have the capacity to alter their heart, we'll call it, and learn this new language that will deepen their understanding of the universe and man's role in it. He uses this tool not to obfuscate but to elucidate and if our response is confusion the proper remedy is not to write off the teacher but rather to sharpen our ability to comprehend. That's what we try to do here on Sundays. Advisedly or not, the Christian method is not going to change.

"And in case anyone was wondering exactly how committed Jesus was to this methodology he immediately starts talking to them about lamps and their purpose, and here it helps to remind oneself of the critical importance at the time of nonnatural light. To those whose soil has produced a bounty he says, *Be like lamps.* Light up the world not just with words but, far more importantly, with your actions. Create a brightness so luminous people will marvel at its source until they can't help but discover truth.

"Jesus's answer to the implied question of *why parables*, his answer in both substance and methodology, is, I would argue, a powerful claim for the primacy of all those human activities we class generally under the term *Art.* For poetry and learning and philosophy and even music, which you might have noticed is another big part of what we do here. The majesty of these tools is not in meaningful dispute, and not just because of their use by the greatest moralist the world will ever know.

"Fittingly, the chapter more or less ends with Jesus contemplating artistic creation aloud, the storytelling oddness of which I don't think has ever been fully parsed. By that I mean that Jesus literally says, *Hmm, let me see, how should I describe the Kingdom of God (itself a metaphor, right?) to you all, what parable shall I create?* then follows with the Parable of the Mustard Seed, perhaps the most accomplished one in all the gospels. Yet that was all two thousand years ago and one of my primary claims here on Sundays has been my belief that humanity must update and sharpen the metaphorical tools it uses to convey this truth of divine transcendence.

"Which brings me, however circuitously, to American football. Because it seems that some time back the mighty, all-powerful IFL went on strike, a strike that despite all predictions continues to this day. Now of course there was a lot of consternation among fans as to what would become of their football Sundays; believe me, you cannot do this job and be unaware of the special role that sport plays on autumn and winter Sundays. Except here comes this little upstart league, the NFL, that frankly no one even knew existed. What's that? Oh, I mixed them?

"Okay, it seems the NFL is the all-powerful and they're the ones that went on strike. Okay, good. Let's see, okay.

"Except here comes this little upstart league, the *IFL*, that frankly no one even knew existed. And look at this, they even have a team here in Paterson. And everyone has a good laugh at it all because surely the NFL is going to come along at any second and crush the whole thing, right?

"But unbeknownst to us all, while we were looking straight ahead with our blinders on, off to the side some people were planting mustard seeds. So maybe you saw some construction take place on the armory or saw an ad on the local public access channel but nothing near enough to make you think you had to question your analysis, which, after all, everyone shared with you.

"Now, admittedly, the vast majority of the stories we humans create through our actions follow predictable trajectories. But who predicted this? Who predicted that later this afternoon the undefeated Paterson Pork would be on national television trying to stay that way? That our armory would've been transformed the way it has into a place of community delight?

"Maybe the few that did are the ones who planted that humble seed early this year and have now watched it blossom into a verdant canopy that for the moment shields us from those harmful aspects of the sun. Maybe when you look at this awesome challenge, becoming the kind of person whose soil is conducive to the flowering of beautiful acts and bounteous love, it seems unattainable, an entirely predictable failure. But change doesn't have to come all at once or not at all. Maybe you aren't that person yet but maybe it's also true that you will be someday. And maybe you'll look back and wonder how it began and maybe you'll identify today in a makeshift church in Paterson as the day you didn't look at the impossibility of it all, you just planted a seed."

Afterward many gather near the entrance, this is customary, to kind of well-wish others, especially the priest. No one mentions the sermon directly to him but it's in the air otherwise and the strong consensus is that, to the extent it was understandable, it was weird. His sermons, plural, are odd really. There's even more agreement, however, that his reference to something purely fun like our undefeated football team was more than welcome, keep that kind of thing coming.

Larger point is the success of the Pork is emanating past the grid-iron and out into the city's crumbling infrastructure; it's not clear what real-life effects, if any, this is having or will have.

22

||||||||||

Elsewhere, well, back at Bellevue, the Theorist has started to draw a following that seems basically religious. He's managed to procure a lab coat and a pointer to go with the whiteboard that somehow materialized that first time and the impact of those accessories on his influence cannot be gainsaid.

Also he's maybe gifted, this dude. He modulates his voice beautifully and is undeterred by the many prolonged patches of audience incomprehension and disinterest. Physically he's quite tall and bony with the aforementioned wild hair that makes him look like a giant praying mantis wearing an electrified wig. And when he makes what he thinks is a particularly pointed claim, that hair reverberates as if duly impressed.

"When last we spoke we saw that the great chasm between what our equations say Time is and isn't and the way it brutally dominates our lives has led some to claim that Time doesn't even exist, that instead the universe is an almost limitless set of indistinguishable Nows of equal ontological value that our puny brains can't help but organize sequentially, though always with a strictly prescribed form of sequentiality, that famous one-way arrow of time. The idea is that we create what seems like the arrow's flight when in fact instants of time are like articles of clothing hanging on a line to dry, a line with no direction, only simultaneity. Now, this is wrong in fundamental ways but, even so, there's more than a kernel of truth in it.

"For example, let's start with the very general premise here. Is there any support for the existence of this kind of delusional process? Of course there is. We saw earlier that even adopting the most simplistic concepts of space and time possible doesn't allow us to meaning-fully distinguish between being in uniform motion and absolute rest or allow us to agree in all instances on temporal concepts like velocity or duration. This is just another way of saying that our most powerful and immediate sense impressions can be greatly deceiving. And when we say something like this we're doing nothing less than referencing the very genesis of science if you think about it. Because past man was certainly justified in concluding, for example, that the earth stood still while the sun bopped up and down around it. Our realization that our own eyes couldn't be trusted did nothing less than spur an intellec-tual revolution. Similarly, couldn't we today be fundamentally in error regarding our sensations of the passage of time?

"First, an initial difficulty with the analogy. Note that with the sun our observations were, in a far more pronounced sense, outside of ourselves. We were collecting and interpreting data and sensa-tions about the world around us and as our methodology improved, through technology et cetera, so did our conclusions. By the way note how enmeshed those kinds of observations were and continue to be with our experience and concept of time: we would see the sun rise in the morning then *later* set in the evening and so on. The distinction is that with Time we don't feel in any deep sense that we are able to fully step away from it to consider it dispassionately like we can with the earth's rotation for example.

"What happens when we try? Who's *we*? What happens when you try? What are *you* anyway? Putting that aside for the moment, what happens is you might find that in a way Time is unavoidably inside you. For example, you'll make that realization over time. You'll begin to make that realization and it will intertwine with the passage of time until you make it fully. This may be a fine point but it's, I think, a valid one.

"I asked you just now what you are, so take a moment to consider it at length. Are you fully and finally just a physical body? If you want to reflexively say yes consider this first. Can't you make observations about your body that have the kind of logical and experiential distance of those earlier observations about the solar system? Take your time but it seems like you can. A human body is a physical object, yes, but that's not the end of the story, right? A basketball is a physical object as well so a human being must be a physical object *plus*. They share characteristics, human bodies and basketballs; but a basketball doesn't have free will, desires, dreams. It doesn't reflect on the nature of time and other mysteries. Let's sum up and say it lacks consciousness. Or I would argue that a better way of saying it is that consciousness never instantiates itself in basketballs.

"We're about to go off in a critical new direction so let me lead with the conclusion in a sense and say that the mere fact that human consciousness so fundamentally experiences Time means that Time necessarily exists and functions essentially as we believe it does; it just does. What about the lack of equational support, you say? You know what else lacks that kind of support? That's right, consciousness! Nothing in the world, nothing biological, psychological, or philosophical, can explain it. Nothing in any physical theory requires it or even sheds any light on it whatsoever.

"So what is consciousness then? It's not like anything else in the universe, though other things may be like it. Consciousness is just itself. Like Time, it's invisible but for its effects. That said, it's far more mysterious. You'll hear things like *No one knows how it arises from purely physical phenomena like neurons* but it doesn't take more than a few seconds' reflection to see that statements like this sneakily insert the unjustifiable presumption that that's where it arises from.

"So if we can't fully explain it, and believe me we can't, what *can* we say about it? Simply this, consciousness is without question the single most powerful and grand force in the universe. I would even go so far as to say that, without it, the universe would not exist.

"Now, I can almost feel your skepticism on my skin so let me explain. I said physics has nothing to say about consciousness in any explanatory sense but that's not the end of the story. And it's actually a remarkable twist. Because what if I tell you that the history and development of quantum physics has been nothing less than the establishment and repeated confirmation of the supreme primacy of consciousness?

"In the interests of brevity, though I assure you there's more, let's start and end with the uncertainty principle, probably the star of quantum mechanics. I know what you're thinking, not again, but it's just so perfect for our purposes. You'll know by now what's so uncertain about it. Go to the extremely subatomic level and you'll find something odd. You'll find that you can't really accurately measure both a particle's position and its velocity. The more accurate you get with one measurement the more inaccurate the other becomes.

"This is commonly misinterpreted as a measurement problem but in fact it runs much deeper than that. It's not just that we can't measure these things accurately and simultaneously. It's worse, these values simply don't exist *until* we measure. What exists instead is a kind of wave of possibilities right up until the moment we measure. What happens then, why don't we find a wave when we measure? Well, measuring somehow causes the wave function to collapse into a fixed value, is the way we look at it. You can see how that seemed insane at the time. How could the act of measuring more properly fall under the heading of creation instead of discovery? What if no measurement ever occurred? What then was the independent reality, the truth?

"I know, this is all well established and kind of trite stuff. But what I want to highlight is how I think insufficient high-level thought has been devoted to the even odder fact, odder than the fact of no underlying unambiguous reality in this context, of what we uniquely mean when we refer to measuring. Physicists here don't mean *measure* in the ordinary sense of the word. If I asked you to measure the temperature of something what would you do? You might grab a thermometer and employ it to see how high its mercury rises and therefore arrive at a number. You'd use a physical object to give me an answer. You wouldn't feel, for example, that you could just intuit a precise answer, right?

"But is that really the kind of measurement we're talking about here, the kind that mandates subatomic collapse? It can't be, right? The uncertainty principle is saying that the uncertainty we've identified infects everything physical. *Everything physical*, you might notice, includes your thermometer. It includes Geiger counters, sheets of paper, and decaying atoms. How then can we avoid a kind of infinite regress of uncertainty? A state where the universe is in a kind of wave state of possibilia that never realizes? The pervasiveness of the principle means you can still use these physical tools as part of your apparatus, but to truly activate collapse, to truly create reality, and the equations bear this out, you need something more, something that is superior and that is not physical and therefore not subject to the uncertainty. In other words, correct, you need consciousness!

"This realization should feel astounding. Now you see why I call consciousness the supreme force in the universe. It literally creates physical reality. That's why we can't determine how it arises out of physical processes. Because it's superior to those processes in every way. Consciousness is not derived from the physical world, more like the other way around! What does this mean for Time? It's about time."

He waits for chuckles that never come.

"It means, for one, no more apologizing if our only empirical support for Time and its arrow resides in consciousness. You say Time is an illusion created by our collective consciousness? Sorry, pal, consciousness doesn't create illusions on such fundamental questions, only reality. This isn't the orbit of the sun here, this is direct unavoidable experience of the type that can't, in the absence of a ludicrous Cartesian evil genius, prove to be false. This much human agreement about an invisible nonphysical entity is like *Cogito ergo sum* and as such just equals truth. If you want precedent I'll take you to the subatomic world, and not coincidentally something else we find there is the manner in which particles called kaons decay, which manner *does* empirically support the arrow of time et cetera.

"But that, besides leading us far afield, would also be backtracking in an unnecessary way. Physics is an attempt to describe the physical world we find ourselves in and it's done that quite brilliantly. I'm reminded of Wittgenstein's lament, however, that even if all scientific questions were magically and satisfactorily answered, still the genuine problems of life would not have been touched at all. In other words, physics and the other sciences are never going to answer the *why* questions that ultimately seem most interesting. This is another way of saying that the tyranny of Time is not going to be toppled through the discovery of an equation.

"However, don't misinterpret, I'm not saying Time is a simple uninteresting tyrant either. I don't deny that the potential for confusion is certainly present. The seeming constancy of the linearity, for example, can lead us to exaggerate its import and demarcation lines. To combat this it can be useful to remind ourselves of a philosophical insight, not my own, that I've always found intuitively attractive. Basically it reminds us that we view past, present, and future as highly exclusive notions without overlap. If an event belongs to the past then it cannot exist in the present or future. Similarly, a future event cannot be past or present and so on. This exclusivity is what creates change and makes it so that the only two changes possible are from present to past and future to present.

"But is it really that unproblematic a division? Because note that there's a sense in which events most certainly do transcend these categories. If an event is past, for example, it was once future and then present. A present event was once future and will soon be past and all future events will unavoidably be also present and past. Present events were future events in the past and in the future will be past. Past events were future events if you go farther back in the past and present if you go less far. Future events will in the further future become present then past. The point is that all events necessarily and simultaneously partake of all three notions and this seems to give lie to the pronounced exclusivity we thought we'd identified.

"This gets more complex but I think in general it's a notion that's onto something vital, essentially the notion that Time is more fluid and malleable than we give it credit for. Forget math, do we not feel the past often far more forcefully than the present? Do you feel a great foreignness to your future or is it something that constantly colors your present?"

Just then Dennings walks in with a look of clear distaste on her face. "That's enough, Doctor," she says sarcastically. "You're riling up my patients, class is over."

"Okay, that's my cue, folks. Next time we'll kind of bring this all to a head and I'll explain why all this matters. How Time is simultaneously more complex than you think but also far more fragile and contingent. Including the shocking revelation that Time is literally running out and how that is the worst possible news for everyone in this room and indeed everyone you know and love."

With that Dennings kind of ushers him out amid no evidence whatsoever that anyone has been riled. This includes Nuno, who stays perfectly still in the corner and still, weeks now, utters not a syllable.

21

||||||||||

The regular season that only feels more irregular by the minute continues, the primary change the consistent dimming of all ambient natural light.

Dia verbally encourages the Pork's Executive Director of Marquee Alteration and Iteration as he shakily negotiates his way up their flimsy ladder to gingerly put 8–0 up on the marquee. The executive director is careful not to look down the whole time.

The Pork's pig is facing off with the Maryland Maul's giant lobster to contest who can do more push-ups. Both put up an impressive number until finally the pig collapses in exhaustion as the lobster taunts him by putting one claw behind his back and continuing with one-armers. On the sideline, Coach Elkins throws down his headset and wonders: "The hell's wrong with this pig anyway?"

Notwithstanding the failings of their mascot, the Pork are an excellent football team. In every game Sims always carries the ball the way Nina taught him. Reeves, Mutola, and the entire secondary are great. Opposing quarterbacks have nowhere to go with the ball so that even though the pass rush is nothing special many coverage sacks ensue. Harris is sharp and the unquestioned leader, although it does appear that getting up from hits becomes more difficult for him as the season goes on.

It's a home game against the Louisville Locust and the wheel has landed on Not in Kansas Anymore meaning extreme, unpredictable winds. The coaches have no headsets as they have all flown off. The goalposts are bowed. In the crowd, parents hold on to young children lest they blow away. Harris drops back, spots a wide open receiver, and throws a pass that gets caught in the wind then travels about twenty yards backward. In the booth, Slim Janders exercises his gift for summary thusly: "That one might've been affected by the fake wind, Jim."

13–0 goes on the marquee, but Dia won't watch as she holds the ladder because of that number's unluckiness.

20

||||||||||

The next day at Bellevue the Theorist is back, that fakakta equationy illustration still his backdrop. Nuno is in the room but looks even more vacant than usual, another update has just been filed with the court indicating that his status is unchanged. Also there's a weird looking orderly present. I don't mean that the orderly's appearance is weird, I mean that he literally looks, as in he observes, in a weird way.

"Let's review a bit first. Last time we saw that quantum physics, if it's to make perfect sense, puts a lot of pressure on our concepts of Time and Possibility. One response has been this notion of a multiverse. You'll recall that, very generally, under this scenario our universe is just one of many that actually exist and they all exist in the fullest sense of that word. These universes are constantly being spurred into existence by the question of what's possible.

"So because we all feel that it's possible that I will suddenly in three minutes attempt an ill-advised somersault in front of you all and land flat on my face then under the proposed multiverse frame-work, three minutes from now, when I don't do that in front of you guys, an entirely new universe will be created, one that is identical to this one we've all lived but only right up to that fateful somersault moment. Because at that precise moment, in this other newly cre-ated universe, I do attempt the somersault, with the aforementioned embarrassing result. In that manner, new invisible-to-us universes are constantly sprouting. I know what you're all thinking, It's going to get very crowded. But it's okay, we have all the room we need. So there are variations on this, but that's the very general idea with multiverses.

"Now, the concept of the multiverse is revelatory. It usefully explains some otherwise troubling math and it has genuine philosophical benefits. It is in many ways a masterpiece of creative human speculation that has attracted significant prestigious support. It is also finely tuned complete nonsense, to the point of gibberish.

"Think of what the multiverse people are saying. They're saying that because it's possible I will attempt a somersault here, and/or for other reasons, then I actually do attempt one in another universe created solely for that purpose. Well, besides the fact that Occam's razor is rolling over in its grave, that none of this even remotely resembles science, no data to interpret, no hope of any so therefore no ability to verify or falsify, there's a fatal logical failure that allows us to summarily dispense with this silly idea entirely.

"In brief, the whole thing depends on it being me who attempts the somersault elsewhere so to speak. But I didn't attempt it, nor did I do any of the other things required for this theory to be true. How do we know I didn't? Just ask me and I'll tell you. I didn't. It's really that simple. When the philosopher G. E. Moore was asked to prove the existence of the external world he said, *Look at your hand, that's it.* I know I didn't attempt that somersault because I experienced not attempting it. Note that this is true no matter how I choose to define myself. If I think I'm just a physical body, nothing more, then it's clear I didn't attempt the somersault and all of you are my witnesses. Of course, no one truly defines themselves as such so let me concede that I am more than just a collection of flesh and bone and say that I have a soul or, if the connotations make you uncomfortable, I am a localized consciousness, that concept again. Now since the primary and indispensable quality of consciousness is awareness, the fact that I am unambiguously unaware of having attempted any somersault means *I* didn't.

"Time for objections. I'm being too literal, the multiverse proponent might say. When I said you attempt the somersault in an alternate universe I didn't *literally* mean you. I meant that a sort of copy of you attempts it and does so in a sort of copy of our universe. This is, of course, ludicrous. What does a copy of me even mean? Physicists say things like this, seemingly oblivious to the profound philosophical problems they create. Suffice to say that like all of you I know who

I am and I know, as well as I know anything, that whatever I am it is both indivisible and not susceptible to duplication. If someone or something does a somersault anywhere I don't care how much that thing looks like me or talks like me it's simply *not* me and as such its actions can never be significant to assertions about me in any meaningful way.

"This is what makes the Derek Parfit problem that everyone seems so impressed by so fundamentally dumb as well. Parfit asks you to imagine a machine that destroys you on Earth then instantly re-creates you on Mars, meaning an exact atomic copy. You use it often to flawless effect, flawless as in every time you find yourself transported, as it were, to your destination. What if one time you opened your eyes and found yourself still on Earth? You tell the guy to try again because you really have to get to Mars for that big meeting and he says he can't because the copy was in fact created on Mars. Here, see for yourself on the monitor. When you wonder aloud what's to become of you, the technician tells you not to worry because you've been poisoned and your body will be expiring in about ninety seconds. When you predictably protest loudly he responds by reminding you that your original body has been destroyed on Earth every single time you've gone to Mars and the only difference this time is the ninety-second delay.

"What now? These are the kinds of fake controversies that can last decades and shake one's faith in humanity's collective intellect. You, the traveler, are perfectly qualified to assert that the continued existence of your consciousness is not dependent on any particular collection of physical particles, having experienced unassailable confirmation of that fact many times. You know for a fact that you are not in the body on Mars that you saw on the monitor because you just aren't. When you look around you don't see the red planet, you see a blue one. In other words, you know that you are more than a body, more than a brain, and that reductive materialism is false. In that case, I suggest you sit back, relax, and see what the next minutes bring for your consciousness, how exciting. There's no *problem*.

"All of this is so plainly obvious that I won't belabor it any further, only sum up: there is one universe, one and only, and we're in it. Also there's only one *we*, you are you and you alone. That said, we are not, however, alone. And, no, I'm not referring to something stupid like aliens.

"I don't have the time or inclination to show my math but understand that the same way there are at least three dimensions to Space, there is more than one dimension to Time. Oh boy, the very imprecision I loathe. Time is two-dimensional, exactly two, how's that for precision? The only people in the universe are located on Earth. That's the answer to the question of *where* all the people in the universe are. The answer to *when* all the people in the universe are is a bit more complicated.

"Everyone in the universe of course feels they are in the now and they are in a sense correct. Remember that these *past*, *present*, and *future* concepts are far more nebulous and porous than most think. However, if the people in this room could observe those in the other temporal dimension it would appear to us that those people were living in our future. On the other hand, if those people could look at us right now we would appear to be living in their past. Hmm, where else have we seen this kind of relationship between the observer and the observed?

"Listen, I am *not* talking about time travel, which is impossible, so put that out of your minds. I'm talking about a hidden dimension, a concept that whether you realize it or not you are fully familiar with. Think of a painting. Staring at one to the exclusion of all other visual stimuli you would be well justified in concluding that space has two dimensions even though the underlying reality is three-dimensional space. The third dimension was hidden from you due to your limited perceptual abilities. So it is with this other dimension of Time.

"Now, if this dimension is inaccessible to us why should we care at all, let alone believe in it? First of all, there's inaccessible and then there's inaccessible. Up until about yesterday, cosmically speaking, humanity couldn't access the moon; I assure you it nonetheless affected the tides much as it does today.

"My point is we're more aware of this extra dimension than we think, but rather than go off significantly in that direction I'll just plant a few seeds that might spark at least the beginnings of recognition. Imagine time travel for a second, which in my experience most readily agree to do, and ask yourself what the status would be of the time spent during the actual travel part of that concept, such as in the machine. When we sleep or are otherwise unconscious, don't we escape the tyranny of time? Is there Time in our dreams? Is it the same one the body in the bed is experiencing? Does it flow and if so does it do so more slowly or faster? Are what we call out-of-body experiences also out of time?

"Putting that aside, I warned you last time that I would have bad news. You know how we humans experience the universe as expanding? Moreover, how many believe it to be expanding at an accelerating rate? This observation has been the impetus for the to-date fruitless search for the so-called Dark Energy supposedly driving this expansion. Well, you can call off the search because the universe is *not* expanding. The data and observations are not so much inaccurate as misinterpreted. What's really happening is not the universe expanding. What we're seeing when we look way out there is Time literally running out and it is physicists' reluctance to accept this fact that has led to all this universe expanding nonsense. There's no acceleration at all, it's Time itself slowing down that makes it look that way.

"Please understand that I am not speaking in metaphor here as my colleagues are wont to do. Time most definitely exists. It functions very close to how we experience it. Its nature is mysterious but mysterious doesn't mean eternal. Time had a beginning with the Big Bang and like all things with a beginning it will have an end. It is slowing as we speak and it is slowing the way your great-grandfather is slowing, with the same ultimate result. It has shed and will shed dimensions. Those two dimensions I've taught you about will become one then none, and the one we're having this discussion in is going to be the first to go!

"Do you understand? This thing is almost over! You are all about to die, if I may put it bluntly though misleadingly. You, your thoughts, hopes, dreams, prejudices, obsessions, not to mention everyone you know and love and all of their store of the above, are about to disappear. Forever!"

This last passage is a bridge too far and it takes all of Dennings's alacrity and athleticism to spring into action in time to preserve the

Theorist's safety. As it is, the whole thing devolves into a bit of low-level mayhem as mental patient after mental patient, literally, tries to get a free shot in before the would-be victim is escorted away from the most imminent danger. The weird-looking orderly gives no indication of understanding the demands of his position and just stands there dumbly. When everything's died down he walks over to Nuno, who could not be a less inviting presence.

"Whoa, what's that guy's damage?" he wonders with a smile.

"Ø"

"Sorry, friend of yours?"

"Ø"

"Nuno, it's me."

"Ø"

"Nuno!"

Nuno looks up through incomprehension. The orderly puts his hand on Nuno's shoulder and that makes him instantly recoil.

"Damn, bro," the orderly says. "You look . . . used up, man. It's me, Solomon. Solomon. Solomon Hanes, yo!"

Nuno turns away and kind of puts his face in his hands.

"I know, what the hell am I doing here? But I would ask you the same thing, dude. When you first got moved here from Rikers I was your biggest defender, man. I says, this is genius. I'm like, dude's already got the get somehow and has taken it with him to Bellevue, where it's going to be a hell of a whole lot easier to break out. Problem is days pass and nothing, then weeks and now this. I don't have to tell you about the legendary impatience of the outfit that's our boss on this thing. Anyway I hold them off and hold them off, *my man knows what he's doing so let him do his thing*, but even that runs out, dig? So let me ask you point-blank, do you have the get? Is this all part of a grand master criminal scheme? If so, I gotta say, what's the delay? I been through every corner of this place, I can't imagine it's holding you, yet you been in here a minute, yo. What's the play here, man? Can I be, like, filled in? There's things on my end, feel me? You got the get?"

"Ø"

"So then? I mean I've held them off nicely but that's starting to feel like a past-tense thing, know what I mean? This is my last play. I says get me in there and I'll talk to him. So here I am to do just that. I'm trying to preserve this shit cause it's beaucoup dough re mi, dig? You're welcome, by the way. I had to actually get this orderly job, you know. Yeah, fine, The Absence hooked me up with the false history and whatnot, but I'm still the one had to do the interview and charm these fucks. Nuno?"

"Ø"

"Nuno?"

"Ø"

"The hell, man? Listen, sorry, I know I been all business but I got limited time here. The Absence doubled the purchase price on us, which sounds great, seven fucking figures, but they need to know, can we do this? Otherwise they're moving on and I don't need to tell you what being fired by them means, they're not gonna leave two freelancers like us who know about this thing, they're not just gonna leave us be, bro!"

"Ø"

"Oh, man, seeing you like this, you in there? Man, you're like all sunken and shit. Seven figures, bro. No reaction?"

"Ø"

"Nuno!" He also kind of grabs Nuno's pajama lapels and starts shaking for emphasis because it really is that urgent. Except that just then Dennings enters to see an orderly she doesn't know shaking one of her favorite patients, favorite because he doesn't talk, and commences the process of unleashing holy verbal hell on said orderly, but for it to get physical she'll first have to work her way through the mass of mentally ill humanity impeding her path. Solomon hears the screams but like someone well practiced in escaping detection he doesn't do the dumb thing where the recipient of a scream turns to face the screamer before running away, he just shrinks into flight and she never sees his face.

When she gets to Nuno she's all apologetic in the manner of someone who fears litigation.

"Are you okay? Mr. DeAngeles, are you okay?"

"Ø"

"I didn't, I can't believe, do you know who that was?"

"Ø"

"Are you okay?"

"No."

"Oh my, you talk! Are you all right?"

"No."

"What's wrong? Can I get you something?"

"Yes."

"Really?"

"You can get that orderly back, I need him."

19

||||||||||

The Pork's pig is inches from the top of a climbing wall when he slips off and is defeated by a humongous hot dog. The hot dog mascot is normally all-beef but this Sunday that specification has been removed to taunt the opponent. It doesn't work and the Pork win. Consequently, the next day's marquee, set up in advance of the probably unchallenging penultimate game, reads a very bacony 14–0.

18

||||||||||

Solomon is enjoying somewhat the sensation of having recently dodged a bullet. If pressed, he probably has as much fear of Dennings as anyone, but his is multifaceted and special. Truth is he's found himself, almost against his will, bucking for that ridiculous Employee of the Week plaudit they give out. Such a thing would never have occurred to him but for a chance comment he overheard in which the person putting up the Polaroid last Friday let slip that it had really been a last-minute decision between the woman depicted therein and *that weird Hanes guy*.

He, Solomon, was that weird Hanes guy! The force of these words had hit him with redirectional force. Was he really Employee of the Week material? Sure, his entire presence there was inherently fraudulent. But the fact is this kind of long-term fraudulence can become indistinguishable from reality. So even though his résumé and various certifications were fictions created and procured by The Absence for a very specific purpose, that had nonetheless been his true self undergoing extensive training in the orderly arts then translating that training into genuine development.

Truth is he'd become invested in the thing. Maybe it was time for a career change. Damn, he was twenty-one. Isn't that the age people graduate and embark on some prolonged legit shit? Point is, he'd successfully run away from Dennings days earlier mainly motivated by his desire to preserve his chances at employee of this week that just started, which award he anticipated would propel him to the stratosphere, or whatever the equivalent is, of world-renowned and commensurately compensated medical orderlies.

Problem is, to have a career, especially the kind where everyone's just kind of fawning over you at all times because of how good you are at medical orderlying, you first have to number among the living and that's problematic at the moment. Solomon's knowledge of the underlying mechanisms is limited but scary enough. He only knows that he and Nuno were given a simple if insane task. Get into Rikers and steal some crazy timeless piece of art that's hidden in there for some reason. Simple enough, but nothing beyond that had really developed simply.

His role was to use his island expertise and connections to assist this Nuno guy in whatever he needed. But what does this nut do to land on the island? Only catch a body in the most high-profile, tabloid way possible, so that everybody's all *Brainiac Killer* and shit. Tell me, could this possibly be the fault of one Solomon Hanes, criminal sidekick extraordinaire? How is his professionalism even implicated?

Months of nothing, remand status then solitary, could this get more implausible? It took all his skill just to hold on to the assignment. Now this. His initial optimism had dissipated, but nothing like its sudden death when he finally got to Nuno, or what's left of him. The urgency of it all and that blank statue in response. This thing, The Absence, it's not like you get a letter from their lawyer informing you that they're exercising their right to early termination under the contract and best wishes in your future professional endeavors and shit. The only thing they like less than failure is witnesses to failure.

Nuno has to know all this. Unless. Unless there is no Nuno anymore. There wasn't one that afternoon few days back, that's for sure. That wasn't the Nuno he'd grown to know and, fuck it, fine, *love*. Not to say that dude would've been all that helpful. Solomon can almost hear him saying *Fuck The Absence, they know where to find me* or some other similarly badass shit. Lots of guys talk like that, difference with Nuno is he means it. And he backs it up. Until one day he wouldn't be able to. But so what. Nuno would go down fighting, better than Solomon can say for himself.

Anyway, almost certainly gone, that magnetic guy. Anyone Solomon's ever seen come back from anything more than brief solitary was the same thing, dead eyes. Way he sees it is we're all utterly and irreparably alone so we have to delude ourselves to deal. People who've done solitary lose that option forever. The empty dark drives the savage truth straight into their vulnerable minds and the result is a kind of premature spiritual death.

Still, he'd make another attempt before running, not *to* anything but away. From The Absence or anything else that would seek to do him harm. *This can still all work out,* the kind of thing he just forces himself to continually mentally recite. Nuno's going to recover, go back there, swipe the get, and break out with it so they can get paid in full. Then Solomon's going to disappear with his share after just saying no to any future jobs, which *is* allowed, or is at least more allowed.

Or none of that'll happen and he'll just have to run like a dog afraid of a bone, is that a thing?

When he finally does get a chance at Nuno he finds him sitting near that mental patient from before with the physics and time running out and shit. Time's running out all right, he needs Nuno to wake up and fast. But as he approaches he realizes something weird or just weirder. This dude they call the Theorist isn't lecturing at large like before, he's actually addressing Nuno directly. Whatever, Solomon's going to have to just pretextually interrupt them and get to this thing. Should he die from politeness? He waits for a lull but this Einstein-wannabe cat ain't pausing for air and Nuno's got that look on his face that Solomon recognizes as extreme disinterest while still processing every single syllable. Wait, isn't that good? Who knows with this motherfucker rapping mile a minute?

"Think of Plato's cave. The premise is famously that inside a cave some humans are held in such a way that they can only look straight ahead at the wall across from them. On that wall they see shadows, their shadowy movements, and how those shadows interact with each other. What they don't see, can't see, is what's happening behind them. Because behind them is a parapet where puppeteers manipulate objects in front of a light source positioned to cast those shadows. Now, if you asked the prisoners to describe reality as experienced by them you'd hear a lot about those shadows and nothing about the parapet et cetera. But that, of course, doesn't change the fact that the parapet and the underlying puppet show are *true* and constitute a deeper sense of reality.

"You see where I'm going with this. We live in a four-dimensional world that is like a shadow caused by a higher-dimensional reality. Many are onto this. They know there's a fifth dimension and that it's curled up and hidden. Problem is most of those many think it's light, when in fact it's a second time dimension. The important thing to realize is that when I say curled up and hidden I'm speaking relatively, meaning Einstein's principle insight remains. To us in this temporal dimension the other one is curled up and hidden. But to those in the other, we're curled up and hidden. We share a great many events and would agree on a great preponderance of factual claims but we are absolutely *not* fully coextensive.

"Maybe it would be useful here to start talking about the eighty-eight iterations of Calabi-Yau manifolds. Eighty-eight. 88. See it in your mind's eye. That particular *untouchable* number, as we call them, that looks like two stood-up lemniscates or infinity symbols. Let's talk about the role that number and these other concepts play."

It is here that Nuno shoots the Theorist a look that's like *Talk about any manifold you wish, it's your safety at issue.* Solomon is close enough to see this look and so fully realize that genuine Nuno is back that he almost, but not quite, barrels forward with a million questions where subtlety is needed. Even the Theorist, who is not known for nonverbal cue receptivity, abandons that course.

"Let's talk about football instead," he says.

"Football?"

"Oh, not sure I've ever heard your speaking voice."

"What voice of mine have you heard?"

"Good point."

"You said football."

"I know what you did, uh, are accused of doing."

"What football?"

"Nothing really, just that football's a kind of shorthand I've developed to help me orient myself and maybe even think through these things. Listen, I can say things to your kind here because, really, who's to judge, right?"

"You're currently not *saying* anything, just throat-clearing bullshit."

"I'm saying there was ample warning. We do things like the Large

Hadron Collider to discover and learn but severely downplay the possibility of actual and tangible effects. I know because I was one of the downplayers."

"What does that mean?"

"It means I was there September 2008 when we first fired that thing up."

"Aw, fuck, man, go sell your brand of crazy somewhere else."

"Look it up, it did not go well. People had said, Try to re-create the conditions of the Big Bang and you just might end up succeeding too well, ending everything in an instant Big Crunch. Well, they were only partially right."

"Uh-huh."

"I'd often wondered, if death turns out to be the expiration of our physical bodies while our souls persist, what would it feel like to those who die in their sleep while dreaming? For me, I can report I felt nothing out of the ordinary. I didn't die of course; that was clear. But I do remember getting back to my hotel as if through a dream. I popped the TV on to some football show. I was no aficionado, I assure you, but I knew enough. Jersey boy, some knowledge is inescapable. At any rate, they were interviewing David Tyree, does that name mean anything to you?"

"No."

"I know it doesn't. Truth is I couldn't have picked David Tyree out of a lineup at the time, the way these athletes ply their trade while covered head to toe in protective garb. But I could tell it was Tyree, I thought, from the context. They were asking him about a once-in-a-lifetime improbable catch that decided a Super Bowl and denied the heavy favorite an undefeated season."

"That's Jolley. You're talking about William Jolley, the catch between his knees to beat the Giants?"

"Yeah, to you it's Jolley."

"What does that mean?"

"I mean that here it describes a famous play by someone called William Jolley."

"*Here?*"

"You're right, I mean *now*."

"Whatever, dude."

"Let me explain."

"No thanks, I'm not interested."

"That's why I said *let*."

"Fine, but make it quick, I have business with that orderly sitting over there pretending not to listen."

"The reason I thought they were talking to Tyree is that about seven months earlier, on February third, 2008, to be precise, I had watched Super Bowl Forty-two, wherein someone named David Tyree made a gargantually improbable catch using his helmet, which catch propelled the New York Giants to a victory over the theretofore undefeated New England Patriots."

"*What?* The Patriots? That never happened. That's likely why you're in here, because you think something like that happened and the rest of the world knows it didn't."

"I assure you it happened."

"Giants lost that Super Bowl. They were the ones going for the undefeated season right up until William Jolley, a two-bit receiver on the Kansas City Chiefs, caught a ball with his knees to beat them."

"You're right."

"You just said—"

"We're both right. I'm telling you that on February third, 2008, I watched a journeyman wide receiver make an exceedingly-difficult-to-believe catch using his helmet to keep the Patriots from going undefeated."

"The Patriots? Do you realize how insane you sound? The laughingstock of the fucking league."

"Not when I'm from. Point is that seven months after seeing that I was in Geneva when humanity first tested a device so powerful people feared it might actually end humanity. Well, it didn't, but over the next few days I made some startling realizations. In short, I realized I was here. Here, Super Bowl Forty-two had just been played and it was as you've described it. Worse, *here* I was alone. I've never cared all that much who won or lost a sporting event, it's fundamentally irrational. Besides physics I had one thing I cared about, just one. I had one thing in life. No, that's understatement. I had a life that was really just another name for one thing: Dawn Collier was my wife."

"Ah, I see. Sorry, man, but this is uncomfortably weird even for you. Think I'm out."

"I started doing math, that's really all I am. I needed to get back. I knew this was about CERN and the LHC but I also couldn't shake this weird feeling that it was also about football somehow."

"That's stupid, or should I say stupider."

"I know how it sounds but I don't say that lightly."

"Oh, I see, you're a careful lunatic."

"How is that proof?"

"You're about to claim fucking *football* has cosmic relevance, that's how."

"Is that so crazy though? Think of the passion and interest it inspires and how logically indefensible it all is. American football is an ugly and brutish activity. It doesn't create beautiful lines and angles like soccer or tennis. It's not pastorally calming like baseball. It doesn't have the technical mastery of sprinting or the physical precision of gymnastics. Maybe something deeper is going on."

"No, there's no hidden depth. First of all, football looks great on television. Something about the helmets and the lights, whatever, it's visually compelling. Also, it's violent. America is the worldwide leader in civilized violence so it naturally fell in love."

"Boxing's more violent and has a level of human drama that football could never approach yet its popularity wanes by the day. Realize that I'm not saying football *causes* anything. Just that there might be this weird spooky linkage. My support for that is admittedly intuitive and anecdotal but it's compelling at least to me because it's based on my very personal and direct experience. The details are almost too painful to recount so I'll just say that I did find myself back with Dawn one day."

"What?"

"Yes, thanks to my LHC connections. And all I wanted of life then was to fix things with her. Remember, from her perspective I had disappeared without warning for almost four years. Well, I could and I couldn't. I'd lost something in my travels, something ineffable but no less painful for it. Have you ever felt that just *rightness* with someone? What choice did I have? It was either make no grand claim to her and just try to repair and regain, or else keep insisting on the truth and be marginalized as insane."

"Jesus, your delusion is well developed, you're going to keep these motherfuckers in here busy for years."

"I won't overstate what I was able to regain with her but it was something and it was more than this, this *emptiness*. So, what happened? Why are we having this conversation?"

"We're not."

"Because one day I look up and they're still playing this stupid Super Bowl business. This time it's Super Bowl Forty-six and they're playing it February fifth, 2012."

"You're quite a fan, aren't you?"

"Yes, but not of football, of numbers. Do you see it? Super Bowl Forty-two started this mess. Four and two, right. Four years later they're playing the Super Bowl on a date that's two days later than the preceding one, so Super Bowl Forty-two on February third and now Forty-six on February fifth, four and two, remember that?"

"Oh, absolutely, sure."

"That's nothing, guess who's playing whom? Of course, the New York football Giants against the New England Patriots and what is widely considered the most despicable football fan base in existence, at least when I'm existing at the time."

"Again with that?"

"Exactly, *again*. What are the chances? A rematch. The Giants aren't even good! They never even make the playoffs, their quarterback looks like a paperboy, yet any time they sneak into the playoffs here they are playing in the ultimate game against a vastly superior opponent. I can accept coincidences but not to that degree; to me I decide this game means something."

"Sure, if you're going to completely invent a game might as well have it mean something."

"So they play the game. I have this deep sense of meaning as I watch but don't really know what to root for. I have various competing theories developing. Patriots were supposed to win four years earlier so if they win this night everything is righted, my time here becomes like a forgotten dream and I have the true Dawn back. Or I'm back where I'm supposed to be, difficulties and all, so another Giants win will just cement my recovery."

"Or nothing that happens on a football field has any real significance."

"Well, that's clearly not true, even if you think everything I've said is gibberish."

"I do."

"Patriots are in control, they're going to win. I feel good, my strong intuition now is that a Patriots win sets things right and that's what's going to happen. Except that here's Eli Manning again dropping back—"

"Who?"

"Exactly. Throwing a prayerful pass and, what's this, yes, a different journeyman receiver making a remarkable catch so that the Giants then win again. There'd be no setting aright of the universe. If the Patriots were supposed to win Forty-two, all Forty-six had done was aggravate the injury."

"Bummer."

"I lived alone. That night I dreamt the Cowboys lost a close Super Bowl Forty-six on a last-second field goal."

"That actually happened, listen to that voice."

"I know it happened. Believe me, I know everything that happens in the NFL here."

"I can't believe I'm saying this but what's happened in their NFL since the two Giants wins?"

"That's just it, I have no idea, understand? I'm here with you and your kind ever since that *dream*. No Dawn, no ascertainable truth, no nothing."

"Quite a plight."

"Yes, quite. With a possible solution however. Though frankly I'm far less interested in solving than I am in resolving, less about a solution than I am about a termination."

"I have to talk to this orderly, see the impatience?"

"You know what Super Bowl's coming up, right?"

"None."

"Fifty. Four years since my last violent dislocation. Want to guess when it's scheduled to be played?"

"It won't."

"You guessed it, February seventh, 2016! Remember the pattern, every four years the cosmically significant Super Bowl is played on a date two days later."

"Hate to burst your bubble."

"Believe me, if this nightmare has taught me anything it's to open your mind and absorb the patterns."

"There's no Super Bowl this year."

"Math doesn't lie."

"How have you missed this strike?"

"That day they're firing the LHC again, you're welcome."

"Are you listening?"

"There's a physical location to this kind of thing too and this time it's Paterson Falls. I'm sorry."

"Sorry?"

"But I'm going to flush it all down."

"Good idea. Wait, what does that mean?"

"I'm sorry, it's not personal."

"What's not?"

"How when they play the game 2/7/16 we're going to fire the LHC and this strain of time we're existing in, and which is verifiably running out, will just stop running altogether."

"I see, the world's fated to end that day and—"

"No, that's a stupid word, no offense."

"It's okay, I didn't invent it."

"There's no such thing as fate. I'm not telling you that I know something that is going to happen; I'm telling you about something I'm going to *do*."

"End the world?"

"One of its two time lines. There used to be more and there's about to be one fewer, leaving just the one."

"Benefiting you how?"

"Ending this nightmare for me once and for all. If this dimension doesn't exist anymore, that means I can't be forced to exist in it. That further means I either won't exist at all or I'll exist where I'm from. Where Dawn's from, where Dawn is, always has been, and seemingly always will be."

"Good luck with that."

"It's not personal."

"I understand you to be saying you're going to kill me, among many others, so it feels pretty personal, I gotta say."

"Never thought of it that way. Talking to you makes it more difficult, I'll admit."

"So now you're not going to do it?"

"Correct, I'm not going to talk to you anymore."

"I appreciate it."

"Except to say I'm genuinely sorry. But when people say they would die for their kids or something like that?"

"Yeah?"

"I never really felt what they meant. But now . . . I would, and will, level the world entire for Dawn. To me, there is no world without her and if external reality has to match my internal state for me to bear this pain then so be it. This fourteen-billion-year-old prayer to a deaf-mute God is going to be abruptly silenced. This silencing will be beautiful in its way because, just like that, it won't matter if the prayer was going to be answered or more likely remain ignored. This hole in me. It's only a hole if it's enclosed by matter. If there's nothing that can be used to enclose nothing then everything is a hole and paradoxically nothing's a hole. I don't have to fill anything if everything is just emptiness."

"Okay, man. I've gone a long time without conversation, which used to be a need, so that probably influenced my decision to humor you this long, but the humoring is over. This is the only time line and in it I'm telling you to leave."

"I will."

"Good."

"But it isn't."

Nuno looks straight at the Theorist, diminished and knowing it. Get crazy enough and maybe you're cured. What he's looking at doesn't look like insanity, it looks like one of those cloud formations that will be different things to different people but dangerous to all. He wants to leave it alone, Solomon is nearby and Solomon is highly readable. He can do this, someone else can get the last word in just this once.

"You're engaging in the kind of nonscience you accused the multiverse people of," Nuno says as the Theorist begins to walk away.

"How so?" And just like that they're enmeshed again, to Solomon's dismay.

"You say there's a hidden dimension. Hidden's perfect because it means we can't see it or disprove it. Unprovability is always the last refuge of the lunatic claim. The lack of evidence becomes the best evidence of how well crafted the illusion is."

"I'm saying I have the evidence, that I've lived it for years."

"Right, *you* have it, exclusively. So when no one else sees it you resort to the limits of subjectivity to explain away all difficulties."

"It's not exclusive to me, it's just most salient in me. If you know what to look for, you'll begin to sense this dual dimensionality everywhere. When you sleep, especially if you dream but even if you don't. The moments just before and after sleep. Certain kinds of drug use or medicinal manipulations. The experience of genuine art, not just its consumption but especially its creation. In fact, a lot of what we call out-of-body experiences are probably better termed out-of-time ones."

"Hmm."

"You see what I'm driving at."

Just then Solomon realizes it's the proverbial now or never on talking to Nuno before the orderly schedule mandates he leave the floor.

"Okay, sorry to interject." He does. "But I have official orderly business to conduct."

"That's not a thing," says Nuno.

"I assure you it is."

"I was leaving anyway," says the Theorist and he does just that.

They watch him leave, very slowly, the way he does everything, then Solomon turns to Nuno.

"Nuno DeAngeles, the real McCray!"

"McCoy."

"What the hell was that nut all on about?"

"Him? He's going to destroy the world."

"That probably bears watching, no?"

"Oh, yeah, right away. Only problem is that guy probably couldn't manage to swing an extra gelatin from the lunch lady in here. I'm saying I think the world is safe from his grand plans."

"Can we talk?"

"You start."

"What are we going to do?"

"Why don't we just wait awhile and see what we *did*?"

"That's one way to go. Another way is we could take steps to try to avoid ending up in the East River thanks to The Absence."

"So panicky, but out of curiosity, what steps?"

"For one, we could do the job we were hired to do. Collect our outrageous fee, a disproportionate amount of which goes to you, and enjoy a life without consummately evil and powerful enemies. Can we please try to do that?"

"Next question."

"Why are you here?"

"Where do you want me?"

"Seems to me there's only two places to be. You're either on that island where that Dalí is or you're out on the street, since I can't believe you'd claim this place can genuinely hold you against your will."

"You said it yourself, the Dalí's at Rikers, what good would being on the street do me?"

"I could ask the same about this place though. What good does being here do?"

"I'm not going back to Rikers."

"We need to go back."

"You and I may have different definitions of *need*."

"Let me be as explicit as possible. The Absence concludes that we are no longer on this job for whatever reason, they will kill us in the most gruesome way possible. You know this, or at least *knew* this. Just to orient you, the latest is that they made some guy's last meal his own fingers."

"Not going back to Rikers."

"Where are you going?"

"Anywhere that's not there."

"Okay, hear me out. First, understand that there's no more solitary on the island for people like you so you'd be going back to cushy general. Second and third, the Dalí's still there. That's another way of saying that a seven-figure payday is there and that's another way of saying complete freedom is there. Complete, Nuno. Money to go wherever you want and do whatever you please. We go back, steal the Dalí, and break out with it to great reward. Think about what you'll be feeling then. What's out there? Freedom, money, that woman you were always talking about."

"Quiet that."

"What's the alternative? A protracted and painful death as a penniless nobody?"

"It didn't work out."

"What didn't?"

"My life. Didn't work out. From the very beginning, a nightmare, just reality for me but then you make the mistake of comparing. I know what you're saying about The Absence but I don't care. I'm not debating you on the merits. I'm saying you might as well be asking me my favorite color for my level of interest."

"Nuno, listen." He looks away slightly. "Shit, I gotta split. Don't do anything rash, man. I'll hit you again in the next few days."

Only once Solomon practically runs away does Nuno see Dennings approaching. This woman, is she going to talk to him? And if so is he going to talk back? Is he ever going to do anything again? He is dead and everything's just trying to catch up to that fact.

"I understand you're back among the talking but just barely. I bet I can get you to say more than two words."

"You lose."

"I'm scheduling you for an assessment tomorrow. It's a mandatory assessment, as in not dependent on your wishes. We are called upon to constantly reevaluate our patients in your position to determine if and when they can resume being prosecuted to the fullest extent of the law; there'll be no shirking of criminal responsibility within the four walls of this fine institution. I'm warning you right now that silence will not be an option. Do I have your attention now, Mr. Dang . . . Dangle Ease, however you pronounce that mess?"

Dennings is going on but truth is Nuno can no longer attend to two things at once and right now he is staring at the Theorist in the next room as he straightens out his bow tie, huh? How is this happening? Theorist is doing that thing where you line up a stack of papers then tap them against the top of a table to create a sharp and orderly bottom line. Now he's placing this in a briefcase, the hell? How is he getting access to this stuff? But none of that compares to Nuno's shock at the sight of this dude cavalierly putting on a jacket and initiating what looks a hell of a lot like his imminent exit.

To Nuno, his sudden desperation makes strange Dennings a bedfellow.

"Hell's that about?" he asks her.

"What? And language, please."

"That," he says, pointing.

"What?"

"That, *the Theorist*, he's being allowed to leave?"

"The what?"

"The guy in the bow tie, with the hair."

"Dr. Epstein?"

"Doctor what? No, the guy with the hair!"

"That's Dr. Epstein."

"You're letting him leave."

"He's free to come and go as he pleases. Let's get back to your situation, because someone who did something as evil as—"

"What're you saying?"

"I'm saying it is fundamentally evil to—"

"No, what are you saying about the . . . this Epstein guy? You're saying he's not a patient?"

"Dr. Epstein is not a patient, correct."

"He's staff?"

"No. I'll pretend you have a right to know this and say that he today completed a research fellowship here, some nonsense about temporal physics and the criminally insane. He's sane, in other words, just like you. That's right, I see right through you."

"C'mon, stop fucking with me."

"Language!"

"It's not nice to mess with the insane."

"No one's *messing*, as you say, with anyone."

"Fine, when's he due back?"

"He's not, that's what *completed his fellowship* means."

Nuno doesn't really know what to believe here except that it is undeniable that this nut screaming about Time for months has just used some of his to calmly walk out of what Nuno thought was their shared incarceration. He searches his mind, this used to be a far more impressive procedure, and try as he might he cannot locate any memory that would definitively establish that this guy they were calling the Theorist was who they assumed he was, a deluded mental patient yammering incoherently. And examining further, had there ever even been any actual incoherence?

All that cognitive dissonance at once but also pure beauty. It was beautiful, beautiful and emotional and all kinds of resonant, the way he'd just elevated and haughtily walked out of static death and into complete freedom and life. There will be time to contextualize it all but in the meantime he forms a clear and dominant thought.

"You're right," he says to Dennings. "I've been malingering, but no more. Find me fit, send me back to Rikers. What the hell, there's no more solitary I hear and it's an island after all. Island as in drinks with little umbrellas and grass skirts, right?"

"Let me get this straight, you want us to find you fit so you can go back to Rikers?"

"Correct."

"In that case, settle in, because you're not going anywhere."

17

||||||||||

Nina and Dia are in their office, two days before the Pork's final regular season game and outside their window the plastic faux bacon numbers indicate 15–0. On the stereo, Dia has undertaken a chronological discographic summing up of the Joni Mitchell oeuvre, deconstructed to date, before embarking on the latest. In Dia's hands are various reports while Nina reads a doorstop of a book with a psychedelic cover and a pitiable attempt to cash in on a sexy word.

The ambient sound in the office is *The Hissing of Summer Lawns*. These are very good sounds to have be ambient. Musically, it's very seductive. Melody is maybe tamped down, when you consider it's Joni. As literature, it's as if we've gone from limited first-person to omniscient narrator and while that probably threw some people off at the time, to Dia it's been like revelatory second sight. Big picture is another masterpiece from an artist working essentially alone who seemed to have found an inexhaustible tap to highest art. In keeping with how often the sublime precedes the ridiculous, the final string machine notes have just reduced to nothing when on comes the television with one of those *zany* sports shows with unjustified yelling and impossibly busy graphics. They cut to a guy on Park Avenue:

The IFL season closes this Sunday amidst uncertainty over whether they will even have a postseason. The incredible popularity of the league has been the surprise of the sports year and was greatly aided by the NFL's cancellation of their season. But last week's announcement that the NFL work stoppage has been settled and that play will resume next September seemed timed to take the steam out of this weekend's tilt in Paterson between the undefeated Pork and the clear-cut second-best team in the league, the Canton Claws.

Also, the NFL is rumored to be playing hardball with those players scheduled to play in the IFL playoffs by warning them of the chance of injury just as the NFL will be filling out rosters for the upcoming season. Because no one believes that the IFL can be a viable competitor to the NFL next fall, those players must think long and hard before crossing the NFL.

Given that backdrop, many are calling this contest the true IFL championship game and likely the only professional football champion to be crowned this year. The Pork will be led by likely league MVP Major Harris, who—

"Shut up, meathead!" says Dia as she kills the television. "All the Claws are playing, I checked."

"Good. We're having a playoffs too. You know the charter. As commissioner I can take over any team that refuses to operate and that's exactly what I'll do. These pansies can't operate at a loss for the mere four weeks it takes to establish a legitimate champion? Fine, they're out and I'll pay out of my pocket. Any player legitimately worried about the risk to their future NFL career can be negotiated with. And if the NFL thinks we're not competing with them next fall they're even stupider than I thought."

Dia doesn't seem placated. She appears to want to say something.

"What?"

"I'm sure it's nothing but the last few times I've tried to pay for something there's been a problem so I had Meyers in accounting look into it."

"And he saw what when he looked?"

"The accounts have been frozen."

"Well, melt them."

"Knew you'd say that, so I had him draft this. It has to be signed by Worthington Gill."

"Ugh."

"Your father."

"Thanks, I'd heard of him." Nina puts down her book and moves hair away from her face. "There's something to disclose, I have to disclose. Not *disclose*, that sounds so distant, it's more like news, good news! Well, news, good is probably in the beholder's mind. It's not a straightforward thing."

"Okay?"

"Yeah."

"Can you orient me to the area of life we're talking about? Is it league?"

"No, not league."

"Then?"

Nina walks to the window. The sky so clear you can sense infinity and how nothing said or not said down here will alter anything higher than a treetop.

"Did I say *not league*? Of course league, right? Yeah, just this frozen thing. Not a problem, I'll see him tomorrow and get the signature, nothing to see here."

"Oh, that's great. The only other thing . . ."

"Yes?"

"Coach Elkins wants Travis out, Travis Mena?"

"Who the hell's that?"

"Travis Mena. He's the pig!"

"Oh, right, and Elkins wants what?"

"He wants him fired because he's never won a challenge and he wants to bring in someone more athletic. He says what happens if one of these games goes into overtime? But I know Travis has been—"

"Hold on. First of all relax, because no one's getting fired from a perfect team. Second, you're with the pig, aren't you?"

"What? Me? No. Well, yes, I guess I am *with* him, but only until I find better entertainment."

"Yeah, right."

"You're right! I'm not like you, Nina, I love that pig! I love Travis Mena! Everyone calls him the pig."

"As you just did."

"But he's so much more than a corkscrew tail, you know? He's a medical resident who left Bellevue because he wants to operate on cleft palates. It's just that he happens to like mascoting."

"For the pork you pine."

"Stop."

"Just needling you. In reality, that's great, I'm happy. Not just *for you* either, plain happy."

"Really? Oh what a relief . . . the last thing, and this will probably seem weird."

"Weirder than you dating a pig?"

"It's just, he really fears you with every bone in his body and with all the marrow inside each of those bones. I don't think he could ever even direct a word at you."

"You want me to warm up to the swine, you got it."

"Actually the opposite. Can you keep it that way? Understand that I've grown to love you like a muh-older sister."

"A molder sister?"

"And I know you would never do it on purpose but I've seen what happens when you give men even the slightest encouragement and . . . well . . . I like my little porcine partner is all."

"You got it, sister. But Elkins has a point, maybe. I mean, *oh and fifteen?*"

"He's training, I think this is the week."

Nina is skeptical, she reopens then soon thereafter closes her book.

"Don't think this is going to end well," she says. But this is to no one in particular.

16

||||||||||

Nuno's latest tack is a kind of juvenile reverse psychology. How he has managed to generate such deep-seated antipathy in Dennings without taking any affirmative action is currently irrelevant. What matters is that he has a great many complex actions to engineer but first he needs to be found fit to proceed and sent back to Rikers.

Days have elapsed with Nuno expounding at length on these passionate monologues intended to demonstrate the clear-eyed sanity of both his positions and his personal position. A disproportionate amount of this speech has been laced with his considerable legal insight, specifically regarding the various roles and rules of the many components of the criminal justice system. The reason is that this is supposed to be the relevant consideration: whether or not Nuno is mentally competent enough to understand his plight and assist in his defense. His every utterance has skillfully propounded that fact yet there he remains, the victim of vindictive whim. Change is necessary.

"I've been thinking," he says. "You're right. Who's the least competent person to judge my sanity? Me. If I'm insane, as you say, then it's just the expression of the judgment of a lunatic and who wants to hear that, right? If I don't think myself insane that's exactly what you'd expect from someone insane. If I feel insane that's enough to constitute insanity it seems to me. Either way I've got to defer to the experts like yourself. Besides, be careful what you wish for. I'm filled with mortal terror at the prospect of returning to Rikers Island. Only my worst enemy would do that to me. You know how many enemies I have there? Not to mention the overwhelmingly oppressive nature of the accusation against me. No thanks, I'm right where I want to be.

Not fit is right. You can't fit me with a life sentence and I won't fit in their cells. *Not fit* fits beautifully, thank you very much."

As he spoke Dennings filled out the form and she now hands it to him while grinning slyly. NOT FIT TO PROCEED, it says, meaning no access to the Dalí and its freedom with Dia and also meaning that he is staring at it wondering what the hell's happened to his mind that he can't even maneuver someone like this.

15

||||||||||

The next day, in the late afternoon, Nina pulls into the driveway of a lavish Texas mansion. Answering the door is a butler who lights up at the sight of Nina.

"Jenkins, I would've thought you'd be on death row by now for slaying Daniel."

"I survived you, I can survive anything."

"I didn't kill you and now look, stronger. Where is little Danny boy?"

"Only your father is here, Ms. Gill."

"Ms. Gill? How'd you like it if I called you that? Enough chatchit, lead the way, sir."

Nina is taken up a flight of stairs and into a somewhat dark room. Jenkins begins to announce her but Nina stops him and goes in alone.

"Hey?"

"Who is it?"

"It's me, Nina."

"Who?"

"Nina! Look at me, it's Nina. What are you doing in pajamas at four?"

Nina gently directs her father's gaze to her face. He looks at her and smiles. She is hurt by what she perceives to be an emptiness behind his eyes.

"Oh, man."

Suddenly the emptiness seems to fill.

"Laura! Laura, I'm sorry."

"No, Pop. This is Nina, Laura was my mother. I'm Nina, your daughter. But you're right, Laura looks like me, I mean, looked like me . . . I mean, I look like her . . . like she did. This is goddamn Nina."

"Laura, I'm sorry, say you forgive. Say you forgive, Laura."

"Pop, it's . . . I forgive you. You're forgiven, Worthington Gill."

He exhales in relief. They sit in silence.

"Nina, you're here! Why didn't Jenkins announce you?"

"He was going to fulfill his contractual obligation to do so but I didn't let him. I let myself in."

"You've settled this thing with Daniel, right, Nina?"

"Who the fuck is Daniel?"

"Oh, I mean your brother, your brother . . ."

"Just kidding. Yeah, it's settled."

"Good. Poor Daniel, I hate an unfair fight." He starts to laugh but it quickly turns into a coughing fit. "Jenkins says you have something for me to sign?"

"Yes, let me explain. The fucking lizard lawyers froze some accounts I need to run the league."

"The league? But Daniel says—"

"No, Pop, not that league. The Pork, remember?"

"Pork? Is it suppertime already?"

"No, listen."

"You listen, Nina. I don't understand what you mean but if you say sign something I'm going to sign."

"No, I need you to understand."

"The only woman in the league making football decisions . . . no one could believe it . . . you should've seen her."

"I am her."

"Nina wants me to sign something? Give it here." He takes out a pen himself but reacts to it as if someone had made it materialize from behind his ear, the life of the mentally impaired is fundamentally magical. "See this pen? Laura bought this pen for me when we were broke and it cost a fortune. It felt like a fortune at the time. To celebrate a minor success. I remember I got so angry then felt bad afterwards, very bad. Later I bought the company that made the pen. Silly things I would do. Buy a company because of a pen to try to prove something. Today I see that it didn't really matter, me buying that company."

"It was a nice gesture, whatever, you did things like that."

"Maybe. Let me sign. The ramblings of an old man."

Nina starts to hand Worthington a paper then pulls it back.

"On second thought, I don't need your signature."

"Are you sure? Because if Nina said sign, Nina doesn't make many mistakes."

"I'm sure, and far as I can tell she makes plenty."

They sit in silence for a minute. Worthington is having difficulty reaching a glass of water. Nina takes it, dries the outside of the glass with her blouse, and hands it to him.

"Nina, thank you again for settling with Daniel. Did you say it was pork for supper?"

"Not sure, but I have to get going."

Worthington visibly deflates.

"I'll be back very soon though."

She kisses him on the forehead and hurries out. He seems confused. She is hurrying down the stairs and to the front door. When she goes to open it Daniel is coming in from the other side with grocery bags.

"Nina, hi! You saw Pop already?"

"Just saw him." She's not meeting his eyes. "I didn't realize. Well, I guess it's been some time. He . . . didn't really know me at times."

"Yeah, I know. He's not that bad really, he has bad moments. The more he sees you the fewer the bad moments."

"He was sorry, *I'm sorry* he says all insistent. Thought I was Mom."

"Yeah, that's one of his things, definitely. He has bad stretches, I think you just caught one."

"Worthington Gill ends like this."

"I wanted to talk to you about this frozen accounts thing and assure you it wasn't my idea. You know I'm no longer even on the labor committee, let alone the point man."

"Yeah, Javitz. We beat him like a drum every year and you let him take the reins."

"I had no choice, you know how things are done there. I told them it was a waste of time anyway, one signature from my father and it's back to unlimited resources."

"Christ, Daniel, you think I would take a signature from him like that?"

"Oh. That's not the only thing either, Nina. They're reaching out to all the agents of your prominent players and putting the word out. No future NFL career of any kind unless they cease playing for the IFL immediately. Same for your prominent coaches."

"Figured."

"And your TV partners too. They're going to create a new schedule of Wednesday night games and offer it to them at a reasonable rate but only if they drop you."

"I have a contract."

"They'll breach it and the NFL will pay. There's no solution, Nina, even if you had the money."

"Guess we'll see. Just don't forget who taught you everything you know about business."

"Pop?"

"Exactly."

"So what's the relevance to this situation?"

"Who said any?"

"Listen, there *is* an offer they want me to make you on their behalf."

"No."

"Listen at least, please. You cancel your playoffs and the NFL buys the IFL as its developmental league. Think about it, Nina, no IFL jobs are lost. It makes business sense and football is a business."

"Business. That's only partially true and that's what you never understood. All those years with Harris at QB when we would knock on the door but ultimately fail, you know what I would see every year in the stands when it was over? An eight-year-old crying. Different one each year. Does that sound like a business and nothing more? Everything you guys came up with. Charging people six figures for the privilege of buying tickets. Having the players wear seven different uniforms in six weeks so the kids would bug their parents for each one. New stadiums paid for by the sweat of people who then get priced out of them. Call it business if you want but eight-year-olds don't cry reading the business section."

"The rest of the league was doing those things. We had to do them just to compete."

"Compete? Who won more games than us?"

"They were making more money, Nina."

"Let them! It was about winning, and I don't mean the revenue race. Winning games so that you create an undeniable good. A community of people who've chosen to align themselves with you and who by some magical process feel better on Monday morning."

"But you still have to watch the bottom line. Look at you. You created a remarkably popular product, no one else in the world could've done it, but you haven't sought to capitalize. It's the last weekend of your season and you're still charging those ridiculous bargain basement prices."

"I don't care, I look in the stands and see landscapers and janitors taking their kids to their first game with their chests puffed out. What do you see in NFL stands? Wall Street pricks checking their phones."

"I don't want to argue, Nina. I accept your offer. The Cowboys are yours in every way, just come back. Close your league, take the NFL offer."

"That offer expired when I walked out of Havisham's office."

"Come on, Nina."

"I don't want the Cowboys anymore, but I'll call you tomorrow about this other thing."

"Okay."

"That it?"

"One more thing . . . I love you."

"That's cheating."

"Maybe, but I need you to know that before you go back into Nina lay-waste-to-everything-in-my-path mode. You're my sister and I love you."

"I heard you the first time."

"And? Reciprocation?"

"Best I can give you is this. I'm not crazy about the Daniel who invented personal seat licenses but I'll love to the last gasp the Daniel who was in charge of squeezing my hand to cross the street. Good enough?"

"It'll have to be."

"Call you tomorrow."

"Oh."

"What?"

"Just that I thought you would stay for dinner. Jill will be back from soccer soon with the boys and—"

"Soccer? Not football? I almost wish Pop was already dead just so he could roll over in his grave."

"I've got these great Wagyu steaks. And I don't know the first thing about it but I'm told this is supreme tequila."

"More cheating."

"Can't help it, I'm desperate."

Nina reverses course and enters the house.

"Let's go, but if that bony Jill screws up my steak we're back to being through."

14

||||||||||

The next morning. Nina has slept on Daniel's sofa after too much tequila and he is trying to rouse her.

"Nina! Nina, wake up. Your phone hasn't stopped, I think it's that Princeton lawyer of yours. Don't you have a game at one? A flight?"

"Yeah, right." She is gathering her things, mildly rushed.

"You have to say goodbye to Pop, haven't seen him that good in the months he's been living here."

"I will."

Nina enters her father's room. He's in pajamas looking out the window. He spots her and smiles.

"Gotta go, Pop. Game at one."

"Game? What time? Who can work this thing?" He is turning a remote control in his hand as if appraising a rare gem.

"Give here, I'll find it and leave it on the channel for you. Remember you're rooting for the Pork. Who *can* work this thing?"

Hours later Daniel notices the time. He leaves his family in the kitchen and goes up to his father's room to tell Nina she's late. He stops at the doorway and looks in to see his sister and their father watching the game together.

"Remember Reeves, Pop?"

"I'm telling you, that guy could cover a rabbit while wearing snowshoes. Is that Major Harris? He still plays?"

"He's our quarterback, that's what I've been trying to tell you."

"You know, of all the quarterbacks we ever had."

"I know, your favorite."

Three hours later Nina looks terrible. Developments on the screen are making her that way.

"One of those games where you dominate everywhere but on the scoreboard. Everything that could go wrong has gone wrong, Pop."

"Still only down seven?"

"Still. Come on, Major, damn."

"Major? Major Harris?"

"Allegedly, I think someone stole his uniform."

"Fourth and twelve."

"Please flood the right, Buford!"

"Complete! Just enough for the first!" These sudden moments of perceptive lucidity from her father are more unsettling in a way than the prospect of an undefeated season going up in smoke. "First and ten for the Pork at the Claws thirty with fifty-eight seconds to play."

"Thank God. Oh, man. Overtime. Coin toss. Dia's pig better come up big, Pop."

"Whose pig?"

With those words is the sight of a Pork touchdown with eight seconds left and the ensuing confirmation of overtime.

"What pig?"

"You'll see. See our undefeated season die suddenly thanks to a painfully unathletic pig. Elkins was right."

In Paterson, Elkins's rightness is exactly the thought occurring to him at the moment. At midfield of the Pig Pen a wrestling ring has been set up. The Pork's pig will wrestle the Claws' giant crab to see which team will get the ball first in sudden-death overtime. The Pork sideline is disconsolate at the prospect of losing their perfect record without even getting the ball in overtime (IFL overtime rules are like old NFL rules and do not guarantee each team a possession). The pig is exhorting the crowd to support him but they are tepid at best. Dia is on the sideline and when her pig looks over at her she smiles and gives the old thumbs-up.

The match begins and the crab is off to a fast start. He lands an ugly gut shot that doubles the pig over. He heaps great abuse on Dia's pig.

"Damn, that crab's definitely not soft-shell," she observes.

Now the crab has applied a sleeper hold on the pig, who soon appears to be out. The ref comes over to verify. He raises the pig's arm and it drops lifelessly (three such drops will signal the end of the bout). He raises it again and it falls. He raises it a third time and it begins to fall except this time the pig (who must be a Hulk Hogan fan) halts the fall of his hand and signals no with his pink finger to the raucous delight of the crowd.

Now the pig has completely turned the match around and is delivering serious punishment to the crab. Finally he delivers the coup de grâce as he raises the crab into a suplex (see, 1980s WWF) and the crab is out cold soon as he hits the ground. The Pork will get the ball first in overtime and the exultant players and Dia congratulate the pig accordingly.

Back in Texas, Daniel hears exultant cheers coming from his father's room and chuckles. A short while later a smiling Nina is coming down the stairs. Her smile lessens when she sees Daniel and remembers.

"Gotta go, Danny boy. The Pork just went undefeated in the regular season. Remember when the Cowboys did that? Oh, that's right, they never did."

"Pop was into the game, huh?"

"At times, at others I think he thought we were watching a nature show featuring giant pigs and crabs. You're right about the greater exposure equals less confusion though, so I'll be back soon."

"What about the Javitz offer? Tell him where he can stick it?"

"No, I guess not. Those NFL pricks leave a girl like me no choice." She bats her eyelashes. "I know when I'm beat."

"You do? There was one more element to the offer but I was afraid to mention it and enrage you."

She stares at him silently. He closes his eyes and says quickly with a pained expression that "you have to admit in a joint press conference that your league is economically unviable because of the low quality of play."

Nina flashes considerable anger at this but then somewhat composes herself.

"Schedule the press conference for tomorrow. I'll say what they want. But all IFL personnel keep their jobs. And if they cross me . . ."

"I'll do it."

"Good boy."

13

||||||||||

The game, epic Crab v. Pig battle and all, had aired on the television in the Bellevue common area and that might've been the only place in the world that hadn't found the entire spectacle all that bizarre. To Nuno, only one visual had really registered. Members of the Pork organization (Dia's multiple attempts at a *Porkanization* label had failed miserably) celebrating on the field and somehow a glimpse of Dia Nouveau that then got extended into eventual horror, like intently watching the beauty of the sun setting into the Mediterranean until someone pokes you in the eye with a stick.

Here the poke was some pencil-necked twerp in a pink pig costume save for the head, which he held to his side like a riding helmet, explaining his coin-toss victory. Who cares except that Dia Nouveau, his Dia, was nearby smiling, always smiling, but a different kind of smile and, yup, there it is, her gorgeous hand landing on the pig's giant right shoulder (what cut is that?) in a way that just desolated Nuno right where he stood in his dingy sanitarium cage.

This, at last, was something like the universe's final insult. Now he had, and *was*, nothing.

Now? With all he'd been through?

Yes, because if someone stripped bare of all human comfort and solace (not just the obvious tangible ones that imprisonment eviscerates but also seemingly insubstantial ones like fraternity or humor) could still be said to have a purpose, his had functioned really as a substitute will to live. Armed with it he was not a victim of suffering; he was suffering because it was the only path to his destination. The Dia destination only worthwhile if he could stand tall to face her when the moment arrived. Dia across from him and everything that preceded that moment will just instantly evanesce into irreality.

But that look on Dia's face, the hand, the glance up.

Maybe the probability of a dream is irrelevant so long as it's not zero.

There's two ways to go here but Nuno so fears the inactive one that he forcefully evicts the image from his mind best he can, then, perfectly coincident with the start of Free Talk, rises to command the room.

"Thank you, friends. Gather round. This is my first time addressing the group so you'll forgive me if my extreme nervousness occasionally reaches up like a damaged hand out of a shallow grave to throttle my tongue into incoherence."

Gathering group: The hell?

"I come to counsel peace. I know that's not what's in everybody's heart right now and I don't blame you. But still I urge patient docility. Truth is its own reward and as such it need not compel action."

"Truth in everything!"

"Yes, that. Thank you, random patient. *Drapetomania* is an ugly word, no doubt about it."

"Truth in everything!"

"Oh, another? We have a veritable Greek chorus forming here, how nice, and apropos. As I said, an ugly word. So you can imagine our seething hatred on seeing it spilt so indiscriminately onto our life-line medical records."

"Truth in everything!"

"Drapetomania, that hideous reminder of our shameful bloody ancestry. The invented *illness* that purportedly caused slaves to run away from their masters against the natural order of things. What can it mean to see that word so plainly asserted under the diagnosis section of our records? Is this to be resurrected at this late date to once again enslave us?"

Nuno pauses as here some murmurs begin to emerge regarding the clear fact that he gives no physical indication of being African American, but before they can really take hold the chorus grows and shouts it all down with

"Truth in everything!"

"Remember the inventor's claim. That the scriptures themselves intended a position for us to occupy and that it is the position of submission. Now, I don't agree. In fact, if that's what the scriptures claim, bring me their writer right now and I'll open his throat!"

"Truth in everything!"

"But of course I abhor violence and would never exhort it. I didn't want to believe it, not me. When experts in the field came to me with *Nuno, you know that since the sixties schizophrenia diagnoses have been weaponized to control black men* I regret to say, shamefully, brothers, that I had ears but couldn't hear."

"Truth in everything!"

"Yes, truth. Everyone here no better than a slave. Pills in a cup instead of leg-irons, but that's small consolation when you have to bow your head to a master. If you were a pig or a chicken it would come so natural, wouldn't it? Same if Dennings and her others were, in some open and notorious fashion, clearly superior beings. Instead we get this. I know I suffer no impairment, yet like that despicable anti-Semitic scumbag Ezra Pound before me, here I am, confined as criminally insane. Must I wait thirteen years as well for legal relief? When, brothers, does it end? Pigs and chickens enslaving angels, prose ruling poetry, the sound of clashing iron drowning out music."

"Truth in everything!"

"You want violence, I know. Your very being bends to it. Only legitimacy can hold us yet we see none extant. In Mexico, for example, it is not a separate crime to escape imprisonment. Sure, they can shoot and kill you but that's only right. It's not a crime because our natures seek freedom the way plants orient towards the sun. A fish will swim and a human will alight for liberty, you may as well blame the oak for standing firm. So you can imagine our reaction when assaulted by such mendacity. Can we help but want, above all, to lash out violently then get out?"

"Truth in everything!"

"Truth, yes, our only consolation. If we're to be imprisoned like so many fleas in a circus at least let us be enlightened fleas. Let everyone here know there's nothing what all wrong with them but still they're held for sport in this curiosity shop. So kick that ball, pull that cart, or best of all rotate that Ferris wheel that reminds us how the passage of time is just a circle with no productive destination so that now your enslavers can dispense with any schizophrenia pretense and just go back to the far more honest and truthful drapetomania. Remember, I counsel peace so this little bit of truth telling will just have to constitute your full reward. Don't listen to those who say that a forceful exit is not only warranted but must be initiated this very second in order to succeed and not result in a savage reprisal that will only make you fleas more miserable."

"Truth in everything!"

"Jump, fleas, jump! Now is the time before they tighten the noose around your suppliant neck so you can't draw the breath necessary to resist!"

It's not entirely easy to describe what happens next since we're limited to Nuno's perceptions and he purposely just steps to the side of the onrushing humanity he has stoked and avoids detailed visuals as Bellevue staff, always beats behind, scrambles to catch up and bar the door so to speak.

What he can't help but sense shortly thereafter is when a fist or something inside one crashes into the side of his head. Doesn't even hurt all that much really but he falls because he's a good player and that's what the part calls for.

And when they corral him into an even more restrictive cell and things seem to be calming down he makes sure Dennings is looking right at him when he yells, *Truth in Everything,* which sort of just restarts everything again and makes it really the height of inevitable when later that night Dennings contemptuously drops a sheet in his cell indicating that he has now been found *fit to proceed* and will be returning to Rikers, to which Nuno responds does this mean he'll miss tomorrow's Free Talk?

12

||||||||||

That night the Porkanization have gathered to celebrate the end of a perfect regular season.

"Is this what you had in mind?" wonders Dia. "You didn't give much detail beyond celebrate."

"Precisely."

"Did you see Travis? Travis Mena the pig?"

"Never heard of him."

"Wasn't he great?"

"Never seen an uncoordinated pig take it to a giant crab any better."

"Oh, here he is! Nina, this is Travis Mena, he basically won today's game for you single-pawedly."

"Yes, well done, but don't get too happy with yourself, up until this afternoon Coach Elkins wanted you turned into cracklings."

"But."

"Dismissed."

Mena leaves quickly and Dia mouths *thank you* to Nina.

"As for you, young lady, we're having a joint press conference with the NFL tomorrow. This is the name and number of the guy who does for them what you do for us, doubtlessly with less skill and panache. Call him and set it up, then be there to stand next to me."

"With the NFL? Everything okay?"

"Everything. We'll talk about it tomorrow, enjoy the party tonight."

Music comes on and the highly skilled dancing already in evidence escalates.

"Ooh, Prince, love him!" says Dia. "Maybe we can get an impersonator if Radiohead won't budge."

"Maybe."

Dia rushes away to join as Major Harris approaches like a challenged sailboat in a combination of inebriation and severe pain.

"So, that went perfectly well," he says.

"A genuine accomplishment, I don't care what letter precedes FL."

"Can I confess something?"

"No."

"Thought so."

"Your birth certificate is fraudulent, you're actually fifty-five."

"No, *what*?"

"Just that the way you played today."

"We won, don't forget."

"Undeniable."

"Hey, you said before the season started something like fight until you have no fight left. Well, let me say that I have very little fight left. Maybe just enough for the next two games and my ring. That's my confession. I want that ring bad. I'm serious, the worst thing about retirement is the way it freezes your career."

"That word again."

"Anywhere I go the last five years. *Do you regret not having won a title? Do you wish you had a ring?* Obviously I'm not going to show any weakness to these scum so it's always I had a great career, many records, no regrets. Not true, it eats me up. I know it's stupid, just football, a *game* after all. But sometimes the explanation's just easy and not at all intellectual. Somewhere along the line I decided I *needed* a ring. That's all."

"You know you have to pay for all these hits later."

"I don't care if I'm drooling in a corner in ten years as long as that fucking ring's on my finger as I do it. It's all I think about. Well, almost. That skirt, my God. So we have this bye."

"More like a bye-bye."

"Maybe we should take advantage and do three days on that island where we—"

"Tell you what. Let's talk tomorrow at this time and if you still want, we'll go."

"I'll still be in want, you'll see."

"You know, playoffs are, like, an American thing really. In Europe, champions are crowned based solely on the regular season, parades in the street and all."

"Europe? Don't you just want some mindless beach? Culture can be so exhausting."

"Since when?"

"Just tired, I don't think like I used to."

"The hell you say. Besides, I was talking about how *there* this would be a championship celebration, there'd be nothing left to prove."

"Proof, exactly! Put that fucking proof on my finger! In the meantime give me this eighty proof."

"I'm saying maybe the undefeated season is all the proof we'll need."

"I'm too drunk to know what that means but if you say so. Playoffs!"

Teammates come and take their drunken leader away. A significant portion of the team is singing and dancing to Prince's "7" and its warning not to stand in the way of Love.

Many dancing at once is a weird thing. There are always some people who try to dance individually but a group aesthetic inevitably trics to take hold. Here, a highly choreographed and synchronized dance gradually emerges that seems highly implausible; until one remembers that what we call Life is essentially organization that gruelingly emerged from indescribable chaos and that the majority of the people on the floor are already primed for extreme collaboration.

11

||||||||||

Rikers Island didn't change, Rikers will never change. Nuno looks up at the same TV in the same spot, even some of the same people. There will always be twelve thousand captives there and the TV will always be set to some kind of athletic development meant to placate them. But Solomon said to meet him there so there he is and there they meet.

Solomon wants to know how Nuno got back but Nuno only wants status data. This offends Solomon, who posits that it wouldn't kill Nuno to exhibit a little friendliness towards someone who has done so much for him. Like? Like soothing The Absence to the point where this could all still happen. There's no *could* because this needs to happen yesterday, Nuno responds. Fine. Still, a little friendliness couldn't hurt. Nuno then exhibits a little friendliness and turns out Solomon was right because it doesn't hurt. The television looks down on these two friends and declares that it is transmitting events from an NYC hotel ballroom where a press conference is forthcoming. The image suddenly jars before stabilizing.

10

||||||||||

Nina almost wipes out a camera, so contemptuously does she enter the location of that press conference. Dia notices her and hurries over.

"This idiot you put me in touch with is genuine moron. He's going around telling everyone that you're announcing the cancellation of our playoffs and shutting down the league." Her laughter isn't met so she just continues. "I told him he must not know our boss."

A young Ivy Leaguey twerp comes up to Nina and hands her a paper.

"This is the exact language we need you to use, Ms. Gill," says the twerp and he leaves.

"That's him! Why'd you let him get away still conscious?"

"Because he knows I can't run an untelevised playoffs without any personnel that envisions a future in the NFL."

"It's true then?"

"That I can't? Yes, it's true."

"Oh, man. All anyone's talking about is winning a championship and getting that ring. Even Travis has been wondering if the pig gets a ring. And the fans, oh."

Just then a tall power-suited man approaches them so that Dia begins to walk away.

"Nina, you look amazing!"

"Hold on a second, Dia. Come back here, maybe you can help us solve this mystery. The mystery, John, is that I don't recall asking for your opinion on how I look. Did you hear me ask that, Dia?"

"No, nothing like it."

"So, John, surely you see my resulting confusion when upon having contact with you for the first time in several years you immediately offer up an unsolicited opinion on my appearance."

"A compliment."

"How? I can only conclude that you must think my appearance is of particular importance to me when I know full well that there is scarcely anything that matters less to me."

"Most women—"

"Care what you think of their looks? I hate to be the one to disabuse you of that notion but ten times no. Maybe you think you're providing a service, in which case allow me to reciprocate. You, like most men, do not look good at all. You appear to be at least ninety pounds overweight, your skin is an orange that is most certainly not a naturally occurring hue, and whatever subterfuge that hair is attempting is not close to being achieved."

"I'm a man."

"Even grading on that curve."

"My appearance is irrelevant."

"Then disappear."

He speeds away to tell as many people as possible. The press conference is ready to commence. Nina takes her spot on the dais with Dia next to her. After some prefatory remarks by the twerp who handed her the paper, Nina approaches the microphones.

"About a year ago I stood here and announced the ascendance of the IFL and that's precisely what it turned out to be. By the end of the just completed regular season we were playing before one hundred percent capacity attendance and our ratings in many instances exceeded those of comparable NFL games last year. However, I must announce today that there will be no IFL playoffs."

Long pause, during which Nina picks up the twerp's paper then puts it down.

"As far as the level of play in the IFL this year, there was one clear-cut best team. The Paterson Pork had one of the very few undefeated regular seasons in the history of professional football. They played and beat every other significant team in the league and, with the exception of yesterday, the games weren't even close. The obvious question on the minds of football fans everywhere is, What is the true meaning of this season by the mighty Pork?"

She pauses again and a great many of those old-fashioned photography flashes detonate, so many she looks like a nascent interstellar being.

"Well, I must give the NFL a great deal of credit because they have agreed to a single-elimination championship game between the Pork and the NFL."

That press conference murmur thing.

"Now, you would think since I am making this joint announcement with Dick Javitz, owner of the anemic Tennessee Titans, that the game would be against the Titans. That is not the case because the NFL agrees that the Pork must face only their best, not a team that hasn't won a playoff game in two decades."

Javitz is furious and his dog will probably pay later.

"So, again, the IFL playoffs have been canceled. Instead, the Paterson Pork and the Dallas Cowboys will meet in a championship game in Paterson, NJ, date to be announced, to decide the football champion of the civilized world. The setting will be out of doors, the fans will be rabid, the tickets will be cheap, the tailgate will be insane, but most importantly, the Pork will win. We thank the NFL for this opportunity to prove what should be obvious to any lucid being: the Paterson Pork is the best football team in the world. No questions. You're welcome, folks."

Dia is following Nina off the stage but makes a quick stop at the microphone.

"And Radiohead will be the halftime entertainment!"

But this was just defiant posturing. That band won't be playing and a lot of people Dia knows and likes are going to be at least profoundly embarrassed if not physically ravaged. She's not Nina. It was dread, really, and a kind of dispiriting impending finality she'd been feeling as she spoke.

9

||||||||||

Seeing Dia again, at least that fucking pig hadn't been there to ruin the view. Dia's now like some kind of movie star, less real than quotidian life's females but all the more powerful for it. Nuno now is like a body that's been accelerated into an attempt at escape velocity, where any slowing would imperil the whole project. The remainder of the world doesn't exist.

Back at Rikers and now legally fit to proceed means a return to court for Nuno. There, his palpable urgency is rewarded when his lawyer tells him that God knows why but the judge has dismissed the indictment against him with leave for the People to re-present.

"God knows why? God knows nothing, I told you months ago they'd screwed up jurisdiction in the grand jury."

They had, though Nuno was wholly uninterested in explaining how he knew. Most crucial was Coin Esquire then serving cross grand jury notice on Nuno's behalf, ensuring that he could testify whenever the People inevitably took the court up on that leave to re-present their case. The prosecutor is rattled and will be re-presenting expeditiously. Way before the forty-five days they're entitled to, Coin says.

So couple days later when Nuno informs Solomon that he will very soon be testifying in the grand jury and that this will be a critical event that will incite a rushed chain of events that can only link seamlessly if Solomon exercises his role properly and on command, part of Solomon is surprised, even skeptical. But most of him just concludes that Nuno is some kind of magical being not susceptible to the usual constraints, and woe to anyone who might disrupt that.

8

|||||||||||

Nina walks towards the entrance to Pork headquarters as a bevy of reporters crowd in front seeking comment on the upcoming game.

"The president is a big Cowboys fan," says one of them. "He says your team has no chance."

"President? President of what?"

"Of the United States."

"Oh, I'm glad we cleared that up, I almost said something untoward. I would say to the president, respectfully, of course, that he can go fuck himself sideways. I say that respectfully, of course."

This will become a significant thing, albeit a thing that Nina will mostly ignore. As she enters the office, Dia is attempting to stay abreast of the intense media requests, only gradually discovering the cause of the sudden explosive increase. Nina offers nothing but just grabs her voluminous scouting material as Coach Elkins walks in in a state of torment.

"Normally I would begin by asking you if you're crazy or something but your insanity seems so well established at this point that I'll save my breath."

"We're gonna win."

"No, we *were* going to win. We were going to win a championship only you forgot who you are and now we're going to be embarrassed in front of the entire country."

"I think I remembered who I am."

"At the expense of about a hundred people who have worked at a goal for almost a year?"

"This is the goal we were working on."

"No it isn't! We had an *achievable* goal, this is nonsense. The ravings of a madwoman!"

"It was this or nothing, Coach." Dia has interjected this to even her own surprise. "Her only other choice was canceling the playoffs and becoming a developmental league for the NFL."

"Then you should have done it, we would all have jobs!"

"You have a job, beat the Cowboys and etch your name in football history."

"That's crazy talk."

"Then leave, Buford. I'll coach the goddamn team in the Global Bowl."

"The what?"

"Just don't expect me to even thank you when we're at the White House."

"Well, I have to interject that I don't think there's any way *that's* happening after what you just said to the president."

"See what I mean? Insane!"

"Call a meeting of the coaches," Nina says in the most conciliatory tone she can muster. "I'll show you what needs to be done and you know I *know* so don't even pay lip service to the opposite notion."

"It's not about knowledge, Nina. We have a two-hundred-and-fifty-pound nose tackle!"

"Two-sixty, and two-fifty of it is heart."

"Won't matter, they're unbeatable."

"No one's unbeatable, Buford. It's a football game. They have some soft guys, and at key positions."

"Soft guys? Soft guys with three straight rings?"

"We're built to beat them. Call the meeting, I'll show you what I mean. What's the players' mind-set?"

"What do you think it is? Except for Harris, Reeves, and Mutola they look like sandlot guys being asked to compete with maybe the greatest football team ever."

"That hasn't played in almost a year, will be overconfident, and is playing a team that will fight for every blade of grass. I like our chances. More importantly we need *them*, when they take that field, to like their chances. We need that, Buford. It's just coaching, same thing you've been doing for thirty years' worth of sleepless days. You don't want to do it for a few more?"

"I didn't say that, Nina. Of course I'll *do* it. I just wanted to be on the record that this is crazy."

"Did you note it for the record, Dia? Coach Elkins believes that trying to defeat the three-time defending NFL champions with the Paterson Pork is insane."

"Duly noted."

"Hear that, Buford? It's on the record."

"So when we win I want a sweet bonus."

"Your bonus is that I will be very involved these few weeks. When's that coaches' meeting again, Dia?"

"Forty-eight minutes."

"See you at the appointed time but not before, Coach. That is assuming you don't resign first for fear of the big bad Cowboys."

7

||||||||||

Nuno is wearing headphones in a Rikers video conference booth with Coin and another incredulous lawyer on the other end. The lawyers have accepted the shock that the indictment has been dismissed and that there will be a brand-new grand jury presentation forthcoming. What they can't abide so far is Nuno's insistence on testifying in front of that grand jury.

They know, and remind him, that it is ultimately their decision whether or not Nuno testifies, the appellate divisions are clear, but he has this way of making people want his approval.

"Cutting to the chase, it's hard to envision anything you could say that would convince the grand jury not to indict you for murder. Given that, why give the prosecution free discovery in the form of your statement?"

"Tell me, Counselor. How you holding up with that murder charge hanging over your head?"

"I don't have any murder charge." Coin is shaking his head, may have been a mistake to bring his supervisor.

"Oh, sorry. My mistake, just that the way you were talking. See, I have had a murder rap over my head for close to a year. So you'll forgive me if I've run out of patience with being falsely accused."

"Falsely? Tell us more about that," says the supervisor.

"Oh, it's tragic. Sobbiest story you ever heard."

"That's just it," says Coin, more practiced in Nuno matters. "I've never heard it. You've never talked about what happened that night."

"Really?" asks the supervisor. "Let's start there, tell us what you'll be telling the grand jury so we can better advise you."

"Hmm, tempting. On the one hand, I increase your efficacy. On the other, I obey the dictates of accomplished, spoiler-free storytelling and make it so the first time you hear it is in the grand jury sitting next to me. See you in the grand jury."

And he hangs up.

6

||||||||||

Nina stands in front of about a dozen coaches with a giant screen behind her demonstrating the concepts as she discusses them.

"This will be a brief overview, questions at the end, please. Tomorrow morning you'll each receive a packet tailored to the position you coach detailing what you'll need to drill into your players so we can execute the game plan.

"Let's start with the defense. We have a severe problem in the trenches. Their offensive line is monstrous. There's a significant danger here that they'll just line up, blow us off the ball, rush for three hundred yards, and beat us by about fifty with us barely touching the ball.

"The obvious move would be to play a lot more 4-3 to get that extra big in there. I think that's obvious but also insufficient. What we're going to do instead is run a Monster 5-2. I know, I know. But we do have it, we ran it as part of our goal line package, maybe one percent of defensive snaps this year. A defensive lineman across from every offensive lineman with two-gap responsibilities. I know it's crazy but it predominated in the early NFL for a reason and we're going to have to run it on at least running downs that Sunday. Before that, we have to start drilling the ever-loving hell out of the package this instant since it's so unfamiliar.

"Even with that, forget eight in the box we need to do nine or at least eight and a half in the box. Reeves and Banks on an island with their receivers, there's no other way. Not just that, they have to play bump and run. Disrupt their timing patterns and make Tom Laney hold the ball waiting for his receivers to release, which in turn means more hits than he's used to taking because no one's ever had the balls to do that against them.

"About Laney, yeah, he's great, so what? He does not like being hit. Fine, no one likes it, but he *really* doesn't like it. To win we have to give him a severe amount of what he loathes. You can't confuse him, so don't try. Hit him and as he's falling hit him again. Sell out to do it if necessary. He'll make some big plays, big goddamn deal, you were expecting a shutout? By the end of the game he'll be looking for an exit strategy.

"On the other side we have to protect Harris. He's running on fumes right now but he's still capable of making the five or six plays we need to win the game. There's no point, at this late a stage, in try-ing to coach up or inspire our offensive line to protect him. They are physically incapable of doing it against this team. No, take the air out of the ball with Sims, who is legit, and when we do have to pass, go max protect. If we have to punt we punt. As I said the reports tomor-row will give you the relevant details.

"So that's strategy, but my bigger concern right now is everything else. This is an undefeated football team walking around like it's some kind of honor to be on the same field with the Cowboys! Well, I don't do deference and neither does my team. I don't care about their three rings, I care about getting our first! Them having three doesn't tell me they're great, it tells me they *were* great. How could they want their fourth as much as we want our first?

"If we lose because they outperform us, so be it. If we lose because your players are in awe or intimidated, your next job in football will be painting the goddamn lines! Oh, and same for anyone caught sleeping or leaving this facility before the game is played."

Some coaches start smiling but stop almost immediately as they realize Nina isn't. Nina leaves the coaches' room for the practice field. Protecting Harris is everything, she thinks. His body is a mess, true, but also he just seems slower in other ways as well.

As she walks out onto the practice field, Sims the running back is walking towards her in uniform, holding his helmet at his side from the face mask. He sees her and immediately grasps his helmet to his heart the way Nina taught him. As he passes, she strikes at it in an effort to dislodge it but it doesn't budge. Near the first sideline a tight end runs an undefended out but drops the pass. Without breaking stride she grabs him by the helmet and pulls him alongside her as she demonstrates with her hands the proper triangle that should be formed to catch a football.

That's all fine and good but there's no attention to detail or neglected fundamental that'll change what's going to happen.

5

||||||||||

```
 1    SUPREME COURT OF THE STATE OF NEW YORK

 2    GRAND JURY OF THE COUNTY OF NEW YORK

 3    -----------------------------------------------

 4    PEOPLE OF THE STATE OF NEW YORK

 5

 6                    V.

 7

 8    NUNO DEANGELES

 9    -----------------------------------------------

10                            NEW YORK, NEW YORK

11                            JANUARY 2016

12

13    BEFORE:

14    A QUORUM OF THE FIRST JAN/FEB

15       2016 GRAND JURY

16

17

18    PRESENTED BY:

19            DILL O. MONTE, ESQ.,

20            ASSISTANT DISTRICT ATTORNEY

21

22

23

24                    DIANE S. SALON

25                    GRAND JURY REPORTER
```

1

2 Q. Sir, would you please state your name and address.

3   A. My name is Nuno DeAngeles. My address for close to a

4 year is wherever DOC has me at any given moment at Rikers

5 Island, how specific would you like me to get?

6 Q. Okay, before your current address.

7   A. Not sure what that address was. If you want, let me

8 out and I'll get you that.

9 Q. That's not necessary. Do you have an attorney?

10   A. While we're on the topic of unnecessary? Yes, I have

11 an attorney.

12 Q. His name and address, please?

13   A. Coin, Edward Coin the last, hailing from parts

14 unknown.

15 Q. You don't know his address?

16   A. Correct, but this is him sitting right next to me

17 and he probably knows it. Are you looking to send him

18 something?

19 Q. Mr. DeAngeles, do you understand that the subject matter

20 of this inquiry of this Grand Jury proceeding is an allegation

21 of a murder which occurred inside the Four Seasons Hotel at 57

22 East 57th Street in Manhattan, on February 10 into the morning

23 of February 11, 2015.

24   Do you understand that? That that's the subject matter of

25 this inquiry?

26   A. I understand that.

1 Q. Do you understand that you are not required to appear

2 before the Grand Jury and testify?

3   A. I do.

4 Q. Your attorney, who is here now, will be present during

5 your statement, during your time in this Grand Jury, but will

6 not be allowed to consult with you during your testimony in the

7 Grand Jury room.

8   A. That's quite all right.

9 Q. You understand?

10   A. I do.

11 Q. If you wish to consult with him, simply indicate this to

12 me and you will be given the opportunity to speak with him

13 outside the presence of the jury.

14   Do you still want to testify?

15   A. Yes.

16 Q. In connection with your appearance here today, were you

17 present with your attorney, Mr. Coin, and did you read and sign

18 a piece of paper entitled "Waiver of Immunity," which read as

19 follows: The People of the State of New York against Nuno

20 DeAngeles.

21   Waiver of Immunity.

22   Grand Jury number 4665 of 2015.

23   I, Nuno De Angeles, pursuant to the provisions of section

24 190.45 of the Criminal Procedure Law of the State of New York,

25 do hereby waive all immunity to which I would otherwise be

26 entitled from criminal indictment, prosecution, conviction,

1   punishment, penalty, or forfeiture, for or on account of, or

2   relating to any transaction, matter, or thing, concerning which

3   I may testify or produce evidence, documentary or otherwise,

4   before the Grand Jury of New York County, in its investigation

5   above-captioned. I do hereby waive my privilege against

6   self-incrimination under the Fifth Amendment of the United

7   States Constitution and Article I, section 6, of the

8   Constitution of the State of New York, a privilege to which,

9   absent of this Waiver of Immunity, I would otherwise be

10   entitled. My testimony, and any evidence I produce, may be used

11   against me in any investigation or legal proceeding before any

12   court, grand jury, agency, official body, or person authorized

13   by law to conduct a legal proceeding.

14   I hereby acknowledge that I have been advised of my right

15   to confer with counsel prior to deciding whether to sign this

16   Waiver of Immunity and of my right to a reasonable amount of

17   time in which to obtain and consult with counsel.

18   I further acknowledge that I have been advised that I may

19   appear in the Grand Jury with my retained counsel or, if I am

20   financially unable to retain counsel, with an attorney who

21   shall be assigned by the superior court which empaneled the

22   Grand Jury.

23   I have conferred with Mr. Coin, whose office address is 40

24   Worth Street, New York, New York, prior to signing this Waiver

25   of Immunity.

26   Did you in fact sign that piece of paper after your

1   attorney read it to you?

2   A.   Could you repeat that? Oh, come on. I kid. I kid out

3   of love. Yes, I signed it.

4   MR. MONTE: Let the record reflect I'm holding an 8 ½-by-

5   11-inch sheet of paper entitled "Waiver of Immunity," which I

6   will now deem marked People's Exhibit 1 for identification.

7   (SO DEEMED)

8   Q.   I just read the waiver to you in its entirety, Mr.

9   DeAngeles, do you understand it and its effect.

10   A. Fully.

11 Q.   Let the record reflect that on the lower left-hand portion

12 of People's Exhibit 1 for identification is the purported

13 signature of Edward Coin, who is present in the Grand Jury room.

14   I will now move into evidence what has previously been

15 deemed marked People's Exhibit 1 and ask that it be so marked

16 by the court reporter.

17   (SO MARKED)

18   MR. MONTE: Madame Foreperson, would you please date and

19 sign the Waive of Immunity in the appropriate spot?

20   (Whereupon, the Foreperson dated and signed the Waiver of

21 Immunity.)

22   MR. MONTE: Thank you.

23 Q.   Mr. DeAngeles, just so the record is clear, you understand

24 that you are not merely a witness in this inquiry but that you

25 are in fact the target and focus of it and as such your

26 statement can be used against you and you can be prosecuted and

1 | penalized with regard to this inquiry.

2 | A. Yes.

3 | Q. The form this proceeding will take is after you're sworn,

4 | you will be allowed to make a statement to the Grand Jury. I

5 | will not interrupt that statement unless it is legally improper

6 | or irrelevant to the subject matter of this inquiry.

7 | After you have made your statement, I will be entitled to

8 | ask you questions, which you will be asked to answer to the best

9 | of your ability.

10 | In view of everything I have said and in light of this

11 | Waiver of Immunity, is it still your desire to testify?

12 | A. Hmm, yes!

13 | MR. MONTE: I ask you to swear the witness.

14 | FOREPERSON: Can you please raise your right hand? Do you

15 | solemnly swear that the testimony that you are about to give

16 | this Grand Jury will be the truth, the whole truth, and nothing

17 | but the truth, so help you God?

18 | THE WITNESS: Yes, solemnly, so help me, her.

19 | Q. You may begin your statement.

20 | A. Call me Nuno, you don't know about me without you

21 | have read the various incendiary articles written about me in

22 | this city's *finer* tabloid publications. I think I'm probably

23 | about twenty years old, and they've been eventful ones to say

24 | the least. I was likely born in New York, but I know I lived

25 | some time in Colombia for whatever reason. No one can deny I've

26 | been very lucky in life. For example, most people get stuck

1 with one mother for the duration whereas I have had a great

2 many answer to that name.

3   Most of them were great, you could tell right away which

4 were the ones that were just in it for the money and which were

5 genuine heart. Didn't matter much either way because becoming

6 accustomed to one meant moving on to the next. Bottom line is I

7 would say that the only thing fostered in your humble narrator

8 lo those many years was something like seething contempt.

9 Q.   Mr. DeAngeles I instruct you that's irrelevant to the

10 proceedings. The Grand Jury is here to investigate the events

11 of February 10.

12   A.   Patience, Monte, really. I can't explain February 10

13 without a little background. Surely you wouldn't deny me that?

14 Anyway, there were fathers too, though far fewer. One of them

15 relates to these events, see, Monte, so let's get to him.

16   I think the idea was I would call him Mr. P but even as a

17 squirt I don't think I ever really flew with that mister shit

18 so it just became P and quickly "Peeps," which looking back may

19 have been a bathetic attempt to approach Pops and those

20 concepts while still maintaining plausible deniability. That's

21 the kind of thing might be unknowable.

22   Tell you what I do know, and this is really none of your

23 business, but Peeps had a soul, man. I saw it, often. I saw it

24 when he would walk me the few blocks to school or bring home a

25 box of donuts since he worked nights and I'd be up, never been

26 able to sleep much.

Peeps was a tiny guy, but I only realized that during phase-two Peeps. See, there were two iterations of this guy in my life. In the first one he was this really mysterious entity who didn't say much but if he perceived I needed something, sneakers or a Band-Aid or just a lift onto something, it was instant. His wife was the effusive one.

Mostly I wasn't entirely sure what was happening. Kids were suddenly calling me Chinese, which I gathered was a thing to be made fun of. Being surrounded by idiots is just another way of saying being part of the human race and you can imagine how especially true that was where I found myself so even I knew we weren't Chinese. I knew the word *Cambodian* and not much else even though I was starting to get the language, I've always had a thing, and it's Khmer if you're wondering. Either way I knew my classmates weren't really looking to embrace geopolitical nuance so I mostly stood silent, I think I kind of emulated him and he always seemed at most only slightly curious about humanity.

What I cared about was the kind of things a captive animal might value. I knew Peeps had to be somewhere that required him to wear a black bow tie at six sharp. So at fiver sharper the three of us would sit in that yellow kitchen and devour whatever humble brilliance his wife had created. Afterwards she'd fill his coffee mug, straighten out his tie, and off he'd go to work. I think it's just the consistency of certain stimuli, especially at that age, that gives them their power.

1   When it ended, like always, it was abrupt. The real
2   mothers were always upset and this was no exception. The
3   difference here was that Peeps was crying, which I had never
4   seen before. I think this was the first time I fully realized
5   that not only was this a bad thing that was happening but that
6   it was a recurring bad thing that had always happened in my
7   life and that would always keep happening.
8   Phase two Peeps, years later, was a bit weird. I'm sure
9   they were the same but I'd changed. The look on his face when
10 he saw me, I don't know what useful I can say about it. Except
11 to say that I loved this tiny wisp of a man and if pressed to
12 give a reason I don't think I could come up with much more than
13 the fact that it was obvious he loved me. Yeah, that kind of
14 self-interesty jive.
15   So still just them two, I bet he couldn't sire kids of his
16 own, he seemed physically broken, and me maybe twelve? Lots of
17 talk that this time there would be permanence, whatever the
18 legal requirements might be, they couldn't go through that
19 again was the idea.
20   This becomes a bit of a weird time. They're looking at me
21 like I'm the innocent cherub they mentally formed in their past
22 and truth is I'm more than a little insane. But it's also true
23 that I am that *to them* and I will not violate that even
24 minimally. Anyway these two are on top of things and get me
25 tested or whatever and next thing I know I'm at this Catholic
26 all-boys prestigious-and-all-that jazz high school, absolutely

1   free of charge, and it's looking like, fine, I'm no angel but

2   we may still get a result that's somewhat angelic, know what I

3   mean? Talking years here.

4   That changes one night when I stop by the restaurant Peeps

5   works at. We're doing that thing where we talk while he works

6   until he goes to a table to refill water or something followed

7   by this horrible crash with a pitcher flying and Peeps kind of

8   caving in on himself all the way to the floor. I rush over to

9   help to see what I can only describe as purified terror on my

10   father's face. Everyone's attending to the old man and worrying

11   on what happened. Well, every-but-one I should say.

12   The customer at the table is not worried, he's angry.

13   Couple drops of water splashed on him it seems and this isn't

14   just his primary concern, it's his only one. I stare at this

15   face, a severe stone that looks like it's been lodged in place

16   to stop up malevolence, and do that thing where you photograph

17   it with your mind. Why I did this was more an intuitive sense

18   of significance than anything else.

19   I guess we somewhat stabilized him but things devolved

20   quickly from there. He wouldn't talk about what had happened. I

21   discovered the strange fact that he and his wife had actually

22   met in the U.S. and only coincidentally shared heritage, she

23   couldn't explain is the point. No one really knew what was

24   going on except that he'd be screaming in the middle of the

25   night and wouldn't be coaxed out of the house for Midas's gold.

26   It all moved so fast, downward. Now I was living alone but

1 I would go by and try to help, give them money, try to get him
2 to go out. But it was either catatonia or low-grade terror in
3 response and there's no real solution to either of those. Next
4 thing she's sick with a brutal quick ending and I don't know
5 what to do with him. That uncertainty doesn't last long because
6 a few days later some doctor at Bellevue is telling me he died
7 of a broken heart. I'm telling him to consider his own safety
8 and lose the metaphors, and he's showing me that it's a real
9 actual thing that people can die from.
10   What the hell had happened? I was, let's say, curious. I
11 didn't have much to run with, just a mental image and an
12 overpowering sense that there was a hidden lattice of meaning
13 and incidental extremity behind it. I'm a big believer in the
14 informational context of faces and I decided I was going to see
15 this one again. And I would, but not before a prolonged and
16 pernicious descent into the nature of human evil.
17 Q.   Mr. DeAngeles, the events of last February 10, please.
18   A.   I think you'll just have to defer to my sense of
19 relevance on this one, Monte, my good man who's been not at all
20 hard to find. Watch, I'm about to plunge right into the heart
21 of the matter. Nazi Germany was a telling place.
22 Q.   Mr. DeAngeles.
23   A.   Okay, how about Rainis Park? Surely you wouldn't
24 begrudge me talking about that lovely place. That's not my
25 usual sarcasm either, it really is quite lovely. As I
26 discovered when my investigation took me to Latvia and one of

1 | the seats of modern human mayhem. Oh, did I say that I was now
2 | engaged in an investigation into what it was had eviscerated my
3 | father's soul that night in the restaurant?
4 | Anyway, pursuant to that I stood in that Latvian park and,
5 | man, I could see it. I saw where, on the fourth of July 1941,
6 | they lined them up, women and children, didn't matter, but not
7 | before taking their clothes from them because, unlike the human
8 | flesh, the clothes had value. The Russians had dug
9 | up deep defensive trenches there, which is why the site was
10 | chosen, that and it being the center of town.
11 | I stood on the edge where a trench had been and looked
12 | down. I want to say that seventy-five years later my mind was
13 | able to clear away the earth that had filled the hole so I
14 | could use its eye and see the abyss. This is where people,
15 | literally hundreds, were taken to the precipice and shot in the
16 | head to fall into that abyss and land on the bodies of those
17 | who went before. The bodies piled up, some still alive, their
18 | final moments choked by corpses. Someone's job was to go and
19 | kick loose those bodies that hadn't made it all the way down.
20 | Q.   Mr. DeAngeles, once again I charge you that this is not
21 | relevant.
22 | A.   You wouldn't think so, I know. Except that looking
23 | down I saw it all, the almost comic horror, and felt a gnawing
24 | familiarity. This barbarism, I'd sensed it before. Then it hit
25 | me, grand jurors. The face in the restaurant that night. It was
26 | too young to have been there, true, but that fucking face was

1 born in that trench. I'd say something like the vermin kicking

2 those bodies down in 1941 and the guy staring down at my father

3 with contempt in that restaurant three-quarters of a century

4 later were consubstantial. Normally none of my business except

5 that you fuck with enough people eventually you're going to

6 come up against the wrong type. This guy had come aground

7 against me, grand jurors, and as much as it pains me to admit

8 it, I'm the wrong type.

9 I started investigating. You'll recall I said my man was

10 from Cambodia and that should've set off more than a few alarm

11 bells because if you're talking about mass twentieth-century

12 horror, nothing exceeds that place. But I know that if I say

13 that for four years in the mid to late seventies Cambodia was

14 essentially an entire country of Rainis Parks, there will be

15 some skepticism. So I apologize that I must here inject a bit

16 of history.

17 In 1975 Cambodia, Pol Pot's Khmer Rouge regime came to

18 power. Now, this motherfucker would basically outdo Hitler and

19 do so more than three decades later. So when you hear those

20 famous hypotheticals about what humanity would've done with

21 Hitler had he survived, or before and during, if it'd known the

22 full extent blah, blah? Maybe take as instructive the example

23 of this unrepentant scumbag. Because not only did he

24 immediately upon taking power institute full bore with no

25 exceptions human slavery, he somehow improbably managed to make

26 that concept, slavery, even worse by barely feeding the slaves

1   and encouraging those in charge to be creative in devising the
2   methods of cruelty by which it would be enforced. That, along
3   with the highly intentional extermination of those deemed
4   undesirable for usually concocted reasons, basically means that
5   Khmer Rouge killed one out of every four Cambodians in about
6   four years. So the equivalent of eighty million Americans, or
7   as if six of you listening to me talk right now were killed in
8   the vilest way possible then buried in shallow graves in the
9   hopes that your bodies would function as fertilizer. So not
10 only did that happen, but afterwards, when the entire globe
11 knew, this piece of shit was allowed to live at liberty and at
12 a peaceful remove from revenge for only about two more decades.
13 This was achieved through the complicity of charming entities
14 like the very government that currently employs Mr. Monte here
15 and cages me.
16 Q.   Mr. DeAngeles, that's enough! Counsel, really. A wide
17 berth is given in these situations but there's still a
18 requirement of relevance and I charge this Grand Jury that Pol
19 Pot has nothing to do with the events of February 10, 2015, at
20 the venerable Four Seasons Hotel.
21   THE WITNESS: Actually, I'm going to sustain your
22 objection, Monte.
23 Q.   That's not the way it works.
24   A.   Because you're right that this isn't about Pol Pot.
25 That's another thing people sometimes don't get. Mao, Hitler,
26 Stalin, Pot, these are all scumbag motherfuckers who deserved

1 to have their throats ripped out and shown to them while they

2 were still alive. But for too long you've all fed this

3 boogeyman narrative to distract from the truth about common

4 humanity.

5   I have no doubt that Pol Pot never caught a whisper of

6 this man I temporarily called father just as Hitler couldn't

7 have told you the first thing about that guy kicking down

8 corpses in that Latvian park. The Hitlers and Pol Pots mandated

9 violence, yes, but it's far more meaningful to say they loosed

10 it. I know it's not in our interests to see it that way. We

11 grab someone from these regimes and when we ask them what the

12 hell they were thinking they say that otherwise they themselves

13 would have been killed. Hearing this makes us feel better.

14 Makes us feel better but that doesn't make it true.

15   Show you what I mean. As I said, I started doing

16 investigative research. This is a talent of mine. Along with

17 the language one I mentioned earlier and maybe combat, which

18 I'll likely mention later.

19   I discovered Peeps was actually Long Pimh. I also learned

20 that, unsurprisingly, he'd been one of the boat people who

21 eventually landed here after fleeing Cambodia when the

22 Vietnamese ousted the Khmer Rouge in 1979. He was an attorney

23 who lived with his wife and children in the capital, Phnom Penh.

24   Problem is first thing Khmer Rouge does upon entering the

25 city is order its immediate and complete evacuation. People

26 like Pimh, educated and urbane, were the prime enemy. Think of

1   the complete evacuation of a major city. Something like two

2   million people had three hours to abandon all their property,

3   there would be no more private property or even money, and

4   start for the countryside, where they would begin their new

5   lives as starving agrarian slaves driven by almost

6   inconceivable violence to meet impossible monthly quotas.

7   A great many never made it, but Pimh and his did. I wish

8   he hadn't. He got to watch several of his children starve to

9   death or in the case of those over seven, taken away for

10 reeducation in the Khmer Rouge way. Worse, he also, in late

11 1978, near the end of this nightmare, got to meet Norodam Matak.

12 Remember that name because my claim is that this fuck was every

13 bit the dark equal of that cocksucker Pol Pot but for his lack

14 of opportunity and capability.

15 Q. Let me stop you right there, Mr. DeAngeles, because I can

16 tell by the grand jurors' reactions that they are uncomfortable

17 with your language.

18   A.   Oh, I'm sorry, folks. I meant that in terms of true

19 moral culpability it can be difficult to intelligently draw a

20 meaningful distinction between someone like Matak and the

21 savage at the top cultivating, endorsing, and rewarding his

22 mind-set. See, in 1978 Khmer Rouge, Matak was a rising star.

23 I'll let you draw your own conclusions on how you become such a

24 thing in a place like that, but at all of twenty-three he was

25 already in charge of his own cadre with an eye toward joining

26 his uncle, the verminous Deuch, who ran the S-21 or "Asian

1   Auschwitz," a former high school in the abandoned city where
2   every day a hundred to a hundred and fifty people were killed
3   in the most debased way possible. This world is full of Mataks,
4   maybe always will be. The only reason it matters to this room
5   is that my father ran afoul of this particular filth.
6   How it happened was Pimh got ahold of some eyeglasses.
7   Khmer Rouge hated glasses. Glasses meant reading and reading
8   meant education and intelligence and there's nothing savages
9   like less than the intellect, except maybe for a fair fight. He
10 took to wearing them in open defiance, who knows what got into
11 him. Matak himself beat him badly but nothing too out of the
12 ordinary. But then Matak personally transported him. Pimh
13 assumed he was being led to his death at S-21, a death he
14 wasn't all that wary of given the disappearance of his pregnant
15 wife months earlier.
16   He was only partially right. His final destination would
17 be S-21, sure, but first there would be a stop along the way. A
18 different village, same as the others with one exception. His
19 wife was in this one, her belly still swollen with their child.
20 A reunion of sorts. But a short one because here's Matak making
21 sure Pimh can see as he pulls Pimh's wife off the work line
22 then he and others rape her in front of him. He then pulls out
23 a giant blade, and this is one hundred percent true so shove
24 your objection up your ass, Monte, which he uses to slit open
25 her stomach and pull the fetus out. He then carries it by the
26 neck to go hang from the eaves of a nearby roof with the

1   others, shrunken and blackened by time. All this in full view

2   of Pimh including the hour or so it takes for his wife to bleed

3   out then get dragged to the nearby field where so many human

4   skeletons would ultimately collect one could build a giant

5   temple to human malevolence.

6   Q.   Does that conclude your statement, Mr. DeAngeles?

7   A.   What gives you that impression, Monte?

8   Q.   You haven't spoken for a while.

9   A.   Do you blame me? Is there any response that would

10 signify? Pimh arrived at S-21, eventually everyone would have

11 arrived there. But this was 1979, very near the end. In its

12 history maybe half a dozen people would enter that place and

13 somehow survive. He became one of them because he realized

14 early on that they would kill, literally, for a confession.

15 Breaking bodies is easy, the idea there was to break wills

16 though. You knew the second you *confessed* to whatever they'd

17 concocted you had outlived your usefulness to them. Garbage

18 gets thrown away, this is universal, so same with you. Your

19 liver was removed from your body and eaten for its supposed

20 strengthening qualities, or your head removed to be employed as

21 decor, or the blood entirely drained from your body for storage

22 and later use.

23   I think everyone knew a confession meant that, but S-21

24 was almost diabolically creative at making you prefer death to

25 whatever torturous existence they'd created for you. Pimh

26 withstood the torture and denied them the only thing he had the

1   power to withhold. He refused to talk in any way and, stepping

2   back, it seems odd that his torturers would even cling to that

3   particular vestige of fair play and think they needed an actual

4   confession instead of just saying he'd confessed and in so

5   doing make it so. The result is he lived, if you can call it

6   that. And when the order came to immediately kill all the

7   inmates because the Vietnamese were close, he managed to slip

8   out in the confusion.

9   Q.   Relevance, Mr. DeAngeles.

10   A.   I think our grand jurors can tell where the relevance

11   is going to lie by now, Monte, even if you're struggling. My

12   father dropped his water, dropped any pretense of a life, when

13   he saw again the face of evil itself. Matak sitting there about

14   to enjoy a comfortable meal that he would have to cater to.

15   It took some time to figure this out, but I did. Matak was

16   now Mark Tam, another way of saying the decedent in this case.

17   Mark Tam was doing very well for himself. He owned several

18   properties, here and abroad. He traveled a lot, apparently

19   being murderous garbage is a cosmopolitan pursuit. I learned

20   everything learnable about this savage.

21   Then I searched my soul, grand jurors. I asked God to help

22   me locate the merciful forgiveness I knew was in there. After

23   all, the events of this world are but a prelude and those

24   seeking justice would do well to remember that the conclusion

25   of human events does not preclude ultimate harmony.

26   Oh no, wait. None of that happened. I remember now. What I

1 actually did was set about devising the vilest revenge I could

2 serve this motherfucker at the first possible opportunity.

3   The night that Monte's all on about, Matak was staying at

4 the Four Seasons before flying out the next morning. This is

5 where people like him stay with the money they steal draining

6 the blood out of our fathers. He'd arranged for two escorts, as

7 in prostitutes, to arrive at his room at eight. This is Monte's

8 hero for you, sex slaves really. When they arrived I was

9 waiting in the hallway by his door. I paid them thrice what

10 they were expecting to cancel their evening's plans then I

11 knocked on Matak's door.

12   To say I was not what he wanted to see when he opened the

13 door would be severest understatement. I went inside, the Four

14 Seasons is quite lovely if you're ever in need, and before long

15 he was in the bathroom chained to the toilet, where someone like

16 him belongs. I told him I'd been in his room earlier, which was

17 true, and asked him how he'd enjoyed his tea. I confirmed to

18 him that he was right that it had tasted funny and I explained

19 why.

20   I explained to him that he was about to join a very select

21 list of people intentionally killed by polonium-210. That's why

22 his tea had tasted funny and that's why he was about to undergo

23 the most excruciatingly painful death possible in the next few

24 hours as his organs basically disintegrated. I said I would be

25 with him every step of the way but definitely not to provide

26 comfort.

1   You see where this is going. I told him who I was, made
2   sure he remembered Pimh and his wife, their unborn child. He
3   began to experience the grimmer physical symptoms and he knew
4   the dire situation he was in. I told him I would give him the
5   same level of mercy he was known for, that I would measure mine
6   out to equal his measure. He knew what that meant and that he
7   would never again see the sun.
8   He melted down emotionally and I made sure to aid and abet
9   his psychic devolution every step of the way. Near the end I
10 handed him a giant knife. I reminded him what he'd done with a
11 similar one and how he and his used to eat their victims'
12 livers for strength. I convinced him his only chance was to eat
13 his own, he carved himself open in an attempt, and I watched
14 him bleed out on the luxury Italian marble of the Four Seasons
15 bathroom, a better end than he deserved but the best I could do
16 under the circumstances. He said nothing. I said I'd see him
17 again in hell and would show him even less mercy there.
18   When the police came they asked what they were looking at
19 and I said I had killed him. This was a lie. Matak killed
20 himself. There'd been nothing truly harmful in his tea, though
21 I had put something novel in there to mimic the symptoms I'd
22 been telling him about. In sum, Matak or Mark Tam committed
23 suicide because he had indigestion. Suicide being a crime, both
24 moral and legal, his last act was fittingly deviant. With
25 respect to this deviant's death the best thing I can say is
26 you're welcome.

```
 1   Q.   Does that conclude your statement?

 2        A.   It does, it concludes it.

 3   Q.   Just so we're sure we understand you, then, your claim is

 4   that you never physically harmed Mark Tam, who you concede died

 5   in your immediate presence?

 6        A.   No.

 7   Q.   So you did harm him.

 8        A.   No, I'm saying it's not a claim, just the unvarnished

 9   truth.

10   Q.   So you say. But you've provided no corroboration for this.

11   You're merely asking us to take your word for this outlandish

12   story. In fact, there's no reason for us to believe that

13   anything you've told us is true, with the Cambodia and the

14   unborn fetus.

15        A.   Does that conclude your question, Monte?

16   Q.   Are you having trouble answering it?

17        A.   Not particularly, it's just that I'm nothing if not

18   polite. First there's the absurdity of you lamenting the fact

19   that I haven't provided corroborating evidence. Aside from the

20   painful truth that this likely constituted legally

21   impermissible burden shifting, a criminal defendant in this

22   country has no legal burden to speak of, your lament relies on

23   either feigned or willful ignorance on your part as to the

24   nature of this proceeding and the tools at my disposal within

25   it.

26        That said, I recognize that among the grand jurors there
```

1　may be one or two who would demand to see the holes in my palms

2　before they'll believe. On their behalf I'm asking the

3　foreperson to request two things before voting. One is the

4　medical examiner's report. This report will confirm the

5　existence of salicoside benzoate in the system of Matak when he

6　died. This is a highly improbable if not unique chemical

7　compound, not naturally occurring in the least. It is a

8　compound I essentially invented for these purposes and that I

9　put in Matak's tea. It causes and here caused severe

10　gastrointestinal distress but no actual injury. Ask yourself

11　how this compound got in his body if I didn't put it there or

12　how I would know of its presence if I were lying.

13　　　　The other thing is to ask to recall as a witness Detective

14　Long. It took him a while but Long now knows who Mark Tam

15　really is, was. And just in case he was Matak, this detective

16　intentionally screwed up jurisdiction during the initial Grand

17　Jury presentation almost a year ago. Recall him and ask him all

18　about Matak, you'll see the favor I did the world.

19　Q.　You know what, DeAngeles? I see no need to ask any further

20　questions.

21　　　　A.　Suit yourself, Monte.

22　Q.　And seeing no questions from the Grand Jury, I thank you

23　and—

24　　　　Okay, I see that several hands are now up, indicating

25　questions from some grand jurors.

26　　　　Now, having had the question whispered to me, I now charge

1 this Grand Jury that it is not a relevant or legally

2 permissible question and for that reason it is not going to be

3 asked of the witness.

4   Another hand. Okay, a grand juror wants to know how you

5 knew, allegedly, that Matak, uh, Mr. Tam, would be at the Four

6 Seasons that night? How you supposedly knew two escorts would

7 be appearing, and how to make that substance? And I would add

8 how you claim to know about events in Cambodia that occurred

9 before you were even born?

10   A.   I think the most efficient way I could answer would

11 be to say that I have operated outside the bounds of the law

12 practically my entire life. I know people, people like me, and

13 I know a lot of proven illicit methods and skills. When I said

14 Matak had run afoul of the wrong person I meant it. As for

15 Monte's point centered upon when I was born, it is, of course,

16 a fundamentally ludicrous one. We all thankfully know a lot of

17 things that predate our existence or occurred outside our

18 direct experience. But forget that for a moment, grand jurors.

19 I know Matak did the things I say he did because he told me so.

20 I spent hours with him before he killed himself and I would say

21 he wasn't exactly ashamed of it all, not to say I was really

22 looking for remorse.

23 Q.   A grand juror wants to know, quote, what it is, then, you

24 were looking for? Why you did what you did?

25   A.   Why? Seems self-evident but okay. In my life I've met

26 maybe half a dozen males I could tolerate. Peeps was a man I

1   loved. This vermin destroyed him in every possible way a human

2   being can be destroyed. What would you have me do in response?

3   Send him a strongly worded letter?

4   I'll start with the obvious. This animal was a cancer that

5   needed to be removed from our world. But there's removal and

6   then there's removal. Matak had come up to his final night,

7   that was beyond doubt, but it was also my job to make that

8   night a special version of earthly hell for him. Unchecked evil

9   has the ability to obliterate everything benevolent. The baby

10 giggling with a rattle, the woman nearby smiling. Evil looks at

11 that and sees easy prey.

12   Evil. What is this predator? Earlier I said that Cambodia

13 became something like one of the premier loci of human evil. I

14 was wrong to use that modifier. There is no such thing as

15 inhuman evil, without humanity there'd be no way for evil to

16 instantiate. The ocean, a shark, a lion, cannot create evil or

17 even channel it, for that you need people. But while it's in

18 that sense man-made, it's also true that something like

19 platonically ideal Evil exists independently. Think of this

20 entity like the invisible radio waves we know are immanent but

21 that are powerless and silent until concentrated in a radio

22 et cetera. Let's say that with some people the reception of this

23 toxic element is just crystal clear.

24   Only two things check that kind of evil in our world.

25 Conscience and violence. Whatever its basis, conscience is a

26 genuine thing in our world and it has a repressive function

1   that offends many. This is what I was driving at before when I

2   said something like Pol Pot didn't create anything in Matak and

3   those many others, it was more like he authorized what they'd

4   always wanted. This is the appeal of ideologies, each one

5   stupider than the last. People want to kill, but what to do

6   about this nagging innate feeling that they shouldn't? No

7   problem, Allah is great and he commands it or gays are an

8   affront to the Bible or communism is historically inevitable

9   and can only be achieved bloodily, fucking troglodytes. All

10   that bullshit can be filed under justification, but we only

11   justify what we want to do and we only feel the need to even do

12   so because of conscience.

13   Matak had no conscience, rare but it happens. That leaves

14   the only other thing that checks this brand of evil: violence.

15   Of course violence breeds more violence but that's not a

16   criticism. It breeds it because that's the only cure for this

17   affliction. You know how you finally tame Macbeth? You put a

18   fucking sword through him before he kills any more children. I

19   wasn't looking to reform Matak or have him experience remorse,

20   I was looking to exterminate him before he pulled the unborn

21   child out of *your* womb and hung it from a roof.

22   That said, it wasn't going to be a clinical operation. We

23   needed him to suffer in the process. Not physical suffering

24   either, that's fucking child's play. I wanted deep-seated

25   psychological agony. But how, given the lack of conscience? The

26   only way was to create existential desolation. If that sounds

1   tame, imagine right now becoming a hundred percent certain that

2   you will die in four hours. Truly imagine it and what you would

3   feel. Now imagine me sitting next to you as the declared

4   responsible party devoting every skillful word to the

5   exacerbation of your internal pain. I half-think he opened his

6   abdomen up just so he wouldn't have to hear me anymore. See,

7   that's the thing about unrepentant scumbag psychos. The only

8   love they experience is for themselves and they have a

9   tremendous capacity for feeling victimized. Someone like that

10   cannot be allowed to leave our world without at least a small

11   dose of the suffering outbreak they created redounding onto

12   them. After all, what if this world is all we get? Someone's

13   going to get away with turning it into their personal sadistic

14   playground? On the other hand, I had to cover my bases in case

15   this isn't the only world. That's why it was important he kill

16   himself, tempting as it was to play a more active role.

17   Q.   Not sure I understand that last part.

18   A.   If something identifiable as Matak continues to exist

19   in some alternate reality I want him to know he was essentially

20   duped into taking his own life, that feels as if it would

21   somehow be more painful to him and deny him some of the

22   comforts of inevitability. I *really* didn't like the guy.

23   Q.   Why not call the police? If everything you're saying is

24   true, he was a war criminal subject to arrest.

25   A.   Oh, Monte. I fear you haven't really been listening.

26   Incarceration? Really? That seems to you a proportionate

1   response? We're having this conversation in America in case you

2   haven't noticed. This country was built on blood and its

3   letting still sustains us. Maybe at Cornell, the safety school

4   you went to, they call campus police when someone gets out of

5   line. I was born into a fucking cauldron with only the

6   occasional person trying to tamp down the flames. When I

7   firefight I use fire, exclusively. Maybe that's not ideal but

8   I've never had any real relationship to water and consumptive

9   flames don't pause while you deliberate.

10   Q.   A grand juror wants to know what assurances you can give

11   that this was an isolated instance.

12   A.   I know what she's worried about. She's worried that

13   if they restore me to a viable life I'll be on the first flight

14   to Cambodia to find and stamp out any other insect that might

15   conceivably have had anything to do with this. Or that I'll

16   train my sights on any of the many similar others roaming our

17   earth in leisure to cosmic offense. In other words, that I'll

18   be a vicious force for global justice so that fewer people have

19   to endure what Peeps endured and all you'd have to do to contribute

20   is vote the right way.

21   While I'll confess to some general thoughts in that

22   direction, I'll just add that I'm done and tired and older.

23   There's a woman I know, the real reason. She's one of those

24   people. Others see her and just want to get closer. Then she

25   talks and emotes and the effect is multiplied tenfold.

26   Physically she's adorable, with these cheeks that just seem

1   unreal. Beautiful too. Also sexy as hell. You get the picture,

2   I won't get too graphic.

3   Point is, with her I'm effortlessly the best version of

4   myself because I just start involuntarily mimicking her, she's

5   that compelling. For the generosity of her spirit and the

6   luminosity of her mind do I love her, grand jurors. The fact

7   that she once viewed me with some semblance of those emotions

8   until we were forcibly parted is like a minor miracle in my

9   life and one that I plan to exploit. The moment this body

10 politic does the right thing I'm going to find this woman and,

11 if she'll have me, start a new day as an artist, thinker, and

12 lover, not a fighter.

13   (Prosecutor conferred with his supervisor)

14 Q.   But as of now you're a criminal, right? You said you

15 operate outside the bounds of the law, did you not?

16   A.   Criminal? Okay. But I never fucked up anyone didn't

17 have it coming and I never fucked up anyone had it coming more

18 than this.

19 Q.   It's also true, is it not, that since this event you've

20 spent significant time in a mental hospital?

21   A. C'mon, Monte. You know I was mad merely south by

22 southwest.

23 Q.   I don't know what that means. But nothing further.

(Whereupon, the defendant, defendant's counsel, Warden Graves,

and Warden Ballard exited the Grand Jury room.)

4

|||||||||

"Hell was that, Nuno?"

"What you read, Solomon."

"You actually went into the grand jury and said that?"

"No, Solomon. I got a court reporter to create a false transcript."

"But . . . you're saying it worked?"

"To a point."

"Be specific, Nuno, how are you a sentenced prisoner now?"

"Try and keep up, man. They indicted me on Trespass Three, a misdemeanor, and I took the max year concurrent with the six months I'd taken for fucking that CO up. They're denying me good time, which means I get out February tenth, what's so confusing about all that?"

"Maybe not confusing but how about insane? You blew out a murder case in the grand jury? Was that stuff even true?"

"Course it was true. Did you miss the part where I swore to declaim nothing but?"

"And they took your word for it?"

"No, but they did what I asked and called OCME and Long, who confirmed everything I said."

"How the hell does a People's witness confirm that Cambodia stuff? Who's he to say?"

"He's a former journalist who became a detective. In the days after my arrest a package was delivered to him with evidentiary support for the notion that Mark Tam was no innocent victim, along with the suggestion that he take steps to delay the grand jury presentation or in the alternative somehow compromise it to leave the door open to a future presentation once he'd fully investigated the claim."

"Holy shit, that's some master-criminal-type interplay, bro!"

"All right, I don't have time for this shit. Let's get back to work, as in the plan."

"You mean we're still doing this shit?"

"Fuck you think?"

"No, it's just that, you just dodged such a huge bullet, I would think you'd be chastened some and shit."

"Oh, is that what you'd have thought? Luckily I don't take my cues from such a delicate sensibility. Meaning, no, I won't be leaving the stolen Dalí painting worth millions on this island when I make my triumphant exit."

"Wow, but you no longer need to break out."

"Correct. I get out the tenth with full legitimacy. That means around then I finally get transferred to where I need to be. Once there, soft place where everyone's about to get out, abundant hours to work with, I'll steal the painting myself and no one will know."

"Wow."

"The rest of the plan's not all that different. I bury, you retrieve. Safeguard it and when I get out few days later we'll go get our exorbitant pay."

"Amazing. But why this grim gravedigging detail, man? My whole life, I don't cotton to that shit."

"Told you, it's a good way. Final exit searches here have become insane."

"But *there*?"

"Why not? Superstition? A natural morgue with no eyes on it. Yeah, there."

"Fine, bro. But I'm telling you, the plot sickens with this shit, burying bodies and whatnot, damn. I guess the trade off that the theft is back on is worth it. The Absence is going to be so happy when we resurrect this shit. Well, happy's an overreach but maybe their threats to dismember me will get less vociferous."

"The Absence has nothing to do with this."

"Oh, fuck you. Is that what that investigation you made me do was all about? That's why you made me find out who hired them? No way, man. That's simply not done!"

"Don't be so dramatic, darling."

"You're saying cut them out and go directly to their client?"

"Yes, but you left out the best part. Go directly to their client and get three million instead of a lonely one."

"At risk of great personal harm. Why, man? A cold mil is a fortune, don't get like that."

"It was a fortune until I heard goddamn Tate got two for a Ryden, who's no fucking Dalí. Since that precise moment, one's lost its luster."

"This is crazy."

"What's so crazy about it? You said it yourself, The Absence canceled with her, they gave up. This is an open job now, we bring it to this Nina woman and she gives us three."

"What makes you think she'll pay three?"

"What makes me? Your conversation with that Jackson Five–loving lackey for one. Or the fact that she's behind the Rio *Two Balconies* theft in 2006 and the 2010 Belgium heist of the *Woman with Drawers* sculpture. Call me crazy but when we reunite her with fucking *Adolescence* she ain't going to be haggling over price."

"Do you even hear yourself?"

"What?"

"Who are you going to have this conversation with?"

"This Nina whatever."

"Yeah, Nina Gill!"

"You say that like it should mean something."

"Because it should! This is one of the most famous people in the country."

"The hell's that about?"

"Jesus, man, where you been?"

"I think you know."

"Right, well, Nina Gill is who you're talking about. Gill recently upended our world by challenging maybe the greatest NFL team ever to a one-game, all-the-marbles death clash, and they accepted! Then she followed that up by telling the president to go fuck himself when he predicted a victory for her opponent!"

"That's this Nina?"

"Yes!"

"The one from that indoor football bullshit?"

"Yeah."

"The Nina every media outlet is currently inveighing against non-stop?"

"Correct, so you see our problem."

"Not really."

"Interest in her right now is sky-high, her every move is being scrutinized. You think in the middle of that she's going to take time to indulge her well-hidden criminal impulses by paying three million dollars for a stolen Dalí that's been missing since 2009?"

"Coincidence is such a weird thing, Solomon. Surprise is built into the concept but somehow that doesn't seem to diminish its force every time its superior commands it."

"Thanks, Aristotle, but you haven't addressed my objection."

"Because it's not worthy of address. A leopard would never consent to the forcible removal of its spots. She needs this. It's need all around. She needs Dalí, we need that bread, and I *need* Dia."

"Still on that? You said yourself she's with that mascot and shit."

"What's *with*? She thinks I'm dead, my resurrection changes everything."

"Now I see your true motivation, it's not that she's a stolen art buyer, it's that her employee can't be far behind."

"I had no idea the two things were linked. But now, holy fuck."

"It's still insane that you think she's going to do this a few days after the Global Bowl."

"The what now?"

"The fucking Global Bowl is on the Sunday before you get out."

"That's not a thing."

"It most certainly is. Don't let the name fool you, it's basically this year's Super Bowl, they're even playing it on the date that game was scheduled to be played on."

"What date is that?"

"February seventh, I guess. In the two thousand and sixteenth year of our Lord."

Solomon continues talking here but Nuno has flown away. He's doing that thing where you try to retrospectively relive conversations that only now seem critical. The dates thing had stuck, the guy'd said something about two and four, right? Every two years, no, every four years a cosmically relevant Super Bowl is played on a date two days later? That's it. Who cares except that at the time no Super Bowl was going to be played at all, let alone on 2/7/16 as required, and now here's Solomon saying that against astronomical odds this other weird thing is going to happen on that date. Again, who cares, but it's also just enough to unsettle.

"Do you think that could actually mean something? Sol?"

"What?"

"That date?"

"Hell you talking about?"

"Remember that Theorist guy at Bellevue?"

"What, that fucking nut with the hair?"

"Yeah, but he was actually a professor."

"Could've fooled me."

"And did. Point is he thinks there are currently two dimensions of time."

"Good for him."

"And that the one we're currently in is slowing to a stop."

"I did feel as though time was crawling, but I just attributed that to the colossal boredom of my life until you just put us back in play on this art heist."

"I think that motherfucker might be right, though. He mentioned sleep and dreams and art. All these things I've always found wildly suggestive. It was convincing in its way. But then like so many things that convince in the moment, I forgot it soon as the onrush resumed. I mean, what if the fuck's right? He says it's not something can be altered but I feel like it is, something he's going to do."

"Do what?"

"I don't know, something about CERN and Paterson Falls maybe?"

"Well, the game *is* being played in Paterson."

"*What?*"

"But I'm sure that's just coincidence."

"Get real, the exact place and time he mentioned? Forget that, what about the fact that he was referring to a game that wasn't even scheduled at the time?"

"Yeah, but what does that really even mean, *at the time*?"

"That's what he would say!"

"You're like those people who fall for psychics or astrologers and their vagaries."

"Am I? Step back a bit. Think how weird this whole thing has been. The NFL is a wildly successful industry. That there would be a work stoppage at some point given the massive revenue involved was entirely predictable. That it would persist to this point, where they would cancel an entire season and its profits and let some ludicrous comedy act fill the void, would be literally inconceivable if not for the fact that we are currently experiencing it."

"What's your point?"

"That . . . I don't know . . . maybe improbability, no matter how much, isn't enough anymore. If anything's permissible that has to include the end of the world, no?"

"So, what? Some giant explosion?"

"Don't think so. He kept saying time's running out. That's different, I think."

"Okay, so time runs out or it doesn't. What can we do about it?"

"Maybe nothing. But this fuck's going to want to be at that game or near Paterson Falls on the seventh."

"So?"

"So maybe we meet him there and talk him out of it. Or something more persuasive."

"You get out the tenth and game's the seventh. Whether time is running out or not, it doesn't work that way."

Nuno is staring straight ahead. Everything that crazy fucker said. But how much was truly crazy and not just the packaging? Bellevue, the hair, the drugs. But the undeniable fact that this professor was confidently referencing a game that not only wasn't yet planned at the time but that no one could have even foreseen. The look in his eye when he talked about his inaccessible wife. The dual time line explanation he claimed to have discovered. He said the math meant it and math has no agenda. If he's wrong and a crank, so be it. If he's right . . .

Nuno turns to look directly at Solomon, in the eyes.

"Don't say it, man. Fucking don't. It would be pure insanity. You're getting out three days later no matter what. It would literally be the craziest thing ever done by a human ever in the history of ever!"

"Change of plans."

"Fuck you."

"I need to break out."

3

|||||||||

Dia is tired. Maybe it's just everything needs to be done is done but also there's a sense of defeat and exhaustion, exhaustion in the literal sense, permeating her world. On the surface it was excitement and distraction that was immanent but surfaces rely on inattention and Dia is currently in a damaging state of superskilled hyperattention.

For example, the fact that the Global Bowl will be played at Hinchliffe Stadium. It's making for a great story, historic Paterson locale, not really in use for almost twenty years. But Dia is privy to the combination of bribery and threatened eye gouging that went into securing approval for its use. What if during the game the stadium collapses into deadly mayhem as the whole world watches? Might put a damper on things.

Similarly, there's the fact that tickets to the game have been restricted to Paterson residents and made available to them free of charge, her idea. Almost immediately came swelling whispers of fraud and other assorted criminality. Just seems there's nothing so well intentioned or admirable that it can't then be corrupted.

Finally, there's the competitive aspect of the game, if you could call it that. A common maneuver in these days before the game is the rounding up of *experts* who are then asked to predict. These experts almost uniformly predict that the Pork will lose and lose badly. Bad enough, but it occurs to Dia that the truest experts on the imminent game are the people in her own building. These people know the Pork roster cold. They know, from very up close, the level of football it's been operating within for five months and the level it might be able to attain on its dreamy best day. Some also have significant intimate knowledge of the particular opponent. These specific experts are not acting and talking like the Pork are going to lose or even lose badly; they are acting like they have to decide whether to take a loved one off life support.

This palpable fear, Dia senses, goes beyond a fear of embarrassment to encompass the fear of genuine and irreversible physical harm. This is especially true where Major Harris is concerned. Nina is saying, in the way people say things while making evident it's no prelude to conversation, that Major seems off. This is not about his body; it's more fundamental, his mind. Medically, he should not participate in even one more play of football. Major has made it clear that he will be participating in however many more plays the Global Bowl provides even if they constitute his last willful actions on Earth. Nina has the ability to prevent this. She is saying she will not.

Maybe it's just Joni has Dia thinking like this. She listens to other stuff now and she misses it, misses being able to listen to that angelic musical poet in that particular way with its mixture of novelty and chronology. More of the exhaustion she feels all around or its cause?

Hejira and *Don Juan's Reckless Daughter* are both masterpieces, the former likely her greatest work, but they are also the final two. Eight straight. Eight nonpareil albums in nine years, all written and produced by just Joni in what was easily the highest individual musical achievement of the twentieth century.

To Dia it'd not been idle melodic literature. The work had merely deepened and broadened her spirit and intellect, that's all. But like all such work it was made by humans and humans are human, meaning two major things. First, that even the most powerful among us is only so temporarily. Here, that means that Joni continued producing sometimes superb music but with a definite diminution that began with *Mingus*, a collaboration that only sexism could argue was not beneath her. This impotence that always asserts itself in the end, why not just go on indefinitely in glorious mastery?

The other thing it means is failings. Joni Mitchell gave a daughter up for adoption, the lyrics are rife with it once you know what to look for. This was either indefensibly wrong or retroactively justified by the eight works. Or neither.

Can't get too caught up in that kind of thing, Dia's decided. The word *biology* should always be preceded by a form of *mere*. Not so for the fact that what Dia feels for the music and for Joni, this person she's never been within miles of and who has no clue Dia exists, is at least a variant of love.

She loves Nina too, might as well get that out of the way, and this one *is* reciprocal. The rest is just human failings and if they decide they're both just going to know something, and know that they both know it, but not harden it verbally or otherwise, what business is that of the rest of the world? We fixate too much on the inalterable past.

It's just, everything ends anyway. So does that deepen or nullify everything that came before? Today, Joni doesn't really create music anymore, she mostly just struggles with a disease some think she herself invented. In a few days people will learn the embarrassing truth about the Pork and by extension the entire IFL. Very few associated with the league will have any viable professional future. A lot of their players, many of whom she considers friends she cares deeply about, are currently enduring significant physical suffering that the game will only worsen greatly. In the case of Major Harris, who is especially critical to Nina, his body is likely to survive only to preside over a death sentence to his mind and personality.

In all cases the past will respond with stony silence. The magic of the albums will endure, true, but so will Nina's decision not to accept the NFL's developmental league offer and to do so in the most antagonistic way possible, without which there would have been an end to the physical damage, future paychecks, and an ambiguous undefeated season to debate in perpetuity however one saw fit. Given the choice between relitigating the past and violently hooking the future and reeling it onto the deck of the present, she will henceforth always do the latter.

She will soon be out of a job and is starting to think that it will be best if she's just *out of* simply everything. The apartment she rents, for example, is in a sense Travis's so she'll have to be out of that. She can buy a place. She has money now, but instead she thinks she'll buy a car. A place stays in one spot and you begin to fill it with meaning, a car can take you to various meanings.

Travis has to be over, she'll tell him after the game, because he's not addition but subtraction and she'll need the full sum of herself to . . . do whatever she's going to do. He's fine, but she's twenty-two years old going around calling someone her *boy*friend, it's all just kind of embarrassing. Worse, when she considers what he must call her. Already she finds herself fulfilling the special obligation of women as far as men are concerned of sublimating aspects of yourself to become a kind of cheerleading confessor: think if a man had achieved what Joni did; think only because none did. Travis Mena's a nice enough guy, but please.

Genius is at least partially a choice, a search. She's a searcher now, but not searching for anything external. Not for anything internal either. It's not a finding, a discovery, or a becoming she wants. She wants to disappear. She's a genius who doesn't know it. A free artist whose medium is humanity and whose greatest work is slowly but inexorably forming. It's what she will disappear into. A life as master-work, that blur between bassinet and coffin. It will be revolutionary and timeless, this work, and it will spread like a contagion.

2

||||||||||

Nuno is on a water vessel moving away from Rikers Island. Doesn't seem possible, but he watches this violent rip of the universe recede from sight and force and he can almost convince himself that it will never again be a thing in his life.

Wrapped around his thigh is an eighteen-inch-by-twelve-inch canvas. On it a very young Salvador Dalí stands next to his seated nurse, Lucia, and the rest of it, Nuno must concede, is pretty fucking killer. More killer is that about eighty years ago some nut ran a brush through some paint and canvas and now this other maniac is going to profit off it to the tune of three millions.

The power of research. Years earlier, bumbling corrections officers stole a Dalí drawing of the crucifixion from Rikers. After much criminal justice system drama, and to no knowledge of the direct perpetrators, it ended up in the hands of the invisible mastermind. This greatly offended one of her rivals. This rival would have his revenge, though. Because when the mastermind followed with a successful theft of *Adolescence*, the prize currently warming Nuno's leg, he was somehow able to deprive her of her hard-stolen unlawful possession and stash it on the very island that had housed his greatest Dalí defeat.

There it remained, no one sure quite where, until credible information placed it at the island's Adolescent (get it?) Reception and Detention Center and its particular bunk for inmates facing very imminent release. So Nuno had gone to Rikers intentionally, it's just that his violent improvisation had cost them a year. And when he'd finally gotten to that building the night before, he found things just as Solomon and the blueprints had predicted. Solomon was good and right and true but the challenge was considerable. The goddamn thing was interwoven into the ugliest drapes you'd ever seen located in the booth where a CO sits to monitor inmates. You had to know what to look for but there it fucking was hiding in plain goddamn sight. The thought that went into this damn thing. The entire drape itself became a paranoiac-critical exhibit that betrayed just how obsessive this revenge was. An early Nuno thought was that if he could find who'd done it they'd probably give more than three just to extend this deranged campaign.

A distraction that would get the CO out of his booth was no big deal. Problem was how do you cut up a drape out of camera view then make it so the CO doesn't notice the change when he returns? His solution was complex but appropriately so. It meant igniting what remained of the drapes to remove evidence of any absence after cutting out *Adolescence*. Before that it meant moving and tampering with a nearby space heater to make it look responsible, all in the ninety seconds or so it took for a sea of eager colleagues to respond to the distracting incident.

Nothing's all that crazy if it works and this one did, though barely. Problem was he now had the wildly valuable get but no Solomon, no great way to move it off the island (the exit search for released prisoners has become extreme), and a cell that gets tossed seemingly hourly so that extraction could not wait for his imminent prison break. This is why he's going to visit the dead. How he can be, as stated, leaving Rikers with a three-million-dollar canvas strapped to his leg yet celebration would be premature.

Problem is his exit is temporary. Leaving an island of grim captivity for one that is arguably worse. Hard Island, Solomon kept calling it, not sure if humorously.

It is growing, that island. Growing into focus for Nuno as he sits on that ferry with surprisingly few fellow inmates and even fewer officers. Grows and grows and seems to gravitationally pull their craft to it. Nuno wonders just what the hell it is he's looking at. Intellectually he knows he is looking at a true natural island, not a man-made atrocity like Rikers, and that makes it somehow worse.

Because there are the clinical facts about Hart Island, like that one, but even as bizarre as those are they only partially prepare you for the sensual experience of actually coming ashore that fetid ground. The seven miles traveled had been traveled in the wrong direction, in every sense. As pure geography, the miles had taken him away from Rikers, true, but they'd also taken him farther from his ultimate goal of Paterson Falls. He also felt the travel had been away from a very sour but at least predictable and orderly reality into disorienting irreality.

Meaning how can all this Hart Island stuff be the case? If the world is just everything that's the case how can it be the case that his includes this? Look, he's got a job to do and he's going to do it, but first *how?* How can it be that the NYC Department of Correction owns this island? That they use it exclusively as a potter's field where the lost and unknown are buried in a mass grave that already holds a million of their brothers and sisters and children? But mostly, what lunatic confluence of events made it the case that the burials are carried out by Rikers Island inmates ferried over and paid fifty cents an hour?

Nuno walks in involuntary formation on that dying ground and tells himself he's there to do something great, not turn into Solomon. Solomon, who blanched every time the plan mentioned his having to go to that island to retrieve what Nuno is about to bury.

Pretty early on Nuno gets what he needs to surreptitiously inter the glorious painting in a place he can easily direct Solomon to later. Following that, he's free to just pretend he's there legitimately, to the extent such a concept could even apply to what is currently happening on that island.

He is digging. Trenches for adults the universe forgot or just never knew in the first place. Makes sense. The cosmos is deaf, dumb, and blind, so how many will move through their personal millisecond time lines without causing so much as a ripple? The nameless million already interred there would be just a start. He knew a kid once, fixated on this kind of stuff, what happens to these people when they die and so on. The answer is bad, worse even than the childish speculations they'd throw out back then.

Then it's all improbably worsened when he is selected to move to a different section of the island for a *special assignment*, the phonetic pronunciation of which creates a great temptation in Nuno to brain the speaker using the shovel in his hand. He's led away and when he arrives at the destination, it's just different. This is where they bury the children. The stillborn and others born into violent brevity and designated for a *city burial*. The small caskets stacked four by five in a trench. Separated from the adults for no reason apparent to Nuno so he decides it's about the formation of the soul and the time required to accomplish it.

Not counting guards, he's with just two others. These two are jousting. This is not said metaphorically, they are literally using their shovels to playfully sword-fight each other, so fencing then. This, Nuno decides, is the most sane thing happening at the moment.

"You two, this really the place?"

"Course it's the place," one says and stops, which allows the other to land a scoring blow. "*Place* is like *now* or *present*, always true when uttered. So, yes, this is the place."

"A stickler, I see. Too bad your decorum doesn't extend to not literally dancing on the graves of dead infants."

"Gravely I say that I see much that's grave but no graves. You, brother?"

"No graves," he says, suspending his shovel to answer.

"Brother?"

"Yes?"

"No, you two, literally?"

"I figure we're all brothers figuratively, so it figures you'd want to litter with the letter of the law."

"Just asking if you two are brothers."

"And answering that we all are."

"Fine, no one agrees, but fine. I'm referring to watching you duel with what appears to be a photocopy of yourself."

"Who, this ignoble dirtbag? You think I'd fraternize with someone like this if we weren't identifiably identical?"

"Jesus Christ, how do twins end up at Rikers together?"

This goes unanswered as the ghastly pair resume their shovel fight. Nuno realizes he won't be getting a straight answer but that's just as well. Of all the senseless things humans fixate on. Watch two people can barely tolerate each other find out they're related and suddenly they're hugging and kissing over their biological quirk. One more fucking thing to keep rejecting out of hand should he ever live on.

Nuno also decides he will not be dropping any infant-size pine boxes into that trench. He moves away. Now there are even smaller cylinders around him and when he responds with a what-the-hell look he is artlessly informed that they are full of severed human limbs that are also to be buried.

This is the precise moment when Nuno suffers not just sadness, or anger, or any other well-established emotion so much as an extreme and profound abasement then complete loss of meaning. The sudden perfectly abiding conviction that the shovel in his hand is no different in kind from the six-year-old arm that'd had to be lopped off to prevent the virulent spread of premature death, an empty arm he was now charged with concealing. That it didn't matter if he buried that gangrenous limb or instead jumped into that trench himself to serve his ultimate purpose as landfill for the mass grave that is our world. Jump in now and foreclose violently the erratic rises and falls of one human pogo stick bounding senselessly as it's buffeted by the universe's unfeeling events.

Here's a leg. Once it ran and leapt and obeyed mental orders. Today it's gone the way of all flesh but not before deserting its host to discover that grim truth. Think of the twins, a collection of limbs waving in the wind as if desperate to get skyward attention. Forget the twins, think of his own hand. Does he keep it alive, this dumb tool? Can it turn on him notwithstanding? Look, a dagger. Can his hand arm itself with it, his arm handle it, to plunge it into his heart in mutinous savagery? Can the heart then object? To whom and how? Can it retaliate? The heart is powerless and the hand all-powerful because the manipulation of matter is all there is and matter is all we are. It's not that everything will end in that mass grave, it's that everything's already a mass grave with some of the corpses dreaming of life.

His dream, he feels, is over. His actions and their reactions will not persist in time. *Adolescence* can stay interred like the arm he just dropped in and worms won't distinguish one meal from the other. He could bury the money there as well and nothing appreciable would change. A rush to the center of the earth with not only no victors or vanquished but also just no tabulation of any kind. The only logically defensible response to any activity that is meaningless in every sense is its immediate cessation. The painting and its secret can stay where they are. Same for his body, caged or free. The people he knows, but only their surfaces. The thoughts and words that began to disappear the instant they formed. He's where he belongs, no need to get back on that ferry. A potter's field for those who never created mourners and he is someone who now sees the folly in creation of any kind. He emerged originally from no one's nothing and that's where he'll return.

He stares at his grave, but it only stares back.

1

||||||||||

In recent death Feniz existed maybe more than he had in life. Reason is that Father Ventimiglia had drummed up business. First he'd guilted Fernandez Funeral Home into a bare-bones service at cost—the only other option was this so-called *city funeral* ignominy he'd never even heard of before. Then he took up a special second collection during the masses to pay for it while encouraging attendees to not just dip into their pockets but also to fulfill their Christian obligation to send off a member of their community, even one who'd been basically invisible to most of them, in a manner consonant with their beliefs.

The result is you could credibly argue that currently gathered in that funeral home's smallest room is a decent showing of humanity, as if for a loved one. What distinguishes it from the home's usual fare is the amount of speculative discourse. Truth is, a clear majority of the mourners just don't know with great specificity what they're mourning. So you hear things like *the guy with the mother with the leg* or *the dude who wouldn't cover up that giant scar on his head.* That last part was widely and graphically understood, as Feniz had undoubtedly spent his final months devoid of all personal vanity so that really the best he's looked in forever is that mock-up of his body in that casket where stage makeup is concealing the fact that his skull had been forcibly wrested open so that its contents could soldier on maybe an extra six weeks.

Not surprisingly in this context, a bit of disinformation here and there also begins to emerge. That means whoever finds themselves most skillfully correcting the record, in this case Sharon, emerges as de facto expert to the point that she even ends up sitting in the front row and taking condolences and when people there wonder at the nature of their relationship, they aren't blood, she's black, he wasn't, the priest said earlier he wasn't married, the consensus that emerges is that Sharon Seaborg and Feniz Heredia were, in the special dual sense of the word familiar to most of that audience, *neighbors.*

How Feniz now exists more than before is that people are discussing his life in a way that almost makes it seem momentous; in the past tense, sure, but still. Then Ventimiglia speaks and intuitively senses that a lot of the usual prosody is inapplicable here. He does say that our world is full of glioblastomas and amputated limbs and faltering hearts but maybe this is all just subtle confirmation that everything physical is ephemerally trivial so that the search for meaning must of necessity look elsewhere.

Left unsaid is that the world is also full of all sorts of nonphysical elements that are even more deleterious. That the world is full of loneliness and rejection and fearful doubt and betrayal and these things aren't so much ephemeral as they are endemic. Sharon's decided those things are fixed realities and maybe always will be. But it's also not a one-sided war, we score our victories where we can.

Sharon has taken the opportunity to bury a suit of Hugh's she's always hated. Maybe there's something to this burying thing. She feels a story has ended. This brings a certain sadness with it but also a kind of excitement at what novel stories may now begin to form. Across from her, near the end of the viewing, is Larry.

"So sad," he says.

"You bought that air conditioner for him. Feels like the kind of thing people should do and that I won't soon forget."

"Was kind of wondering if, maybe hopeful, Celia de Cervantes would be here."

"Who?"

"The call that night? The guy impaled at the bus stop? You pick up the call and the guy's from Paterson, a double coincidence I still can't fully believe."

"Right, what about it?"

"Just that I've been debating for like a year whether to talk to her about that night."

"And you thought she might be here why? Because she's from Paterson?"

"I know."

"Along with a hundred and fifty thousand others?"

"I know, but the coincidences start to pile up until you almost grow to expect them."

She stands there kind of absently gathering her things sensing he really wants to talk but not sure how much she really wants to listen. He is suffering, albeit moderately, so maybe a slight invitational look wouldn't kill her.

"You know?"

"What do you want to say to her, Larry?"

"Not sure."

"Good thing she's not here then."

"Her husband, can you imagine? Thing is, we're standing there facing each other. I know what's coming. Worse, he knows. There's just no way. What do you do, you know, when there's not even the pretense of hope? We spoke, his wife, kids. Right before the end he startles. He's looking past me and crying out. It's his mother, the unmistakable way men act then, and after some surprise he's telling her he's coming, Mami, to join her. All with pauses where she's apparently speaking to him."

"Terrible."

"Sure, but there was also something about it I couldn't let go of so I did some digging."

"On what? He knew what was coming and naturally thought of his dead mother."

"That's just it, she wasn't dead. Well, okay, she was dead but he didn't know, no one knew."

"What are you talking about?"

"I'm talking that as Jorge de Cervantes was uttering those final gasps at his mother about a reunion, he had every reason to believe she was alive and well in Manizales, Colombia. Everyone did because she lived alone, meaning there'd been no one to report the fact that days before she'd collapsed and died on her kitchen floor. In fact it wasn't until a family member went to her home to report the grim news about her son that everyone's grief was somehow made even worse. And the Colombians didn't even tell family members here in America about her death until after Jorge's funeral, not wanting to compound the grief. So not even any of Jorge's family members could have known at the time he was talking to her dead spirit. You see what I'm driving at?"

"I do."

She starts to walk away. The day is over. Later, Hugh is taking Donnie to that game or whatever, the Global Bowl in Paterson, doesn't seem very global if they can just walk there. Does she want to be alone tonight or with a girlfriend(s) and wine? Already she misses Feniz, presickness Feniz, who would have expertly and comically feigned interest in the game out of some misguided loyalty to Paterson or something. Dumb fuck, couldn't do a simple thing like keep the cells in his brain from turning on him. Guy spoke to his dead mother. What business is that of hers? But Larry has followed and wants an answer. Should he seek out the wife, isn't it a comforting disclosure?

"I don't think so," she says. "These things happen. They may mean something, maybe not."

"But isn't meaning itself comforting?"

"When something ends, just gotta accept it. What about anything in life makes you think that trying to resurrect or relive some shit is even a good idea? Leave that woman in peace. She probably just starting to get over it, last thing she need is your nosy ass dredging that business all up again. Everything, Larry. Everything, like this conversation, ends."

"Yes, everything. But maybe only to be reborn," he counters.

But she has left and truth is he hadn't really put all that much of his steam into this declaration.

ZERO

||||||||||

The area near a stadium in the moments before a big game. Almost easier to name the Paterson residents who aren't there with the food tents and the attempts to throw footballs through tires and the Major Harris jerseys on bodies not conceivably comparable to Major Harris's. The forecast is for the hardest rain that ever fell to fall but coming from east over the Atlantic and maybe not even reaching the field before the game is over.

Hinchliffe Stadium looks legit. True, a lot of it is façade but even its harshest critic would concede that these are good moments for the city of Paterson.

The genuine Major Harris sits in the locker room wondering what the greatest ever single-game achievement by an NFL quarterback is. He knows his history. Joe Namath beat the Colts in what's still considered the greatest upset in history and even predicted it beforehand but if you look closely at the game he wasn't actually all that instrumental in the victory. Phil Simms went 22 for 25 in a Super Bowl but truth is he had a vastly superior squad, and anyway no one thinks he was even close to as good as the guy he was quarterbacking against.

No, if he does this, has the right three hours, it will be the greatest thing ever done by his position. So even just the fact that the universe's atoms collided in precisely the right way to give his collection of atoms that chance is celebratory if you think about it. But Harris is not in the business of celebrating opportunities, only results, and the only astounding result here would be a win.

Then what? Don't think like that. Then peace, that's what. A lifetime hearing that he doesn't come through in the big spot, a function largely of not having come through in the big spot, and he can rationalize it all he wants but he also can't help but have internalized some of it as well. He somehow wins this game and all that shit disappears. This wouldn't be like winning a Super Bowl, this would be like winning Life and winning is always a kind of ending.

They once asked a player if the Super Bowl was the ultimate game and he rightly wondered in response how *ultimate* it could be if they play it every year. This is different. This game really never will be played again, making its significance incomparable, and as far as Major is concerned dig a hole right there on the field and drop him in it if he doesn't win it.

This is entirely consistent, however, with Major's deep, bone-marrow understanding that he and his team are about to get their heads bashed in before an obscene number of witnesses. He knows this but is committed to defiance and knows as well that there's something off about him mentally now that probably won't be coming back, which means hereafter he'll likely be becoming more and more like a child, with a child's understanding of things like whether or not he won this game that's about to be played. If he dies on the field that's fine too as long as it's not drawn out and humiliating with Nina watching his slow devolution.

Nina is outside the locker room preparing to address the team.

Dia is in some press area at the stadium talking up the game's *globular* import while instantly realizing that this is improper usage.

Nuno is impatiently awaiting the final count at ARDC so he can finally effect his year-in-the-making escape.

Solomon currently has it worst by far. He is in an odd-looking boat of some sort that is quite speedy but whose seaworthiness he has begun to doubt gravely and the faster he goes the graver the doubts. He is about a nautical mile from Hart Island, not that he knows from any measurement like that or any other seafaring shit for that matter. Goddamn millions at stake and he feels like he's playing Bumper Boats with the unit that's going to be pulled from rotation immediately following his use.

The closer he gets the less resistible the urge to veer off and go home. In three days Nuno would get out legitimately and they could calmly go there as free citizens to dig up the get. This has so many advantages it practically screams necessity, but for some hairy lunatic Nuno is ascribing mystical qualities to saying here comes the moment of truth. Nonsense of course, and Solomon is highly tolerant of all faiths and creeds and whatnot but he also doesn't warm at all to this mass grave business and's been clear about that from the jump. And also it's starting to rain pretty damn hard and he's getting soaked, man.

Not in Paterson though, where an incomprehensible February sun lasers down on everyone. This means the gridiron is in perfect condition but perfection is relative because here it includes perfect traction and the last thing the Pork want is the Cowboys being able to push off with eviscerative zeal. Like all pigs they want a slop fest, one where skill and nuance are lost and the efficacy of savage will is bolstered.

Nina looks out the window at that fiery ball signaling that the universe is conspiring against her and her contempt manifests in a violent application of the blinds. She's not going to think about it, just walk into that room and tilt at it all.

"You already know everything I'm going to say but truth doesn't weaken from repetition so I'm going to say it again. I know you guys like to watch your all-sports networks, listen to all-sports radio, and devour everything written about you. If you've done that the last few weeks you can't like what you saw and heard. No one out there gives you even a slight chance. Well, I've forgotten more about football than they'll ever know and I say not only do we have a chance but I *expect* to win.

"I'm not saying we're a better football team than the Cowboys because we're not. But we can and will be better than them *today*. They are better than us but what specifically are they better at? Are they better at huddling up before and after plays? Are they better than us at television time-outs or at picking up their teammates after a play? No. They're better than us when the ball is in play, those intermittent seconds between when the ball is snapped and the ref whistles the play dead.

"Well, let me fill you in on a little secret. When I did this for those pansies over there I once had someone reduce the game film of a game we'd lost to just those seconds, those seconds when the ball is actually alive and in play. You know what the result was? Eleven minutes.

"A three-and-a-half-hour football game reduces to eleven minutes that actually decide who wins or loses. Are you going to sit there, knowing all the work we've put into this season, the bloodshed, the bones snapped, and tell me that you can't bind yourself to your brothers and collectively outperform another group of men for just eleven minutes?

"If you feel you *can't* I'm going to pause now for you to say that out loud. I want everyone in this room, and more importantly *you*, to know that you don't think yourself capable of eleven great minutes.

"I don't know about you so-called men but if I look across from me and see someone who thinks they're better than me at something, anything, I want to punch them in the face. If you feel different, if you're going to look at the guy across from you during this game and feel admiration or respect or awe then don't play. Leave your information with their agents, maybe they'll hire you to water their lawns when this is all over.

"Eleven minutes. Be better than them for eleven minutes and you're better for life, for as long as humankind populates this place. I still say there's a championship in this room. But no one's going to hand it to you. You have to go out and take it. Take it the only way anything ever gets done in football, in life, by force. Take it and you'll never have to let it go. Take it for everyone in your life who helped you up when you were down or to spite those who tried to keep you there. I don't care what your motivation is because they don't want it like we want it, they can't. Take it. Take it or die trying or don't come back to this room afterwards because this room is for fighters. Go!"

The players storm out of the locker room violently and the home crowd roars at their sight. Harris is last to leave and he wants Nina.

"Listen, the championship rings go to the owner and then he, or *she*, distributes them to the players."

"Your point?"

"Just that I've decided life is a comedy and any comedy worth its salt ends in, you know, and I also thought that maybe . . . if you owed me a ring . . . it might help." He hands her a diamond ring. "Understand, that's all this is."

"Not sure I can accept it if that's all it is, remember my moral objection to superstition."

"Would you accept it if it was more than that?"

"Is it?"

"If I knew you'd accept it."

"I'd only accept it if I knew it was more than that."

"I would only accept more than that if . . . wait . . . are we doing this or not?"

"Damn, Major, you pick a hell of a time to get all soft on me. Will you please go out there and get the ring that matters! And try to stay alive, last thing I need is to be widowed before we've even decided on the appetizers."

He leaves. Life is weird. All she asks is that it give her this one measly football win, is that too much to ask? Also that that nut with the strange name show up with her damn Dalí. Hell was his name?

God damn goddamn Nuno, thinks Solomon. If the damn thing is buried where he says it is then where the hell is it? Rain is falling like a motherfucker, general all over that vile island but seemingly nowhere else. Falling and falling like a universal letting that won't cease until it reaches empty. The deluge is such that Solomon is essentially shoveling mud around, which is very taxing and he's not the strongest guy and he's kind of even crying because any time he displaces earth, water rushes in to replace it; water's coming in and in and in a way that feels like the end of the island until Solomon's shovel no longer displaces anything, it just fulcrumy sinks its operator into the sucking ground and its new vacuum divot, which then quickly fills to sink him deeper until he's just slogging through the excremental muck human activity can't help but continually produce.

This is not something that can be done, he decides. Those things exist, they just do. If Nuno had charged him with turning invisible or flying like a bird he would fail and this is no different. Course it's unlikely Nuno will see it that way and he has that presence thing that can make you question little concepts like reality and human limitations. The rain builds, which he would not have thought possible.

He is wading through thigh-high diseased water to that crazy boat and he has made an executive decision. The decision is abandonment, which is a legal defense. *Adolescence* is gone, our planet swallowed it whole, and when he doesn't arrive to pick up Nuno only to tell him the get is gone, he'll be doing him a favor. He can go back to his cell to no one's notice and just get out in a few days lawfully. Money isn't everything, but existence is. This grandiose nonsense notion of having to reach Paterson Falls in a few hours or else! exists only in Nuno's head and that's where it will stay. So much rain that Solomon decides he'll just stand in one spot and let it drown him.

What conks him out of his absent reverie is a floating casket to the midsection. Bizarre of course but who's got time for anything but pushing it out of the way and continuing towards the boat? Except here come reinforcements. Casket after casket noisily piercing the surface tension of the floodwaters to form an undulating grave site. The biblical force of the water has summoned all these silenced corpses out of their terraneous prison to serve as premonitory flotsam.

Solomon is nearing a kind of horrified catatonia when he finally reaches the boat. It won't start. Surrounded by caskets so that the boat begins to look like just another receptacle for the dead. Won't start and the dead closing in.

What strikes his boat then is a familiar cylinder.

Impossible.

But that's what it undeniably is.

The adorned tube Nuno was to use to bury the Dalí. He lifts it onto the boat to find that it's somehow fused with some other far grimmer tube. He can't separate them or open either one, but the important thing is they're on the boat costing him his excuse for not proceeding to Rikers and anyway he's about to die so nothing physical matters.

But then the boat starts and he guns it in the general direction of Rikers and Nuno. Away from Death and its drowning pool and towards Life, and freedom, and wealth—the deafening soundtrack the violent cycle of water, from sea to sky then back.

. . .

In the parking lot and concourses they pipe in the radio pregame show:

"We are coming to you live for the last time this season from the Pigsty in beautiful Paterson, New Jersey, location of the first ever Global Bowl between the IFL champion Paterson Pork and the three-time defending NFL champion Dallas Cowboys.

"You say you want story lines? How about Nina Gill, whose diatribe against the sitting president has been viewed tens of millions of times in just two weeks, going against the franchise her father built from practically scratch and the most successful sports league in human history?

"How about Major Harris? A former NFL legend and one of the very greatest to ever play the position going against his former team. A team that cut him to avoid paying a roster bonus then went on to win three consecutive championships with his replacement, Tom Laney. Coach Buford Elkins in a similar position.

"As for the Cowboys, what more can be said about them? Is quarterback Tom Laney the greatest ever? More than a handful think so and today is another opportunity to add luster to his brilliant career.

"That's the story off the field. On it? Are we in store for a mismatch, the greatest upset in the history of professional sports, or something in between?

"Joining Slim and I today is former NFL great and broadcasting legend Tim Livetree. Tim, make a case for the Pork."

"I can't, Jim. I guess Laney could break his hand on the first play of the game or Coach Tesseract, who has a history of high blood pressure, could stroke out during the national anthem. Even then I think the Cowboys would win handily with the backup and maybe a cheerleader calling the plays."

"Okay. Slim, how do the Pork win this game?"

"No chance. Wait, are we on the air? Oh. Yeah, no chance, Jim."

"Okay, well, as far as the rules are concerned we are operating under primarily NFL rules meaning none of the mascot duels or Weather Wheel shenanigans that IFL fans grew to love. One holdover from the IFL, no replay challenges, all referee calls are final.

"As for the weather, not good news for Pork aficionados, who undoubtedly were hoping for the kind of severe weather the Pork grew accustomed to

playing in and that might've evened up the odds a bit. Instead, it is a sunny forty-two degrees here in Paterson and the forecast is for more of the same.

"All right, I see we're about ready to start. The Cowboys have won the toss and have elected to receive."

Nuno knows the count is done and that Solomon might even already be waiting, but he's also undergoing a kind of existential paralysis. There's been a change in him as he approaches his legitimate release date and he can't help but feel it's been a diminution. A species of fear. If he just stays put and fully absorbs inaction they cannot keep him past Wednesday and they can never put him back in. He would have the approbation of society at large behind him for maybe the first time in his life.

He knows he should just close his eyes in that bed and shut out the outside world but every time he tries he keeps seeing two faces. Dia's he could look at forever but it's that damn Theorist, man. He knows that guy wasn't lying. Deluded, insane, maybe; but that dude believed every word he was saying, boy. And there's just a way a face looks when it's reflecting deep truth. If he doesn't get out right now he thinks he will never see Dia again.

Anyway there's just something about waiting versus doing that he can't ever abide, so he starts moving. Speaking of doing, there's one quick thing he has to do before leaving that haunted isle and if it's true that he's not going to be doing many more things then that only adds to the urgency. Result is that through a series of convoluted but beautifully precise steps he is soon alone in a room with an inmate in protective custody.

"Who in the hell are you?" asks this inmate.

"I'm the last person you're ever going to see, sorry."

The cornered inmate, Dell Morkevich, is looking at Nuno and that little bit of defiance from the beginning is already long gone because he better sees what's before him.

"Why do you say that?" is all he can manage.

"I say that because I am here on behalf of Jorge de Cervantes."

Morkevich tries to scream but some one or thing has stolen his breath.

"Don't," says Nuno, and just like that it no longer seems possible he will. "There's nothing you could say. Although, to be honest, there's probably something I could reassess."

"Huh?"

"You drove your car straight through a man, what did you think? Oh, I know what you thought. You thought your world is full of countless examples of savagery opposed by mere process and that this would be no different. I should punch my fist right through your heart this instant to show you how wrong you were. Who would fault me? Except . . ."

"Yes, that, except! Except, man, except."

"*Except* you? Why should I? Because you're more pathetic than active? That's what's bothered me about your case from the start. Little fucking mouse bouncing off the sides of your cage when denied your sugar pellet. Now your head's clear to what you did but the memories cloudy. Justice would be a crystalline repetitive loop in your head of you killing a family that defied all the odds of this cesspool and generated beneficence."

"Didn't mean to, man, please."

"Yeah, the world's full of *didn't mean to*. Poor substitute for *didn't*. Still. If everything's evil maybe less evil will have to pass for good. Time was, we would've never had this interaction, just the damage. Now I don't know. I just don't. I don't know if I *know* anything anymore is what it is."

Afterward Nuno is literally in a shithole. All the Porta Potties on the common grounds are rounded up and stored near the island limits at the end of the week. Nuno is currently in one as it's rudely transported along with many others by a half-asleep driver. Thing is, it hasn't been properly emptied so now every listing sloshes liquid blue shit all over him and he has to just bear it silently for fear of discovery.

Once the movement stops he is looking at a slight crack in the top of the tube that allows him to monitor the progress of the DOC searchlights. Dark to light then dark in oscillating regularity. Just has to time the darkness to cover his sin. He thinks forty-two seconds. When the next ones start he'll go.

But they come and he doesn't. He can't because something's blocking the door from swinging open no matter how much force he uses.

The only way is out the top of the tube and a violent exaggeration of that crack. He attempts this through repeated open-hand blows while standing perilously and without leverage on the bowl. He falls in several times and can never quite get the whole top off but he does eventually manage to open a hole that maybe would fit a human? He sits to build up strength for the imminent passage.

When the next forty-two seconds arrives he is pulling himself up into the hole, the serrated edges tearing open the flesh on his palms. He's having trouble getting his shoulders through. The light's coming and at the last second he has to quickly drop down out of view. He's cut and injured and covered in shit and may not even have enough strength for another attempt.

When he next squeezes partially through that gory opening he gets stuck. The light is swinging back like a pendulum and when it arrives it will illume an orange half man being swallowed by a giant plastic worm full of shit. In desperation, he can neither free himself *out* nor retract back *in*, he just swings his weight to topple the whole wriggling worm over, milliseconds before the searching globe of a photonic eye passes the vacated space overhead.

The worm's gastrointestinal contents flood onto Nuno's lower half and he retches violently. From behind the tears in his eyes the world is just refracted energy that never forms solids. In a positive, however, the slime around his abdomen acts as lubricant and he is excreted by and from the tube, the sewagey afterbirth following closely behind to drench him in postnatal humiliation.

Nuno rises out of that elemental mire. Slow and unsteady, like the recently undead or a supernatural swamp being. He staggers forward. One foot in front of the other is all he has ability for now. He reaches the meeting point. No Solomon yet, if ever. He sits and rests his head on a nearby metal container. Some rust flakes off and adheres to his face. His many wounds are deep and filled with mud and shit. Better to have not been born into this world in the second place, he thinks.

The Pork kick off amid flashing bulbs and the Cowboys' returner takes a knee in the end zone to the delight of the almost unanimously pro-Pork crowd. In Nina's owner's box is Worthington Gill with Jenkins and another attendant and assorted other Pork personnel and family members. Nina is in a partitioned section of the box with the only person she'll consent to have near her, Dia. The radio game call is audible. Nina checks the sky again.

"Sunniest day of the winter too. Even God's against us."

"Coach Elkins wanted the grounds crew to inundate the field yesterday so their offensive line would have trouble getting traction. I said you wouldn't approve. Was that right?"

"It was, because I'm an idiot."

The Cowboys take the ball at their twenty. On first down they hand to their halfback, who runs to his right and towards the intended gap between his all-world guard and tackle. The violent collision of helmets and pads, the sound of breath being involuntarily expelled, groans of pain and frustration. By the time the Cowboy runner arrives at the line of scrimmage his guard and tackle have practically subsumed the Pork player across from them. He easily gains twelve yards before Reeves brings him down by his ankles.

This is a sequence that is repeated without fail on this initial drive of the game. Without having to even risk a pass or facing so much as a third down, the Cowboys repeatedly hand the ball to their running back, who every time seems to run for at least four yards before a Pork player can even make contact with him, so massive and skilled is the Cowboys' offensive line and so physically overmatched is the Pork defense. Soon the Cowboys are at the Pork fifteen on second and three.

This is precisely the kind of physical domination those of us in the know expected, Jim.

Another run right up the gut for twelve and that Cowboys running back gets up laughing and taunting. Before the next play, the Cowboys' center tells the Pork defensive line the exact location of the run called. When his running back then runs in that exact direction but untouched into the end zone, he has made his point. Evident on the Pork sideline is not frustration but something like fear that they may be powerless to in any way slow this epic embarrassment.

"They just need to adjust to the shock of that level of play," Nina says. "Couple first downs here and we'll be okay."

She says these things more to herself than anyone else, which is fitting because Dia doesn't hear any of it.

After a kickoff through the end zone, the Pork have the ball at their twenty. They hand the ball to Sims, who is hit almost before he can even take the handoff for a loss of three yards. On second down the player across from the Pork center drives him back so quickly at the snap that the center can't really transfer the ball to Harris, resulting in a fumble that Harris desperately recovers amid much physical abuse.

"Third and long, damn."

Harris drops back to pass but is given no time. He has to throw the ball away before his receiver has come out of his break. Following the incompletion, two Cowboys defenders appear to take an extra step or two before unloading vicious hits on Harris, who flies backward and bangs the back of his head on the turf as he lands. Nina winces.

"Something we forgot to note is that the Global Bowl is being officiated by IFL not NFL referees. Unlike the NFL, the IFL does not take steps to protect its quarterbacks above other players and what you just saw there is rarely called a penalty whereas in the NFL it would probably result in a roughing the passer penalty and fifteen yards."

"That's bad news for Harris, Jim. At forty-four I wouldn't expect him to be able to take too many more of those. This ain't the Albuquerque Armadillos anymore."

"Also means Tom Laney is going to have to take those hits as well though."

"Well, I suspect the Cowboys will do a far better job of protecting their quarterback on the rare occasion they even have to pass. Remember that their first drive featured eight runs and no passes."

After a barely executed punt, the Cowboys have the ball at their forty. Three more violently successful running plays ensue, during which a Pork tibia is shattered, a Pork Achilles is ruptured, and the ball is placed at the Pork thirty. Nina has seen enough.

"Move the safeties up even more, this is humiliating!"

Whether coincidentally or not, that's exactly what Elkins does. Mutola and his partner at safety are in the box within seven yards of the line of scrimmage. Laney sees this and audibles into a passing play. At the snap, the Pork cornerback (Banks not Reeves) misses his jam at the line. The Cowboys receiver streaks right by him down the sideline and Laney lofts a perfect pass to him in the end zone to give the Cowboys a two-touchdown lead.

When the Pork get the ball again, it's just more of the same. Sims has nowhere to go on runs and on passes Harris either gets sacked or leveled violently the second he releases the ball. After one particularly violent hit, the hitter tauntingly tells Harris not to bother getting up, that at his age his health is more important than any game. Harris doesn't respond and it takes a while for him to meekly get up.

This is true futility. And what's responsorially building in the air now is a kind of generalized obloquy. Question is how to specialize it and whom to direct it at with assaultive vigor. Although not too hard to identify the two *ladies* responsible for putting poor Paterson directly in the crosshairs of another ignominious calamity. Right about now the town wants to skip the guilt phase and go right to fixing a penalty for these two shapely rogues.

Mentally, Nuno is at the end of a skewer. The flesh on his face is falling off and dropping into a waiting cauldron below that sizzles when fed. His face is disintegrating off the poker, which then starts stabbing at the remaining flesh in attempted reconciliation.

He opens his eyes. His visual field is at first dominated by the end of a stick that grows and recedes, grows and recedes, but offers no informational content. Who is he? Or what? What's his name for example?

"Nuno!"

No, that can't be it. But the other end of that stick. *That* he knows is Solomon. Solomon is a saint really, if you give it more than a moment's consideration. Look at him there. An angelic emblem of freedom. Not subject to human foibles or frailty. No past-tense acts that can disinter at any moment to harm the present. Fitting that this will be his last earthly sight.

"Let's go, man! You alive or what?"

He is, but none of this is really signifying properly. Now Solomon is literally dragging him in a way, rolling him down the slight hill towards the concealed vessel.

"Get in the water, man. Get in to snap out of this."

He does and starts to sink and probably drown and Solomon can't believe he came all this way just to watch this and is that actual shit on his hands now?

Except that after a bit Nuno's head pops up. He climbs into the decrementing boat. He is perfectly nude having stripped underwater and the shedding means a cold so hostile to life that he has just traded one kind of death for another. Solomon doesn't know where to look. He just tosses Nuno the waterproof bag of clothes and starts to drive. Is it called driving when it's a boat?

On their third possession the violent assault of the Cowboys continues. No one is laying a finger on QB Laney the few times he even has to pass and fairly soon they are inside the Pork ten threatening to take a three-touchdown lead.

"If you're a defender of the IFL or the Pork this has to be embarrassing. They're not even competitive."

"The effort is certainly there, they just seemed overmatched really."

"It's not over yet, gentlemen. Still thirteen minutes to go in the first half."

As he speaks the Cowboys' running back is carrying two Pork players into the end zone.

"Okay, it's over."

"Twenty to nothing Cowboys and this crowd is stunned. Now look at this! Coach Tesseract is leaving his offense out there to go for two with a twenty-point lead. The handoff to Jacobs and he is in! Twenty-two to nothing, Cowboys."

"Just when you thought it couldn't get more embarrassing for the Pork, Jim, Coach Tesseract finds a way."

"Can we change this, please?" Solomon asks of the portable satellite radio Nuno insisted on.

"No. To what even?"

"Oh, I don't know, to the news maybe? See if they're freaking out about two lunatics escaping Rikers on a half-assed boat?"

"Does it matter, Sol?"

"Matters a hell of a lot more than this dopey mismatch!"

"The game has metaphysical import." Nuno is shivering his way to death.

"Aw, not that again."

But, yes, that again. Like a deathbed confession and through a brain-fever haze, Nuno details how despite the absence of causation the game is like an announcement and how he fully expects to find the Theorist there at the Great Falls thinking he's some kind of master of closing ceremonies. And is this really the fastest this thing can go to try and prevent it?

Here Sol's a little bit insulted because truth is he knocked it out of the park with how fast this thing is, evident to anyone observing how, like a veloce missile, it savagely cuts through the immanent black. Cuts through, but nothing on the other side except more black. No orientation in time or space. No promise or hope. Although that also means no disappointment.

No observer either. Just you to, in a sense, confirm its reality.

At twenty-two to nothing the stadium, and the world it's a part of, senses a developing atrocity. Still, there's an inevitable optimism that comes with lining up to take a kickoff. The ball will soon be ours and who's to say we can't do great things with it?

Except that here before the optimism can even begin to swell, the Cowboys are attempting an audacious onside kick, one they recover insultingly easily. The Pork sideline is funereal. The Cowboys' offensive line is coming back out, literally laughing.

In the owner's booth Nina is shaking her head and not really daring to watch as Laney delivers a perfect pass to his tight end in the seam that goes to the Pork two before Mutola drags him down. First and goal at the two for the Cowboys.

"What have I done?" she laments.

In a frantic audible compelled by a secretive source, the refs call an official time-out. What'll follow will be the longest commercial break in televised sports history as various corporate entities scramble to air their commercials while any eyeballs at all remain available.

The man-made starlight overwhelms them. They've progressed out of Queens's waters and into the solar shock of Manhattan's. The tip of that island lures them magnetically and Solomon even slows as if deferring to gravitation.

"Some people look at natural beauty or deep space and feel small," he says. "That's a far more appropriate reaction to something like this, don't you think? I mean, look at it! Who did this? It sure as shit wasn't me. What have *I* done? What will I do? Worse, what will I have done?"

"You will have accelerated this boat if you want to keep doing."

"I thought you were sensitive, man. No reaction?"

"I feel like the wisest man in the universe. Not because I know I don't know anything, but because I know there's nothing to know. These bells and whistles. The pretense of critical activity. Shouts into a void and I feel the ultimate victory of silence as it builds all around us."

"But it's not truth at large, man. It's just your internal state. Because to look at you, swear to Christ, you're fucking dying. We need to cancel this whole thing and get your ass to a hospital."

"Lost your mind? Get me to the falls, you can all thank me for saving your lives later."

"You're delusional, man. Everything you been through? It's understandable. But I've recently communed intimately with the dead myself, brother, and chain of command is chain of command and our destination is that ridiculous stadium for our bread."

"Chain of what now?"

"Command, bro. Every seafaring vessel can have but one captain and this captain's not gonna let you get all Ahab about some ridiculous end of days time's running out bullshit when we're this close to a god-damn yearlong epic score."

"We're only close if I'm wrong."

"You want proof of that, being wrong? You yourself said the Pork have to win."

"So?"

"So have you been missing the part where they're getting forcibly sodomized on the field of play by the best football team that ever lived? They ain't winning shit. Twenty-two to zilch and fucking Tes-seract is clowning them with onside kicks, two-point conversions, and other assorted embarrassments."

"Good point maybe."

"See? Feel better?"

"No."

"Great, let's go get our fucking dough re mi."

Cowboys with the ball, first and goal at the Pork two, when play finally resumes. On first down, for the first time all game, the Cowboys' run-ning back is hit in the backfield for a loss. The crowd barely reacts, what's the point? When a similar play occurs on second down though, the crowd stirs a bit; and when on third down the Pork manage to stop the Cowboys at about the half-yard line the crowd is maybe even defiant for the first time.

But not as defiant as Tesseract, who decides his team will go for it on fourth down in yet another thinly veiled slap in the face at the Pork. The crowd is genuinely energized by events on the field. Could the lowly, put-upon, and impotent Pork be about to strike their first effective blow? And struck on whose behalf?

The fourth-down play call, in an apparent concession that the Pork cannot just be easily overpowered anymore, is a fade into the right corner of the end zone. The pass is good but Reeves blankets his receiver and at the last possible second gets his hand in between the receiver's two to knock the ball away. Reeves shakes his head negatively to the receiver, who points to the scoreboard as they get in each other's faces. The Pork have somehow held and will get possession of the ball at their one with five minutes to play in the half.

They're in Newark Bay, among a great many other things the final resting place of the powdered parts of Elsie Heredia. Until now Solomon has been able to convince himself that he and Nuno are like representatives of early man boldly penetrating uncharted waters to set new boundaries for future aggressions. What now kills that illusion is the detritus of a species consuming itself.

Moving north, from the union of the Passaic and Hackensack rivers to following just the Passaic, Nuno unconscious but his chest heaving to confirm his continued existence, Solomon can accurately say he is abob some of the most polluted water on the globe. The primary smell is of chemicals dying and this modern River Styx is threatening to consumptively eat away at the boat until it's just him and Nuno swimming in flames.

Then there's the fact that they are now moving against nature and this subtle change in flow has slowed their ascension to the point that the vessel's engine is smoking and complaining. If Nuno ever comes to he'll humor him and say they're going to Paterson Falls. Where's the harm? The Great Falls is as likely as Shangri-la the way they're looking.

First and ten, Pork. After halfhearted play action, Major takes a deep drop into the end zone. The offensive line is immediately under siege but somehow holds up long enough for him to deliver a perfect pass over the middle to his tight end for twenty. This is the Pork's first first down. They are out of the shadow of their end zone and the crowd is getting louder.

On the next play, the players seem more relaxed as they execute a perfect halfback screen to Sims that goes for twenty-five to almost midfield.

"Perfect call," says Nina in the owner's box, allowing herself for the moment that this might not be the most mortifying day of her professional life.

Maybe the crowd, maybe the first experience of any success, but the Pork seem energized as Sims runs hard around left tackle for nine yards. He gets up exhorting the crowd.

"The Pork showing a little life now as the crowd reacts."

"This ain't over yet, Jim, despite what Tim says."

With ten seconds left in the half the Pork are at the Cowboys' twelve. Harris drops back as two Cowboys come through unblocked. He takes a vicious hit from one but spins away to his left. Now the other player grabs him and he is struggling with him to stay up and release his throwing arm. At the last possible moment he frees the arm and manages to release a bullet into the end zone, where it is caught by a Pork receiver to make the score (following an extra point) 22–7 Cowboys.

That play was all heart and will by Harris and we, uh, the Pork, may not be dead yet!

Everyone is celebrating except Harris. Even Coach Elkins is excited as the halftime gun goes off.

"Nobody moves a goddamn muscle!" he says. "There's nothing to talk about in there! We stay right here until they come back. They need to know we're not going anywhere. We're just getting goddamn started! Nothing to goddamn talk about. It's not what we're doing that has to be changed, it's *how* we're doing it. Do it harder, stronger, *beat* them literally! No one moves."

After some initial confusion, the players stand on the sidelines. They will wait there until the Cowboys return.

"We're back and this is something you've never seen before. The Pork will apparently not go into their locker room at halftime."

"You know what, Jim? For three goddamn years NFL teams going against the Cowboys in the playoffs have gone into their locker room at halftime then come out and lost, so might as well try something different."

"Maybe so, but what comes to mind when you say that is deck chairs and the Titanic.*"*

"Hell's all that about?" a waking Nuno demands.

"This thing's about had it, man."

"No, the radio."

"Will you forget the radio, dude? We're about to sink to our watery demise here!"

"Fucking Pork scored, didn't they?"

"Yeah, big deal. They scored a touchdown. It took about seven lucky breaks and everything they could muster so now the final score will be something like fifty to seven instead of them getting shut out."

"Fucking Theorist, man."

"No, that has nothing to do with anything right now."

"We gotta go straight to the base of the falls, there'll be no time for anything else."

"Yeah, okay, whatever you say. I'm sure this fine craft will deliver us from evil to glory."

"Falls, right?"

"To the falls!"

But not much mechanical happens in response to this human roar. Because the thing really is failing. Failing to go forward at a reasonable rate and even taking on water. It's not going to make it, which means Solomon and Nuno won't either. And, yes, the motor then gasps out its final declaration to leave the living. There'll be no falls, no stadium, nothing. Nothing will be.

Solomon is placid and thinking on how they might still deliver the Dalí. Nuno is at the motor trying to resuscitate it. Suddenly he tears it off and drops it in the water to sink. Solomon feels the same way but at least he's not melting down like Nuno, who's now violently kicking at the sides of the craft until the thing's about to tip. Where's the professionalism?

"Yo!"

Now he's gone and broken it, this nut. He's pried a plank off and is breaking it in half over his knee.

"The hell, man? Calm down."

"I couldn't be calmer," Nuno says, handing him half the board. "Start paddling and I'll get even calmer."

"You crazy?"

"We're like five football fields away. Think of that preindustrial Man you're so fond of, you reckon he just floated in one spot?"

Solomon catches on and soon the thing's moving again at a decent clip. It's more than the 1800 feet of five football fields but it's a distance and distances were made to be traveled. Occasionally Nuno has to prod Sol, literally, to get him to paddle harder.

The first thing is the natural roar. These differ in kind from their artificial counterparts mainly in their independence. You listen and just know the earth's been making this complaint since way before you and will continue to do so long after.

Here, it's the sound of voluminous water crashing down from a height of eighty feet. Crashing down in constant replenishment as if powering Life itself.

Nuno and Solomon stare at it dumbly from below and appear to have relinquished even volition itself. The vestigial remains of their vessel, drifting them right into the violent teeth of this thing.

"Steer, man!"

"You see this dude anywhere?"

"Hell you talking about?" Then he jumps into the water.

This is only somewhat strange to Nuno, who in truth has been expecting precisely this kind of mental breakdown. But he snaps out of it just in time to see Solomon's wisdom. It's either jump off or get flushed. He jumps.

The two of them swimming, if you can call it that, in icy water. They canine their way to the edge somehow, Nuno overcoming Solomon's head start and arriving first ashore.

From there they watch their once proud vessel suffer extreme aquatic abuse. Beset and battered, every time it looks like it might escape another swell is there to smack it back into the liquid fusillade. Here and there a small piece will break off and escape the whirlpool until it's all just small pieces heading to Newark, no evidence they ever constituted a larger whole.

"The Dalí to a watery grave," says Nuno.

"Christ, Nuno, give me more credit than that." He is untying something from his waist and now holds up the two fused watertight tubes from before. "I'd sooner go to my own grave."

Nuno is impressed and Solomon's grateful to have a plaudit to savor as he is abashedly realizing the whole Falls versus Stadium controversy has been senseless since the stadium appears to be about five hundred feet from where they're standing.

"We can walk from here, let's go."

They are ascending stairs, natural and man-made, to street level, but Nuno is going half steam at best.

"The hell, man? Let's go! This how you move towards three million?"

"Don't get it, where is he?"

"He's at home watching the game, or he's at CERN, or he's at a different facility because he's a mental patient and not at all who you think he is!"

"No, I watched him walk out."

"Fine, I believe that *you believe* you saw that. Under a haze of psychotropic medication! After solitary confinement, a medieval practice that will one day be outlawed! Forgive me if I favor reality over your severely-damaged-at-the-time perceptual skills."

"No, the math works. Works today when I'm perfectly lucid."

"What are you, Sir Fig Newton? Here's what works! This goddamn Dalí that's going to get us three million but only if we get to that stadium now!"

"I don't know."

"I do! I know that money's there. I know that woman you never shut up about is there. That's right, motherfucker! Dia Nouveau, you see her here? She's in the very same luxury box we have tickets to. Want to see her or stare at these rocks?"

Nuno takes one last look around then follows Solomon towards the stadium. He can't deny his own fundamental weirdness, so who's to say? Of course he'd feel a hell of a whole lot better about his decision but for a fleeting sight out of the corner of his eye as they lose visual contact with the area: a seeming halo of white hair bobbing up and down then descending in the direction of what feels like the base of the falls.

The halftime entertainment is Radiohead. They seem surprised as anyone as they mill on a stage at midfield playing "Paranoid Android." The Pork remain on the sideline as instructed, exhausted and watching through pain. In the owner's box, Nina and Dia aren't really speaking or eating or much of anything really.

At 3:33 of the song it would appear the song is over after a flurry of electrical guitar activity. But now lead singer Thom Yorke has an acoustic guitar in his hand and he and some bandmates are singing melismatic aahs.

The tonic C minor chord but a shifting tonality between that and D minor and things have slowed too.

Everyone at Hinchliffe is silent. The sky is darkening. Dia looks up at it with mounting awe.

"Radiohead's going to make it rain," she says.

Rain on Paterson and all its denizens and from a great height.

♫   ♫
Come on rain down . . . on me
♫   ♫

Players and fans start to sense it. They turn their palms up to feel drops of water. It mounts and the cheering too and both growing apace.

Solomon and Nuno are a block away and Solomon can be said to be freaking out a bit.

"Oh, man. This is that insane rain from Hard Island following my ass here. This shit's about to get real."

"Relax, it's rain."

"You don't understand, this rain's not playing. Shit's about to liquefy everything you know and hold dear."

They can hear the music but are stopped at the gate. Even though they have two passes that say they're entitled to admission to the owner's box, security is rightly suspicious.

A torrential downpour indeed begins. Radiohead is not dissuaded.

♫   ♫

God loves his children, yeah

♫   ♫

The ground is becoming soft mud. It is either raining everywhere on the globe or only above this stadium. Regardless, this kind of rain emulsifies what it lands on and makes it easier for the weak to resist the powerful.

The Cowboys smugly return to the field determined to prove that the touchdown just before the half was a fluke.

"I don't understand the words you are speaking, we demand immediate admittance as specified by these floppy yellow laminated passes!"

"Excuse me, sirs. If you'll just be patient while I confirm. Your names again?"

"Funny, I don't see the part on these passes saying you need to confirm. So I'm curious what's driving this insulting skepticism."

"What's driving it is you two look like something the cat refused to touch long enough to drag in."

"Only because your negligence has exposed us to the elements, good sir!"

"Names?"

"Once again, I am Solomon Gill and my suddenly tight-lipped cohort here is Nuno Entrapagin . . . son . . . stein! We are Nina Gill's nephews and I for one cannot wait until she hears how you treated her family. Imagine, her only nephews left to absorb the full wrath of Mother Nature's hydrodioxide vengeance!"

"Protocol is protocol, sir."

"Good, you absolutely should start working on your defense. And make it a vigorous one, let me tell you. Because I'm sure you've heard how our aunt's known for her generous patience."

He's citing a phenomenon well known to the listener.

"Fine, just go!"

And they do, working their way through the concourse, negotiating crowds formed by fans seeking shelter from the deluge, their ultimate goal of the owner's box never farther for being near.

The Pork take a knee on the second-half kickoff. On their first play, Sims takes a handoff and, like a man possessed, breaks three or four tackles for fifteen yards. The piped-in radio call is haunting Nuno, who just wants to feel confident in the obvious Cowboy win.

You can analyze your cover-two-zone blitzes all you want, Jim. But I know one thing, pigs love freaking mud!

Harris takes two more vicious hits on consecutive plays and upstairs Nina wonders what happened to max protect that suddenly we're using empty set. What she doesn't know is that now Harris is calling his own plays after steamrolling Elkins into agreement. This is the equivalent of a protracted suicide by collision.

Third and thirteen at midfield. The Pork have to find some way to keep this drive alive.

Seeing nothing downfield, Harris is forced to swing a pass out to one of his small receivers for about five yards, well short of the first down. The receiver is hit immediately but manages to keep his feet. He struggles free just as a second defender blasts him. He still fights forward, however, and, even after a third defender joins in, manages to drag the far bigger men about four yards forward, where he fully extends his right hand with the ball to barely cross the marker. First down! The crowd appreciates this to say the least. The drive will continue, the rain shows no signs of abating.

Nuno and Solomon are lost. They don't realize they've passed the owner's box thrice and are actually closer to where they first came in than anywhere else.

Meanwhile, the Pork just keep barely extending their drive with the clock continually running until they arrive at the Cowboys' five-yard line and a pivotal fourth and goal. They must decide whether to kick the field goal to make it 22–10 or go for it on fourth down.

Overseeing it all, Nina wants to go for it. Eleven minutes are gone and being down twelve's not sufficiently better than being down fifteen. Also, at least go down defiantly.

Harris drops back as Sims picks up a violent blitzer. With all the congestion of a drastically reduced field there is no one even arguably open. In desperation Harris pulls down the ball and starts running, first up the middle then, after crossing the line of scrimmage, to his right, where there's fleeting daylight. Seemingly the entire Cowboys defense is now converging near the goal line as Harris approaches. Seeing no other option, Major leaps into the air, where several players unload on him, spinning him like a helicopter blade until he lands on his head and right shoulder in the end zone for a painful touchdown. The main environmental reaction is shock.

"The extra point is good and how many people would've predicted the Pork would be down only eight at this late stage of the game?"

"They still have to show they can stop Laney and the Cowboys' offense, Jim, and I don't think they can."

"You may be right but I'll venture that the soaked people in this arena are starting to think they can and that may just be enough."

Nuno doesn't really care what everyone around him is feeling. His feeling is that this isn't really very funny anymore. A one-score game going into the fourth is not funny. So when he sees someone walk by who definitely has never worked a day in his life he instinctively grabs Solomon and they follow him. Right to the goddamn owner's box as he suspected.

Once there, it's security problems again. But this time Nuno handles it, telling the lackey to tell Ms. Gill her special delivery is here but that there's a special instruction requiring COD or the package is to be marked "absent." Exactly like that, the lackey is told. This gets them into an anteroom of sorts, where Nuno asks Solomon to level with him.

"I look like shit, right?"

"Well, we emerged from a literal cesspool so, yeah, pretty much."

Nuno's thinking maybe get the money tonight and see Dia tomorrow, assuming there is one. The lackey comes back in and says to hang tight.

"They're giving us the runaround, bro!"

"Easy, Sol. She *is* currently engaged in maybe the most important football game ever played."

"I don't buy it. Look here, my man." He is prying open one of the canisters. "Your boss is going to be mighty happy indeed when she casts her eyes on *this*!" And he promptly pulls out a withered severed arm.

"Oh, shit!" he yelps and drops the black stump as the lackey rushes out screaming bloody security.

"Yeah, I was gonna say, I think you're opening the wrong one."

"Fuck! Now what?"

"Now security escorts us out and you answer questions about what you're doing with that little treat there."

But it's Nina instead who walks in.

"You two sure have a way of announcing yourselves. Tell me why I should care, you may have noticed I'm a bit occupied at the moment."

The extreme beauty of this woman, her preternatural self-possession. Solomon is literally struck dumb. Nuno is not.

"If you're busy we could come back later," he says. "Or we could just go to Stamp instead, since truth is it's costing us money selling to you and not him. Is your deputy here? Maybe she can handle our transaction."

"I see no evidence of a potential transaction. Where's the star of our show?"

In one motion, Nuno drops his outermost garment to cover the severed limb and picks up the correct cylinder. When he then pulls *Adolescence* out, the room, especially Nina, lights up. She is inspecting it closely, her face is flushed.

"Okay," she says.

"So?"

"So the money's close by. Wait here and soon as the game ends we'll conclude our *business*, albeit funny business, relationship."

Solomon is objecting nonverbally but Nuno is acquiescing and taking back possession of the painting.

"Now if you'll excuse me, I'd like to get back to winning a global championship."

"Oh, one more thing."

"Yes?"

"The price has gone up."

"I don't think so."

"It's now three plus some dry clothes."

"We can do that. On one condition."

"Which is?"

"Stay away from my . . . deputy."

Fourth quarter. Cowboys have the ball but Tom Laney is frustrated. The Cowboys' running game has been hurt by the mud. Forced to pass and with Reeves and Banks effectively jamming his receivers at the line, he must hold the ball longer than he wishes and as a result he is getting hit with alarming frequency by players who are not showing him the deferential respect he's grown accustomed to in the NFL.

Finally, from about midfield, he is going for it all in an attempt to end the game. With Reeves running stride for stride with his receiver he nonetheless uncorks a deep post pattern. Mutola is charged with over-the-top help but he has bit on a tight end crossing pattern designed to draw him forward and free the deep middle. As the ball is released, Mutola realizes his mistake, adjusts, and breaks deep.

Reeves is with the receiver but the receiver has inside position and the ball appears to be perfectly thrown. At the last moment Mutola gets in position and despite a push in the back from the receiver jumps up and makes a spectacular one-handed interception ending the Cowboys' drive.

Harris promptly completes three downfield passes (absorbing a vicious hit after each) and the Pork are at the Cowboys' forty.

Following an incompletion on third and eight, Harris takes another hit and when he rises to go to the sideline his right arm is limp by his side from an injured shoulder. The rain has subsided.

Elkins sends out the field goal unit.

"Not sure about this decision, a fifty-eight-yarder in these conditions seems like a tall order."

"No taller than what's transpired to this point, Jim! I say the little prick makes it."

"Okay, well, I hope the delay was working on that one as Donald Grimm, the Pork kicker, is gonna line it up when we come back with five minutes to play and his team down eight."

Dia and Nina only somewhat commit to watching this. Travis

appears in the doorway and Dia decides she wants to settle that thing first before watching her professional dreams disintegrate. But first:

"Can our kicker even make it from fifty-eight?" she asks Nina.

"*Can* is a strange word, I guess he *can*."

Dia takes Travis to a privatey corner of the box. She informs him that regardless of what transpires in the next five football minutes, whether she becomes an in-demand star or a penciled-in footnote, she will be getting in a car and putting a lot of varied asphalt under its tires. She couldn't help this little bit of base poetry but immediately recognizes its ill-advisedness. Point is, Travis, whatever she does here-after, she will do alone in peripatetic solitude.

What's terrible is when Travis reacts as if receiving a literal blow. As in he actually drops to one knee and his eyes tear up, an objectively reasonable reaction given everything Dia but, to her, over the top. She channels Nina and together they conclude that this is unfortunate but also confirmatory. And understand, Travis, that this is not personal; there's not a person in the world she would link herself to right now (untrue). The very imminent FGA gives everyone involved a much-valued excuse to terminate this frankly brutal exchange.

Nina, Dia, and Pork-based others have their faces basically pressed against the glass for this weird kick that decides nothing conclusively but still feels symbolically rich. The kick is up and it travels like a wounded bird of some sort. It does not stop traveling, however, until it lands on the wet crossbar and skids over for three points. 22-17 Cowboys and the television broadcast of the game is focused on the incredulous face of their coach.

In the adjoining room, Nuno sees it on the TV, throws his hands up, then puts his head in them. Leading up to this, Solomon had grown introspective while Nuno furiously vacillated. Solomon had been doing that thing, for the last time, where he engages in solilo-quized narrative rumination for the seeming benefit of no one.

"Can you believe it, man? Think where we were, Nuno. And now this shit is really happening. Three large, I gotta say, you are one bad man. Don't think on it too much, bro, just enjoy it. That feeling, yo. Motherfucker, I went through literal hell, understand? On that island, man. I feel like I know what it is to die now, dig? What's left in this world for me to fear? When you've seen it empty its bowels on you like that? Look who I'm talking to. You know better than anyone. They shouldn't a did you like they did with that solitary, man. That's the one thing they can't do to people. Kind of move fuck someone's shit up good. But you just absorbed that blow whole, man. Then transmogrified it and whatnot into gold, three million dollars' worth! We been through a lot together, dude. That's a bond not so easy to break. Feels like we won't be going through a lot more though now. Rich people don't have adventures like we did, right? Traversing those troubled waters, the world trying to capsize us. It wanted to swallow us whole, man! Motherfuckers. Fuck all of them really. Not all of them, I guess. That crazy chaplain was all right. I mean, Jesus freak and all, but the good kind, you know? Y'ever wonder about someone like that poor sap? No women or drink or crime or running away or any of the other finer things. All the poor saps of the world, man. Wish I could give them all three large."

Nuno heard none of this because he'd just before seen the kind of sight that reduces you to a blank. He hadn't been sure whether he even wanted to see her. But the repeated sound of her voice, like musical notes from a siren. What's the right time and scenario for a revelation like this? Then he peered in, saw her face, and a concept like *right time* became immediately senseless.

How can faces be so unique? So many of them awash in the world you'd expect massive repetition. Instead each somehow manages its particularized story, no two exactly alike, a stunning fact that no one but Nuno seems all that stunned by. That perfect face? Thank God only Dia has it because it melts him and everything around him.

When he recovers, the enormity of the moment strangles him in a way that breaking out of jail and all his other assorted mayhem hadn't. He knows that going into that room might cost him millions. That it may result in his return to jail. But he also knows that in many ways Dia Nouveau is what his entire life's been about. He sees her, he can't help *but*. He is staring. What he cannot quite believe is that she will soon see him. Maybe she's about to say, *Great to see you again, move on, pal.* Who knows?

He knows, that's who. He knows Dia wouldn't do that, not to him.

That some version of what he's going through is soon to flood over her and that their mutuality will then suspend every other process the world over. That she will remember he's a mess, but also that he'd never let that mess get on her. Or maybe he's not even a mess anymore.

When he starts to walk into the room he sees the vilest thing he's ever seen and this is a guy with quite a list of extreme visions. Some gangly guy is on one knee in front of Dia with tears in his eyes and shock in hers. Nuno recoils as if witnessing a spontaneous live vivisection. This must be that pig mascot guy. Dia Nouveau, *the* Dia Nouveau, is going to marry some guy who dresses up like a pig?

This revelation tilts the globe and not in a favorable way. There's only one possible reaction to this. Dia cannot marry Porkboy. This is easy enough to accomplish. Show her your face and proceed from there, he thinks.

But he never does. He just keeps thinking how unlikely it is that what's best for Dia aligns with what's best for him, or even with what he desperately needs. Is it true that the sight of him would likely derail, as in the movies, their suboptimal nuptial plan? It feels true.

But it also feels selfish. If there's such a thing as deserve, maybe Dia deserves some pussy who gets on his knee and cries from the emotion of proposing. To be loyal and pusillanimous and uncomplicated. And best of all predictable. Nuno? No one deserves that.

That decisive inaction leaves Nuno to it. The desolation of being the only person left in the world, all that love in vain. Dreaming of loneliness and sounding thoughts into a silencing void. Dying alone. When the ridiculous kick then went through the goalposts it was like a confirmation. But knowing what's coming is like another form of freedom so he just sits there calmly to watch more of the ignorant dance of elapsing time.

When the Cowboys get the ball back, after said field goal that no one has yet fully processed, they get several first downs that partially deflate what was an insane crowd. Now it's third and four for the Cowboys at the Pork twenty-two with a minute fifty seconds to play. The rain has stopped, is that an emerging moon?

Just before the snap, Dylan Reeves seems uninterested. He's just staring. Actually he is recognizing something in the formation the Cowboys have lined up in for this critical play. Countless hours of film study have allowed him to pick up on the small detail that is the tight end's particular positioning of his feet. He believes the play will call for his man to run an immediate slant that will clear the area for their tight end to run a six-yard out. The defense they're in calls for man-to-man but when the first steps of the Cowboys at the snap seem to confirm his suspicion, Reeves decides to gamble. Timing it perfectly, he waits until Laney commits to the throw, leaves his receiver alone, and streaks as fast as possible to the place where the pass should be. He is right and makes an easy interception that he manages to return to the Cowboys' forty-five!

Down only five, the Pork have the ball on the Cowboys' side of the field with a chance to take the lead. After two successful passes by Harris, the ball is incredibly at the Cowboys' twelve with forty-two seconds to play. How is any of this happening?

The call is a draw to Sims, who takes the ball to his left and finds a nice opening. He appears to have a fairly clear path to the end zone and a Pork victory. The fans erupt in cheers, Nina and Dia rise in expectation, and behind the play Major raises his hands to signal what is about to occur.

But at about the four Sims forgets himself and allows the football to extend away from his body in his left hand. A Cowboys cornerback, engaged in a block and unable to make the tackle, reaches his left hand out and is able to poke the ball loose just before Sims crosses the goal line. A pileup ensues but the Cowboys have recovered the ball.

A near-catatonic Sims is walking back to the sideline joined by Harris, who pats him on the helmet.

Oh, God bless his soul, Sims must be sick. After struggling with fumbles last year, he had not fumbled once this season.

The crowd is horrified. In the owner's booth, Mutola's son is crying. Dia's eyes are welling up with tears.

"It's not over," Nina says despite knowing it is. "We have all our time-outs left. If we stop them we can get the ball back with about fifteen seconds left."

On the Cowboys' sideline, players are celebrating and the coaches are congratulating each other. Many fans are gathering their possessions. While this is occurring, the Cowboys have gained nine yards on three carries, each followed by an immediate Pork time-out. After a Cowboys punt and a short return, the Pork take over at the fifty, down five with sixteen seconds to play and no time-outs. Nina was accidentally right, it wasn't over.

In the Pork huddle, Major Harris can barely speak he is so damaged but he manages to exhale his words through clenched teeth.

"Still time, ladies. Don't even think of quitting. Get out of bounds if you can, but if not we have to rush into a spike play. 49 Z out 82 seam on three, break."

Harris drops back. He's looking to make a sideline throw but the Cowboys know this and are only allowing passes to the middle of the field, where the clock will keep running and time will keep disappearing. Finally, no choice, Major releases a pass over the middle (taking a shot to his right shoulder immediately after) and his receiver takes it to the Cowboys' twenty. But the clock is running!

Now the Pork are desperately rushing to the line to spike the ball and stop the clock. 8 . . . 7 . . . 6. The clock is at three when the Pork snap it and Harris instantly spikes it with his left hand to stop the clock with 0:01 to play.

"Harris spiked that with his left! I think his throwing shoulder's shot, Jim!"

"The Pork have time for one last play from the twenty, anything short of a touchdown and they lose the game!"

The Cowboys' defensive players have relaxed expecting an offensive huddle by the Pork. Harris, however, has kept his team at the line of scrimmage and is signaling the play from there. He is signaling with his left hand as his right hangs limply at his side. The face mask on his helmet has become partially detached.

The snap and Harris drops back holding the ball, by necessity, with two hands. He has time at first but then the pocket breaks down once again. He is buying time and limping to his left.

Just before the Cowboys can deliver the knockout blow he spots something. Taking the ball in just his right hand he brings it back and throws it as hard as he can, screaming in agony as he does since it feels as if his arm's just been detached from its socket.

The millisecond the ball is released a Cowboys defender launches himself forward helmet-first into Harris's face mask. The face mask gives way on impact and the defender's helmet goes right through into Harris's face to shatter his nose, bounce his brain off his skull, and resect substantial parts of his lips.

But Harris was just able to follow through and the resulting ball is a perfectly tight spiral slicing through the air towards the back left corner of the end zone. A well-covered Pork receiver is in the area but he is quickly running out of room in which to make the play.

The defender reaches up and slightly tips the pass, redirecting it a bit into the face of the intended receiver. The receiver quickly manages to raise his right hand and wedge the ball against his neck. The defender immediately pulls that hand off the ball but the receiver then uses his head to pin the ball to his shoulder. His left foot lands inbounds just inside the sideline and he contorts his body to tap the right toe seemingly inbounds. As he falls out-of-bounds he turns his body to show the referee that he has controlled the ball the entire time without his hands but using his helmet and shoulder pad.

The referee jogs towards the goal line to make the call that will immediately decide the winner as there is no instant replay. After a seeming eternity he raises both hands and signals touchdown and a Pork victory of 23–22.

Delirium, but not pure because almost scary in its illogic.

Harris is unconscious on the ground, it's not that he will never remember this, it's more that he never experienced it in the first place.

The Pork Win the Global! The Fucking Pork Win the Global!

Nuno is running.

The crowd is spilling onto the field. A great undulant beast. Spilling everywhere and possibly even growing as it flows outward like a superkinetic wave. Larry Brown and Hugh Seaborg and Nelson and his cousins and Donnie with a giant foam finger and Simon in his collar and every other Patersonite who'd squeezed into that enclosure expecting so little, all now components of that wave. The sound of car horns and the sight of people coming out of their homes just to feel the air.

Nuno is running in fits and starts, narrowly avoiding atomic collisions, not always clear on his direction.

The rest here is a kind of samizdat-threnody; its author obvious but the network or other means by which it was preserved then disseminated not overly clear:

Second he released that pass I felt I knew what was up. Ball's in the air and I'm booking out of there, trying in my head to estimate the distance back to the falls. Problem was everything to that point, everything except Dia, was in a soft-focus haze. Now I had superpowers of perception but all they helped me see was obstacles everywhere. It felt like people were being poured all over me by some evil puppet master, anything to keep me from my destination. I had the thought that we're all just billiard balls anyway, even destined for the same pocket. But that only energized me to fight my way through even harder.

Coming out of that mess I hit the street outside the stadium with no concept of where to next. I realized I'd only followed Solomon before, not really aware of what surrounded me. I looked up through the pandemonium and saw the temporary eyes of the GL©BAL B©WL sign staring back down at me. It was this sight I'd first seen earlier with Solomon so by moving myself to match that initial vision I was able to orient myself to the proper course.

I also knew I was right because I was running fast as I could and tangibly sensed the world opening up in a way. I knew it was just that I was moving away from crowded architecture towards open nature but I swear it also felt like some postmortal drift into a new reality. I thought how my one-sided view of Dia before was what it must be like to die, continue to exist, and watch the living move on. Reason enough to reject the Ventimiglias of the world, if not on the merits then on aesthetics.

I reached the falls and saw nothing. I don't mean that I didn't see anything, I mean that I affirmatively saw Nothing.

But then life emerged from it. First I saw was the hair. Down at the base of the falls like a spectral unnatural charge. I screamed down to him to freeze, which sounded stupid even to me and even before the *z* sound could resolve. At any rate, he didn't. He looked up at me and maybe smirked. I was a good distance away.

Descending into this hole, everything drenched so that several times I almost lost all tactile control and plunged straight to the violent bottom, the Theorist, maybe just Dr. Epstein, growing larger in my sight and now maybe actually frozen for all the movement he expressed, I was suddenly overcome by the sensation that I was in a performance, but one without an audience, so therefore empty.

I fell a few times. Probably broke some things, tore others. My wounds were serious but it was more the psychic harm I'd suffered in the luxury box, that horrid sight.

I somehow got to where he was at the base.

The sound was cacophonic. The volume of rainwater had been extreme and now the swollen river felt it could inundate the world starting with us two. I had to scream.

"The hell, man? Don't do it!"

"You are some sight. This world, I'll give it to it, full of surprises. Nuno, was it?"

"Still is."

"You seem badly injured. Guess it doesn't matter anymore."

I saw that in his hand was a sci-fi device of some sort and understood instantly that the fate of the very universe rested in my mangled hands.

"Don't do it, man. Don't activate that goddamn thing!"

"What, this?" he asked, raising it up in an obviously malevolent manner. "You can have it if it concerns you so much." And he tossed it high in the air at me.

I don't mind saying the pressure was extreme. The device formed its parabola and, yes, I made the visual connection to the earlier Harris ball. I tried, I knew the stakes, but it had been a physically grueling sequence and I wasn't expecting the pass. I managed, barely, to get a hand on it, but it bounced off and hit the ground. I turned away from the blast but there wasn't one. I picked it up carefully. It looked familiar but its theoretical and interstellar underpinnings remained a mystery.

"What is it? Deactivate it!"

"It's from before your time, kid. They're called transistor radios. How else would you have me monitor the game?"

I tossed it away.

"You were right about the game," I said.

"I was."

"Right about the game, and the math, and about Time."

"I was, and am."

"So now what?"

"Now we run low on Nows, sorry."

"Look, man, I've kind of forsworn violence but I can't let you do anything crazy either."

"No offense, but you don't look fit to do anything violent in your condition."

"You'd be surprised, but I'd rather talk you out of it."

"What is it you want to talk me out of?"

"I know you miss your wife and everything with her. I know, intimately and recently, what that feels like. But I don't think we get to level everything and everyone in response."

"I agree."

"Good." I was feeling better.

"What makes you think I don't?"

"Facts are facts, Doc."

"And which do you view as the most salient ones here?"

"The fact that you are standing here at Paterson Falls for one. I have a mind that tends to trap detail and one it trapped is you expecting something calamitous at this very spot in conjunction with a football result no one but you would've dreamed of, those facts."

"Yes, all true. But what I was referring to was like an opportunity. Look at it this way. What I thought would happen very likely did. It just went on ahead and happened without me. Another way of saying, of course, that from my perspective it never happened at all. Along with the sad concession that, to me, my perspective is the only one that matters. I missed the train back to Dawn Collier, the train back to life. To a very similar world where David Tyree made that catch and they're obsessed with end-of-the-world scenarios but don't know why. I will never see my wife again. There's nothing lower than that."

"Well, I'm sorry, but I'm glad to at least hear you talking in the past tense. You realize, I take it, that you have to accept this, no matter how painful. That you can't do anything drastic."

"Do you really still not get it? I know what I told you but I was never going to *do* anything. There's nothing can be done. If there was, I'd do it. I was just rhetorically advancing the conversation before when I agreed with you, because I absolutely *would* maliciously level everyone and everything extant if you told me Dawn would see me again."

"Easy, Doc. You missed this train, maybe you'll catch the next one. After all, you have a history of catching them, who else can say that?"

"No, that part of the math remains true and has even been recently confirmed. That was the last train. Ever."

"Hell's that supposed to mean?"

"It means what I told you all, way back at Bellevue. This time is running out."

"That's not a thing."

"It most certainly is and it's coming. Or leaving, I guess."

"You're saying we're all gonna die?"

"Not exactly. Dying is something that happens within Time itself. This is not that. But it's not living either."

"You seem pretty calm about it."

"Told you. Dawn Collier is in another reality. I won't bore you with the math except to say that you can't get there from here. I can't go *there* and that means that *here* I can't go any lower. There's only two states worthy of deep analysis, existence and its negation. I reject one, leaving only the other."

"What will it feel like?"

"It won't feel, feeling also relies on Time. I'm sorry, Nuno, but you hear all those people up there celebrating? I think I'm going to ascend to them and join in. Assuming I can get there in time. Just seems like a fitting way."

He turned and left and I sat on a wet rock.

Didn't really know what to do. Except I was sure I could never physically work my way back up to street level. No one was around. The sound of water clashing with more water grew louder. The moon was out and it was an unprecedented supermoon that lit everything into heightened existence. I had the feeling it was even palpably growing, fired at us to knock us off course.

Solomon had said something like the things he and I had been through had created an insuperable bond. I wondered if something like that could be true of more than seven billion people. Billions dropped into existence with no say in the matter then abandoned.

Dumbest thing people say is when they try to minimize the importance of human events or even humanity itself by pointing out the ridiculous dimension of the universe, its size and age et cetera. Dumb because we never claimed to be the physically biggest or the oldest or the most resilient. We bring intelligence and reflection and self-awareness and imaginative creativity. Only rubes value size or endurance over that.

Everything of even mild interest. Every musical passage. Every poetic phrase. Everything prosaically kind or prophetically benign. Everyone attuned to all that everything, and everyone feeding it to them. Every atom redirected to assist everybody and the many loci of consciousness preserved as a result. Every act of play or sound of mirth. Every useful speculation or moment of insight. Everything that was a beneficent thing and that was traceable to this common source existing everywhere every moment of every day. All of it now seemed of a piece. Everything was testimonial and all of it had been a form of melodic protest.

I could hear revelers above me.

I started screaming that I was down there, invisibly but undeniably.

"I'm here!" I would scream, again and again.

"I'm here," I said.

I think I wanted them to come get me so I might contribute.

But mainly, I think, even then, whispering aloud, we really just wanted it to be True.

Recursive Fissures

Ice was everywhere, with glaciers that moaned as they cracked and melted and refroze and did this often enough that the recession of one glacier in particular created a moraine that disrupted what had until then been an unimpeded river, so much a disruption that it formed a lake that later offshot into a new river that eventually reached and cascaded over a columnar collection of basalt—columns formed two hundred million years before—to create a confluent fall; and water will fall and fall there, fall without cognition or intent but fall for ten thousand years.

A Note About the Author

Sergio de la Pava is the author of the novels *A Naked Singularity* and *Personae* and is a public defender in New York City.

A Note on the Type

This book was set in Janson, a typeface named for the Dutchman Anton Janson, but is actually the work of Nicholas Kis (1650–1702).

Composed by North Market Street Graphics,
Lancaster, Pennsylvania

Printed and bound by Berryville Graphics,
Berryville, Virginia

Designed by M. Kristen Bearse

DATE DUE

Fic
Pava

Pava, Sergio de
la, author
Lost empress

WITHDRAWN

Mechanics' Institute Library

3 1750 03444 6370